PRAISE FOR RANDY SINGER

"Singer skillfully loosens the strings and reweaves them into a tale that entertains, surprises, and challenges readers to rethink justice and mercy."

PUBLISHERS WEEKLY on *The Last Plea Bargain*

"Another solid, well-crafted novel from an increasingly popular writer. . . . Its nonfiction origins lend the book an air of reality that totally made-up stories sometimes lack."

BOOKLIST on *The Last Plea Bargain* (starred review)

"*The Last Plea Bargain* is a superbly written book, hard to put down, and easy to pick back up."

THE VIRGINIAN-PILOT

"Singer's superbly researched plot charges out of the starting gate on page one and doesn't rest until literally the last page."

CROSSWALK.COM on *The Last Plea Bargain*

"If you're looking for a mystery full of rich details and realistic scenarios, you will enjoy Singer's latest. It is easy to see why Singer reigns with Christian legal thrillers. You'll be guessing till the end."

ROMANTIC TIMES on *The Last Plea Bargain*

"Intricately plotted, *Fatal Convictions* is . . . an exciting legal thriller with international overtones. In addition to the action and rich cultural information, realistic characters carry the action to its exciting conclusion."

FAITHFULREADER.COM

"Singer's legal knowledge is well matched by his stellar storytelling. Again, he brings us to the brink and lets us hang before skillfully pulling us back."

ROMANTIC TIMES on *Fatal Convictions*

"Get ready to wrestle with larger themes of truth, justice, and courage. Between the legal tension in the courtroom scenes and the emotional tension between the characters, readers will be riveted to the final few chapters."

CROSSWALK.COM on *Fatal Convictions*

"Great suspense; gritty, believable action . . . make [*False Witness*] Singer's best yet."

BOOKLIST (starred review)

"A book that will entertain readers and make them think—what more can one ask?"

PUBLISHERS WEEKLY on *The Justice Game*

"Singer artfully crafts a novel that is the perfect mix of faith and suspense. . . . [*The Justice Game* is] fast-paced from the start to the surprising conclusion."

ROMANTIC TIMES

"At the center of the heart-pounding action are the moral dilemmas that have become Singer's stock-in-trade. . . . An exciting thriller."

BOOKLIST on *By Reason of Insanity*

"Singer hooks readers from the opening courtroom scene of this tasty thriller, then spurs them through a fast trot across a story line that just keeps delivering."

PUBLISHERS WEEKLY on *By Reason of Insanity*

"[A] legal thriller that matches up easily with the best of Grisham."

CHRISTIAN FICTION REVIEW on *Irreparable Harm*

"*Directed Verdict* is a well-crafted courtroom drama with strong characters, surprising twists, and a compelling theme."

RANDY ALCORN, bestselling author of *Safely Home*

DEAD LAWYERS TELL NO TALES

DEAD LAWYERS TELL NO TALES

RANDY SINGER

TYNDALE HOUSE PUBLISHERS, INC., CAROL STREAM, ILLINOIS

Visit Tyndale online at www.tyndale.com.

Visit Randy Singer's website at www.randysinger.net.

TYNDALE and Tyndale's quill logo are registered trademarks of Tyndale House Publishers, Inc.

Dead Lawyers Tell No Tales

Designed by Dean H. Renninger

The author is represented by the literary agency of Alive Communications, Inc., 7680 Goddard Street, Suite 200, Colorado Springs, Colorado, 80920. www.alivecommunications.com.

Luke 19:10, quoted in chapter 2, is taken from the Holy Bible, *New International Version*,® *NIV*.® Copyright © 1973, 1978, 1984, 2011 by Biblica, Inc.™ Used by permission of Zondervan. All rights reserved worldwide. www.zondervan.com.

John 15:13, quoted in the epilogue, and 2 Corinthians 5:17, quoted in the acknowledgments, are taken from the Holy Bible, *New International Version*,® *NIV*.® Copyright © 1973, 1978, 1984 by Biblica, Inc.™ Used by permission of Zondervan. All rights reserved worldwide. www.zondervan.com.

Dead Lawyers Tell No Tales is a work of fiction. Where real people, events, establishments, organizations, or locales appear, they are used fictitiously. All other elements of the novel are drawn from the author's imagination.

Library of Congress Cataloging-in-Publication Data

Singer, Randy (Randy D.)
  Dead lawyers tell no tales / Randy Singer.
    pages cm
  ISBN 978-1-4143-8675-1 (hc) — ISBN 978-1-4143-7558-8 (sc)
1. Ex-convicts—Fiction. 2. Lawyers—Crimes against—Fiction. 3. Murder—Investigation—Fiction.
4. Christian fiction. 5. Legal stories. I. Title.
  PS3619.I5725D34 2013
  813'.6—dc23   2013001140

Printed in the United States of America

19   18   17   16   15   14   13
 7   6   5   4   3   2   1

In writing this book, I was reminded how fortunate I was to have great mentors in my legal career. I've dedicated this book to them: Palmer Rutherford Jr., Conrad Shumadine, John Pearson Jr., and Bruce Bishop.
I hope someday to be a lawyer worthy of your investment.

PROLOGUE

THE SCREAMS WOULDN'T STOP.

They were ear-piercing, pathetic cries for help. Pleading. Begging. The voice belonged to Fatinah Najar, the woman he loved. Once a beautiful and enchanting voice, it was now distorted by pain and fear, pleading rapidly in Arabic, denying that she knew anything her interrogators were asking about. She was in the next cell over, another dark, mildew-covered hellhole just like his, smelling of feces and vomit. They had set it up so he could hear everything.

The Syrian guards questioned her in low growls.

"Do you work for the American CIA?"

"You are in love with Mr. Phoenix, no?"

"What have you told him?"

There was a sinister rhythm to their interrogation techniques. Sean heard them ask questions, then make accusations, their voices calm and deliberate, letting Fatinah know emotions were not part of the equation. Her denials were breathless, racked by sobs. She begged them to believe her. This would go on for half an hour, maybe more—accusations and denials. The calm voices promising her that if she just told the truth, it would all end.

But she never did. She stayed strong. Loyal.

Eventually new voices were added to the mix, loud and threatening. They cursed at Fatinah and described what was coming next, their words crescendoing into angry shouts.

Then the voices would drop again in resignation. "We can't help you if you don't tell the truth."

That's when the man in Sean's cell, a giant Syrian military officer with an unkempt black beard, his body covered with hair, would snuff out his cigarette and remove Sean's gag. Sean's legs were spread, his ankle irons bolted to the floor. His arms were stretched wide and his wrists shackled to the wall so that his entire body formed an X.

His arms had long ago gone numb. But the guards hadn't yet laid a finger on *him*. He was an American. A suspected CIA operative, to be sure, but an American nonetheless. And he knew that at this very moment the State Department was quietly negotiating his release. Its success would depend, in no small part, on whether he and Fatinah could maintain their composure and not give the Syrians anything to work with. He hoped against hope that the State Department would negotiate Fatinah's release as well, although that part was complicated. Either way, they wouldn't stand a chance if Fatinah admitted anything.

He reminded himself of this in the most anguishing moments of all, the silence that engulfed both cells as his captor extinguished his cigarette and stood to untie the gag.

He got right in Sean's face, his breath nastier than the ambient stench of the cell, and he quietly demanded information. He had a tape recorder and made no effort to hide it.

"Do you want to know what happens to your girlfriend next?" he asked. His voice was casual and conversational, as if the matter was of small importance.

"She hasn't done anything. She doesn't know anything. Let her go. Keep me."

The Syrian grunted. "Ah, you Americans. So noble. So heroic." He shook his head in mock sadness. "But so unable to keep your hands off our women."

It was Sean's fault that Fatinah was enduring this torture. He had befriended her, then recruited her, and ultimately he had fallen in love with her. She now worked with Sean and the CIA. She had used her charm and beauty to extract confidences from one of Syria's most powerful leaders. Her name, in Arabic, meant "captivating, a restless intensity that defies relaxation." She had proven to be that and much more to the Syrian general, a man who liked to boast about his exploits to a lover he was desperate to impress. But when he caught this same woman with Sean, the gig was up, and lust turned into rage.

Now the rage had turned into a psychological experiment. How could Sean and Fatinah be broken? How could they be made to talk?

"Your lover is feisty; she likes to fight back. But we bring in fresh men every time," Sean's captor said. He smirked as he talked, finding a perverse enjoyment in the pain he read on Sean's face. "And you have such power, my American friend. You can stop all this—all these things I must describe to you in detail so you will know what is coming next. You are the one man in all the world—" he made a broad, sweeping motion with his hand, a little faux drama as he toyed with Sean—"who could stop this poor creature from suffering more."

He placed both hands on the wall behind Sean and leaned in toward his captive. "Do you work for the American Central Intelligence Agency?"

Sean shook his head.

"Do you love the woman in the cell next door?"

"I've told you. We're in love. There's nothing wrong with that."

"Has she shared any secrets?"

"We all have secrets."

"Clever. But you know what I mean." The big man took a step back, sighed, and then began describing, in exquisite detail, the abuse and torture that would happen to Fatinah next. Sean closed his eyes and tried to shut out the images being implanted in his brain.

When the Syrian was done painting his brutal picture, he gave Sean a few more minutes to think it over. Sean took advantage of the opportunity to shout encouragement to Fatinah.

Shaking his head, the Syrian stuffed the gag into Sean's mouth and taped it back in place.

When Sean's shouts could no longer be heard, the Syrian spoke to the men in the next cell. "Mr. Phoenix claims to know nothing," he shouted. "He says we should ask Fatinah instead. He says we should do whatever we want with her."

The man sat down and lit up another cigarette. A few minutes later, the piercing screams began again.

///

The interrogation continued for two days before Sean Phoenix was released. Unharmed. Untouched. His national security secrets still safe.

He was debriefed at the U.S. embassy, where he learned that the State Department had disavowed any knowledge of Fatinah Najar and her relationship with Sean. They had not tried to negotiate her asylum or pressure Syria into releasing her. The only issue they had addressed with Syria, in the strongest possible terms, was their desired release of an innocent American businessman named Sean Phoenix. He was not a spy, according to the State Department. And falling in love with a Syrian woman was not an international crime.

The strategy had been determined at the highest levels. The director of the CIA had personally instructed the American negotiating team to admit nothing. He was confident that Sean and Fatinah would not crack. The director's right-hand man, a lawyer and bureaucrat who had never put his own life in harm's way, had convinced his boss that trying to negotiate Fatinah's release would be tantamount to admitting she was a spy. It would create an embarrassing international incident. Sometimes you had to sacrifice one for the good of all.

After his debriefing, Sean returned to his flat in downtown Damascus. He had been told to pack his belongings for a flight back to the U.S. the following day. Instead, he put together a battle plan. The Syrians had confiscated his guns and ammunition when they had captured him, so he would have to buy new weapons on the streets of Damascus. He wasn't an explosives expert, but he knew how to make crude bombs out of fertilizer. In the wee hours of the morning, he would launch his one-man attack on the prison. He knew his odds of success were infinitesimal, but he would rather die trying to free Fatinah than live with the knowledge that he had done nothing.

At midnight, three agents burst into his flat and told Sean that his flight had been moved up. There was a loud argument, followed by a fight. They carried him out unconscious. He woke up on an airplane headed to Germany.

///

Within thirty minutes of setting foot on American soil, Sean was meeting with the CIA director personally. The man called Sean a hero and talked about the sacrifices that had to be made so that the rule of law could prevail. He regretted that he couldn't award Sean a medal, but he knew Sean would understand. Anonymity was part of the bargain. He was sorry they hadn't been able to do more for Fatinah. She had not made it out alive.

The director talked about giving Sean some time off and a new assignment at higher pay. But Sean turned in his credentials. He walked out of the director's office and made a list of every person, both Syrian and American, who had played a role in Fatinah's death. He vowed to cross those names off the list, one at a time, as he exacted his revenge.

Sean was tired of hearing about the rule of law and the cost of freedom. He was sick of pompous men who lived and worked in luxurious surroundings spouting off about high-minded concepts that would cost them nothing.

Patriotism. Democracy. Freedom. They were all ploys to get men like Sean to do the bidding of those in power. And when the power brokers had their backs to the wall, people like Sean and Fatinah became expendable. Assets to be written off. Another casualty or two. Another exercise in damage control.

Sean Phoenix was done with it. There had to be a better way.

1

ATLANTA, GEORGIA

LANDON REED EMERGED from his two-year prison sentence into the muggy warmth of an August morning wearing the jeans, gray T-shirt, and sandals that Kerri had dropped off the day before. He squinted as he left the dingy interior of the Fulton County jail and stepped into the crisp, brilliant light of the sun. He held a paper bag containing the suit and shoes he had worn to court two years earlier when he pleaded guilty. There were sunglasses in the bag as well, but Landon had decided not to wear them, concerned they might send the wrong message—a former all-star college quarterback still trying to play it cool.

He had been sentenced for his role in a point-shaving scandal, and it was not surprising that only one former teammate came for his release— his best friend and center, a mountain of a man named Billy Thurston. While Landon served his time, Billy had been drafted by the Green Bay Packers.

The media formed a semicircle around Landon, cameras rolling to capture the scene. The same reporters who had crucified him two years earlier were back to record his moment of freedom and to rile up the Southeastern University fans all over again. Landon didn't hold it against them. He had changed in prison, his bitterness replaced by contrition. But he didn't expect people to understand.

He held it together as he hugged his mother and older sister. They didn't say anything, mindful that the cameras would capture every word. Kerri waited in line, just as she had waited for two years, true to her word, enduring the scorn of most of her old friends. On her hip was the little girl Landon knew would grow into the same kind of strong-willed, independent, beautiful woman her mom was. Maddie had been born after Landon started serving his term. He had never held her outside the prison walls.

Landon and Kerri had scripted this moment. There would be a brief hug; then Landon would say a few words to the press about how much he appreciated Kerri's loyalty. He would answer a few questions. They would keep it low-key. The emotional dam would burst later.

But when Kerri stepped forward to hug him, the script no longer mattered. She started crying, though they had agreed she wouldn't cry and neither would he. Unbidden, tears rolled down his face as well. Kerri buried her head on his shoulder, and they held each other for much longer than they had planned, with little Maddie right there between them, an arm around each of their necks. For the old Landon, the hotshot quarterback of three years ago, this public display of emotion would have been embarrassing. But the new Landon was beyond all that. Once you've been humiliated in the national press, crying in public is no big deal.

The questions started even before the little family disengaged. Kerri handed Maddie to Landon, and when he turned to face the reporters, his little girl turned her back to them, hiding her face in Landon's chest, holding on for her life. It was all overwhelming for an almost-two-year-old.

"What're your plans now?"

"Are you going to play football again?"

"What do you have to say to your teammates and coaches?"

He took them one at a time. "I'm pretty sure my football career is over." *Who would want me?* "I'm grateful for everyone who stood with me during these last two years." He put his free arm around Kerri's shoulder. He nodded toward his mother and sister, standing on the other side of him. His mom, always a slender woman, looked wiry and gaunt, with tears streaking her face. Prison had aged her even more than him.

"I'm sorry that I let my teammates and coaches and fans down. I know I can never undo the damage I've done to Southeastern University or my own reputation."

Kerri held her head high, as if she were standing next to a prince. His mom and sister kept their chins up as well.

"I'm incredibly grateful to Kerri for waiting for me these past two years. I certainly wouldn't have blamed her if she had moved on to someone else. In terms of what I'm going to do, one of the first things will be tying the knot."

Kerri had her arm around his waist and gave him a little squeeze. The questions kept coming and he patiently addressed each one. Reporters were a cynical lot. Marriage, yeah, yeah—that's quaint. But what about a comeback on the gridiron?

"Are you saying you haven't been contacted by any NFL teams?"

"That's what I'm saying."

"Are you planning on attending any tryouts?"

It was Billy Thurston who decided enough was enough. He stepped between Landon and the microphones and made a little announcement. "Let's respect this family's privacy and let Mr. Reed go about rebuilding his life," he said. And then, as he had done so many times in the past, he cleared a path for his quarterback to follow.

The reporters took this as a cue to ask the same questions louder, shouting at Landon and the others as they worked their way toward the parking lot. Landon, no stranger to the spotlight, knew the drill. Once you've decided the press conference is over, keep your head down, ignore whatever they say, and just keep moving.

They had almost completed the gauntlet when Landon spotted Bobby Woolridge, an older reporter from the *Atlanta Journal-Constitution* who had always been more than fair. Bobby believed in redemption and had written a piece a few months ago about Landon's jailhouse conversion. Unlike the others, Bobby didn't assume it was just part of a sophisticated PR campaign.

"You going into the ministry?" Bobby asked.

Landon grinned a little and kept walking. "No, Bobby. I hardly think I'm qualified."

"How are you gonna feed your family?"

"I'll figure something out," Landon said. He was tempted to tell Bobby. Sooner or later, it would all come out anyway. But he and Kerri had talked about this. They would keep their plans private until this new wave of publicity had washed over. He had finished his undergrad degree in prison. Now they would start a new life miles away from Atlanta, in a town with lots of history but few SEC football fanatics.

"Good luck," Bobby said.

Billy had double-parked his Land Rover, and they all hopped in, leaving the media behind to snap a few final pictures. As they pulled away, Landon could feel the pressure in his chest begin to loosen. He was a free man again. He could do whatever he wanted.

"Where to?" Billy asked. "Pizza? Burgers? The Varsity?" For Billy, it was always about food.

But Landon had a commitment to keep. "Trinity Church," he said. "We've got our best man and flower girl in the car. No sense giving the bride a chance to change her mind."

Kerri was sitting in the back with Maddie. She leaned forward and placed a hand on Landon's shoulder. "She's had two years to think it over," Kerri said. "She's not getting cold feet now."

They had been planning this day for six months, and Landon couldn't believe it was finally here. It wasn't exactly a dream wedding, but Kerri didn't seem to care. Even her parents' refusal to attend hadn't fazed her. They would have each other, she had said. What else did they need?

That afternoon, the minister at the small church Kerri had been attending made it official. Kerri Anderson became Kerri Reed. And when they made their vows, pledging to stick with each other for better or for worse, the minister actually paused for a moment and turned to Kerri.

"I think you've already got this part down," he said.

Kerri was beaming, as was Landon. And they didn't stop smiling until long after the minister pronounced them man and wife.

Later that day, Kerri said it was the most romantic wedding she could ever have imagined. With just the seven of them in the small sanctuary, it somehow felt more private and intimate. She had been smiling, she said, because it felt so surreal she almost had to pinch herself. The three of them were officially becoming a family. She was Mrs. Landon Reed. Maddie would have her daddy home.

Landon didn't tell her the reason he had been smiling. Like Kerri, the whole experience had felt like a dream. The entire two years behind bars, he kept thinking that any day Kerri might come to her senses, find somebody else, and bolt. She was beautiful and smart with a larger-than-life personality. But she kept coming back. And now, Landon was married to her.

That was enough to make any man smile. But there was also one other thing.

The honeymoon would start that night.

2

THE CHARACTER AND FITNESS COMMITTEE of the Virginia Board of Bar Examiners is made up of five lawyers with the unenviable task of determining whether law school graduates who have passed the bar exam have also demonstrated, by clear and convincing evidence, that they possess the character and fitness required to practice law. In lawyer-speak, the members of the committee are looking for men and women "of such good moral character as to be entitled to the high regard and confidence of the public." As a practical matter, it is the committee's job to stare down would-be lawyers who have demonstrated a propensity to lie, cheat, or steal—or in rare cases, commit more violent crimes. The committee hears the evidence and makes a recommendation to the Virginia Board of Bar Examiners—a thumbs-up or down—for the aspiring young lawyers with checkered pasts.

The committee meets in a large courtroom on the second floor of the State Corporation Commission in Richmond. The members set up shop behind a table in the well of the courtroom, and the lawyer getting grilled sits just below the judge's dais in a single chair facing the committee. There is no table or witness rail to hide behind; the young lawyer is totally exposed. Some of these young men and women bring their own attorneys. Others who cannot afford lawyers take their future into their own hands, representing themselves. For those who lose, it will be the only case they ever try.

Landon Reed had talked to several lawyers, but none would take his case. Three years after his release from prison, he sat in front of the committee wearing the better of the two suits he owned, his six-foot-three-inch frame draped over the chair. He felt more vulnerable than he had at any time since his sentencing five years earlier.

It was the job of the committee's lawyer to summarize the areas of concern. His name was Jeffery Henderson. He was a studious-looking man in his early forties with a calm demeanor, and he had been fair to Landon throughout the process. He read from some prepared notes while the committee members stared. Landon recrossed his legs and folded his hands together, his heart beating against his suit coat like it might pop out of his chest at any moment.

During his two and a half years at William and Mary Law School, Landon had rolled out of bed every morning with the knowledge that it would one day come to this. The student loans, the all-nighters before exams, the summer courses so he could graduate six months early, and the stress on his marriage would all be for naught if three of the five lawyers seated before him decided he didn't have the purity of character necessary to be a lawyer.

A lawyer! As if there weren't thousands already unleashed on the public who would make Landon look like a patron saint.

"The committee has received your letters of recommendation and your written submission," Henderson said calmly, his formal words accentuating the gravity of the moment. "The purpose of today's hearing is to inquire about your conviction on two counts of conspiracy to commit sports bribery. The underlying acts involve alleged point shaving while you were the quarterback for the Southeastern University

Knights and specifically involve two games against SEC opponents Kentucky and Vanderbilt during your junior year at the university. You pleaded guilty to those counts and served two years prior to starting law school at William and Mary. In addition, you had five traffic infractions during the time you were at Southeastern."

Landon had always gotten a kick out of the traffic infractions. Like most college athletes, he had a lead foot and had racked up more than his share of tickets. But that wasn't why they were here today. Landon had been the central figure in one of the biggest point-shaving scandals in college football history. He had admitted to intentionally shaving points against two SEC schools in games his team had dominated. But the real controversy had swirled around the SEC Championship Game, a game that Southeastern lost to Alabama—a game in which Landon had thrown three interceptions.

He had steadfastly maintained his innocence on that one. And the prosecutors could never prove anything different.

The first question from the panel came from the one person Landon had pegged as a possible ally. His name was Harry McNaughten, an ornery old criminal-defense lawyer who reportedly suffered from cirrhosis but kept outliving everyone's expectations. He was thin and somewhat jaundiced with leathery skin and receding gray hair that swept back over his ears. His high forehead, elongated face, and Roman nose reminded Landon of the statue of George Wythe, one of Virginia's founding fathers, that dominated the sidewalk at the entrance to William and Mary Law School.

McNaughten was on the committee because criminal-defense lawyers had revolted after years of not having one of their own sitting on the panel. It was widely believed that he brought a liberal and lenient voice to the proceedings, and Landon was banking on his vote.

"I think the question on everyone's mind," Harry said, his voice raspy, "was why you did this. Heck, I know a lot of lawyers who would have given their left arm to play quarterback in the SEC. And you sell your team down the river for a few thousand bucks." Harry leaned back in his chair and eyed Landon down his long nose. "It just seems incomprehensible to most of us."

Landon swallowed hard before responding. He wanted to argue the point. Technically, he hadn't sold out his team—he had only shaved points in games he knew they would still win. But it *was* wrong, and everybody knew it. Unless he fell completely on his sword, he wouldn't stand a chance.

"Nothing I'm about to say should be construed as an excuse for what I did," Landon began. His voice was shaky, and it made him more self-conscious. "I take full responsibility for my actions. As an athlete, I can think of nothing more detestable than working against your own teammates—even in games I knew we could win. But at the time, in my twenty-year-old mind, I was more focused on myself than on my teammates. I had just found out that my girlfriend was pregnant, and we didn't want her parents to know. We didn't know if we were going to keep the baby. Neither of us had enough money for her to see a doctor unless she went on her parents' insurance, and I thought that maybe . . ."

Landon's voice caught and he swallowed hard. He looked to the front row, where Kerri was staring at him, her head high as it had been throughout the entire ordeal, a look of dignity and pride accentuating the beautiful almond eyes. She wanted this for him perhaps more than he wanted it for himself. He couldn't afford to choke up now. The committee members would think he was just putting on a show.

"The point is, I was desperate for cash, and this was the only way I knew to get some. I thought I was good enough to be able to shave a few points but not cost my team the game. None of that makes it right, and I'm ashamed of what I did. I brought disgrace not only on me but on the team and on Kerri as well. The reason I get emotional about it is because I let down the people who cared about me most."

"What kind of lawyer do you want to be?" McNaughten asked. The others seemed content to let Harry take the lead.

"I've thought about that a lot," Landon replied. The shakiness in his voice was gone, and he tried to keep his tone soft and humble. "I would love to be a criminal-defense lawyer but probably not for the reasons you might expect. One thing I learned behind bars is that most men serving time have given up hope. You can see it in their eyes, their posture, their outlook on life. I know this might sound a bit Pollyanna-ish, but I think I could give my clients a small infusion of hope.

"I know what it's like to have the full weight of the law come down on you and to feel like everybody's turned against you. But I also know that our system is set up to give men and women a chance at redemption. I would tell my clients that if they take complete responsibility for what they did, they can change. That someday they can actually make something of their lives. And if they see me representing them in court, they'll know it's not just a pep talk."

There was so much more Landon wanted to say, but he knew this was not the time. This group of lawyers had heard it all before. Like so many other felons, Landon's story was one of spiritual redemption. At the lowest point in his life, he had started attending a prison Bible study led by an ex-felon turned law school professor named Mason James. Mace, as the inmates called him, shared biblical stories of men who had served time in prison and had become heroes of the faith. Joseph in the Old Testament; Paul in the New. Moses had been a murderer. David was an adulterer. "There's hope for men like you," Mace had said. But it required confession and repentance and faith in Christ.

Landon had stiff-armed the message for six months but was eventually convinced by the man's lifestyle. Mace never missed a week of Bible study, never tired of coming back, and spent his time defending men who couldn't afford a lawyer. It inspired Landon to one day do the same.

The story that finally got through to Landon was the one about Zacchaeus, a tax collector. Like Landon, he had cheated a lot of people, but this didn't keep Jesus away. Zacchaeus welcomed Jesus into his home, paid back everyone he had cheated—four times over—and Jesus assured him that salvation had come to his house. When Jesus was criticized for hanging out with a tax collector, his explanation seemed as much for Landon as for Zacchaeus: "The Son of Man came to seek and to save the lost."

Motivated by that message, Landon had written a letter to every one of his former teammates and coaches asking for their forgiveness. Some had ignored him. Others had responded with harsh words. But most, including Landon's former head coach, had responded graciously. In fact, Landon had included a letter from his coach in his submission to the Character and Fitness Committee.

The youngest lawyer on the committee was a blonde litigator who had graduated from the University of Virginia and was working for one of the big Richmond firms. She had been riffling through some papers while Landon was speaking about his desire to be a defense attorney.

"One of the things that this committee looks for is whether the applicant has paid his or her full debt to society," she said, looking up at Landon. "I know that plea agreements often involve concessions from both sides and that the defendant pleads guilty to less than the full scope of his wrongdoing. So my question to you, Mr. Reed, is whether there were any other games where you attempted to affect the outcome for which you did not plead guilty?"

Landon knew the question was coming. Every fan in the SEC suspected he had thrown the championship game.

"Those are the only two games. I gave my best effort in every other game and, for that matter, in every other practice."

"Some of us have a hard time believing that," Harry McNaughten interjected. "A lot of folks betting on Southeastern lost money on the championship game that year. It wasn't your best day."

"It was probably my worst game," Landon admitted. "But I tried to win."

"How many interceptions did you have your entire junior season?"

"In the regular season—seven."

"How many in that game?"

"Three."

"And how many fumbles?"

"One."

Harry nodded, as if the point was obvious to everyone. "I asked Mr. Henderson to bring a few TVs in so we could watch something," he said.

Landon had noticed the television monitors in the courtroom. One was on a stand facing him; the other was off to the side, pointing toward the committee. Lots of courtrooms came equipped with television monitors, and Landon hadn't given them a second thought—until now.

Harry pointed a remote at the television. "I've watched that entire championship game," he said. "Those first two interceptions weren't really your fault. One of 'em got batted by your own receiver. The second one, you were under a lot of pressure. And that fumble on the last drive of the game—well, you got blindsided when your protection broke down. But this third interception, on a critical drive with just a few minutes left . . . it looks pretty suspicious."

Harry put on a pair of reading glasses and fiddled with the remote but couldn't seem to get the video started. He passed the remote down to Henderson and mumbled something about technology. In the awkward silence, Landon fidgeted in his seat, his leg bouncing, then caught himself. He knew he had to stay calm under pressure.

"If we can get this thing to work," Harry said as if the televisions were the Hadron Super Collider, "would you mind watching this play and telling us what happened?"

"I'd be glad to."

Henderson hit the remote, and the video flicked on. "Figures," Harry said.

Landon watched the nightmare for the first time in years. The night after the game, ESPN had replayed the interception over and over, though by then Landon had been too drunk to worry about it. Later, it had become a staple for ESPN's coverage of the point-shaving scandal. Landon estimated that every sports fan in America had probably seen the play at least twenty times.

Southeastern was behind by one point and driving down the field with just under three minutes to play. Vegas had Alabama favored by four, so Landon's team was beating the spread. Despite the prior interceptions, Southeastern's defense and special teams had kept them in the game.

On this play, the protection was good, and Landon's favorite receiver was running down the sideline, step for step with the defensive back. But the throw was short and well behind the receiver. The defensive back glanced over his shoulder and broke on the ball, picking it off and sprinting nearly fifty yards into the end zone. The crowd roared, and the commentators were momentarily speechless.

"You hit him right in the numbers," McNaughten said, referring to the defensive back. "That ball must've been a good five yards short. Now, we're not experts on football here. But I think this committee would like an explanation about how a quarterback with a rocket arm like yours could throw such a wounded duck."

LANDON KNEW IT LOOKED BAD. He had heard it all before. But with his career on the line, he had to make them understand.

"Can I stand up and demonstrate something?" he asked.

The committee members looked at Henderson, who shrugged his approval.

Landon rose from his seat. "Mr. Henderson, would you mind standing up here for just a minute?"

The committee's attorney furrowed his brow, hesitated, and then joined Landon in the well of the courtroom.

"Kerri, can you help me out too?"

His wife practically jumped at the opportunity.

Landon guided Kerri to a space in front of one end of the committee's table and placed Henderson right next to her. He moved to the other end while a few lawyers on the committee crossed their arms.

"Let's assume that Kerri's my receiver," Landon said. "She's running down the sideline, looking over her shoulder just like you saw on that film. Mr. Henderson's the defender, and he's running right next to her. But he can't be looking back at me or he'll lose contact with her. So he watches her eyes to determine when I've thrown the ball.

"Um, Mr. Henderson, would you mind turning your head so you're looking at Kerri?"

Reluctantly, Henderson did so.

"Now this is what we call a 'read pass' because I'm supposed to read the defender and decide whether to throw the ball on my receiver's back shoulder or whether my receiver is a step or two ahead and I can throw it out in front of him. If the defender is step for step, like he was on that play, I'm supposed to throw the ball just behind my receiver and toward the sideline for what's called a back-shoulder throw. My receiver's looking at me, and he should slow down right at the last minute while the defender keeps going a step or two."

As Landon was explaining, Kerri, who had been a sports announcer in college, stepped back and pretended to catch an imaginary ball. She was slender and in great shape, and the men on the panel followed her every move.

"But on this play, my receiver thought he had the defender beat, so he kept going." On cue, Kerri took a few steps in the opposite direction. Henderson just stood there, clearly not anxious to play along. "The defender turned at just the right time to break on the ball. So what looks like a horrible pass was really just a massive miscommunication."

Harry McNaughten tilted his head a little as if he might be buying it. He had his glasses off, holding them in his right hand. "Can we run that tape again?" he asked.

After Landon, Kerri, and Henderson took their seats, the committee watched the tape one more time.

"Hold it! Right there," Landon said. "Just before I let go of the ball, you can see that the defender and my receiver are step for step. Now watch—I'll throw it to his back shoulder, and the defender's head turns right when I do. He makes a break on the ball while my receiver keeps going."

Henderson rolled the tape forward, and it unfolded just like Landon said. McNaughten stuck out his lip as if he might be considering the matter. After a few beats of silence, he moved on to other areas of questioning. They grilled Landon for another thirty minutes and then asked if he had any closing remarks.

Landon thought about it for a moment and almost passed on the opportunity. What else was there to say? But he had worked so hard these past three years, and Kerri was sitting on the edge of her seat, waiting for him to pull a rabbit out of his hat. He couldn't just stay silent.

"I appreciate the chance to come in here and answer your questions. And I want you to know that I totally trust whatever this committee decides. When I went to law school, I knew that I might never actually get a chance to practice law. If you decide that I'm too much of a risk, I'll understand. My actions have consequences, and I'm prepared to accept whatever you say those consequences should be.

"But I can promise you this. If you recommend me, I won't let you down. Other lawyers might take their license for granted. But every day I go to work, I'll remember that I'm fortunate to even have a license. I'll remember that you were willing to take a risk on me and give me a second chance. And I'll remember what happens if I'm ever disloyal to the people who trust me. I know how much I hurt my teammates and my coaches and my family. There's no amount of money that could ever make me do that again."

Landon looked down at the floor, satisfied that he had said everything he wanted to say.

"Thank you," Henderson said. "We'll be in touch with you in a few weeks."

///

It was a long and quiet ride home from Richmond to Virginia Beach. Landon spent the first fifteen minutes beating himself up about the answers he had given and the answers he should have given, second-guessing just about everything he had said. It was typical windshield wisdom, the clever things you think up on the drive home. Kerri tried to cheer him up by telling him how proud she was of the way he had handled the hearing. If she was ever in trouble, she said, she wanted him to be her lawyer.

"In fact, I want to sign a contract right now. If we ever get a divorce, I'm hiring you to handle my side."

But Landon continued to sulk. So Kerri took another approach.

"You're right—you were terrible. They've probably sent an e-mail out already denying you admission to the bar, if not for being a cheat, then for being a terrible lawyer."

"Probably," Landon said.

"Nothing like a good pity party," Kerri replied.

Silence took over until they crossed the Hampton Roads Bridge-Tunnel and Landon reached over to hold Kerri's hand. "I just can't stand the thought of what I put you and Maddie through if I'm never going to be able to practice law," he said softly. "I'm not very good at being Mr. Mom."

"It's all going to work out," Kerri said with her usual self-assurance. "Besides, you make a great mom."

"Thanks for being there today."

Kerri laced her fingers through his. "You really are going to be an awesome lawyer," she said.

"If I only get the chance."

4

AS A BOY, LANDON REED had always loved the holiday season. His mother, a single mom raising two kids, never had much money for presents. But Christmas still meant time off from school and a few toys under the tree. When Landon reached high school, December was filled with state playoffs in football, culminating in back-to-back championships his junior and senior years. In college, the month was filled with conference championship games that led up to the bowl season.

But during the last several years, all of that had changed. Christmas in prison meant staring through the bulletproof glass at Kerri and his new baby daughter, wishing he could hold them. Only once, a few weeks after Maddie's birth, had the guards made an exception and allowed Landon to hold her. His mom and sister visited at Christmas too, driving all the way from the Florida panhandle just to spend one hour with him—the maximum allowed under prison rules.

After his release, December brought law school final exams and the annual buildup to the SEC Championship Game. The commentators would rehash the controversy surrounding Landon's three-interception performance. Had he thrown the game or hadn't he? They would show each of the picks (and sometimes the fumble on the final drive for good measure), dutifully note that Landon had only pleaded guilty to throwing the regular-season games, and then state that he had been unavailable for comment on the story.

This December held its own special perils. If the Character and Fitness Committee gave him a thumbs-down, it would be one more reason to hate the month. On the other hand, a positive response could be a turning point. And it was becoming harder not to get excited about Christmas when looking at the world through the eyes of a child who had just turned five.

On the good side, Landon had obtained a few painting jobs that generated some extra income for the holidays. He watched Maddie while Kerri worked the early shift, then headed off to paint when Kerri got home. Two nights a week he was at the gym, training three local high school quarterbacks. Landon and Kerri were like two ships passing in the night throughout the entire month. And they still had no word from the Character and Fitness Committee.

By Christmas Eve, Landon's mind was occupied with other things. At noon, he piled into the minivan with Kerri and Maddie and, as part of a local ministry, began taking presents to six separate families whose fathers were in jail. The Reeds gave the presents to the moms, who now had some Christmas gifts to give the children from their dads. The women were especially excited to see Kerri, who was something of a local celebrity as a WTRT personality. Plus, Kerri had been in their shoes. Half the time, she was choking back tears as they drove away.

On Christmas morning, Kerri rolled out of bed at four so she could be on the air by six. She hated working Christmas, but she couldn't turn down the double pay. Besides, it was a chance to work the anchor desk—a welcome break from her normal role as a field reporter.

Landon woke with her and quietly fixed some coffee, trying not to awaken Maddie. It would be hard enough keeping her enthusiasm in check until Mommy got home at noon.

Two hours later, Landon settled in to watch the morning news and thought about how blessed he was. On the screen, Kerri was gabbing about some feel-good story with a gray-haired male reporter who had outlived his TV prime, a guy you hardly noticed because your eyes were immediately drawn to Kerri's long, dark hair and piercing blue eyes. Even though they glammed on the makeup, she still had that fresh, girl-next-door look. Landon had always believed his wife could have been a model, but she was more of a tomboy and didn't like the anorexic look that the modeling agencies preferred. He watched the way she commanded the camera, her eyes sparkling and her face lighting up as she flashed the big smile that viewers loved. She had a lazy left eye that drove her crazy when she reviewed her own tapes, but Landon found it endearing.

Maddie woke up at seven, and Landon fixed chocolate-chip pancakes. The next five hours were the slowest of young Maddie's life. Every noise outside their rented condo generated a mad dash to the front door to see if Mommy had come home early. Each of Maddie's presents was lifted, shaken, and subjected to endless speculation. *How the Grinch Stole Christmas* held her attention for only fifteen minutes. And so, after exchanging three text messages with Kerri at a few minutes after twelve, Landon broke down and allowed Maddie to open a present.

"Why don't you open this one first?" he suggested. It was a small, flat package that didn't look like it would be a lot of fun. But after waiting all morning, Maddie was not going to argue.

"Okay," she said, tearing into it. She pulled out a small card with Kerri's handwriting on it.

"What does it say, Daddy?"

"It wants to know if you've been a good girl."

The question, a no-brainer in Landon's mind, seemed to stump Maddie. She scrunched her little face into deep concentration. "I tried," she offered.

"Then it says that your best Christmas gift ever is waiting right outside the front door."

Maddie looked at Landon and lowered her eyebrows in curiosity. Gifts were supposed to be wrapped and under the tree. She hustled to the front door and cracked it open a few inches. Then, with Landon standing behind her, the video camera on his cell phone rolling, she threw open the door and squealed.

Kerri was standing there, holding a furry, light-brown puppy that looked like a lion cub.

Maddie placed both hands over her mouth and let out another whoop. "Can I hold him?" she asked.

"Let's let him run around a little first," Kerri said. She had just picked up the little guy from their neighbors, who had agreed to take care of him on Christmas Eve so they could surprise Maddie. Kerri walked into the condo and gently placed the puppy on the carpet. He stood there for a moment, looking from one human to the next, trying to make sense of his brave new world.

"Oooh," Maddie cooed. She knelt down next to him and started petting him. "Does he have a name?"

"That's for you to decide," Kerri said.

Before they opened another present, the furry little ball had darted around the condo several times, wearing himself out, and been christened with a name: Simba.

Simba was a showstopper. Maddie lost interest in anything else under the tree. In fact, it wasn't until almost one thirty, after Simba and his new owners had taken two walks outside (and after one accident on the carpet), that the final gift was opened.

Kerri had changed into jeans and a sweatshirt, modeling the new furry slippers that Landon and Maddie had given her. "Oh, wait," she said, "there's one other gift I almost forgot."

She disappeared for a moment and brought a box from the bedroom closet wrapped in Christmas-tree paper they had bought on sale after the holidays the previous year. It was the size of an old computer box, and it had Landon's curiosity piqued. He would be a little frustrated if Kerri had violated their agreement on the amount of money they were supposed to spend on each other. They had school loans to pay, and painters didn't make much money.

Still, Landon smiled as he tore away the wrapping paper and opened the box, only to discover a smaller box inside. *One of those routines.* There were three boxes total, each separately wrapped, each smaller than the last. Inside the smallest box was a manila envelope, which was also wrapped. Inside that envelope was a smaller business envelope that was wrapped in the same green Christmas-tree paper.

Landon held it in his hand and looked up at his wife.

"Open it, Daddy," Maddie said, squirming with excitement.

Landon's left hand started shaking a little. He didn't want to get his hopes up, but what else could it be? And why would Kerri have gone to all this trouble if it wasn't good news?

"Is this what I think it is?" he asked.

His wife shrugged. Always the tease.

He opened it carefully, slowly. He said a prayer. He unfolded the letter and started to read.

The Character and Fitness Committee of the Virginia Board of Bar Examiners has reviewed all material relative to the issues of character and fitness surrounding your application. The Committee finds that you have proven by clear and convincing evidence that you possess the requisite character and fitness to practice law.

He read it twice just to be sure. He wanted to pinch himself to see if he was dreaming. Kerri had tears in her eyes. Maddie was jumping and cheering. He gave them both a hug.

That night, with Simba sleeping in his crate next to their bed, Landon and Kerri celebrated their greatest Christmas ever. "After all," Kerri said, "we can afford to have another baby now that you're going to be a hotshot lawyer."

5

THE DAZZLE OF CHRISTMAS turned into the dreariness of a January filled with depressing news. While waiting for the Board of Bar Examiners to affirm the recommendation of the Character and Fitness Committee, Landon bombarded local law firms and public defenders' offices with applications. To distinguish himself from the dozens of other applicants, he put on a suit every day and personally hand-delivered the paperwork. The receptionists all smiled and politely told him they would give his application to the hiring partner, but Landon never received even the first call.

After three weeks of rejections, he started exploring the possibility of hanging out his own shingle. But among other problems, that would take start-up money, something he and Kerri didn't have. Somebody had to pay for the malpractice insurance and a website and business cards and license fees and who knew what else.

His painting jobs mostly dried up after the first half of January, leaving Landon to split his time between training high school quarterbacks at night and playing Mr. Mom (along with the Dog Whisperer) during the day.

House-training Simba was about as successful as landing a legal job. Landon resorted to spreading blue plastic on top of the carpet in the condo so it would be easier to clean up after one of Simba's many accidents.

The sole piece of good news in January was the playoff march of the Green Bay Packers. Landon had always been a Cowboys fan himself, but Billy Thurston was now starting for the Pack. It was enough to turn the entire Reed family into cheeseheads.

Each Sunday, the Reeds attended a church that met in the Westin Hotel in the Town Center area of Virginia Beach. On January 20, they went out for lunch after church to the Gordon Biersch Brewery because the place had lots of big screens and a rowdy atmosphere for Landon and Kerri to take in the beginning of the NFC Championship Game. Maddie liked eating at the high tables in the middle of the restaurant, and the place had a kids' menu with some of the best mac and cheese in town. The Reeds planned on watching the first half of the game there and driving home at halftime. The entire family, including Maddie, had worn Packers jerseys to church.

Things started going south toward the end of the second quarter, as Landon was finishing his last chicken wing. Uncharacteristically, the Packers quarterback threw his second interception of the half, and this one was returned for a touchdown.

The booth directly behind Landon's table was occupied by three loud and obnoxious 49ers fans. After an explosion of high fives, the biggest among them couldn't let it go. "That's two interceptions this half!" he proclaimed during the commercial break. "At that rate he'll have more than three for the game."

"And he'll prob'ly fumble on the last drive," said his buddy.

Kerri shot Landon a look. It wasn't the first time they had been through something like this.

"Yep," said a third voice, "wonder who's paying him."

Landon watched Kerri's face tighten, the storm clouds forming in her eyes. It was a look that generally meant he and Maddie should seek immediate shelter. "Let it go," he whispered. Ignoring him, she turned and stared at the men in the booth.

"You got something to say?" she asked. Her lips were tight in anger, her jaw set. *Great,* thought Landon. There would be no backing down now.

"You talking to me?" the big man asked. The group's spokesman looked like he weighed about 250. He was a Grizzly Adams type with a scruffy black beard, a bald pate, a 49ers jersey, earrings, and a forearm full of tattoos. He held his arms out—a peace offering. "We're just talking amongst ourselves."

He took a swig of beer but kept his eye on Kerri. She stared back.

"That woman can talk to me all day long if she wants," quipped his friend. This guy was shorter, with the high and tight haircut of the Marines. He wore a tight red T-shirt showing off ripped arms and a washboard gut. He and Grizzly bumped fists.

"Grow up," Kerri snorted, turning back to her table, her eyes on fire. "Let's get out of here," she said to Landon.

"Can I go potty?" Maddie asked.

Kerri grunted in frustration.

"Don't worry about it," Landon said, keeping his voice low and calm. "Go ahead and take her. We'll leave when we're ready. You can't let jerks like that run us off."

Kerri sighed and helped Maddie off her stool. The men at the booth stared unabashedly as Kerri and Maddie walked away.

"Wouldn't mind getting inside that Packers jersey," the Marine said. Landon scowled at him.

"Probably hasn't had a real man in a while," said the third man, a younger guy with wavy blond hair who looked like he'd just stepped out of a frat party.

Landon shook his head and reminded himself how much was at stake. The Character and Fitness Committee had recommended him to the Virginia State Bar. If he got into a fight now, he would jeopardize everything he had worked for in the last three years. He had learned to swallow his pride, one of the many consequences of what he had done. He took a drink of soda and turned back to the television.

But the boys at the booth weren't done. Grizzly staggered over to Landon's table, accompanied by the Marine. Frat Boy didn't join them.

"I played a little football back in the day," Grizzly said. He slurred his words and looked unsteady. "Used to have season tickets to the Knights. Consider myself a proud alum."

Just my luck, Landon thought.

The Marine had carried his beer to Landon's table and set it down, as if he might be joining Landon for lunch.

"You know what I can't stand?" Grizzly asked. Landon tried to ignore him, leaning to the side so he could see the game over the big man's shoulder.

Grizzly shifted a little, blocking Landon's view. "I can't stand prima donnas who have the God-given ability to play for a team that I would have given my first child to play for, and then they sell out their teammates. Know what I mean?"

Landon didn't say a word. Out of the corner of his eye he saw Kerri and Maddie returning from the bathroom. This was going to be trouble.

"All right, he gets it," Frat Boy said. He had approached Landon's table and put a hand on Grizzly's arm, nudging him back toward the booth. But the big guy was too drunk and belligerent to retreat so quickly. He shook his friend's arm away and, in an exaggerated move, knocked Landon's glass over, spilling the drink on Kerri's plate.

"You are such a jerk," she snapped, arriving at the table. She let go of Maddie's hand and pushed Grizzly aside to grab her keys and cell phone from the table.

Grizzly took a stutter step back and regained his balance to hover over Kerri. "Darn, you're cute when you're mad," he said, smiling. He put an arm on her shoulder to turn her back toward him.

Kerri looked shocked, but before she could say anything, Landon snapped. He jumped from his chair and caught the man with a right cross. He had learned a thing or two about fighting in prison, including the element of surprise.

The Marine gawked for a second, stunned, and then took a swing at Landon from the side. Landon blocked it, grabbed the Marine's collar, and pulled the man's head down while raising his own right knee and driving it into the Marine's face. Blood squirted from his nose.

Grizzly had not gone down. He wiped the blood from his mouth and grabbed Landon from behind, wrapping him up in a bear hug. Frat Boy and the Marine started punching Landon as Kerri screamed, trying to pull the big man off. By the time the bartender and a few others had separated the combatants, Landon was crumpled on the floor with Kerri kneeling beside him. Maddie was crying.

The police arrived ten minutes later, after the 49ers table had paid their bill and cleared out. Kerri wanted to press charges, but Landon refused. For him, it was just another sad chapter in the ongoing saga of the point-shaving scandal. The dental bill for repairing his three lower front teeth the next day cost nearly fifteen hundred dollars.

Five days later, a sheriff's deputy showed up at Landon's condo with a subpoena to appear in Virginia Beach General District Court on a charge of assault and battery. As it turned out, Landon wasn't the only one who required dental work. Grizzly's name was Kirby Wingate, and he claimed that Landon had started everything, chipping one of Grizzly's top front teeth when he threw the first unprovoked punch.

If the truth about the assault came out in court, no judge would convict Landon. But who knew what Wingate and his friends would say?

Landon couldn't afford an attorney and would have to defend himself. Because his application to practice law was now before the Virginia Board of Bar Examiners, who could either accept or reject the recommendation of the Character and Fitness Committee, he knew he would need to inform them about the charges. If he lost, he could kiss his law license good-bye.

6

IN VIRGINIA, General District Court has jurisdiction over all misdemeanors. Under a unique aspect of Virginia law, the victim or police officer initiates the case and testifies—the Commonwealth's Attorney doesn't even get involved unless the case is appealed. The person who files the complaint chooses the original return date for the first hearing. Sometimes a trial is actually held on that day, but often the case is rescheduled for trial at a later time. Kirby Wingate had chosen February 4, the day after the Super Bowl, as the original return date for Landon's assault charges. It was all Landon could think about while watching the game the night before. But what did it matter? The Packers had been knocked out during the championship game two weeks earlier.

Wingate had apparently called the paper as well. The article appeared on page two of the local section, reminding readers about Landon's role in the point-shaving scandal and informing them of his current application to acquire a Virginia law license. Kerri wanted to sue Wingate for defamation, but Landon scoffed at the thought. "Kerri, when you google my name, there are already four pages of articles about the point-shaving scandal. I'm pretty much defamation-proof."

"What's that supposed to mean?"

"That my reputation's so shot it would be hard for anyone to make it worse."

"That doesn't make it right."

Landon and Kerri arrived at court early and squeezed into the third row of a packed gallery. After twenty minutes, while the judge was processing a line of people requesting continuances, somebody tapped Landon on the shoulder.

It took Landon a second to make the connection. The man was an older lawyer, dressed in a well-worn blue pin-striped suit. He had a long Roman nose, dark eyebrows, a high forehead, and wavy gray hair tucked behind his ears.

"Mr. McNaughten," Landon said, surprised.

"Can we meet in the hallway?" McNaughten asked in a gruff whisper.

"Sure."

"You might want to bring the missus."

Outside the courtroom, they found an out-of-the-way corner. McNaughten introduced himself to Kerri, who said she remembered him from the hearing. "We really appreciate your committee taking a chance on Landon," she said. "You won't be disappointed."

Landon wanted to thank McNaughten as well but thought it might be a breach of protocol.

"That's actually why I wanted to talk to you," McNaughten said. "I was waiting upstairs to have some motions heard in circuit court, and I read the newspaper article. I worked too hard convincing my committee members to give you a chance to have it all get sidetracked now. Have you got a lawyer?"

Landon was gratified to learn that McNaughten had been in his corner. "I was going to handle it myself," Landon said.

"Bad idea," McNaughten replied. "You get this judge on the wrong day and it's a twofer."

"A what?" Kerri asked.

"A two-for-one. An assault on your record and, as a bonus, you get denied by the Board of Bar Examiners."

Landon knew it was true. Yet he had never been short on confidence. Deep down, he was relishing the chance to cross-examine Kirby Wingate.

"We can't really afford a lawyer," Kerri said.

"You can't afford *not* to have one," McNaughten responded. "Tell you what—I'll take your case today, and we'll figure out a way for you to pay me later."

Kerri looked at Landon, her eyes lighting up. Landon was skeptical. Anything too good to be true usually was.

"What's your rate?" Landon asked, as if it really mattered.

"Four-fifty an hour. But for you, I'll knock it down to four hundred. You go back in there and tell the judge that I'm representing you, and she'll set the trial on the contested docket for two this afternoon. Shouldn't take more than an hour to try the case. Another thirty minutes or so right now for you to tell me what happened."

Kerri looked at Landon with a face he had seen before when the woman discovered a bargain. "We really need to do this," she said. Landon agreed but felt a little wind leave his sails, as if Kerri had just benched him for the big game.

He and Kerri spent the next fifteen minutes briefing McNaughten on the fight. They tried to keep it concise. The meter was running.

"Did you bring your dental bill?" McNaughten asked.

Landon pulled it out of his suit-coat pocket. "Right here."

McNaughten patted his pockets and found a pair of reading glasses. He put them on, glanced at the bill, then stuffed the bill and glasses in his pocket.

"This should be fun," he said.

7

OVER LUNCH, Landon and Kerri debated why Harry McNaughten would want to take their case. Kerri's theory made the most sense—the man smelled some cheap publicity. Regardless, they were both glad to have him aboard.

When they returned to court, they sat through three other contested cases before the clerk called Landon's. Judge Tyra Lee, a striking young African American jurist, had all the witnesses stand to be sworn in. Landon joined Harry McNaughten at the front of the courtroom, standing to one side just below the judge's dais. Kirby Wingate and his buddies stood on the other.

"Nice of you to join us today, Mr. McNaughten," Judge Lee said.

"Couldn't resist a little fun," Harry said. "And I'd like to sequester the witnesses."

Judge Lee asked Wingate's buddies and Kerri to step into the hallway until they were called by a deputy. Landon was pretty sure Kerri would try to melt the others with her stare.

The police officer told the court that he had not witnessed the event but had arrived after the fight was over. Judge Lee then turned to Kirby Wingate and said, "Why don't you tell me what happened?"

Wingate had tried to dress the part. He had on a suit and tie for the occasion, though he couldn't quite get his shirt buttoned at the neck. He hadn't bothered to trim his beard but had ditched the earrings. His face was red, especially his broad nose, but Landon couldn't tell if that was from a lifetime of drinking or from nerves. Unlike Landon, he had not yet been to the dentist, and his front tooth was chipped at the corner.

He spoke in a conversational tone, a different man from the obnoxious fan of a few weeks earlier. He had obviously rehearsed his little spiel. He explained that he and his friends were 49ers fans and that Landon and his family were Green Bay fans. The two camps had been going back and forth during the first half, "talking a little trash," according to Wingate. Things got particularly heated when the second interception was returned for a touchdown.

When Kerri and Maddie went to the bathroom, Landon had called Wingate and his friends out. "He'd probably had a few too many drinks," Wingate explained. "I walked over to the defendant's table, and that's when I recognized him."

Wingate testified that he had been a Southeastern Knights fan his whole life. "So I said to him, 'Hey, ain't you the one that threw those ball games a few years ago?'"

That's when Landon got upset, Wingate said, and the two of them had words. Landon knocked over a drink. About that time, Kerri returned from the bathroom and started cursing at Wingate. "I'd prefer not to repeat her exact words, Judge. But anyway, she came up behind me and grabbed my arm and tried turning me around to face her. I put my hands up in the air, like this, basically saying, 'I don't know what you're doing, lady, but you're crazy.' And the defendant over there—" Wingate leaned forward, looking around McNaughten and pointing at Landon—"just hauls off and coldcocks me in the jaw."

Wingate took a half step forward and bared his teeth for Judge Lee.

"Chipped my tooth. To be honest, shocked me for a moment. I mean, that guy went berserk. He kneed one of my buddies in the groin and then started going after the other one. So I just grabbed him from behind to basically pull him off, and his wife is screaming and clawing at me, and somehow the defendant got punched—not by me, Judge— and fell to the floor. After that he stands up, and he and his wife start accusing me and my buddies of all kinds of stuff. So we just left so there wouldn't be any more problems."

Landon had spent two years in jail and another two and a half years in law school. He wasn't exactly naive, but it still shocked him to hear a guy like Kirby Wingate come into court, raise his hand to tell the truth, and spew out such bald-faced lies. He frowned and shook his head, hoping the judge would notice.

Harry, on the other hand, seemed amused. He grinned a little and snickered at the big man's testimony, giving the judge a sideways look. *Are you really buying this, Your Honor?* Judge Lee ignored him.

When Wingate had finished his story, Judge Lee turned to Harry. "Any questions, Counselor?"

"I might have one or two."

8

"HOW MUCH DO YOU WEIGH?"

"About 265."

"Height?"

"Six-one."

Harry took a step back. "How much would you say my client weighs, and how tall do you think he is?"

"I dunno. Maybe six-two or six-three. One ninety. I always thought he was a little thin for an SEC quarterback."

Harry stepped up between the two men and inched a little closer to Wingate. The big man's neck was turning a darker red. "So you're telling me that this guy—a skinny quarterback—calls you and two of your buddies out in the middle of a restaurant just because you're talking trash about his football team?"

"Must've been the beer talking."

"You saw him drinking beer?"

"Several."

"With your own eyes?"

"Like I said, he was sitting right in front of me."

For Landon, it was hard to resist a smile. After their meeting that morning, Harry had sent Landon home to get the receipt from his lunch at the Gordon Biersch Brewery. Harry took it out of his pocket and made a big show of checking three other suit-coat pockets before he found his glasses. He surveyed the receipt and then showed it to Wingate.

"Your Honor, I'll authenticate this when my client testifies, but I'd like to ask the witness about it."

"Go ahead," Judge Lee said. She had her hand over her mouth, as if studying the situation. Landon suspected she was hiding a smile.

"You know of any reason why those beers don't show up on my client's bill?" Harry asked.

Wingate shrugged. "How should I know? Maybe the bartender gave him a break after the fight."

Harry gave that a moment to sink in. "Do you have your receipt for that day?"

"Didn't know I needed it."

"I see. But it would show a few beers, wouldn't it?"

"Maybe. But I hadn't been drinking. They might have put our whole table on one tab."

"Uh-huh," Harry said. He shifted his glasses to the top of his head. "You had two friends with you, right?"

"Yep."

"They're out in the hallway, correct?"

"Yes."

"Now, Judge Lee here has to decide who started this fight. On the one hand, we have three men who came up to my client's table when his wife went to the bathroom. Those three men might have some drinks on their tab. Then there's my client. A skinny quarterback who had consumed no alcohol. And you want us to believe that my client took on all three of you just because you threw your hands up in the air when you turned and looked at his wife?"

To everybody in the courtroom, and especially Landon, the idea sounded ridiculous. McNaughten had a way of rephrasing the issue to make his case.

"I'm just saying what I saw."

"And you remember specifically how this fight happened—blow by blow?" McNaughten's voice was incredulous, mocking the witness.

"Your boy coldcocked me. I remember it like it was yesterday."

Harry pulled out Landon's dental bill and handed it to Wingate. "If you remember everything so well, who threw the punch that chipped three of my client's teeth?"

Wingate just stood there, not wanting to rat out his friend. "I didn't see that part."

"But you were holding him?" Harry said, his voice rising.

"Like I said, I was trying to pull him away from people, so, yeah, I grabbed him from behind."

Harry snorted. "Mr. Reed," he said to Landon, "would you step up here for a moment, please?" He then turned back to Wingate. "Put your arms around my client in a bear hug."

Wingate looked at Judge Lee. "This is stupid," he said.

"All right," Harry said. "I'll do it." He grabbed Landon from behind. "So now, you're holding my client like this, and he's defenseless, and somebody just nails him in the mouth but you don't know who it is?"

"It happened fast. I didn't see it."

Harry let go of Landon. "Isn't it true that you recognized my client as a former SEC quarterback involved in a point-shaving scandal and came over to his table in order to talk trash?"

"No, that's bull."

"And when his wife came back to the table, you started harassing her?"

"That's not true either."

"And when my client tried to protect his wife, you held him so your buddies could punch him in the face and kick him in the groin until he collapsed on the floor?"

"You tell a good story, Mr. McNaughten. But that's not the way it happened."

"And for that we have your word; is that right?"

"You've got my word."

///

The next two witnesses fared even worse. Harry poked holes in their stories and highlighted inconsistencies between them. Nobody seemed to know how Landon's teeth had gotten chipped, and Harry hammered that point relentlessly.

Landon started to relax. This case was going nowhere, and Harry was flat-out having fun.

After all three men testified, Judge Lee turned to Kirby Wingate. "Do you have any more evidence, Mr. Wingate?"

He looked confused, as if maybe he was missing something. "Nope. That's about it. That's the way it happened."

Judge Lee nodded at Harry. "Looks like the prosecution rests," she said.

Harry took his reading glasses off the top of his head, folded them, and put them in his pocket. "I move to strike the evidence," he said. "It's obvious that Mr. Wingate and his friends are lying. But in addition, nobody testified as to whether this alleged crime took place in Virginia Beach. As the court knows, venue is an essential element of any criminal case, and without such testimony, the court should dismiss the case with prejudice."

Judge Lee was already writing on the warrant and didn't bother looking up. "The court agrees. Mr. Wingate has failed to prove his case. The case is dismissed with prejudice."

She stopped writing for a moment and glared at Wingate. "I don't know why Mr. and Mrs. Reed didn't file an assault charge against *you*. But I can tell you this, Mr. Wingate—if they had, and if you had come in here and testified the way you did today, I would have given you the full year allowed by law."

Landon could tell that Wingate didn't like being lectured by a woman. He clenched his jaw and stared at the judge.

She banged her gavel. "Next case," she said pleasantly.

In the hallway, Landon and Kerri thanked Harry profusely. "It may take some time," Landon said, "but we're going to pay you every dime. You certainly earned it."

McNaughten handed Landon a business card. "You got a job offer yet?"

"No."

"I've got a few things I need some help with," Harry said. "Come to my office at nine tomorrow morning, and I'll put you to work at fifty bucks an hour. Once you pay off my bill, we'll talk about where to go from there."

"Are you serious?" Landon asked.

McNaughten looked around and lowered his voice. There was a reporter waiting patiently off to the side to talk with Harry and Landon. "Look, when I started practicing law, I had a lot to prove. Nobody in my family had even gone to college. Nobody cut me any breaks. I like hiring people who have something to prove. You put on a good case in front of the Character and Fitness Committee. If you work hard and keep your nose clean, you'll be a heckuva lawyer someday."

Landon didn't know what to say. He'd been looking for a legal job for weeks and had pretty much given up hope.

"Thank you," he said. "For everything."

Harry took a step closer. When he spoke, his lips hardly moved. "Next time, don't turn your back on the big guy. One good knee to the groin should put him down. Then you can take care of his buddies."

"I'll try to keep that in mind, sir."

9

ON MONDAY NIGHT, Landon hunched over his computer and learned all that he could about Harry McNaughten's law firm, McNaughten and Clay.

Harry was a criminal-defense attorney who had been in the trenches for forty years. He seemed to specialize in cases that were considered unwinnable, occasionally shocking pundits with a not-guilty verdict. The managing partner of the firm, a man named Brent Benedict, was a former Navy pilot who did mostly appellate work. He teamed with a third partner, Parker Clausen, who was not only a lawyer but a published novelist. Earlier that year, one of Clausen's novels had hit the lower rungs of the *New York Times* Best Sellers List. Landon checked out the reviews, most of which skewered the book, so that he'd be able to talk intelligently with Clausen about his writing.

The firm had originally been founded by Harry McNaughten and a woman named Emma Clay. She had retired after an accused rapist she and Harry defended was set loose and attacked the same woman six months later. Emma Clay had given her keys to Harry, walked out of the office, and started raising horses in Pungo.

The bios of the lawyers told Landon a few things about their personalities. Clausen's talked more about his novels than his work as a lawyer. He bragged that he had a Mensa-level IQ and had graduated with high honors from the University of Virginia School of Law. According to his bio, his books were favorably compared to Tom Wolfe, though Landon had searched the Internet in vain for such a comparison. In the firm pictures, Clausen was always dressed casually. He was a big man, probably weighing three hundred pounds, with long gray hair that he pulled back in a ponytail.

Brent Benedict was Clausen's polar opposite. Buttoned-down, with a military haircut, his bio read like somebody had sanitized it and scrubbed it and then sanitized it some more. Brent listed all of his legal accomplishments—rated AV by Martindale-Hubbell, named one of Virginia's "Super Lawyers" for appellate work, past chairman of the Appellate Section of the Virginia State Bar, and so on. He had a long list of complex appellate cases to his credit, and his bio contained links to all the opinions. He was a lawyer's lawyer, and Landon hoped he would have a chance to work with the man.

The head shot that generated the most conversation in the Reed household was of the firm's associate, Rachel Strach. Rachel's wavy blonde hair could have been featured on a shampoo commercial. She had big blue eyes, brilliant white teeth, and thick red lipstick. In the photo, she was glancing longingly over her shoulder at the camera. If lawyering didn't work out, the woman could be a model.

"What kind of lawyer puts a glamour shot on the firm web page?" Kerri asked.

"She probably doesn't look anything like that in real life," Landon said.

Kerri checked out Rachel's Facebook profile and found several pictures of Rachel in a bikini. "You need to keep your distance from that woman," she warned.

Landon got up from his computer and looked over Kerri's shoulder at her iPad. He gave her a kiss on the head. "You've got nothing to worry about."

Landon spent most of his time that night trying to get a feel for Harry McNaughten's law practice. Harry's claim to fame was the infamous defense he had mounted a few years back for an alleged assassin working for a government-contracted security firm called Cipher Inc. The defense Harry had employed was a classic case of jury nullification, a high-risk strategy where a lawyer tries to get jury members to ignore the law and follow their emotions.

10

SIX YEARS EARLIER
NORFOLK, VIRGINIA

EVERYTHING SEAN PHOENIX had worked so hard to build in the years after his release from that Syrian prison came down to this—closing arguments in front of a jury of his alleged peers, chosen from the cities and towns of the Eastern District of Virginia. The reputation and future of Cipher Inc., the company he had personally founded, were on the line. The lives of millions of people around the globe would be impacted.

Following 9/11, two government contractors had risen to prominence. At first, the most notorious was Blackwater USA. Founded by Erik Prince, a former Navy SEAL, the company had purchased more than seven thousand acres near the Great Dismal Swamp on the Virginia–North Carolina border and had trained thousands of mercenaries. Blackwater had received more than $1 billion in government contracts up until five Blackwater guards were charged in the shooting deaths of fourteen Iraqi civilians. An avalanche of unfavorable media coverage followed, as well as a criminal trial against the guards and a slew of congressional hearings.

Blackwater's problems opened the door for Cipher's rise to prominence, though Sean did a good job keeping most of the firm's actual work from public view. Cipher had thousands of employees working out of branch offices in more than thirty countries. The State Department sometimes called on Cipher agents to interrogate foreign combatants in ways that U.S. soldiers could not under current U.S. policies. Cipher operatives also provided a reliable source of intelligence-gathering on competitors of their multinational clients. And sometimes, the U.S. government would call on Sean and his team to perform "off-the-books" operations that were too politically volatile for the U.S. military to attempt directly. This much was clear: the age of terrorism had placed more of a premium on intelligence-gathering than infantry boots on the ground. Over time, Cipher Inc. had supplanted Blackwater as the most influential, despised, discussed, and mysterious company on the planet.

Cipher's effectiveness depended on secrecy and a sophisticated web of informants in nearly every major city in the United States, North Africa, and the Middle East. Now it all threatened to come undone. A former operative had turned against the company and claimed that he had personal knowledge of Cipher's role in the recent assassination of a Sudanese official named Ahmed Al-Latif. Working with U.S. Attorney Elias King, that operative had provided enough evidence for King to charge both Sean Phoenix and the alleged triggerman, an agent named Daken Antonov, with conspiracy to commit murder.

Sean had hired a big D.C. firm and paid through the nose for the best defense money could buy. Antonov had hired a local Virginia Beach lawyer named Harry McNaughten. Neither Sean nor Antonov took the stand. Their lawyers admitted that Antonov worked for Cipher Inc. but denied that Antonov had anything to do with Al-Latif's assassination.

Antonov was one of Sean's best operatives. He had bushy eyebrows that came to a V just over his nose and eye sockets deeply shadowed by his bulging forehead. This, coupled with the long sideburns that ran along the bottom of his jaw, had earned him the nickname Wolfman within the Cipher organization. He was deadly efficient at what he did and seldom left any traces. The Wolfman was the last agent Sean could afford to lose.

But Elias King was a pit bull of a prosecutor, and he built a methodical case with internal Cipher documents and eyewitness accounts of the assassination. Things looked good for the prosecution until the cross-examination of the government's main informant by defense attorney Harry McNaughten.

Instead of directly attacking the government's case, Harry focused on the atrocities in the Darfur region of Sudan, atrocities that Al-Latif had authorized. Harry showed photos of children dying of disease and hunger. He asked about the killing fields and the systematic raping of women and the loss of more than a million innocent lives. He showed a bloody photo of a young Sudanese boy who had lost both hands during a bomb attack. Elias King objected to nearly every question, and there were more than a few shouting matches, but Harry made his points. And finally, as Harry McNaughten rose to give his closing argument, the entire courtroom seemed to hold its collective breath in anticipation.

He took his place in front of the jury without a single note. He hunched over the podium, his wavy gray hair and spindly frame giving him the air of a man who had seen more than his share of suffering and injustice. He didn't bother buttoning his suit coat, his casual demeanor a stark contrast to the stiff bearing of Sean's own D.C. lawyer and the intense staccato presentation of Elias King.

"You've seen the pictures," Harry said. "You've seen what Al-Latif and his men did to thousands of innocent women and children. Now, I'm not admitting that my client had any role in his assassination. But even if he did, should we convict him of murder?"

Harry let the question hang out there for a moment. The judge had only allowed this line of defense after hours of arguments by the lawyers the preceding day, based on Harry's theory that international law could trump these murder charges. Because of the court's ruling, Elias King was forced to swallow his objections, and he sat at the prosecution table with a frown on his face, seething as Harry did his thing.

"There was another murder trial many years ago. It was technically a court-martial, growing out of an incident in Vietnam known as the My Lai Massacre. Lieutenant William Calley, the platoon commander, was prosecuted for giving an order to slaughter innocent civilians. They were all herded down into a ditch and . . . *bam-bam-bam*." Harry acted like he had a machine gun, pointing it into the ditch. "They just mowed 'em all down.

"But there were other men prosecuted for that slaughter as well. Do you know what their crime was?"

Harry surveyed the jury from right to left. He was out from behind the podium now, nothing between him and the jury box. "Their crime was that they allowed the massacre to happen. Because even in war, you don't allow somebody to kill babies and rape innocent women.

"There is something called the Universal Declaration of Human Rights, and the United States is a signatory. I for one am glad we are. That charter acknowledges universal principles, and one of those is that we all have a responsibility to protect the most innocent and vulnerable among us from the atrocities of war."

Harry was old-school and didn't use PowerPoint. Instead, he pulled out his most gruesome pictures, blown up and mounted on poster board, and quietly placed them in front of the jury. He walked back behind the podium.

"There is no doubt that somebody assassinated Ahmed Al-Latif. Did it stop the atrocities shown in these photographs? No. But did it slow them down? Possibly.

"My client didn't assassinate this Sudanese official. But whoever did, they shouldn't be prosecuted. They should be congratulated."

"Objection!" Elias King said.

The objection was sustained, but Harry didn't seem to care.

"I take no joy in showing you these photographs. I take no pride in describing the unspeakable horrors that took place in Sudan. But that's the real world. And just because Mr. King wants to pretend it doesn't exist—that won't make it go away."

"Objection!"

"Sustained. You're pushing it, Mr. McNaughten."

"Sorry, Your Honor." Harry lowered his voice. "George Orwell once said that people like us sleep peacefully in our beds at night only because rough men stand ready to do violence on our behalf.

"Now, I know what Mr. King is going to say in his rebuttal. No international law authorizes the assassination of another country's government officials. We can't allow people to become vigilantes and take matters into their own hands. But when he's giving that rebuttal argument, ask yourself these questions: 'How long do we have to wait to bring someone like Al-Latif to justice? How long do we allow him to play judge, jury, and executioner—along with torturer in chief—before somebody does something about it?'"

Harry McNaughten lowered his voice another notch until it was a barely audible growl. "If you acquit my client, you'll sleep peacefully tonight knowing that you have done the right thing."

It took the jury less than three hours to do exactly what Harry McNaughten had suggested. And since the alleged triggerman was acquitted, Sean Phoenix was acquitted too. Before leaving town the next day, Sean stopped by the offices of McNaughten and Clay. He put Harry on retainer and hired Brent Benedict to handle a few of Cipher Inc.'s cases working their way through the appellate courts.

"Men like me need defense lawyers like you," Sean told Harry.

"That informant almost took you down," Harry said. "Men like you need to be more careful who you hire."

///

Prosecutors are expected to win the big cases, and for Elias King, the handwriting was on the wall. The Al-Latif fiasco, coupled with a presidential election that put King's party on the outside looking in, led to a change in the U.S. Attorney for the Eastern District of Virginia. A year after losing the biggest case of his career as a prosecutor, King moved to the "dark side," representing white-collar criminals as a partner at Kilgore and Strobel, one of Norfolk's oldest and most distinguished firms.

King's tenacity and work ethic served him well in the private sector, and before long he had become one of the top criminal-defense attorneys in the region. And, in the eyes of his successor, one of the most despised.

That was why, six years after Al-Latif, when the Feds received an anonymous tip about insider trading being orchestrated by a partner at Kilgore and Strobel, it didn't surprise the new U.S. Attorney to find Elias King's digital fingerprints all over the anonymous offshore accounts. The man was using information about deals being pursued by firm clients to buy or sell stock of those clients' companies before the deals were made public. The firm lawyered up, as did Elias King. His first call was to his old nemesis, Harry McNaughten.

"After the Al-Latif verdict," Elias said, "I always said that if I ever got into trouble, I would call you."

"Everybody gets lucky once in a while," Harry said.

They met, Elias paid Harry's retainer, and the two analyzed what little they knew about the government's case.

"Based on what you've told me," Harry said, "I'll be surprised if they proceed. Without a witness to tie it all up, there's just too much speculation."

But in that initial meeting, Elias didn't tell Harry everything. He ignored Harry's admonition that defense lawyers needed to know every detail about their clients' lives, both good and bad, that might affect the case. Elias was used to being in control. In his view, certain things needed to remain private.

He didn't tell Harry about Erica. Or about the affair. Or about the fact that his wife, Julia, had found out.

It would prove to be a costly mistake.

11

FORTY-EIGHT HOURS AFTER the initial shock, Erica Jensen still couldn't believe she was pregnant. *That* certainly wasn't part of the plan.

Did she love him? Yes. But that hadn't been part of the plan either.

When she first started working with Elias King, she had expected him to be controlling and demanding. Manipulative. Win-at-all-costs. The man had a reputation.

She found him to be just the opposite. He was winsome and humble. Yes, he was competitive. But he was also committed to justice and to his clients. He was older than Erica. Yet he had a presence, something magnetic about the way he threw himself into his causes. She hadn't thought men like that still existed.

In the last two days, everything had changed. On Saturday, Erica learned she was pregnant. On Sunday night, Elias's wife found out about their affair. Which brought them to this pivotal day. Earlier, at the office,

Elias had told Erica they couldn't see each other anymore. Couldn't even work together. He would find another place for her at the firm.

In some ways, it made her respect him more. Commitment. Family. These were the things that mattered most.

And now, Erica had her own little family to consider. There was a life growing inside her. A little boy, maybe. She wondered if he would be like Elias. Regardless, he would need his mom. She couldn't give this baby up for adoption. She would raise the child herself, giving him enough love for two parents. But first, she had to be able to live with herself.

There was a saying: "The truth shall set you free." She reminded herself of that as she picked up the phone and called the U.S. Attorney's office. She asked for the person in charge of the investigation at Kilgore and Strobel, and her call was transferred to Mitchell Taylor, an assistant U.S. Attorney for the Eastern District of Virginia.

"I've got some information about the insider trading case you're investigating," she said. "I'm willing to testify if you give me immunity."

"Who is this?"

"I'd rather not say over the phone."

"What type of information?"

"We need to meet in person. I'll explain everything then."

"How do I know you're legit?" Mitchell asked. "You need to give me something I can check out."

Erica gave him enough information to convince him that she was to be taken seriously. They argued for a few minutes about the logistics, but the assistant U.S. Attorney eventually agreed to Erica's conditions. She knew the investigation was too important for him to pass up a chance at this meeting. And he didn't know the half of it.

///

Later that night, Erica played the game well, sharing a drink with her visitor as if nothing had changed. It wasn't until her vision started blurring that she realized she had been drugged. By then, her mind was in quicksand, the world spinning around her, the betrayal complete. Her last thoughts were not about her lover but her baby. She put a hand over her stomach, as if to protect the tiny embryo, growing in what should have been the safest place on earth.

"I'm pregnant," she muttered, but she wasn't even sure the words were coming out right. "Please don't hurt my baby."

12

LANDON GOT OUT OF BED EARLY Tuesday morning and would not have been more excited if he had been starting work as the attorney general of the United States. He was a firm believer that everything happened for a reason. The hearing before the Character and Fitness Committee. The brawl at the Gordon Biersch Brewery. His representation by Harry McNaughten in General District Court. All of this had culminated in an opportunity to show McNaughten and Clay what he could do. He had sent out hundreds of résumés, but God had orchestrated events in a way that Landon could have never anticipated.

Kerri was taking a personal day so she could take care of Maddie and look for a day care. She got up early and fixed Landon breakfast, and he felt like a superstar. He arrived at the firm parking lot at eight o'clock and immediately liked the feel of the place. The firm was housed in a classy brick building with pillars on the front portico that made it look like a miniature version of a courthouse. It was on Laskin Road, the gateway to the oceanfront, less than a mile from the beach. He entered through glass doors with the firm name stenciled on them and met a young African American woman manning the front desk.

"I'm Landon Reed," he said. "I'm supposed to start work today for Mr. McNaughten."

The nameplate on the granite countertop that surrounded the reception desk read *Janaya Young*. Janaya had curly black hair, a round, pudgy face, and black-rimmed glasses. There were pictures of Janaya and two young boys who appeared to be twins on the shelf behind her.

"Was he expecting you?" she asked.

"Yes."

Janaya put on her headset and dialed an extension but apparently got no answer. She dialed a second number, which Landon assumed was McNaughten's cell phone.

"He's not in yet. Why don't you have a seat in our waiting room, and I'll let Mr. Benedict know you're here."

Just off the main reception area was a sitting room with a fireplace and some funky-looking striped beach furniture. The fireplace had a beautiful oil painting displayed over it—a sailboat in the Caribbean—and there were bookshelves on each end that prominently displayed Parker Clausen's books right alongside more notable legal-thriller authors such as John Grisham and Michael Connelly. Landon had a seat and glanced around. The entire office had hardwood floors and crown molding. There was marble trim around the fireplace. It had the feel of casual success, and Landon decided that he could get used to working in a place like this.

He sat on a green couch with pink striped pillows for five minutes before Brent Benedict, the firm's managing partner, came into the room. Landon's palms were sweaty, and he was a little surprised at his own nervousness. He had played in front of packed stadiums, but he was wound tight about his first day at a new job.

Landon stood and shook Benedict's hand. Benedict wore a pressed white shirt and red tie. His black shoes looked like they had just been shined, and his perfect posture, along with precise and aggressive movements, showed that the man was still military at heart. His face was starting to display the first signs of age, a few wrinkles spiderwebbing from his eyes, but he had a firm jaw and the bearing of a former officer. He didn't sit down.

"Let's go back to the conference room for a minute," he suggested.

Landon followed him past the reception area into a large conference room with built-in bookshelves and an enormous slate table. Windows in the back overlooked a wooded area around a quaint pond.

Benedict had no papers with him, and he took a seat at the head of the table. Landon sat in one of the side seats.

"We've tried to call Harry, but we can't reach him right now," Benedict explained. "He's got a hearing this morning in Norfolk Circuit Court, and he's notorious for being hard to reach by cell.

"I'm the managing partner here, and Harry didn't mention anything about hiring a new associate. We have processes in place and budgets and those types of things. One partner is not authorized to bring on a new attorney without the approval of the others."

Landon felt his heart pump a little faster but knew he could straighten this out. "It's a bit of a long story," he said. "And I guess I'm not exactly a new hire, but here's what happened. . . ." He ran through the saga as quickly as he could. Benedict listened without expression.

When Landon finished, Benedict shook his head a little. "Sounds like Harry," he acknowledged. "But regardless of how it came about, Harry can't just hire an associate without the firm's approval. And even if you were just going to clerk for us at fifty dollars an hour in order to pay off your legal bill, you're technically still an employee. We would have to do all the paperwork and put you on the payroll. We'd have to set up an office and a computer. Frankly, we're not in a position to do that right now."

"Maybe I could just clerk for free for a few weeks. If you like my work, you could decide whether to put me on the payroll then."

Benedict glanced at his watch. "Look, I don't know what Harry was thinking, and I'm sorry if he got your hopes up. But at this point we're just not going to be able to use you."

Benedict stood and Landon did the same. *Everything happens for a reason,* Landon reminded himself. Maybe God was trying to protect him from something disastrous lurking just beneath the surface.

"Thanks for your time," Landon said.

///

A few minutes later, as he pulled out of the McNaughten and Clay parking lot, Landon called a homeowner who had wanted two rooms painted by the end of the week. Landon had called the day before to cancel the job, explaining that he would be starting at a law firm instead. He hoped she still needed someone to complete the project.

THAT NIGHT, Landon hit the weights hard, working out with the three high school juniors he was training to play quarterback at the next level. The frustration seeped out of his body as the sweat poured off him.

He pushed the boys harder than he had in weeks. After a grueling weight session, they focused on footwork and technique in the gym for forty-five minutes, videotaping the kids' throwing motions and breaking down the film. He liked these kids; two of them had a legitimate shot at playing Division I ball and had already earned several offers. The third was a sleeper and needed to have a good senior year. Landon had been working out with all three since last summer and not once had they questioned him about his SEC Championship Game.

Landon didn't allow cell phones in the gym, so it wasn't until eight o'clock that he picked up his iPhone and saw the two missed calls from a number he didn't recognize. He checked voice mail and was surprised to hear a message from Harry McNaughten. "Landon. Give me a call on this number. I need your help on something right away."

When he returned the call, Harry was brusque. "Where are you?"

"At the Norfolk Christian gym on Thole Street."

"I need you to meet me at a client's house in Chesapeake. The police are conducting a search, and I need as many sets of eyes as possible."

Before Landon could ask questions, McNaughten provided the address and the client's name: Elias King. Landon recognized the name as the prosecutor on the Al-Latif case. Now he was Harry's client? As Landon threw on his Packers sweatshirt and started cutting off lights in the gym, Harry provided a quick debriefing.

Elias, a former prosecutor, was working at Kilgore and Strobel, a large Norfolk firm. A few months earlier, a federal grand jury had been convened to investigate insider trading by the firm. King was believed to be the main target. Now King's paralegal, a young woman named Erica Jensen, had been missing for more than twenty-four hours.

"Elias still has some friends in the prosecutor's camp," Harry said. "Apparently Ms. Jensen was scheduled to meet with the assistant U.S. Attorney today and hasn't been heard from since last night. They suspect Elias has something to do with her disappearance."

"I can be there in thirty minutes," Landon said. "But I'm wearing sweats."

"Be here in fifteen," Harry said. And then he was off the phone.

///

Elias King lived at the end of a cul-de-sac in a large brick house that reminded Landon of a fortress. Tonight it was under siege. Three marked police cruisers and two Crown Vics were angled against the curb. A tow truck sat in the driveway. One of the officers stopped Landon at the front door. "You can't go in there. We're conducting a search."

"I'm Mr. King's attorney," Landon said, self-consciously aware of his sweatpants, sneakers, and large, hooded Packers sweatshirt.

The officer shook his head. "His attorney's already in there."

"I work with Mr. McNaughten," Landon said, sidestepping the officer.

He found Harry upstairs in the bedroom, snapping pictures with his phone while two policemen tore the place apart. Clothes were strewn everywhere. The mattress was off the bed. A woman whom Landon assumed to be Elias King's wife sat in a chair in the corner, a blank expression on her face.

"Elias is in the garage," Harry said. "I need you to go downstairs and document everything they touch. Take notes on whatever they bag."

"Yes, sir."

Landon hustled downstairs and found two plainclothed officers in what appeared to be Elias's study, wearing plastic gloves and bagging evidence. Papers were scattered everywhere. One of the officers was bent over a drawer of hanging files. Landon snapped a picture with his iPhone and then tried to get a better angle and a close-up of what the officer was looking at.

But the other officer, all six feet five inches and 250 pounds of him, stepped in front of Landon.

"Get that camera out of here," he said.

"I'm Mr. King's attorney," Landon responded, keeping his voice even. "Let me see your search warrant."

"'Let me see your search warrant,'" the officer mimicked. "Must have seen that line on TV."

His partner didn't respond; he seemed focused on something he had found in the drawer.

"Let me see your bar card," the larger officer said to Landon.

"I got a phone call while I was working out. I don't have it with me."

"Then you need to leave."

Landon switched his iPhone to video. "My name is Landon Reed. It's now 8:25 p.m. on February 5, and the Chesapeake police are conducting a search at the home of Elias King. The officer standing in front of me is trying to block my view while his partner searches through Mr. King's desk. We will, of course, contest the chain of custody for any and all evidence gathered in this manner."

The officer put his hand in front of the phone. "Nice try, Counsel," he said. "But nobody's stopping you from going anywhere you want."

With that settled, Landon spent the next ninety minutes taking pictures and videos, asking questions that went unanswered, and otherwise making a pest of himself as the police completed their search of the King residence. Afterward, as the officers were huddled in the driveway watching the tow truck operator hook up a Chrysler 300M, Harry pulled Landon aside to provide some additional details.

"According to Elias's source, the cops received an anonymous tip last night that somebody dumped what appeared to be a large body bag off the high-rise bridge on the Intracoastal Waterway. The description of the vehicle matched Elias's car."

After the tow truck and car left, the police officers talked among themselves for a few minutes and then headed toward their squad cars. One of the officers lingered behind and approached Elias.

"I'm sorry it has to be like this," he said.

"You're just doing your job," Elias responded.

After all the officers left, Harry and Landon talked with Elias and his wife in the driveway. Mrs. King's face was taut, the corners of her mouth pulled down. She closed her eyes for a beat, as if that might somehow wash away the memories. Elias still had on his white shirt from work, his tie loosened, his sleeves rolled up to the elbows.

"I don't trust the cops," Harry said. "They may have installed some listening devices in your home. Don't talk out loud about anything having to do with Erica Jensen inside."

Mrs. King nodded. She looked shell-shocked.

"Elias, I'd like to meet for a few minutes. What about the IHOP on Battlefield Boulevard?"

Elias turned to his wife. "You going to be okay?"

Even though she had thrown on a winter jacket, she was hugging herself and shivering. Landon noticed that she kept her distance from Elias. "I'm fine."

She thanked Harry and Landon for coming. Her son, who looked to be about fifteen, was standing in the garage doorway watching.

"Jake and I can start cleaning up," Mrs. King said, her voice emotionless and resigned. "You can take my car."

Harry and Landon headed to their cars in the cul-de-sac. A few curious neighbors were on their porches.

"Just a little misunderstanding," Harry said loud enough to be heard by everyone. "The party's over. You can all go to bed now."

14

LANDON ARRIVED AT THE IHOP first and waited in his truck until he saw Harry pull up. He grabbed his iPad and walked over to meet Harry in the parking lot. Landon was hoping to get a few minutes to mention the less-than-enthusiastic reception he had received at the firm that morning.

"How's that for an exciting first day at the office?" Harry asked as Landon approached his vehicle.

"Beats research," Landon said.

Harry was holding two legal pads and handed one to Landon. "People say I'm a little paranoid," Harry said. "You will be too after you see what the government does to convict some of our clients. Lose that iPad and use this. Every digital keystroke leaves a fingerprint someplace in cyberspace. In our line of work, we don't like fingerprints."

Landon took the legal pad and wondered if all high-profile criminal-defense lawyers were this paranoid. He hadn't heard anything about these kinds of precautions in law school.

Regardless, Landon dutifully put his iPad back in his truck and went into the restaurant with Harry. "I'd like that booth in the corner," Harry said to the young woman seating them. He motioned to a booth that had nobody on either side. Before they sat, Landon had to brush some crumbs off the bench on his side of the booth and a waitress had to come and bus the table, but the spot seemed to suit Harry just fine. The two men ordered coffee, and Landon took off his sweatshirt, bunching it in the corner of the bench. Landon mentioned the run-in he'd had with Brent Benedict that morning.

"Show up tomorrow at eight thirty," Harry said. "Instead of going to the main doors, go in the door on the far right, which is a separate entrance that leads upstairs. If I'm not there yet, Janaya can let you in that outside door. The only rooms up there are my office, a conference room, and a couple of war rooms. Pick one of those war rooms as your office and start cleaning it up. When I get there, I'll deal with Benedict."

Landon should have felt a rush of adrenaline knowing that he would have a place to work in the morning. But the prospect of joining a firm that seemed so dysfunctional took the edge off his euphoria.

He took a few notes on the case while they waited for Elias. When Elias appeared, Landon slid over and Elias sat next to him, placing his briefcase under the table.

When he had first seen Elias, Landon knew that the man reminded him of someone. Now it struck him—a younger version of Eliot Spitzer, the former governor of New York. They had the same pointed face and prominent nose. The same receding hairline and large ears. And the same rock-solid jaw and penetrating blue eyes. Elias was still wearing his white shirt, though he had taken off his tie. He hung his overcoat on a hook at the booth.

Harry introduced Landon, leaving out the part about Landon's checkered football career. Elias stared as if trying to place the young lawyer.

"Did you play football for Southeastern?" Elias asked.

Landon felt his face redden a little. The question always had deeper meaning. *Are you the quarterback who betrayed his teammates? Are you the one who put money ahead of winning football games?*

"Guilty," Landon said. "Hope you weren't a fan."

"I don't watch football," Elias said with what sounded to Landon like a fair amount of disdain. "But I watch trials."

"I sat on the Character and Fitness Committee that reviewed Landon's bar application," Harry interjected. "He tried one heckuva case for himself. I know you're not a big believer in redemption, Elias, but this young man has changed."

Landon felt a wave of gratefulness wash over him. There weren't many people willing to stick their necks out for a former felon, rushing to his defense. Perhaps it came from Harry's job, always looking for the best in his clients.

Their waitress returned and the men stopped talking. Elias ordered water. When the waitress left, Elias turned to Landon. "You're lucky to be working with this man," he said. "Harry McNaughten is a legend in the prosecutor's office. He was a pain in the rear to have on the other side of a case, but a legend nonetheless. That's why I hired him. And he's a pretty good judge of character."

Harry seemed uncomfortable with the accolades and ready to get down to business. He leaned forward a little, his raspy voice barely above a whisper. "How did you know they were coming?"

"One of the secretaries in the Chesapeake Commonwealth's Attorney's office used to work in the U.S. Attorney's office when I was there," Elias said. "She gave me a heads-up."

Landon couldn't decide whether he should take notes on this or not. Given Harry's paranoia, he decided against it.

"What else did she say?" Harry asked.

Elias took a quick look around. Must be everybody on the defense side was paranoid, Landon decided. "She was pretty nervous, so it was hard prying much out of her. Erica Jensen didn't show up for a meeting with the Feds this morning, and nobody could find her. They started calling the locals to see if anybody knew anything. They found out that the Chesapeake cops received an anonymous tip about somebody dumping a body into the Intracoastal Waterway last night. The car description apparently fit mine. They put two and two together, and the Commonwealth's Attorney got a search warrant for my house and car." Elias shrugged. "That's all I know."

"Is your source going to keep you in the loop?" Harry asked.

To Landon, it seemed like the wrong question. He wanted to start with *Did you do it?* But that was probably just his law student naiveté. He would watch Harry's more sophisticated choreography and try to learn from it.

"I doubt it." Elias took a sip of water. Neither Elias nor Harry seemed the least bit bothered about the ethics of having a source inside the Commonwealth's Attorney's office. To Landon, it made the insider trading allegations against Elias seem more credible. "She said she couldn't talk to me about the case after this. Said she knew I didn't do anything wrong and wished me the best."

Harry grunted. It was not the answer he wanted. "Do you have an alibi for last night?" he asked.

"I was sleeping."

"With your wife?"

Elias shook his head and frowned. "Separate rooms."

This elicited a grimace and a second grunt of disapproval from Harry. "And that will be her testimony?"

Elias stared Harry down. "I'm not going to ask her to lie."

"Okay. But why are you sleeping in separate rooms?"

There was an uncomfortable moment of silence as Elias played with his water glass, thinking. He looked up at Harry when he delivered the news. "She found out about Erica."

"Found out that you were fooling around?" Harry asked.

"Yeah. Julia found some text messages two nights ago, on Super Bowl Sunday."

Harry scowled and made another note. "You sent text messages?"

"I know," Elias said, cutting Harry off. "I wasn't exactly thinking clearly."

Harry shook his head and took a sip of coffee. He fished around for his reading glasses, found them, and made a couple of notes, torturing everyone with the silence. "Did you go to Ms. Jensen's apartment last night?"

"No."

"Talk to her on the phone?"

"I called her a couple of times. She didn't answer."

Harry took off his glasses, rubbed his eyes, and thought about the next question. "You have any idea where she is?" he eventually asked. "Is there a chance she could just show up someplace tomorrow?"

"I've been calling her all day," Elias said. "I told her yesterday that Julia found out about us. I told Erica we had to break it off for the sake of my family. I wanted a shot at restoring my marriage. She said she understood."

"And then she called the Feds and said she wanted to meet with them," Harry said.

"Apparently."

"And you knew nothing about this meeting?"

"No. Just found out about it today."

"Your source didn't tell you about it earlier?"

This time Elias waited a moment to answer, setting his jaw. Landon could tell the man wasn't used to being questioned like this.

"No."

Harry spent the next fifteen minutes quizzing Elias about his affair. How long had it lasted? Who else knew about it? How did it start? What did Erica say when Elias told her it was over?

When Harry asked how many times Elias and Erica had sex, Elias bristled. "How is that relevant?"

Harry put down his pen and took off his glasses, setting them on the table. "Do you really need a road map?"

Elias sighed. "No."

"Then how many times?"

"I'm not sure. Maybe six or eight over a four-week period."

"Where?"

"Why does that matter?"

"I'm trying to figure out who else might have seen you."

"Nobody."

And so it went, Harry probing and Elias reluctantly answering. Landon wasn't sure, but it seemed like Harry was trying to subtly demonstrate the weaknesses of their case, and how the prosecution would attempt to cross-examine Elias. No questions were off-limits; no aspects of the affair could remain private.

Finally, mercifully, Harry changed the subject. "Let's start with a list of what we saw the cops take," he suggested.

For the next twenty minutes, the men compared notes on the items the cops had bagged. Conspicuously absent was any mention of computers, cell phones, or tablet devices.

Harry noticed it too. "No computers?" he asked.

"They took my work laptop a few weeks ago," Elias replied. "But they didn't get my replacement laptop or my other devices." He patted his briefcase under the table.

"What's the inventory?" Harry asked.

"My laptop. An iPad. An iPhone."

Harry leaned back and thought about this for a moment. Landon knew that there would be a gold mine of digital information on those devices. Phone calls. Internet searches. E-mails and texts.

"What about Julia's computer?"

"She hid it. The cops don't have it, but she wouldn't give it to me, either."

"Cell phone?"

"Same."

"What's she hiding?" Harry asked.

"Nothing," Elias said. "It's just that right now she doesn't have the greatest amount of trust in me."

I wonder why, Landon wanted to say, though he kept his mouth shut.

Harry finished his cold coffee. "All right. Landon, you'll be the new custodian of Elias's computers and cell phone. Don't let them out of your sight. You sleep with them under your pillow. You take them with you to the bathroom. They never leave your side. Tomorrow I'll give you the name of a guy who can download everything from the hard drives and memory cards. You stand there looking over his shoulder and watch him do it. Got it?"

"Sure," Landon said, though he didn't like it. He vaguely remembered that one of his law school classes had addressed this type of situation. He didn't know if it was ethical to withhold evidence from the prosecutors.

"You sure you don't want to hold on to it?" Elias asked Harry.

"Landon's more than capable," Harry said.

Using his leg, Elias slid the briefcase toward Landon. Landon reached down and secured it against the booth. He would go home and research the issue. But in the meantime, he would do what Harry said. The man trusted Landon, and Landon would return the favor. At least for now.

A few minutes later, Harry picked up the bill, and the three men went their separate ways, with Landon carrying the briefcase. To him, it felt radioactive.

Maybe he wasn't cut out to be a defense lawyer after all.

15

KERRI WAS WIDE AWAKE and ready to talk when Landon arrived home. He had called her a couple of times to update her on his little adventure, but he hadn't wanted to say too much over the phone.

Now he outlined the basics of the case, being careful not to tell her anything Elias King had said. Attorney-client confidences could be lost if you shared that information with a spouse.

When he got to the part about holding King's computer, iPad, and iPhone, Kerri furrowed her brow. "Is that legal?" she asked.

"I'm going to research it tonight," Landon said. "But Harry's on the Character and Fitness Committee, and he's been doing this for forty years."

Landon could tell from his wife's facial expression that she wasn't buying it. "Then why didn't he keep the items himself?"

Landon didn't have an answer for that one. To be honest, he felt a little sleazy carrying around items that might be incriminating evidence in a murder investigation. But he hadn't wanted to question Harry in front of a client.

"Who knows?"

"You don't even have your bar license yet," Kerri said, as if Landon might have somehow forgotten that minor detail. "You can't afford to have any missteps."

"I'll be careful," Landon promised. But he might as well have been talking to a wall.

Kerri had a million other questions about the case and the job offer. Landon didn't know much about the job offer, and he had to be careful not to disclose too much about the case. He fired up his computer on the kitchen table, a subtle hint that he needed to get to work. Kerri finished putting up the dishes and took a seat at the opposite end of the table.

"Do you think he did it?" she asked.

"I don't know. That's why we have trials," he said.

Landon kept his eyes glued to his screen, but he knew Kerri wasn't satisfied.

"I'm not sure if this is the right firm for you. Maybe God is trying to tell us something. You show up for the first day of work and nobody knows who you are. Now you get this evidence from some client who probably killed a young paralegal in his firm and the partner wants you to keep it secret. The whole thing doesn't seem right."

Landon knew he probably shouldn't argue with her. She wasn't really trying to debate the issue; she was just trying to work through her feelings out loud. She had been overly protective of him since the day he got out of prison—her main goal in life was to make sure he never went back.

He typed in a few keystrokes to begin his research and then stopped. "What are my other options?" he asked, looking up.

She had her hands on the table and studied them for a moment. "I don't know. We can keep doing what we're doing. I'd rather have you not working at all than working someplace where you might get in trouble."

"You think it was just coincidence that Harry McNaughten took our case in General District Court? You think that whole bar fight thing was just a random act that *just happened* to lead to my first job offer?"

Kerri frowned. Landon, the astute lawyer-to-be, was turning her own arguments back on her. She was the one who had claimed to see God's hand in all these seemingly random circumstances.

"Let's take it one day at a time," Landon suggested. "We'll both pray about it and see how we feel at the end of the week. How much trouble can I get in between now and then?"

"Do you really want me to answer that?"

Landon stayed up until two in the morning researching the issue of a lawyer taking possession of incriminating evidence. The law in Virginia appeared unsettled. Lawyers had an ethical duty not to divulge confidences of a client. But when a client brought them incriminating evidence, some courts had ruled that lawyers also had a duty to turn that evidence over to the police.

He would have a heart-to-heart with Harry McNaughten first thing in the morning. He slept that night with the briefcase under his bed. He woke up twice to take Simba outside, his mind racing with the implications of what he was about to do. In law school, criminal-defense law had seemed noble and even heroic. But in real life, the waters were murky and the game was played on the fringes of morality. Landon didn't know if he could live in this kind of world.

Finally, after the second walk with Simba and after staring at Kerri for a full ten minutes while wondering what to do, he started praying and quickly fell asleep.

16

ON WEDNESDAY MORNING, the chaos that would become Landon's new life exploded in earnest. Because Kerri had stayed up waiting for Landon the night before, she got a late start for work. She dashed out the door at four thirty, juggling her car keys, coffee, and makeup. "Don't forget to feed Simba and take him out," she said over her shoulder.

"I love you, too," said Landon.

Three minutes later, Kerri was back for her cell phone. Her footsteps fell heavy when she was frustrated with herself, and it woke Simba up. He barked wildly until Landon shut him up with puppy food. By then Maddie was up and claimed to have a tummyache and didn't want to go to day care.

"We'll see how you feel when we get there," Landon said. Maddie pouted, her bottom lip sticking out in a look that usually melted Landon's heart, but this morning he didn't have time for it. Simba seemed to realize that something strange was up, so he protested by relieving himself at the front door while Landon was trying to fix

Maddie's hair. It was enough to make the pope cuss. But Landon bit his tongue—little ears were listening.

An hour later, the first stop of the morning was the doggy day care Kerri had chosen the previous day. Simba, normally rambunctious and playful, suddenly turned shy and fearful. He dug in his heels while Landon pulled him forward on the leash, sliding the little dog along on the tile. Landon finally gave up and carried Simba to the large warehouse where about thirty other dogs were already milling around. The girls taking care of the dogs were nice enough and acted happy to see Simba. But when he went through the gates and into the play area, the other dogs barked and sniffed him and generally mauled the new kid on the block. Simba tucked his tail, and it all reminded Landon too much of his first few days in jail, just trying to figure out how to survive.

"He's scared," Maddie said. She had begged to come with Landon and watch as they dropped Simba off.

"He'll be okay," Landon said cheerfully. He snatched Maddie into his arms. "Simba's going to make all kinds of new friends."

The second stop didn't go much better. Maddie got real quiet and big tears formed in her eyes. Her tummyache came back with a vengeance, but Landon took her inside anyway to meet the friendly daycare workers. They showed her some of the games in a corner of the room and introduced her to a few other little girls.

"This might be a good time for you to slip out, Mr. Reed," one of the aides suggested.

By the time Landon hit the law firm parking lot at eight thirty, he was already exhausted. The forecast called for scattered showers throughout the day, but the rain was already heavy, and the wind was whipping it sideways. The wind chill was probably below freezing. Landon parked in an out-of-the-way spot and grabbed his overcoat from the backseat. He hopped out of the car with Elias King's briefcase, threw the overcoat on over his suit, then half jogged to the building. Though he hadn't seen Harry McNaughten's car in the parking lot, he was hoping for the best.

He tried the door on the right that led upstairs, but it was locked. He walked through the double glass doors of the main entrance, and a grinning Janaya greeted him.

"I see you don't take no for an answer," she said.

Landon wiped his feet on the welcome mat. "I worked with Mr. McNaughten last night. He told me to come in today and go upstairs, but the door is locked. He said you could unlock it for me."

"Why don't you have a seat and I'll let Mr. Benedict know you're here," Janaya said, using her pleasant receptionist voice. She twisted her face and then flashed some dimples. "I'd love to let you upstairs, but I like my job. I'm sure Mr. Benedict will say it's okay."

"How about I just wait in the parking lot until Mr. McNaughten gets here," Landon suggested. "I don't have the same confidence in Mr. Benedict that you do."

But Janaya was already out of her seat and heading back to the managing partner's office. "I'm sure it will be no problem."

Two minutes later she came back with a dour look. "I don't think Mr. McNaughten has spoken to Mr. Benedict," she explained. "Why don't you have a seat and I'll give Mr. McNaughten a call."

Landon was beyond frustrated. Somehow, he had known this was the way it would come down. He sighed and plopped himself in a chair located against one of the lobby walls. He was no more than eight feet away from Janaya and listened as she left a message on McNaughten's voice mail.

"I'm really sorry, but he didn't answer. I'm sure he'll be here soon."

Landon stood. He felt like an idiot. "Tell you what—I'll just wait out in the parking lot. I've got some things I can work on until Mr. McNaughten shows up."

"Are you sure you don't want something to drink?" Janaya asked. "It's cold outside."

"It's cold in here."

Half an hour later, it was raining even harder, and Harry McNaughten was still nowhere to be found. *Must be nice to show up for work at nine,* Landon thought, checking the clock on the dashboard.

While he was waiting, the main doors of the building opened, and a nice-looking blonde whom Landon recognized as Rachel Strach emerged with an umbrella. She had on heels, tight black pants, and an equally tight turquoise sweater with the top two buttons strategically unfastened. She held her umbrella at an angle, pushing against the wind, and scrambled to Landon's car. He rolled down his window and the rain started blowing in.

"Hi. I'm Rachel Strach," she said. "Mr. McNaughten called Janaya back, but she's helping on an appellate brief right now. If you'll follow me, I can get you settled in upstairs."

When Landon had first seen Rachel's glamour shot on the Internet, he had assumed that she wouldn't look as good in real life. In his experience, women with beautiful hair, who posed for their head shots with an over-the-shoulder look and a sultry smile, were not above a little airbrushing as well. It was, he had assumed, a picture from five or ten years ago, and the real-life Rachel would not be half as stunning.

He was wrong. The picture didn't do her justice. She had a glowing white smile, a soft Southern accent, and eyes that lit up when she talked. She immediately exuded an air of trustworthiness. Landon put himself on guard.

"Thanks," he said. He rolled up his window and grabbed the briefcase. They shared the umbrella as they hustled back across the parking lot, though it didn't keep either of them very dry.

Once inside, Rachel shook out the umbrella and climbed the steps in front of Landon. He kept his eyes down as he followed.

The space upstairs was nothing like he had imagined. There were offices on both sides with glass windows separating them from the large middle area. That space contained a few workstations separated by movable dividers, along with three or four filing cabinets and a few card tables with files strewn everywhere. Each of the offices and the small conference room, all visible through the glass windows, seemed to be overflowing with documents, folders, legal pads, notebooks, and law books.

"How many lawyers work up here?" he asked, looking around.

"Just Harry."

Rachel gave Landon a quick tour, which lasted about five minutes. The last office on the left was Harry's. The second room on the right was the conference room, which had a round table in the middle and built-in bookshelves lined with a uniform set of tan law books and a smaller set of black code books. Landon recognized them, like relics from some museum, as the Virginia Case Reporters and a hard copy of the Virginia Code. *Who uses law books anymore?*

"Harry doesn't use Westlaw?" Landon asked, referring to a computer program that provided cases and statutes from all fifty states.

Rachel chuckled at the thought. "Computers are just a fad," she said. "There's nothing like the smell of mildew from a dusty law book."

"Is the whole firm that way?"

"Downstairs, we're virtually paperless," Rachel said. "It's like another world."

"Yeah, they call it civilization."

Rachel circled back past Landon to the office at the top of the steps. "Harry said you could use this office. I'll help you clean it out."

"You don't have to do that."

Rachel gave him a look. "Things are crazy downstairs right now. I could use a break."

The pair spent the next thirty minutes moving files and papers and black binders and two stray sets of reading glasses out of the office. They dusted off an old desk with ink stains and water marks marring the wood and adjusted the desk chair, which squeaked when Landon sat in it. They pushed a filing cabinet into one corner and cleared off a small round table in the other. The back windows overlooked a wooded area and a pond. For a first-year associate, the space actually had some potential. Landon felt a small stab of pride. He wasn't a lawyer just yet, but he was getting there.

By the time they had finished clearing the office, Landon had started to relax around Rachel. She liked to talk. She had a great sense of humor and didn't take herself too seriously. She asked about Landon and his family, and Landon told her about the traumatic day-care gauntlet he had run that morning. She touched him on the arm a few times when they were talking, a natural gesture in the flow of things, nothing overly flirtatious. She didn't seem to have any idea about Landon's past.

"You like sports?" he asked.

"Not really," Rachel said. "I do a little running and Pilates, but that's about it."

By ten o'clock, when Harry finally arrived, Rachel had gone back downstairs.

"Like what you did to the office," Harry grunted. "You might want to put something on the walls."

"I was hoping to have a bar license to put there soon," Landon said. It was a hint to see if Harry had any inside information, but Harry ignored it.

"Give me a minute to settle in, and then we'll talk about the King matter," Harry said.

Landon's first day at work flew by. The best part was when Harry explained that after his consultant downloaded the data from Elias's phone and computers, they would turn the devices over to the Commonwealth's Attorney. Landon breathed a huge sigh of relief.

"In case you didn't notice, I don't trust the cops," Harry explained. "I didn't have any intention of holding on to these things. I just wanted to make sure we got the data before the cops messed with it."

The worst part of Landon's day was when he and Harry went downstairs to process Landon's paperwork. Landon waited in the reception area while Harry and Brent Benedict argued behind the two smoked-glass doors separating the reception area from the conference room. They emerged grim-faced, but apparently Harry had succeeded.

"Brent will sit down with you and go over the terms of your employment," Harry said. "Meet me back upstairs when you're done."

Benedict wasn't much for chitchat. He offered Landon a salary of $60,000. The firm would pay half of Landon's health insurance. The idea of working off Harry's legal fee was apparently no longer on the table—Landon was becoming a full-time employee!

"Your continuing employment is contingent on getting licensed to practice law," Benedict said. "And even if you get your license, you're still an at-will employee, meaning we can fire you at any time for any reason."

"I understand," Landon said.

The firm wasn't exactly big on warm fuzzies, but Landon had been a football player. Freshman players at Southeastern had been required to stand on the table and sing the school fight song. They got razzed and chewed out all through camp. This was nothing by comparison.

"Brent is actually a pretty nice guy," Rachel explained when Landon ran into her that afternoon. "But he's military. And he tries to come across as tough the first time you meet him."

"Mission accomplished," Landon said.

17

BEFORE LEAVING WORK THAT DAY, Kerri Reed dialed the number for the Cipher Inc. executive offices. Through persistence and frequent references to Harry McNaughten and "my husband's law firm, McNaughten and Clay," she was eventually patched through directly to Sean Phoenix.

This was her moment, and she swallowed the lump in her throat. Phoenix was notoriously enigmatic. He had never granted a media interview.

"Mr. Phoenix, my name is Kerri Reed. My husband works at McNaughten and Clay, and I work for an NBC affiliate in the Norfolk market. I'm intrigued by what your company does, and I think it's unfair that you get all this bad press. I'd like to help you tell your story. I'd like a sit-down interview. You can trust me to be fair and do my best to explain Cipher's side of things."

When she finished her pitch, there was an uncomfortable silence.

"You want a sit-down interview?" Sean Phoenix eventually asked.

"Yes. I know it's your policy not to do them. But I think people need to hear from you."

"Do you have a doctor, Ms. Reed? An ob-gyn, for example?"

The question caught Kerri off guard. "Yes," she said tentatively.

"How would you feel if he or she decided to sit down with a reporter and talk about your intimate medical issues?"

Kerri didn't answer. This was different, but she didn't want to argue with the man.

"That's what I thought," Sean said. "Our clients would feel the same way."

Kerri knew her request was a long shot, but the answer was still deflating. It was also patronizing, which made her even more determined.

"I wouldn't ask about specific clients," Kerri promised. "I just think people need to understand that Cipher Inc. plays a legitimate and critical role in the geopolitics of our day."

"Look," Sean said. "I appreciate your husband's firm. They do very good work. And whether it's genuine or not, I appreciate your concern about our company's public image. But I don't do interviews."

"Okay. But if you ever change your mind, you can reach me at this number."

///

Sean Phoenix put his headset in its cradle next to the phone and stared at the number on the screen for a few seconds. Kerri Reed was actually right. Cipher Inc. got slammed in the press on a weekly basis because people had no idea what the company did. For the first ten years of Cipher's existence, Sean had just assumed this came with the territory. When your product is intel, you don't do public interviews.

But lately, he had started to change his thinking. Why not apply the same tactics to his firm's public relations that he did to its intelligence operations? The key was having the right people in the right places—people who appeared to work for someone else but whose allegiances actually ran to Cipher.

He could personally make or break the career of any journalist. If Cipher Inc. had anything, it had exposé stories about certain companies it could feed to a journalist—stories that would reveal the dark secrets of the competitors of Cipher's clients. You want reliable anonymous sources? Cipher Inc. had them in spades.

He looked up Kerri Reed on the Web and was intrigued. He watched one of her news segments. She was good-looking and articulate. She had the "it" factor. He did a quick background search. The woman had waited two years for her boyfriend to get out of jail. Loyalty. It was a valued strand of Cipher DNA.

He had his team run a more thorough background check. Two hours later, he reviewed the complete dossier, which contained more information about Kerri Reed than even her husband knew. Sean liked the woman. She had potential.

He called her on her cell phone, a number she had not given him. "How does this Friday sound?" he asked.

18

TWELVE YEARS EARLIER
DAMASCUS, SYRIA

SEAN PHOENIX HAD PLANNED this moment for three years. He had
lived it in his mind, over and over again, carefully dissecting every detail.
It was like a movie he had watched multiple times, noticing something
different with every viewing.

They were celebrating the culmination of an arms deal. He had
already shown his counterpart the cache of weapons, the warehouse full
of AK-47s, the surface-to-air missiles, and the most sophisticated new
explosives.

Like a good actor, Sean had become his character. He had grown
out his hair and beard, an unkempt snarl of black that he had neither
combed nor trimmed in two months. A good makeup job had changed
his nose—broadened it and darkened the color, the nose of a chronic
drinker. He wore camouflage and Army boots, and his band of men all

did the same, giving them the look of hard-core mercenaries. Still ugly Americans, to be sure. But they would not be recognized.

The transaction was going down in Damascus, and so the deal itself would have to wait. First they were required to gorge themselves on Mediterranean cuisine at a private meal. Falafel. Tabbouleh. Hummus. Shawarma. And always, copious amounts of arrack, a translucent, milky-white alcoholic drink as strong as whiskey.

Sean's guest had not changed much in the past three years. He was a hairy man, loud and obnoxious. He had the same rotten teeth and stumpy neck. The same wiry beard and sunken, probing eyes. When he laughed, his features remained dark and his expression quickly returned to a scowl. He even smelled the same—the foul odor of a man who devoured garlic and spices and never bothered to shower.

And of course, he still smoked. Four cigarettes before they started dessert.

They talked through an interpreter, also a member of Sean's team. There were four Syrians and four Americans. After attempting to talk with each other at the beginning of the meal, the dialogue quickly devolved into two separate conversations—the Syrians talking to each other in Arabic, the Americans speaking in English. The Syrians were louder, more animated, and on a few occasions erupted into intense arguments.

Sean waited until the meal was over and there was a lull in the two circles of conversation. He slid closer to his Syrian counterpart and looked at the interpreter across the table.

"Ask him if he remembers Fatinah Najar," Sean said to the interpreter. Under the table, the Americans all placed hands on their pistols.

Even before the translation, the mention of Fatinah's name caused a dark storm to cross the Syrian's face. His neck tightened, and his head swiveled toward Sean, as if he were seeing him for the first time.

"Why would you want to know?" the reply came back.

"Ask him if he remembers how she died," Sean told the interpreter.

The Syrian stared at Sean from a few inches away, and everyone around the table tensed. The Syrians knew more English than they had been letting on. One of them put down his drink and surveyed the faces of the other men. But the element of surprise was with the Americans, and before the Syrians could respond, they had guns in their faces.

Sean's three American friends stood, circling behind the Syrians, pointing their guns at the bases of their targets' skulls. They demanded that the Syrians put their hands on their heads so they could be disarmed. One Syrian foolishly reached for his weapon. A gunshot quickly followed, spraying the man's brains on the table. The eyes of the others widened in shock as the Americans disarmed them.

Sean's counterpart had not moved. His hands were still on the table, and one of the Americans had a gun aimed at his forehead. Sean reached over, took the Syrian's gun, and tossed it to a fellow American.

"Do you remember how she died?" Sean asked the man, leaning toward him. He knew this man spoke enough English to comprehend.

The Syrian scoffed, then spit in Sean's face.

Sean made no effort to wipe it away. "You cut out her tongue," he said. "You watched as she bled to death."

The man smiled. "I could tell you more of what we did. Very fine lady, your girlfriend."

Sean grabbed the man's beard with his left hand and pulled him closer. He could smell the cigarettes and garlic, and then, as he stared at the man's leathery skin and the pores on his face, it seemed Sean could hear Fatinah's voice in the distance. She was pleading again, her voice cracking, proclaiming her innocence, her bravery keeping Sean alive. But there was no remorse in this man's eyes, no hint of fear, no attempt to negotiate for his own putrid life.

"I have a message for you," Sean said. "It's from Fatinah."

He yanked the beard, and with his right hand Sean thrust a dagger into the man's gut. He twisted and sliced until the Syrian's eyes went blank. Gunshots followed, and the other Syrians slumped dead onto their plates.

Sean rose and pulled out a worn index card, yellowed and frayed.

He crossed the Syrian's name off the list. There were only two names remaining, and each would require a far different approach. They would also take considerable time.

So much time, in fact, that the list would double in size before another name could be eliminated. Vengeance had a way of multiplying.

And sometimes, of turning violently back on its originator.

19

FRANKLIN SHERMAN WAS a short fire hydrant of a man whose perpetual scowl had carved deep lines into his forehead and jowls. With a thick neck and trapezius muscles that sloped down from the base of his skull, he looked like a fifty-year-old weight lifter squeezed into a business suit.

He served as the chief deputy prosecutor for the city of Chesapeake and had earned the nickname "the General" from the defense bar. It was an obvious play on his last name and a subtle reference to the scorched-earth tactics he used to put criminals behind bars. Nobody had ever caught the General doing anything explicitly unethical, but he certainly walked right up to the line. In Sherman's black-and-white world, there were good guys and bad guys. His job, reduced to the nub, was to make sure as many punks as possible spent as much time as possible behind bars.

Prior to law school, the General had spent ten years on the street as a beat cop. He had seen some things. And he was still a beat cop at heart. He had a great disdain for all defense lawyers, but especially for men like Elias King, men who had once served as prosecutors before selling their souls to the defense side of the street, one retainer at a time.

On Landon's second day at McNaughten and Clay, the General took center stage. He was holding a press conference on the Elias King case. Landon watched from his new firm's large conference room on a big-screen TV, along with Harry McNaughten. Erica Jensen's body had been found at the bottom of the Intracoastal Waterway, directly under the high-rise bridge on Route 168. They knew where to look, Sherman said, based on an anonymous caller who had reported someone dumping a body bag off the bridge.

"Erica Jensen worked at the law firm of Kilgore and Strobel," Sherman said. "The description of the vehicle from the source matched a vehicle driven by one of the firm's attorneys, Mr. Elias King, who was also Erica's boss. That car has now been impounded, and we are conducting a careful search of the trunk and interior. The victim's body was stuffed in an L.L. Bean bag along with seventy pounds of metal weight-lifting plates designed to weigh down the bag. Final autopsy results should be available by the end of the week. Preliminary results show contusions on the victim's neck, indicating she may have been choked to death. There does not appear to be evidence of a sexual assault."

When he finished his prepared remarks, Sherman fielded questions and gave away as little information as possible.

"Is Elias King a suspect?"

"He's a person of interest," Sherman said, his face betraying no emotion. "We know that Erica Jensen had a meeting scheduled for two days ago with federal prosecutors who are investigating insider trading charges against Mr. King. Ms. Jensen was killed Monday evening, the night before that meeting. Our investigation is ongoing, and we are pursuing several leads."

"Do you expect to make any arrests in the near future?"

"I'm not prepared to say."

And so it went—thrust and counterthrust—Franklin Sherman controlling the flow of information while feeding the media vultures enough morsels to help them convict Elias King even before his arrest.

Harry watched in silence, his eyes narrow with contempt. His color looked off to Landon, more jaundiced than normal under the bright lights of the conference room.

"We've got work to do," Harry said, turning off the TV. Landon followed him back up to the second floor and received a new set of marching orders on the King case.

Harry was right about having work to do. And it wasn't just on the King file. Landon had been shocked during his first day to see how many cases Harry was handling and the chaotic nature of the firm's filing system. Harry seemed to keep everything straight in his head, but most of the files were either missing documents or were scattered all over the various rooms of the second floor. Landon didn't know if he could ever get it organized.

Landon had already learned that there was a big difference between the way things worked on the first and second floors at McNaughten and Clay. The first-floor lawyers, who specialized in appellate law, had neatly organized files and tidy offices. Most of their documents were stored electronically and easily accessed off-site. Parker Clausen, the lawyer who did most of the brief writing, spent a lot of time working from home.

By contrast, the second floor looked like it had been hit by several tornadoes. Documents and files were spread everywhere. It was hard for Landon to even get an accurate list of the fifty-plus active files being handled by Harry. And Harry had apparently never heard of the green movement. He made hard copies of everything, real scraps of paper that he could hold in his hand and scribble on with his red pen.

According to Rachel, the differences in style had apparently led to some heated discussions between Harry and Brent Benedict. Ultimately, they agreed that Harry would run the upstairs the way he wanted and the rest of the firm would function the way Benedict wanted.

But Landon planned to change all that. Every night, he would take one file home and divide it into neat subfiles, separating out the pleadings from the correspondence and the legal research from the attorney notes. He would develop a reporting system to stay on top of each file and a computerized calendaring system so that Harry's pocket calendar wasn't the only place important dates were noted. Harry McNaughten might be a genius defense attorney, but he didn't know the first thing about office management. Landon was new to the firm, but he understood a thing or two about working within systems and how to organize things.

///

Franklin Sherman didn't waste any time initiating the biggest arrest of his career, orchestrating events in spectacular fashion. On Friday afternoon, somebody tipped off the media, so the television cameras were rolling when Elias King, former federal prosecutor, was escorted from his office in a Norfolk high-rise, hands cuffed behind him. He was shoved into the backseat of a police car, and thirty minutes later, for the second time in two days, Sherman held a press conference on the case.

After adjusting the microphones down to fit his height, Sherman announced that he would be charging Elias King with first-degree murder. He showed the press two large poster-board blowups of photos of the trunk of Elias King's car. The first photo showed a faint impression on the carpet that matched the shape and size of the two thirty-five-pound plates that had been used to weigh down the L.L. Bean bag Erica Jensen had been found in. The second showed four small indentations. They matched up, the General said, in both size and location, with the impressions that would have been left by the two small wheels on the bottom of the L.L. Bean bag as well as the two small knobs at the other end of the bag. He had a replica of the bag there for the press to see. It was over four feet long and looked like a bright-yellow body bag. The General showed how, when the bag was laid flat on the floor, the only four points touching would be the wheels and the small plastic knobs. Not only that, but investigators had found a strand of Erica Jensen's hair in the trunk. He hypothesized that it might have gotten caught on the handles or zipper of the bag when her body was stuffed into it at her apartment and then fallen off in the trunk.

There were also a number of text messages and e-mails that Sherman said supported the charges, though he refused to go into any detail.

"I'm going to the jail to meet with our client," Harry said. "I need you to go talk to his wife and kid. Make sure they don't make any statements to anybody about anything. See what you can find out about his alibi. And see if the Kings happen to be missing any L.L. Bean bags or weight-lifting plates."

20

IT WAS A TWENTY-FIVE-MINUTE DRIVE to the Kings' house in Chesapeake. On the way, Landon got a call from Harry with further instructions about his assignment.

"I hate trying cases in the press, but I'm going to have to make some kind of statement. See if Julia King is going to support her husband. I need to know whether Elias parked his car outside or in the garage. And talk to his kid—what's his name?"

"Jacob."

"Right. Talk to him separate from his mom. Do whatever it takes to convince him that his dad is innocent. Make sure he doesn't talk to the cops or his friends or post anything on Facebook, and no texting or tweeting anything about his dad's arrest."

Landon heard the sound of a car horn through the cell phone and assumed Harry had cut someone off. Harry cursed at the other driver. In Harry's world, the best defense was always a good offense.

When they hung up, Landon started tackling another problem. Kerri was in D.C. to interview Sean Phoenix. Landon was supposed to get off work early to pick up Maddie and Simba at their respective day cares. But Landon couldn't just call Harry and explain that he had to drop everything on this murder case because of day-care issues. Harry wasn't the most enlightened boss.

Landon called a few friends from church, but they were unavailable. He even tried the moms of the high school quarterbacks he had been coaching. Nobody was in a position to drop everything to pick up Maddie. And it was pushing five o'clock.

As a last resort, he dialed Rachel Strach and asked if she could pick up Maddie and Simba.

"I'd love to do it," she said. "But won't the day care require something in writing?"

Landon hadn't even thought of that. The day-care operators were strict. He doubted if a phone call would suffice.

"You have my permission to forge my signature," he said. He felt a catch in the pit of his stomach, but what else could he do?

"I promise I'll take good care of them," Rachel said enthusiastically. "I'll call you as soon as I pick up Maddie, and then we'll have a girls' night out."

"You're a lifesaver," Landon said.

He had a few minutes before arriving at the Kings' house to call or text Kerri. But he decided he would save that conversation for later.

///

Julia King was expecting him. Jacob was still at school, working out in the weight room with some other athletes, and would get a ride home with a friend.

"Believe it or not, he wants to be a quarterback," Julia explained when they settled into the family room. "He's five-eleven and barely weighs 150 pounds. All elbows and knees, and his coordination hasn't caught up with his growth. But he's got his dad's competitiveness. . . ."

Julia looked like she had been through the emotional wringer. Her eyes were red and watery, and if her hair had been brushed that day, it must have been first thing in the morning. She had gone soft in her middle age and had streaks of gray in her hair. According to Harry, Julia had taught at Tidewater Community College before Elias took his job with Kilgore and Strobel. The past few years she had been a devoted stay-at-home mother and wife. Elias had rewarded her by cheating with Erica, a thirty-four-year-old legal assistant with a sharp intellect and a triathlete's body.

Landon and Julia spent their first few minutes talking about the upcoming legal procedures. "You probably know how all this works from living with Elias," Landon said.

"Not really. We never talked much about his job."

Landon did his best to give her a preview of what lay ahead, though most of what he knew came from studying for the bar exam. There would be an arraignment the following morning. Bail would be set. Next would be a preliminary hearing. They were probably looking at a trial date in late summer or early fall.

"You really think this is going to trial?" Julia asked.

Landon didn't have a clue. "We need to prepare like it will. But our first concern is posting bond for Elias. We need to discuss what assets might be available."

"How much are we talking about?"

"Harry doesn't know yet," Landon said. Harry had given Landon some worst-case scenarios. He knew Julia would be stunned. "Could be several hundred thousand. Even a million. You would need collateral for 10 percent of that."

She stared into space. "I don't know if we have that much," she said. Her voice was tight; worry lines framed her eyes. "Elias handles the finances."

"I know Harry's talking to him about this as well," Landon said, trying to keep things hopeful. "We can circle back to that later. The main thing I wanted to address with you is your husband's alibi."

Landon paused for a moment and watched as Julia looked down. This was a delicate area. How far was she willing to go to protect her husband?

"We know the anonymous tip came in during the early morning hours of February 5, so that would have been late Monday night, early Tuesday morning. Was Elias with you that night?"

Landon had asked the question exactly as Harry had instructed. They knew that Elias and Julia had been sleeping in separate rooms. But Harry wanted to ask an indirect question so he could see whether Julia was willing to defend her husband.

She stared at her hands, playing with her wedding ring. When she looked up, her eyes were wet. Her shoulders sagged under the weight of a marriage falling apart in a very public way.

"You want to know if I'm going to stand with my husband," she said. "Play the good wife." She spoke with a firmness of conviction that surprised Landon. "My husband sleeps with a younger woman that he's now accused of murdering, and you want to know whether I'm going to back him up."

She looked past Landon and waited an uncomfortably long time before continuing.

"Do I really have any choice? He's my husband, Mr. Reed. He's Jacob's father, and we once loved each other. I won't lie for him. We were sleeping in separate rooms on Monday night. But I doubt he could have left the house without my knowing."

Landon nodded his head. He felt her pain but had no idea what to say.

"He didn't kill her," Julia continued. She shifted in her seat, became more erect, and brushed a stray strand of hair behind her ear. She would make a good witness, Landon thought.

"I've lived with the man long enough to know when he's telling the truth. He slept with her—" Julia choked a little at the bluntness of her own words—"but he didn't kill her."

"How would you describe Elias's temper?" Landon asked. "Has he ever struck you?"

Julia seemed taken aback by the thought. She waved it away. "We've both got tempers," she said. "But did he ever hit me? I wouldn't be here if he had." Her lips curled into a meager attempt at a smile. "Don't ask him whether I ever hit him," she said. "Unless we're not counting slaps."

"Sunday night?" Landon asked.

She nodded. "I'll never be able to trust him again," she admitted. Her voice was softer now, almost a whisper. "Erica Jensen destroyed our lives. With a little help from my husband, obviously. But I'm not ready to raise Jacob on my own. . . ."

She stopped there, and Landon jotted a few notes. There were other, less sensitive areas, and it was time to move on.

He found out that Elias generally parked his car in the driveway. Landon had Julia take him upstairs so he could get the layout of where everybody was sleeping that night and how easy it would have been to hear the car start. Jake's room was closest to that end of the house.

They were back in the family room when Julia's phone buzzed. "Excuse me," she said. "This is Jacob."

After she said hello, she fell silent and Landon watched her face go dark as she started firing questions. "What happened? . . . What do you mean you're okay? . . . Why did you do that?"

She ended the conversation by telling Jacob she was on her way. "Everything's going to be okay," she promised.

She stood to leave. "I'm sorry, Mr. Reed, but Jake's at Chesapeake General Hospital." She was already heading toward the kitchen to grab her keys. "He got in a fight and is getting some stitches over his eye."

When she had her keys, she turned to face Landon. "The thing is, Jake never gets in fights. That's one thing that he and Elias would argue about. Elias wanted him to stick up for himself more."

She didn't have to state the obvious. The boy had probably been sticking up for his dad this time. It was no coincidence that Jake had ended up in the hospital the day of his dad's arrest.

"Do you need a ride?" Landon said.

Julia shook her head. "Thanks for asking. But I'm fine."

Landon bit his lip for a second and knew it would be so much easier to just leave. He could take Maddie off Rachel's hands. Maybe he could talk to Jake tomorrow or the next day. But Harry had been adamant. He would be calling Landon's phone all night until he got an answer as to whether Landon had talked with Jake. The boy's father was being accused of murder. Some things couldn't wait.

"I really need to talk to Jake," Landon said. "Can I follow you to the hospital and meet with him for a few minutes?"

Julia exhaled and looked at Landon as if she couldn't believe his audacity.

"I don't want him to go through high school without a father," Landon said.

Julia headed for the front door. "He's still in the emergency room," she said. "I'll meet you there."

21

WHEN KERRI ARRIVED at Cipher Inc.'s headquarters on the outskirts of Manassas in northern Virginia, she was impressed, though not surprised, by the security. She stopped at the guard station, produced her credentials, and watched as the unsmiling man checked a list and punched some data into a computer. He asked her to pop the trunk and then looked under the car with a mirror on a long, angled rod. He asked three questions: the street address of her childhood home, her mother's maiden name, and Maddie's birthday. It was unnerving, Kerri thought, to have so much information about her available on the Internet.

When the guard waved her through, she drove down a long, paved road lined by trees. She noticed nearly a dozen tree-mounted cameras monitoring her progress and a few gadgets that were probably heat and motion detectors. At the end of the road she encountered a large electric fence topped with barbed wire. She spoke into a speaker at the gate, a pleasant woman answered, and the gate eventually swung open.

Kerri wondered if the Pentagon was so well guarded.

Cipher's headquarters was a five-story smoked-glass building, surrounded by a massive parking lot and a row of bulky concrete barriers designed to shield against suicide bombers. She parked, checked in at the front desk, and pinned on a bar-coded name tag.

Five minutes later, Sean Phoenix stepped off the elevator and gave her a firm handshake. If Daniel Craig ever tired of playing James Bond, this guy could take his place, Kerri thought. He was almost embarrassingly handsome with the chiseled look of an actor they might use for an Army recruiting video. He had a strong jaw, a perfect symmetry to his face, and to top it all off, dimples when he smiled.

He wore a tight black T-shirt that showed off the cable-like muscles of an endurance athlete rather than the bulky muscles of a weight lifter. He looked surprisingly young for a man in charge of such a massive operation.

"Thank you for giving me a few minutes of your time, Mr. Phoenix," Kerri said.

"There are two rules," Phoenix said crisply. "First, you'll need to leave your phone and any recording devices at the front desk. The only camera allowed is the one your cameraman brings in. And second, please call me Sean. My dad is Mr. Phoenix, and I'm not answering any questions about him."

Before the interview, Sean took Kerri on a guided tour of the building, and before long she had lost her sense of direction. He greeted people by their first names, introduced them to Kerri, and had them tell Kerri what they did.

The building was packed with analysts sitting in cubicles and young executives in small glass offices on the perimeters. Kerri had imagined an operation far different from this. She had pictured the massive war rooms featured in the movies with suspended televisions and maps lining the walls. This place looked like one of the Big Four accounting firms.

"Many of these folks are former CIA operatives or former Navy SEALs or have some other type of special-ops background," Sean explained. "A lot of them just scan websites, databases, and chat rooms so they can collect and analyze publicly available data. As a company, we monitor activities in more than sixty countries and communicate in more than a hundred languages. We've got Fulbright Scholars and Rhodes Scholars and even a few graduates of Southeastern University."

They ended the tour in Sean's office, another place that defied expectations. It looked much like the other offices in the facility except that it happened to occupy prime real estate on the fifth-floor corner overlooking the front parking lot. The walls contained a few sterile pictures and diplomas but no hint of personal information or family photographs.

The WTRT cameraman, Rob Stokes, had driven to Manassas separately and was already setting up his lighting and backdrops. A makeup artist did her magic, and Sean and Kerri took their places in two seats facing each other. Rob tested their mikes, then adjusted the backdrops to eliminate shadows.

Sean had agreed to a thirty-minute interview, and Kerri knew she had to get right to the point. She introduced Sean, thanked him for giving her a tour of the facilities, and then hit him with her first zinger.

"There are reports that you left the CIA because you fell in love with a Syrian woman who served as a spy for our country. My sources tell me that when she was discovered by the Syrians, the CIA disavowed her, leading to her torture and death. And that's supposedly why you left. Are any of those reports true?"

Kerri was not surprised when the man didn't flinch. She had watched tapes of his hearings in front of congressional subcommittees, and she had read transcripts of his testimony in court. He was basically unflappable.

"As far as rumors go, those are fairly tame ones. We have employees who scour the Internet every hour of the day, and we've learned how to separate fact from fiction. There are organizations who know how to plant a rumor and then seed it on other sites so it looks like it sprouts and grows spontaneously.

"But those rumors are false. I left the CIA because, at heart, I am an entrepreneur. Companies need effective intelligence in order to survive in a multinational world. We know how to provide that. As a bonus, we know how to get paid doing it."

Kerri checked her notes to make sure she had the data right. "I found six separate lawsuits in the past seven years that were filed against Cipher Inc., and several reports of threatened lawsuits. You had a tortious interference-with-business claim seven years ago, three patent-infringement claims six years ago brought by competitors of your clients, another lawsuit filed two years later by the relatives of a government official in Sudan who claimed that Cipher operatives killed that official, and one suit three years ago claiming that Cipher stole confidential information from competitors of your clients. All of these have been settled out of court." She paused for effect. "That seems like an awful lot of litigation."

"There are an awful lot of lawyers," Phoenix responded, flashing a quick smile. "All of those lawsuits were frivolous, and we've never had a verdict entered against us. But, Kerri, your husband's a lawyer, and you know how much lawyers charge. In fact, your husband's firm has represented us on several occasions. Some of those cases were dismissed by judges before they ever went to trial. Others we settled. The math is pretty simple. The cost of defending ourselves, even though we did nothing wrong, combined with the loss of focus on our main business, drove us to settlement. I'm a businessman. Those were business calculations."

Sean hesitated for a moment, and Kerri thought he might leave the answer there. She was going to probe about a few of the cases, particularly the one arising out of Cipher's alleged role in the assassination of the Sudanese official. But Sean Phoenix wasn't finished.

"But in case there are any plaintiffs' lawyers watching this interview," Sean continued, leaning forward, "they should know that I've changed that philosophy. I'm tired of being blackmailed through a legal system in which the rule of law has become the rule of lawyers. Don't get me wrong, Kerri—there are a lot of good lawyers out there. But for the vultures who think they can make a quick buck by filing these types of cases—" he looked directly into the camera—"we're done paying just to get the matter behind us. I've adopted a new motto, one you might have heard before: millions for defense but not one penny for tribute."

Sean leaned back, message delivered. *Let the snotty-nosed plaintiffs' lawyers chew on that for a while,* his expression seemed to say. He relaxed and turned to Kerri for the next question.

She found herself wondering if Cipher Inc. had been recently threatened with a massive lawsuit—if perhaps this entire interview had been arranged by Sean to deliver a single message. *Don't mess with our company. We're done paying just to avoid the costs of litigation.*

"Can you tell me whether or not your company has any active contracts with the CIA?"

"If we did, that would be classified information."

"What about the intelligence-gathering arms of other countries' governments? Do you work for any of them?"

"That would be classified too."

And so it went, one question after another, Sean stonewalling her at every turn. When the interview was over she thanked him, and he escorted her to the front door.

She left thinking she knew less about Sean Phoenix than when she had arrived. She had seen only what he wanted her to see, been told only what he wanted her to hear. She glanced in her rearview mirror as she left the facility. There was a story here, no doubt about that. And she would dig until she found it.

22

THE PHONE CALLS STARTED when Landon was on his way to the hospital. He knew that Kerri had probably finished her interview and now wanted to check in on Maddie. He ignored the first two, but by the third one he could feel the desperation coming through the phone.

"How's my girl?" Kerri asked after Landon answered. It was the voice of a mother at the beginning stages of separation anxiety.

"She's good," Landon replied.

"You guys having a movie date?" Kerri asked. "Nothing like *Tangled* for the 943rd time."

Time to change the subject. "How was the interview?"

"I'll give you a blow-by-blow when I get home. Can you put Maddie on the phone for a second?"

It was, he knew, the moment of truth. He could have said that Maddie was in the bathroom, that he was in a bad cell zone, or any one of a half-dozen other stall maneuvers. But his relationship with Kerri was based on honesty.

"Actually, I'm just getting ready to go into the hospital to see a client. Somebody else is taking care of Maddie for a little while until I get home."

There was silence on Kerri's end. Landon decided to wait her out.

"And you were going to tell me this when?"

"I just did."

"This client can't wait until next week?"

"It's Elias King's son. He got in a fight today at school. Harry said I had to talk with him before Elias gets home."

"I don't understand why this is such a crisis. Who's with Maddie, anyway?"

That was the question Landon really dreaded. But he couldn't run from it now. "Rachel," he said casually. He made it sound as if Rachel babysat for Maddie once a week.

"Rachel who?" Kerri's tone turned accusatory. There were strict rules about who could babysit Maddie, a clearing process that would make the FBI proud, and extensive instructions. Rachel had never been considered for the list.

"Rachel Strach from work. It's just a couple of hours, and I've been checking in every twenty minutes."

This response generated another patch of stony silence. "You're kidding, right? I don't even know Rachel Strach."

"I called everyone, Kerri." Landon's voice became a little testy as well. He wasn't the one who had gone running out of town. "Nobody else was available. They're having fun. They're fine."

"I don't get this," Kerri said. "If you couldn't watch her for even a couple of hours, you should have told me. I would have helped make some calls or we could have talked about it or something. I don't want some strange woman taking care of my child, especially when I don't know anything about it."

"*Our* child," Landon said. "And she's not some strange woman. She's the one person at the firm besides Harry who's taken me in and helped me get acclimated. And I'll be home as soon as I get a chance."

They sparred for a few more minutes and then hung up without a single *I love you.* Landon quickly called Rachel, who assured him that Maddie was doing just fine. They were having a blast, Rachel said. "Take your time. And by the way, your daughter is adorable."

Generally, Landon would say something like, *Takes after her mother.* But right now, he wasn't feeling it.

"Thanks," he said.

///

Jacob King was biding his time in the Chesapeake General emergency department. He sat on a bed behind a curtain, a gauze bandage covering a cut over his left eye. Julia stood next to him. The kid looked like a younger version of Elias—the same sharp angles on the face, the same curly black hair. Jacob's hair was longer and not yet receding, and he had the spotted complexion and droopy eyes of a teenager, but there was no doubt this was Elias's boy.

"Jacob, this is Mr. Reed," Julia said. She turned to Landon. "I told him you were a college quarterback."

They shook hands and Landon noticed that Jacob had long fingers and a strong grip for a skinny kid. "Your mom tells me you're a quarterback too," Landon said. "Maybe we could toss the ball sometime."

"Sure."

"How did your team do this year?" Landon asked.

"We basically sucked."

"He played junior varsity," Julia said, quickly coming to his defense. "Most of the good kids from his grade were moved up to varsity." She caught herself. "Except Jacob, of course. They already had a good varsity quarterback."

The small talk was off to a rough start, and Landon decided to get to the point. He wanted to talk with Jake alone, as Harry had instructed, but he was already pushing his luck by interviewing the kid in the hospital. He decided to plow ahead with Julia present. "As your mom's probably told you, my firm represents your dad. And I need to ask you a few questions if that's okay."

"I know."

Unlike most fifteen-year-olds, Jacob looked Landon straight in the eye. He had a wary gaze, at least in the one eye that wasn't swollen nearly shut, but he didn't seem to be intimidated.

"We know your dad's innocent," Landon said. "But the only way we can defend him properly is if everybody in your family is 100 percent honest with us. We can deal with stuff as long as we know about it ahead of time. But you've got to shoot straight with me, okay?"

Out of the corner of his eye, Landon saw Julia reach out to take her son's hand, but Jacob pulled back just a little. He was trying hard to be the man, and Landon's heart went out to him. Landon's own father had run off with another woman, abandoning the family when Landon was in elementary school. It had been Landon, his sister, and his mother against the world. Jacob might experience a similar situation soon.

"I understand," Jacob said.

"You feel up to answering a few questions?"

"Sure."

For the next ten minutes, Landon quizzed Jacob about the night of February 4. Jacob didn't remember anything out of the ordinary. If his dad had driven the 300M out of the driveway that night, Jacob was pretty sure he would have heard it. He claimed to be a light sleeper. He was certain his dad's car had never left the house.

"I noticed you guys set up a weight room over the garage," Landon said. "Do you happen to remember if you have any thirty-five-pound plates?"

Jacob scrunched his forehead, trying to remember. "I don't think we have thirty-fives."

"Are you sure about that?"

"Pretty sure."

"The reason I'm asking is because there were a couple of thirty-five-pound plates weighing down the bag that contained Erica Jensen's body," Landon explained.

Jacob shrugged. The information didn't change his answer.

A nurse stepped into the curtained-off room and asked Jacob how he felt. She said the doctor would be able to stitch him up in a few minutes. She took his vital signs and looked behind the gauze bandage at the butterfly Band-Aid she had used to hold the cut together.

When she left, Julia spoke first. "Can we finish this sometime next week?" she asked. "He's probably been through enough trauma for one night."

"Sure," Landon said. "And, Jake, we're going to do everything we can to get your dad acquitted. I know your father and I know his reputation. Your father's a good man. And Mr. McNaughten is a *really* good lawyer."

Jacob nodded, his eyes glued on Landon.

"So why don't you let us do the fighting," Landon continued. "It doesn't do anybody any good for you to wind up in the hospital."

"Yes, sir," Jacob said.

When Landon left the hospital, he felt the full weight of the case bearing down on his shoulders. He was sorry for young Jake. And he knew that Julia King, her life already shattered by an affair, could hardly cope with another crushing blow. He hoped, for the family's sake, that Elias King was innocent.

And he hoped, for everyone's sake, that he and Harry could prove it.

23

LANDON WAS STILL THINKING about the case when he pulled into the driveway of his condo. When he entered, he heard Rachel announce, "Daddy's home!" Maddie came running and Simba went into a barking fit. Landon dropped to one knee so he could give his daughter and dog the attention they both craved.

He looked up at Rachel in the midst of the chaos and thanked her for taking care of his little girl.

"We had a great time," Rachel said.

Maddie quickly agreed. She started listing all the things that she and her new friend Rachel had done. It had been girls' night in. They had played games—Chutes and Ladders, Candy Land, hide-and-seek, and tug-of-war with Simba. They did dinner and a movie. And there were still three slices of pizza left for Landon.

Rachel hung around for a while as Landon ate and talked to her about the case. Simba curled at her feet and she rubbed his belly with her toes. As she got ready to leave, Landon thanked her profusely and tried to pay her.

"What kind of a girl do you think I am?" Rachel teased.

"Seriously," Landon said, "I owe you. If I can do anything for you, just let me know."

"Maybe you can buy lunch sometime," Rachel said.

"That's the least I could do."

He stood on the front stoop and watched Rachel get into her car. She beeped as she drove away.

"Let's finish the movie!" Maddie exclaimed. The two of them snuggled on the couch while Simba tried to jump up and join them.

"No, sir!" Landon said, pushing the little puppy back to the floor.

Maddie opened her mouth to protest but then apparently thought better of it. Landon was pretty sure he knew why—she didn't want to rat out a coconspirator. Landon had noticed a few strands of fine yellow fur on the couch. No wonder the little guy seemed to like Rachel so much.

///

When Kerri finally arrived home after a bad night of traffic on I-95, it was nearly midnight. But she was still wide awake and wired for a good fight. Landon had no right to leave Maddie with a woman Kerri had never even met. What if something had happened? If Landon wasn't going to be able to take care of Maddie, why hadn't he said so when Kerri first called? She was already starting to hate his new job and the way it had squeezed her own responsibilities, making her feel even more guilty when she couldn't be home with her daughter.

She slipped into the condo, trying to be as quiet as possible so she wouldn't wake Simba. The lights were still on, largely because she was the only one in the house who ever bothered to turn them off. At least the TV was off. Everyone was apparently asleep. She took off her shoes and headed back to the bedroom. If she and Landon were going to have a fight, they might as well get it over with.

Landon wasn't there.

For a brief moment of panic, she wondered if something had happened. She quickly walked down the hall to Maddie's room, and her answer was sprawled out before her.

Landon was lying on Maddie's bed, mouth open, snoring softly. He had Maddie's favorite book, *The Velveteen Rabbit*, open on his chest. One of his legs hung off the bed, his foot resting on the floor. Maddie was curled up next to him, her hair spread across the pillow, covering her face. Simba had curled into his own little ball at the foot of the bed and looked up at Kerri, knowing he'd been busted.

Kerri stood there for a moment and felt the frustration seep from her body. She carefully lifted the book from Landon's chest and placed it on the shelf. She leaned down, moved the hair out of Maddie's face, and gave her a kiss on her curly little head.

She snapped her fingers at Simba and whispered, "Down." But the little guy just stared back. *Who, me?*

She shook her head at her incorrigible dog and her equally incorrigible husband. But she had lost the will to fight. She turned off the light and headed back to her own bedroom. She had waited two years for Landon to get out of prison. She could surely wait eight hours to talk to him about Rachel.

24

ELIAS KING'S BOND HEARING took place on Monday morning, after the former prosecutor spent a weekend in an isolation cell in the Chesapeake city jail. Franklin Sherman argued that the very nature of the crime—killing a possible witness in a federal investigation—should prevent King from getting bonded out. Harry countered that Elias had deep roots in the community and didn't pose any flight risk.

Both lawyers did their share of grandstanding, and the judge ultimately granted bail in the amount of $1 million. If Elias posted bond, he would be required to wear an ankle monitoring bracelet and would be confined to his home except for meetings with his lawyers. He had already been suspended from his firm without pay.

It must have been a good decision, because neither side was happy with it.

Harry and Landon met with Elias at his home later that afternoon, after he had posted bond. Elias looked like a beaten man, sobered by his weekend in jail. It seemed to Landon as if the man were on some kind of antidepressant medication—his mood was flat and without affect, very different from prior meetings. Landon remembered how despondent he had felt when it became obvious that he would spend two years in prison. And that was nothing compared to what Elias was facing.

The press had already tried and convicted him. Tantalizing details about the commonwealth's investigation had been leaked, and hints of an affair between Elias and Erica were in the air. Harry had imposed a gag order on the entire defense team until they could get their bearings. For two days, the news media had camped out in the cul-de-sac in front of Elias's home and shouted questions at anybody who came or went. For two days all they heard was, "No comment."

Harry outlined the big questions in the case at Monday's meeting, but they were coming up empty on the answers. How could somebody have stolen Elias King's car and planted the evidence? Who would want Erica dead? Why would somebody want to frame Elias?

And for Landon, the biggest question of all was the one that went unasked: Did Elias really do it?

Progress *was* made in one important area. After using most of his savings to post bond, Elias promised to borrow from his retirement account and through a line of credit secured by his house in order to pay Harry's $100,000 retainer. Harry would send monthly bills based on his rate of $400 per hour (and $195 for Landon). Each month, Elias would be required to pay the bill without touching the $100,000 retainer.

The reason for this arrangement was understood by everyone but was also left unsaid. Criminal-defense lawyers wanted a retainer at the end of the case if they lost. Clients were not happy forking over large amounts of money for attorneys' fees expended in a losing battle. It was far easier to simply deduct the amounts billed at the end of a long trial from a big retainer.

As the meeting was breaking up, Elias turned to Landon and asked for a favor. "As you can imagine, Jake is really struggling. He's mad at me and has withdrawn into a shell. But Julia says that his eyes lit up when he learned that you were a former SEC quarterback and would be working on the case. Would you mind saying a word to him on the way out?"

A former SEC quarterback. Landon knew what that really meant. If Jake hadn't already known about Landon's history when they first met, he would have googled Landon and found out about the point-shaving scandal. Six years later, and it still made Landon's stomach clench every time the subject came up. "Sure. I'd be glad to."

The two quarterbacks ended up in the backyard throwing the football. The cut over Jake's left eye was healing nicely, though he still had a pretty good shiner. He threw the ball with a sidearm motion and an awkward windup that exacerbated a slow release. But for a skinny kid, he had a surprisingly strong arm. And when Landon suggested some changes in his throwing motion, Jake proved highly coachable, soaking it all in, trying hard to mimic what Landon showed him.

"Your release point is too low," Landon said. "Bring your arm up straight over your head; keep your elbow right next to your ear."

Jake tried, but he had years of bad form to overcome.

"It's okay," Landon said. "It doesn't happen overnight."

The next thing Landon wanted to see was the kid's footwork. He had Jake do a few five-step drops and a few seven-step drops. Landon saw a younger version of himself in this awkward kid with the skinny frame and lots of potential. Because nobody had ever worked with Jake on his footwork, he was slow and ungainly. Jake needed to watch himself on film. Even then, it would take lots of reps before the new footwork became natural.

"You've got to put some meat on that body," Landon said.

"I know."

"And you've got some footwork issues. I work out with a couple of high school quarterbacks on Tuesday and Thursday nights. You want to join us?"

Jake's face lit up as if he had just been drafted into the NFL. "Are you serious?"

"I'm not sure how long I can keep doing this with my new job, but you're welcome to come for as long as I stay at it."

It was the first time Landon had seen Jake smile, a grin full of braces and a row of top front teeth that seemed a little too big for his mouth.

"Tuesday night at seven thirty at the Norfolk Christian gym," Landon said.

"I'll be there."

///

On Friday, Landon was in his office making phone calls to people who had known Erica Jensen. He asked everyone the same questions. Did she have any enemies? What do you know about her background? Did she ever talk to you about people who had threatened her?

Everybody gave the same answers. Erica had no enemies. Everyone loved her. Nobody would want Erica dead other than Landon's client.

"Landon!"

It was Harry shouting from two offices down the hall. He never used the firm intercom system but just barked Landon's name with his trademark rasp.

"Yes, sir!"

"You got a second?"

Landon walked down to Harry's office, moved some papers from the chair in front of Harry's desk, and took a seat.

"You think you can pull fingerprints from an object that's been underwater?" Harry asked.

Landon thought about this for a moment. He didn't have the foggiest idea. "Seems like it would be pretty hard. Especially if it were brackish water like the Intracoastal Waterway."

"You might be surprised," Harry said. "If something's been in the water for a few days, you can almost always pull a print. The water acts as a preservative. The main thing is to use chemicals to pull the print."

"Mmm," Landon muttered, because it seemed like Harry wanted him to say something.

"You'd expect a prosecutor to know that, wouldn't you?" Harry asked.

"Yeah, probably. Especially one who lives around here."

Harry nodded. "My point exactly."

He stared at Landon for a second, and Landon knew some kind of punch line was coming.

"So would it surprise you to know that they pulled two prints off one of the thirty-five-pound plates in the L.L. Bean bag?"

Landon felt like he was being cross-examined. Like maybe Harry was practicing for the trial. *If Elias King, an experienced prosecutor, was going to submerge a body using weights, don't you think he'd use some that didn't have his fingerprints on them?*

"Did the prints belong to Elias?" Landon asked. He had learned the best way to answer one of Harry's questions was with a question of his own.

"One of the prints belongs to Elias. But not the second one."

"Did they find a match for that one?"

Harry shrugged. "*They* didn't find a match. But that's where you come in. You've got a good relationship with his kid, right?"

"With Jacob. Yes."

"Next time you're lifting weights or training him up or whatever you do, grab something he touched. Use a paper towel and don't touch it yourself. We need to get one of the kid's fingerprints."

Landon balked at the idea. He wasn't going to abuse his relationship with Jacob to gather evidence. What was Harry thinking? "Is that even ethical?" Landon asked.

"What do you mean?"

"I can't develop a relationship with Elias's son just to collect incriminating evidence."

Harry leaned forward. "First of all, I'm not asking you to collect incriminating evidence. I'd be shocked if Jacob's prints *weren't* on those plates. He told you they didn't have that size plate in his weight room, but my guess is they did. If his print is a match, it means he's a liar, not a murderer. But if that's not his print—then we've really got something. We find out whose it is, and that person becomes prime suspect number one."

Landon could see where this was headed. Elias would know that fingerprints would be preserved underwater. But his wife wouldn't. And if her fingerprints were on those plates, they might have something.

"And let me make sure you understand one other thing," Harry said, as if he were reading Landon's thoughts. "We have one client in this case. We haven't been hired to protect Jacob King or Julia King or the family dog. It's our job to do everything possible, within the bounds of the law, to defend Elias. And if that means collecting incriminating evidence against his son or his wife, then that's what we do. That's why we get paid the big bucks."

Landon just stared at Harry. He was right, of course. But there had to be a better way to practice law. Landon wanted to learn from Harry, but he didn't want to wind up so cutthroat, so jaded. *Couldn't you be a criminal-defense attorney and still have a conscience?*

"Any questions?" Harry asked.

"I think I get it," Landon said.

25

TEN DAYS AFTER ELIAS KING'S ARREST, Franklin Sherman released the final autopsy. He sent a copy by PDF to Harry McNaughten and within an hour released it to the press. In a slight departure from character, Sherman passed on a press conference. The autopsy itself was bombshell enough.

Landon found out about it when Harry yelled down the hall and called Landon into his office. The older lawyer rubbed his face and leaned back in his chair as if weary of life. His eyes drooped more than normal, and his spotted skin showed the residual damage of too many Virginia Beach summers. His wavy gray hair—what was left of it—was slicked back behind his ears. But even with all the pressure he was under, he still had a look of smug determination, as if he knew he would ultimately prevail.

"Just got off the phone with Elias," Harry said. The weariness of arguing with his client was evident in his voice. "He's been prosecuting too long. Wants to start making our case in the press. He doesn't understand that the more he protests, the guiltier he looks." Harry shuffled some papers and then stopped, locking on Landon. "You want to be a criminal-defense lawyer?"

"Yes, sir."

"Really?"

"Yes, sir," Landon said.

"A lot of young lawyers say that's what they want to be. Sounds glamorous when you're in law school and you're listening to professors who have never tried a case waxing eloquent about our wonderful system. But it gets dirty down in the trenches."

Landon didn't respond. He knew Harry didn't expect him to. The man liked to think out loud, using Landon as a sounding board.

"But you're different from most young lawyers I've encountered. You've been on the receiving end of our system. You know what it feels like when everybody runs away from a defendant like they've got the plague. Somebody's got to stand up for the accused."

Landon knew exactly what Harry meant. Most of Landon's friends had deserted him. Even his own defense lawyer had done a halfhearted job. "Yes, sir."

"And you can cut out the 'yes, sir' stuff. Good criminal-defense lawyers respect nobody. They challenge everybody."

Landon was a Southern boy. He almost did another *yes, sir* but caught himself. "Okay."

Harry tossed a document on top of a disorganized pile of paper in front of Landon. "Before you pick that up, let me tell you one thing," Harry continued. He was in teacher mode now, a role he relished. "At the beginning of every high-profile case, there will be an avalanche of negative publicity. It will seem like your client is getting crucified in the press, and you'll want to respond. But at that stage, when everybody wants blood, you can only make things worse.

"Your job is to hunker down and absorb every blow. Think Muhammad Ali and his rope-a-dope. After a while—and in some cases it takes longer than others—the public gets tired of beating up on the defendant, and then they want to hear the other side. But you've got to let the anger play out first. That's why I wait to make my cases in court."

"Makes sense," Landon said, because he couldn't think of what else to say.

Harry pointed at the document. "Okay, now you're ready to read that."

Landon picked up the autopsy report and absorbed the details. As expected, the cause of death was strangulation, not drowning. That part of the autopsy, along with the existence of contusions around Erica's neck, had already been touted by Sherman. But the toxicology results were new. According to the certificate of analysis received from the state lab on Friday, Erica's hair had tested positive for a substance known as gamma-hydroxybutyric acid.

"What do the hair results mean?" Landon asked.

"That's GHB. A date rape drug. It metabolizes quickly, so it's not always present in the blood or urine, but it can be detected in the hair for up to six months."

Landon nodded, and Harry tacked on an afterthought. "Most people don't know that," he murmured.

It was, Landon knew, another reference to Harry's favorite defense. A prosecutor would have known that information. But a prosecutor's wife or someone trying to frame a prosecutor might not.

Landon also knew what the prosecution's response would be. Elias King didn't expect the body to be found. He wasn't worried about the hair-testing results or fingerprints on metal plates or any other such thing. No body, no prints, no hair—*no crime.*

Landon flipped the page, and his mouth dropped open. This was why Harry was making such a big deal about the autopsy. The hair testing was nothing by comparison.

Erica Jensen had been pregnant.

Landon tried to keep his composure, but the revelation felt like a gut punch. He wasn't just defending somebody who might have murdered a legal assistant. He was defending somebody who might have murdered his lover when he found out she was pregnant with his child.

"Is it his?" Landon asked.

Harry shrugged. "They haven't done the DNA yet. But what do you think?"

There was no way around it. "Probably," Landon said.

He tried to absorb the implications. Did Elias know about the pregnancy? If so, why hadn't he said something? Were Landon and Harry defending a baby killer?

"Look on the bright side," Harry said. "Under Virginia law, killing a pregnant woman counts as two murders. We can double our fee."

"Great," Landon mumbled.

26

ON TUESDAY EVENING, Landon arrived early at the gym with a brand-new curl bar. He had purchased it that afternoon and wiped it down carefully before he left his condo. When he got to the gym, he carefully placed twenty-five-pound weights on both ends—perfect for Jake. The three high school juniors Landon mentored were curling twenty pounds more than Jake, and this would keep the boys from having to switch weights so often.

It would also allow Landon to get a good, clean set of fingerprints.

When they had finished working out, Julia was not outside waiting for Jake as she had been the prior week. Jake stepped away from the others and called her. When he returned from making his phone call, he shoved his hands into the pocket of his hoodie and hung his head.

"Your mom on the way?" Landon asked.

Jake hesitated. "She's running a little late."

"But she is coming?"

Jake shrugged his shoulders. "I'll be fine. You can go ahead."

The kid was a terrible liar. Besides, Landon had to lock the building, and he couldn't leave Jake standing outside in this weather.

"Why don't you let me take you home?" Landon asked. "It's not that far out of the way, and it would give me a chance to check in with your dad."

Jake pressed his lips together. "All right," he said. He made another phone call as Landon locked up the gym.

On his way out, Landon looked at the curl bar but cut off the lights and left it behind. He could always circle back later and get it, he told himself.

They talked football for the first twenty-five minutes on the way to Jake's house. They were almost there when Jake mustered the courage to change the conversation.

"Can I ask you a question?"

"Sure."

He looked out the side window and took a deep breath. "Do you think my dad did it?"

Landon wanted to give the kid some reassurance. He could sense how badly Jake needed it. But he couldn't lie to him. Deception had put Landon in jail once. He had promised himself that he wouldn't walk down that path again.

"Your father's a good and decent man who has spent his life upholding the law. The case against him is highly circumstantial, and Harry's one heckuva lawyer." Landon paused, sensing that Jake needed more. "There aren't any guarantees, Jake. But I believe we're going to win this case."

Jake considered this in silence for a few minutes as they pulled into the Kings' neighborhood. "But do you think he did it?" Jake eventually asked. "Did Dad kill that woman?"

The kid was smarter than Landon gave him credit for. He could sniff out a bluff, and he obviously wanted Landon to play it straight. "I don't know," Landon admitted. "I just don't know."

Jake seemed satisfied by the honesty and nodded his head ever so slightly. "I'm glad you're his lawyer," Jake said.

They rode in silence until Landon turned into the Kings' driveway. Landon admitted to Jake that he really didn't need to see Elias that night after all. "I'll see you on Thursday," Landon said.

"I'm not sure I'll be able to come."

"Why not?"

Jake had one hand on the door handle but stopped before getting out. "My mom and dad had a pretty big argument last night. My mom's going back to New Jersey to stay with her parents for a while. She wants me to go with her."

Landon could see the pain on the kid's face. Choosing between a mother and father was never easy. But it was excruciating under these circumstances.

"Are you going?" he asked.

"I don't want to," Jake said softly. "My friends are here. And I feel like my dad needs me."

Landon didn't like the fact that Julia was heading to New Jersey. It would look better for the case if she hung in there with Elias. But that wasn't Landon's main concern right now. He saw deep pain on young Jake's face, his entire world falling apart.

"You need a ride Thursday?" Landon asked. "I could pick you up."

Jake made a meager effort to decline but Landon insisted. It might be the only way Jake could get there.

Jake thanked Landon, got his stuff out of the rear seat, and headed into the house.

He walked slump-shouldered, facing a divided household and an impossible choice. *Poor kid,* Landon thought.

///

That night, Landon and Kerri talked about Harry's request for Jake's fingerprints.

"You're not going to do it, are you?" Kerri asked.

Landon explained how it might help Elias and Jake. Maybe they could prove that somebody else's fingerprints were on the weights.

"If that's the case, why don't you just ask Jake for his fingerprints?" Kerri said.

"Because at trial, Jake might have to take the stand. If he's asked whether he gave us a fingerprint to test, it would look like we're hiding something if he doesn't also know the results. And Harry's not sure yet that he wants Jake or Elias to know the results."

"Listen to yourself," Kerri said. "And think about this as a father. Would you want your lawyers taking secret fingerprints of your son so they might use them to accuse your kid of murder? Or just as bad, so they might accuse your wife?"

"My kid, definitely not," Landon said. "My wife, maybe."

Kerri gave him a *not funny* look. They both knew she was right. And Landon had no intention of going back to the gym and picking up that curl bar. It wouldn't be a pleasant meeting with Harry, but Landon wasn't going to compromise his principles. Not this time.

"Are you ready to have an unemployed husband?"

"Yes," Kerri said quickly. She gave him a kiss. "I already miss your cooking."

27

THE AUTOPSY HAD BEEN THE LEAD STORY on every local newscast
Tuesday night and was still part of the news cycle on Wednesday morning. The *Tidewater Times* gave it a front-page headline. Landon watched
his own wife read the story on WTRT. They used B-roll with stock
photos of Erica Jensen from her firm's website and a video of Elias King's
arrest. Kerri looked directly into the camera and spoke in dramatic tones
about the autopsy results. She mentioned "the date rape drug GHB"
and the fact that Erica was pregnant. "DNA tests on the fetus have not
yet been completed," she said.

Landon knew she didn't have any choice in the matter. Kerri's
colleagues had begun calling the King case "the gift"—the story that
kept on giving. Just when things seemed to settle down, Franklin
Sherman would release another tantalizing piece of evidence. "The
gift" guaranteed that even a slow news day would have an interesting lead story.

Harry only spent a few minutes in the office that morning, just long enough to pack his satchel for court and ask Landon a question.

"Did you get the fingerprints?" he asked. He was standing in the doorway to Landon's office.

Landon shook his head. "I couldn't do it, Harry. It just didn't feel right."

Harry frowned. "We'll talk later." He turned and headed down the steps.

///

Landon was deep in thought, drafting a motion and staring at his computer screen, when he looked up and noticed Brent Benedict at his door. The firm's managing partner looked serious.

"Can you join me for lunch?" Brent asked.

Landon glanced at his computer. It was twelve thirty and Landon was definitely hungry. But Brent Benedict had never asked him to lunch before. In fact, Landon couldn't remember Brent even setting foot on the second floor since Landon started working.

"Sure," Landon said. He grabbed his suit coat from the back of his door and followed Brent down the steps.

"I thought we'd go to Bella Monte," Benedict said.

It was an Italian place just a few doors down from the McNaughten and Clay building. According to Rachel, the firm used it for client lunches. She said it had the best lasagna and meat loaf around, and the owners seemed to know everyone in the community. Landon had never been there.

He and Brent walked across the parking lots without talking, and Landon wondered if he was being fired. It seemed a little too coincidental that he had stood up to Harry that morning and was now being escorted to lunch by the firm's managing partner. On the other hand, employers didn't usually take you to lunch just to hand you a pink slip.

On the way, two F/A-18 Hornets from the nearby Oceana Naval Base passed overhead. Their roar had become a customary part of life in

Virginia Beach for Landon. He had grown used to stopping conversations and waiting for the jets to pass over, splitting ears with their rumbling "sound of freedom." Newcomers to the Beach would plug their ears and look up at the jets. But Landon was already past all that.

"Is that what you flew? Landon asked as the jets trailed off toward the ocean.

"It's classified," Brent said.

Landon couldn't tell if Brent was kidding, so he stuck his hands in his pockets and walked on in silence.

When they arrived at the restaurant, Landon followed Brent to a back table where the rest of the firm waited. Harry McNaughten was there. So were Parker Clausen and Rachel. Even Janaya.

"Hey, Landon," Rachel said. "Have a seat."

The others had already ordered drinks, and everyone except Harry had a glass of wine. Harry was drinking some kind of dark beer. A waitress showed up and Landon ordered a Diet Coke.

The lawyers all chatted as if they did this every day. Clausen wanted to talk about his latest book, but nobody seemed to care. Rachel asked Harry some questions about the King case. Janaya asked Landon how Maddie and Kerri were doing.

The small talk continued until the waitress came to take their order. It was the first time Landon had seen the firm this relaxed. It seemed like the lawyers might actually like each other.

When the shop talk started in earnest, it focused on an upcoming hearing in the Eleventh Circuit Court of Appeals in Atlanta, Georgia, on behalf of Cipher Inc. The three lawyers on the downstairs floor were scheduled to fly out later that day on a private Cessna the firm occasionally leased. Brent Benedict would be arguing the case, and Rachel and Clausen were going along for research purposes. It seemed to Landon a little extravagant to send three lawyers on such an excursion, when only one would be actually speaking before the court. But Cipher Inc. could certainly handle the charges.

When the main course finally arrived and the wineglasses were refilled, Harry asked for everybody's attention for an important announcement.

"I'd like to propose a toast," Harry said. "To the newest member of the bar."

Harry raised his glass and the other lawyers did the same. Landon stopped in midtoast, his eyes wide.

"Just found out from a friend at the Board of Bar Examiners yesterday," Harry said, his mouth curling into a smile.

The lawyers clinked glasses and took a sip. For Landon, who had said a prayer about this every night for the last two weeks, the moment seemed surreal. He could keep his job. Once he got sworn in, he could officially practice law. He immediately thought about telling Kerri, how she would react, knowing that their sacrifice had paid off.

Still, one could never be too sure in these matters. "So you're saying I'm in?" Landon asked Harry.

Harry looked around the table. "Are there any other lawyers here waiting to hear from the Board of Bar Examiners?"

The others smirked and shook their heads.

"Then I guess I'm talking about you. Congratulations."

Landon smiled broadly and toasted everybody again, one by one. They congratulated him and gulped down their beer and wine. They were starting to grow on him.

"They'll let anybody practice law these days," Harry said.

///

After lunch, Harry and Landon returned to the office, trailing the others.

"I thought I might get fired," Landon confessed. "For failing to get those fingerprints."

Harry's expression didn't change. Perhaps he was considering it after all.

"It's good you've got your principles," Harry said. "That's one of the reasons I hired you. But you're overanalyzing this. Our client needs us to find out whose fingerprint is on that weight. And at this point, I don't want somebody who might be testifying to know that information."

"I understand that," Landon said. "It just felt wrong trying to deceive Jake."

"Don't worry about it," Harry said. He was a little out of breath from the walk. "I'll get the fingerprints some other way."

28

RACHEL STRACH NEVER GREW TIRED of flying in the cockpit of the Cessna Citation Mustang the firm leased from time to time. The plane was trimmed out with a white leather interior and could carry four passengers. For this trip, Parker Clausen was riding alone in the back, while Brent manned the controls and Rachel stayed up front as his "copilot."

She and Brent put on the headphones and chatted away once they reached cruising altitude, after he had switched off the mike to the outside world. For Rachel, the soft purr of the jet engines seemed to drown out all of the tension and chaos that was part of a busy law firm. Here, cruising above the clouds, they could talk about personal matters, and Brent opened his life like a well-worn book.

Brent was good-looking, in incredible shape, and a powerful attorney. But none of those things had first attracted Rachel to the man who was nearly ten years older than she. Instead, it was the side of Brent that others never got to see, the part that he buried beneath his military demeanor and tough-guy veneer. The guy had a heart. He was a sucker for romance and adventure and fairy-tale endings. She had seen it first on a road trip, when the two of them had gone to see *The Vow* together. He had cried, though he'd tried to mask it. She was hooked.

The movie showed marriage the way it was supposed to be, he'd said when they shared dinner together afterward. "I'd give anything to start over again."

There had been rumors about the Benedicts' marriage when Rachel had joined the firm five years earlier. It was Brent's second. His first had fallen apart during a six-month deployment. His wife informed him about the other man by e-mail.

It took Brent five years to get over the heartbreak and find Stacy, a woman who had already burned through two marriages and brought kids into the relationship. They met at a cocktail party. He was a promising young attorney, and she was an interior designer, the daughter of a wealthy Virginia Beach developer. She married Brent, quit her job, and began working on her tennis game. The marriage quickly soured, though they managed to tough it out for ten years. But Stacy knew she wasn't getting any younger and eventually insisted on a divorce, citing irreconcilable differences. They separated and agreed to work things out without getting lawyers involved.

That lasted until Brent suggested what he thought was a fair proposal for child support, spousal support, and equitable distribution. Stacy was insulted, made an appointment with the most aggressive divorce lawyer in Virginia Beach, and the war was on. Brent's stepchildren, who had never learned to call him Dad, alleged that his strict disciplinarian ways constituted abuse. Stacy's attorney, a woman named Carolyn Glaxon-Forrester, claimed Brent was hiding assets, and she demanded access to all of McNaughten and Clay's financial data.

The case became a bone of contention at the firm and made every one of Brent's victories bittersweet. The more money he made, the more support Stacy wanted. And Glaxon-Forrester kept dragging out the proceedings, demanding more information about the legal fees and profits of McNaughten and Clay.

It was against this backdrop that Brent unburdened himself in the skies over South Carolina. "I don't know why it has to be like this," Brent said, his voice forlorn. "I don't hate Stacy. I just don't feel anything for her anymore. There are times when I want to just fire my lawyer and tell Stacy I'll sign anything her lawyer drafts, just to end it. But I don't even think that would satisfy her. It's like her whole life is about getting revenge for all these perceived slights during our marriage. If the divorce proceedings ended tomorrow, I don't think she would know what to do."

Rachel listened and let Brent talk things out. She knew he wasn't really looking for advice; he just wanted a sympathetic ear.

"The first time your marriage fails, you blame it on the other person. I mean, she couldn't wait six months for me to get back from deployment? But the second time, you have to look at yourself. Maybe I'm a poor judge of character. Or just a terrible judge of women. Stacy's certainly not perfect. But I loved her when we first met. She was vulnerable then, coming off her second divorce. Things were different."

"You've always been a sucker for a damsel in distress," Rachel said.

Brent gave her a sideways glance. "Meaning?"

"The Sergeant case. Their motion to compel."

She didn't need to say more. It was the first hearing Brent had allowed her to handle in federal court. The opposing lawyer had accused Rachel of hiding documents and being unethical. Brent had jumped to her defense and almost started a fistfight in the hallway after the hearing.

"You've been a great mentor to me," Rachel said. "And you've given me every opportunity I could ever ask for. So I wouldn't say you are a terrible judge of *all* women."

"Just the ones I end up marrying," Brent said.

"Details," Rachel said.

They flew in silence for a few moments, and Rachel started thinking about the what-ifs. Apparently she wasn't the only one.

"I wish I'd met you ten years ago," Brent said. "It might have saved me a lot of heartache."

On too many occasions to count, Rachel had wished the same thing.

Brent had always been good to her. Protective, encouraging, nurturing. She had endured her own turmoil in the five years since she joined the firm, churning through several boyfriends, one of whom was emotionally abusive. Brent had threatened the man with his life if he ever laid a hand on Rachel.

"I know what you mean. But you know what I've concluded?"

"What?"

"I'm just glad I know you now."

She reached out and put a hand on top of his. She wasn't trying to shatter some new barrier; they had grown accustomed to the casual touches that signified something deeper than friendship. But this time it was an unspoken promise. She left her hand there for a long time, and neither of them spoke.

That evening, Rachel and Brent checked into the hotel, changed clothes, and spent an hour in the workout room. Parker Clausen had his own agenda. He headed to the bar, had a few drinks, and retired to his room to work on the next chapter of his great American novel.

After their workout, Brent and Rachel went out to dinner. Brent ordered an expensive bottle of wine. He had a case to argue the next day, but in typical Brent Benedict fashion, he had prepared well in advance. Besides, the hearing was the furthest thing from either of their minds. In fact, during the hour-and-a-half dinner, neither said a word about that case or any other. There were more important things to talk about. Personal things. And on the cab ride home, Rachel slid next to Brent and he wrapped his arm around her shoulders.

In the hotel elevator, she slipped him a key to her room. "Give me ten minutes," she said.

He was military, so he arrived right on time. He knocked softly and she let him in.

They woke together in the morning.

29

ON SATURDAY MORNING, Maddie woke up early and snuggled in bed with Landon and Kerri. Landon relished these times. Saturday was the only morning left when he could enjoy time with Maddie and lounge around the house. Even on Saturdays, there was work to be done. Though he would usually head into the office later on, Saturday mornings were reserved for father-daughter bonding.

As usual, Maddie squirmed around in the bed with the never-ending energy of a five-year-old. This made Simba restless, and before long he was determined that it was time for him to eat. Because Kerri had to be the first one up every other morning, it was an unwritten rule that Landon would take care of Simba on Saturdays.

He took Simba outside, fed the little beast breakfast, and then fixed chocolate-chip pancakes with Maddie. They poured the pancake batter into a metal cutout on the griddle, shaping the pancakes into small Mickey Mouse heads. They used chocolate chips for the eyes and mouth and nose. When the pancakes turned just the right shade of brown, Maddie flipped them from the griddle onto their plates. They smothered the pancakes in syrup and got everything sticky. Then they snuggled on the couch and put in a Disney movie.

Landon's cell phone rang at eight thirty, but he let it kick into voice mail. It rang again ten minutes later, and he couldn't keep himself from checking it. Harry. The man wouldn't be calling on Saturday morning unless it was something really important.

When Landon called Harry back, he ran into his boss's usual reluctance to talk about anything over the phone. "Can you come into the office for a few minutes?" Harry asked. "And if Kerri's not working, can you bring her with you?"

Landon hesitated. He wanted to set some healthy boundaries for his family, which was nearly impossible with a guy like Harry. The man ate, drank, and slept law.

"If I come in, Kerri will have to stay with Maddie," Landon said.

"Bring Maddie, too," Harry replied. "It'll just take a minute."

The matter didn't sound debatable. So an hour later, Landon dragged his entire clan, absent Simba, into the office. The first thing he noticed was the bright-yellow L.L. Bean bag sitting in the second-floor hallway.

Harry stepped out of his office to greet them. "Thanks for coming in," he said to Kerri. "This will just take a minute."

The L.L. Bean bag was stuffed full of books, reams of copy paper, and black three-ring spiral notebooks from other cases. There was a scale next to the bag.

"I need you to help me figure out what this thing weighs," Harry said to Landon, his voice characteristically gruff.

"Why do you talk funny?" Maddie asked.

"Shhh," Kerri said.

Harry frowned and asked Landon to stand on the scale first without the bag. Harry put on a pair of reading glasses and knelt down, his nose a foot or so from the readout.

"One ninety-five," he said. He pointed to the bag. "Now, let's see what this sucker weighs."

Landon picked it up, using his legs more than his back. It was bulky and heavy, but he managed to get it over to the scale.

"What's 318 minus 195?" Harry asked.

"One twenty-three," Kerri said.

"Math wizard," Harry mumbled approvingly. He jotted down a note.

They off-loaded some ballast until the bag weighed exactly 120, Erica Jensen's body weight.

"You mind trying to pick that up?" Harry asked Kerri.

"I will," Maddie said.

"No, honey. Let Mommy do it."

But she had a hard time. She pulled on the straps and could drag the bag a little but couldn't lift it far off the ground.

"Those concrete walls on the bridge are about three feet high," Harry said, his arms across his chest, chewing on his reading glasses. "And at the very least, somebody would have to lift that dead body up there, balance it on the concrete abutment, and put two thirty-five-pound plates into the bag before dumping it in the canal."

"Hold that thought," Kerri said, her hand up. She took Maddie by the hand, shot Landon a *What's wrong with this guy?* look, and led Maddie down to Landon's office and out of earshot of Harry McNaughten. "This is where Daddy works," Landon heard her say cheerfully from down the hall.

"Whose body was in the bag?" Maddie's voice came trailing back.

"Oh yeah," Harry said, as if he had just that moment noticed Maddie. "Sorry about that."

Landon shrugged. Harry was Harry. There was nothing Landon could do about it.

"You think your wife's stronger than Julia King?" Harry asked, after Kerri and Maddie had disappeared toward Landon's office.

"By a long shot."

"Me too. Meaning that if Julia did it, she didn't act alone."

Landon still couldn't imagine Julia killing Erica Jensen. But Harry was right about one thing—if she had, she would have needed help disposing of the body.

"How much can her kid lift?" Harry asked.

Landon shook his head, dismissing the idea as preposterous. "Jake King did not help his mom dispose of Erica Jensen's body," Landon insisted.

"Yeah," Harry sighed, sounding unconvinced. "You're probably right."

After ten minutes in Landon's office, Kerri and Maddie headed home. Harry gave Landon a ride home after a full day at the office.

"Is every Saturday going to be like this?" Kerri asked that evening.

"Only until we get this Elias King case behind us," Landon said.

But even he didn't believe it.

30

WHEN RACHEL WALKED into Landon's office on Tuesday morning and took a seat in one of his client chairs, he could tell she was out of sorts. Her eyes were red and puffy, and her skin was marked with small red streaks on the side of her neck. She still had the fresh cover-girl good looks and bewitching figure that turned men's heads, but her brow furrowed with worry and her mouth turned down in a frightened little frown.

She would make a terrible poker player.

"Have you got a second?" she asked.

Landon normally welcomed interruptions from Rachel, but today he was swamped. Still, she had been kind to him when he first arrived at the firm. He owed her.

"What's up?"

"I need to show you something."

Rachel placed some photos on Landon's desk. She watched intently as he shuffled through them.

The first was a picture of Rachel and Brent Benedict at dinner, leaning toward each other. It looked like she was mesmerized with what he was saying. The second was a picture of Brent entering a hotel room with number 1217 on the door. The photo was stamped with the time and date. February 20, 10:05 p.m.

The third showed Brent and Rachel leaving the same room, and it was stamped 7:30 a.m. on February 21—the date of the hearing in front of the Eleventh Circuit Court of Appeals. They were both smiling.

Underneath the photos was a copy of Rachel's receipt for room 1217 at the Hilton Hotel in Atlanta. Landon noticed that all of the documents had been identified with exhibit stickers.

He also noticed the guilt-stricken look on Rachel's face and decided not to judge her. She had come to him for advice, not a lecture.

"I thought this was a no-fault divorce," Landon said, referring to Brent and his soon-to-be ex-wife.

"It is. Or at least it was." After a few beats, Rachel lifted her eyes to his. "Can I hire you as my lawyer for this conversation?"

Landon knew she wasn't serious. It was lawyer-speak to ensure that what they said would remain forever confidential, protected by the attorney-client privilege. "Sure."

"Brent has already been deposed several times by his wife's attorney, who's basically the Lord Voldemort of divorce attorneys. Yesterday afternoon she took a supplemental deposition, which was supposed to be confined to questions about his assets and how much he made at the firm. Instead, she asked Brent whether he was having an affair."

Rachel paused, looked past Landon, and drew in a breath before continuing. "He denied it. That's when Stacy's lawyer showed him these."

Landon sighed and rubbed his temple. One of the firm's partners had apparently lied under oath, not to mention the fact that he was having an affair with an associate.

"Are you sleeping with him?" Landon asked softly.

Rachel stared at the desk and nodded. *People can be so stupid,* Landon thought. Even aside from the morality of it, they should have just waited a few months.

"They're going to depose me next," Rachel said.

The dilemma was obvious. Rachel could either lie under oath to protect Brent or destroy him by telling the truth. "He says we're the only ones who know what happened in that room," she continued. "If they had more photos, they would have shown them to us."

"But you can't lie under oath," Landon said. He made eye contact with Rachel. This was serious.

She didn't say a word for a few seconds. When she spoke, her voice registered more resignation than resolve. "I know."

"How can I help?"

"I'm not sure. I guess I just needed somebody to talk to."

Landon thought about what could be done. Perhaps she could take the Fifth. But was adultery even a crime in Georgia? Maybe they could talk to Brent Benedict and get him to change his prior answers. Not likely.

He noticed her eyes tearing up. He took a box of tissues from the credenza behind him and placed them on the desk. She took one, dabbed at her eyes for a moment, and straightened her shoulders. She wadded the tissue in her fist.

"You can't lie," Landon repeated. He needed to fortify his witness. "You've got your whole career in front of you."

Rachel shrugged. "Seems to me like my career is shot either way."

///

For Sean Phoenix, lying was an art form. You don't move up the ranks of the CIA without a little misdirection here and there, and you certainly don't become CEO of Cipher Inc. without learning how to lie as effortlessly as breathing.

But lying under oath in front of a congressional subcommittee made even Sean Phoenix a little nervous. He was a master at not showing it, of course. He could lie to anyone's face without flinching, his pulse and breathing constant and unchanged. But it didn't mean he enjoyed it. He saw it as a necessary evil, an occupational hazard, something to be tolerated for the greater good.

"No, Senator, our organization has never knowingly participated in the assassination of a foreign official."

"No, Senator, we do not torture enemy combatants under orders from the U.S. government or any of our country's allies."

"That's correct, Senator; I'm denying we even have contracts with the U.S. government."

The senators were all such fools. They believed America could play by its self-imposed rules of civility while all her enemies launched terrorist attacks and used suicide bombers to kill innocent civilians. Meanwhile, they argued that those attacks should be answered with United Nations resolutions or economic sanctions to uphold the high-and-mighty principles of democracy and self-determination. But Sean Phoenix was a realist. It was his job to keep the good senators safe so they could live in peace and harass him with these ridiculous questions.

Such was the world of politics.

But in the real world—the Machiavellian world of power and ambition—the victor still wrote all the rules. No matter how the victory was achieved.

So Sean Phoenix sat for hours before the Senate Select Committee on Intelligence, telling one lie after another. He even feigned righteous indignation a time or two. His denials were firm and unbending and full of the conviction of a man who believed he was making the world a better place.

He found it ironic that a high-ranking official at the State Department called him less than forty-eight hours later. There was an issue in Iran, and the State Department needed it handled discreetly. The usual procedures for plausible deniability would apply. Cipher's role in the operation—indeed, the firm's very link to the government—could never be made public. It wasn't quite a *Mission Impossible* "this tape will self-destruct in five seconds" assignment, but it might as well have been. Sean Phoenix and Cipher Inc. would be handsomely rewarded if they succeeded. But they would also be flying alone. The U.S. government would not raise a finger to help them if things went wrong.

An Iranian pastor had been sentenced to death for apostasy. He had become a cause célèbre among American evangelicals, and the U.S. president's popularity was taking a hit because there was nothing he could do. The State Department wondered if Cipher Inc. had any operatives on the ground. Perhaps they might engineer a renegade prison break for several prisoners that would, coincidentally, end up freeing the pastor. If the pastor were whisked out of the country, he could be granted asylum in any number of places. But it would be important for diplomatic reasons that the U.S. government never be connected to the efforts.

This was exactly the type of assignment Sean Phoenix needed. He had been waiting for something noble, something the public would love if the truth ever got out. A good spy covered his own back. If the public forgave Oliver North for lying to a Senate subcommittee, how much more would they forgive Sean Phoenix, provided they knew he was pursuing a higher good—like rescuing Christian pastors from beheadings in Iran?

He would need a member of the news media he could fully trust to carefully document his efforts. His media contact would have to agree to embargo the story and not release it without the authorization of Phoenix himself. And that authorization would never be given unless there was a breach of security and his lies under oath were exposed.

From his office, he dialed the cell number for Kerri Reed. He had already decided that she would be useful for any number of reasons.

"How would you like the story of your life?" he asked.

"I'm listening."

31

THE OTHER SHOE DROPPED on Friday, the first day of March. This time it was the Feds—a twenty-three-count grand jury indictment against Elias King for insider trading. Mitchell Taylor, the assistant U.S. Attorney in charge of the investigation, didn't play games like the General. There was no perp walk. No press conference.

There didn't have to be. The eighty-two-page indictment said it all.

The Feds had received an anonymous tip about insider trading at the law firm of Kilgore and Strobel three months earlier. With the concurrence of the firm's managing partner, a district court judge had issued a sealed search warrant and secretly appointed a commissioner to review the hard drives of Kilgore and Strobel lawyers. The commissioner's job was to look for evidence of insider trading while preserving the attorney-client confidences of the firm's clients.

It had taken weeks to access the attorneys' computers without their knowledge and copy all the hard drives. Another two weeks to go through the data. And ultimately, according to the indictment, only one lawyer was implicated.

The indictment claimed that Elias King had been setting up anonymous offshore companies in the Seychelles Islands and using those companies to conduct stock-option trades from accounts in the Caymans. The trades all involved Kilgore and Strobel clients that were about to participate in a merger or announce some other significant corporate event. To anonymously capitalize on the insider information, Elias had put together a maze of companies and accounts so dense that nobody could have figured it out without the information provided by the anonymous tipster.

The indictment alleged multiple violations of the Securities Exchange Act of 1934, as amended by the Sarbanes-Oxley Act of 2002, as well as associated claims of wire and mail fraud, tax evasion, and general securities fraud. Each count of insider trading carried a penalty of up to twenty years in prison and $5 million in fines. In total, Elias was looking at the possibility of more than 460 years behind bars and more than $115 million in penalties. It occurred to Landon that having the Feds prosecute you for violating the securities laws was more hazardous than having the commonwealth after you for murder.

That thought wasn't lost on Harry McNaughten either. He quickly requested that Elias fork over another $50,000 retainer, which Harry said was a bargain because everybody knew that federal cases were twice as hard and twice as expensive as state court cases.

The money hit the firm account just in time for Harry to show up at the bond hearing. The Feds had already seized every dime in the Cayman accounts and now wanted another $500,000 bond to guarantee that Elias didn't flee the country.

Harry railed against the notion, just as he had in state court, but his client had already become one of the most reviled men in the commonwealth. What surprised Landon was not that the judge set bond at half a million, just as Mitchell Taylor requested, but that Elias King was able to pay it.

"He borrowed the money from his in-laws," Harry later explained.

"Julia's parents?" Landon asked. The woman had left town shortly after learning about Elias's affair, but now she was helping her husband stay out of jail?

"It's old Jersey money," Harry said, as if that justified taking every dime of it.

Landon just shook his head. Perhaps he had underestimated Julia King.

32

AS SHE DROVE NORTH on Interstate 95 early Saturday morning, the day after Elias King's federal court arraignment, Kerri couldn't help but feel a little guilty. Saturday mornings had become a bone of contention in the Reed household. Kerri normally had the weekends off and resented the fact that Landon was now expected to be at McNaughten and Clay on Saturday as if it were any other working day. That new schedule left Kerri to get up and take care of Simba and Maddie, sacrificing her one day to sleep in. It also meant that Landon's father-daughter time with Maddie was gone—the latest sacrifice offered to the firm.

The issue had sparked an intense argument after Kerri's phone call from Sean Phoenix Thursday evening. This could be her break, she had told Landon. She had to go to D.C. Saturday morning. She would be gone for a couple of days. Landon would have to watch Maddie.

Friday night, after the indictment, Landon asked her to postpone the trip. "I'm meeting Harry first thing in the morning," he said.

"Then you better pack some crayons," Kerri said. "Because I can't take Maddie with *me*."

They traded barbs for a few minutes, both convinced that they were the one always making the big sacrifice. They had fallen asleep last night facing opposite walls. Now, as she drove north in silence, her stomach clenched when she thought about the way they had treated Maddie like some kind of disease—"You take her!" "No, you take her!" In truth, she was a great kid and Kerri missed her already.

So maybe she was a horrible mother and wife, but Kerri still knew she couldn't turn down this opportunity. Sean had thanked her for the news story she had done on Cipher Inc. after their previous interview. He'd said it was the first balanced story he had seen about his company in years. And then he had asked if she wanted to see the real inner workings of the place. This weekend he would be directing an international espionage assignment so confidential that she couldn't release the story unless he gave her written permission. If she was interested, she should pack for a two-day trip and meet him at Cipher's headquarters at 9 a.m. on Saturday morning.

If she was interested?

There were hundreds of reporters just like Kerri, toiling away in small-time media markets, hoping one day to land the Big Story. They were all good-looking, eloquent, young, and ambitious. Those were the givens. They were also highly competitive and extraordinarily bright.

But none of that guaranteed success. The news business, Kerri had learned, was not a meritocracy. Survival of the fittest didn't necessarily apply. They were all fit. They all would have made Darwin proud. But the ones who made it to the top needed a little luck. A local story that blew up on the national news. A confidential source nobody else had. Somebody in power who entrusted them with an exclusive.

Kerri could sense that this was her time. As she sped north in the early morning darkness, she worked hard to convince herself that it wasn't just about her career. She wanted this for her family, too. Landon was working at McNaughten and Clay because he had no other options in the Hampton Roads market. But there were better firms out there in D.C.— which also happened to be the Holy Grail for television reporters.

As she took the bypass around Richmond, her melancholy thoughts about family faded and she started feeling some unmitigated excitement about the day ahead. She knew there was more to Cipher Inc. than she had previously reported. More to Cipher than *anyone* had reported. How many people got to see the inner workings of an international espionage operation?

At the same time, she didn't quite trust Sean Phoenix. He was, according to all reports, a notorious ladies' man. The comparisons to James Bond reached beyond the fact that they were both spies. But Kerri was a big girl. When it came to men, she could handle herself.

It was 6 a.m. In another hour, Maddie would wake up, and she and Landon would fix chocolate-chip pancakes before heading to the office. They would spend the day together in Virginia Beach. Meanwhile, for all Kerri knew, by the time the sun set on this day she could be on the other side of the world.

///

Harry McNaughten greeted Landon with a frown when he saw Maddie trailing in her dad's wake.

"Hey, Mr. Harry!" she said. "You want to watch a movie with me? Or play hide-and-seek?"

"Sorry," Harry said dourly. "I've got lots of work to do. And so does your dad."

"Why do you have so many whiskers?" Maddie asked.

Landon had noticed that Harry didn't shave on Saturday mornings and that his gray stubble grew in at an alarmingly fast pace. But leave it to Maddie to ask about it.

"Men have whiskers," Harry said. And then he turned to Landon. "When you get her settled, I've got a boatload of work for you on the King case."

Landon reached down and picked Maddie up. It was always easier to control kids when you were carting them around. "Come on, girlfriend, let's get you set up in Daddy's office."

Once Maddie was out of the way, Harry morphed into mentor mode. Landon had seen it a few times on Saturday mornings, when there was less time pressure than during the week. Harry would act like Socrates, quizzing his young pupil and dropping pearls of wisdom here and there. Along, of course, with a few choice words about the harsh realities of life as a criminal-defense lawyer.

"How do you think we should handle the preliminary hearing in state court?" Harry asked.

Landon hadn't really thought about it. He knew that preliminary hearings were generally used by defense lawyers for discovery—to learn as much as possible about the prosecution's case while showing almost nothing about their own case. He also knew that judges generally had no problem finding probable cause so the case could proceed forward, especially on evidence as strong as the General had here. He said as much to Harry and suggested that he and Harry should probably not even call any witnesses, to avoid tipping their hand.

"It's a trick question," Harry said, which pretty much went without saying because almost all of Harry's questions were trick questions. "We're going to waive the prelim. Know why?"

"I don't have the foggiest idea."

"Because we've got to try the state case before the federal case. It's our best chance of winning, and we can't afford to have Elias sitting there at our defense table having already been convicted of insider trading. That's why we fast-track the state case and stall the Feds."

"Daddy!" It was Maddie calling from down the hall.

Landon grimaced. "Be right back," he said.

A few minutes later, with Maddie's little crisis resolved, Landon was back in Harry's office. This time the quiz focused on the best defense for Elias King.

"Lack of proof beyond a reasonable doubt," Landon said.

"Circumstantial evidence. All those things you told me about how a prosecutor would know better than to leave this trail of evidence. Fingerprints can be preserved underwater. Drugs show up in hair testing. That type of thing."

Harry grunted, which Landon took as a *not bad* grade. "Then who did it?" he asked.

"We don't have to prove that," Landon countered. "Could have been a lot of people."

He hadn't finished his answer before Harry was shaking his head. "No, no," Harry said. "That's what they teach you in law school." He rubbed his hands over his face and back through his hair.

"If we're going to claim some other guy did it, we'd darn well better tell them who did it and how they did it, and we'd better have a darn good motive."

There were only two possibilities, Harry said: somebody set Elias up, or Julia King did it. And if Julia King did it, she would have needed help disposing of the body.

"We're going to talk a lot about a setup in the first part of the case," Harry said. "Starting with opening statements. 'Did the prosecution even consider the fact that my client might have been framed? Do you know how many drug dealers and murderers would love to see Elias King spend the rest of his life behind bars?' You see, Landon, that gives us a chance to highlight Elias's good side—to talk about what he did as a prosecutor. But then, after the prosecution has presented its case and shown all the reasons it couldn't have been a setup, we spring a surprise."

Harry leaned back, pleased with his own brilliance. His elbows rested on the arms of his chair, his hands tented. "The wife did it. Sure, she needed someone to help dispose of the body. May have been Jake. May have even been Elias. But he's not on trial for accessory after the fact."

Harry motioned with a hand, slipping into closing-argument mode. "Hell hath no fury like a woman scorned, and all that stuff." He grinned a little. "Trust me, Landon, I know."

Landon didn't like where this was headed. Too many holes. If Elias was involved in disposing of the body, he wouldn't have chucked it off the high-rise bridge. He wouldn't have stuffed it in a bag with weights containing his own fingerprints. And Landon certainly couldn't see Jake helping his mom dispose of the body. He just wasn't that kind of kid.

"You know why it's got to be Julia rather than an attempt by somebody to frame him?" Harry asked.

"No. I actually think that somebody framing Elias makes more sense."

"Then answer this," Harry said. "Why would somebody who was trying to set up Elias kill Erica? Whoever killed Erica knew about her meeting with the Feds the next day—that couldn't have been a coincidence. And if they knew about that, they would have known that if Erica stayed alive, Elias would be spending the rest of his life in a federal pen for insider trading. Why would somebody who wanted to frame Elias kill the one witness who could have helped put him away for life?"

Landon thought about this for a second and couldn't come up with an answer. Help came from an unexpected source.

"I've got to go to the bathroom," Maddie said, standing in the doorway. Landon wondered how long she had been there.

"Okay," he said, and shrugged at Harry.

An hour later, after Landon had scolded Maddie twice for running up and down the hall, Rachel Strach came upstairs and squealed with delight when she saw Maddie. She must have noticed the frazzled look on Landon's face, and she offered to take Maddie off his hands for a few hours.

"Where are you going?" Landon asked.

"Shopping. Girls always go shopping."

Landon protested a little—"You don't have to do that"—but didn't put up too much of a fight because he was worried that he might actually win. He made Maddie promise to behave and not ask for anything. Then he slipped Rachel twenty dollars so she could reward Maddie for good behavior.

As the two girls walked toward the stairwell, he saw Rachel push a strand of hair back behind Maddie's ear. Earlier that morning, Landon had tried to fix Maddie's hair the way Kerri did, in a cute little ponytail that sat on top of her head and flopped around. But he had been wholly unsuccessful. The ponytail hadn't stayed in place, and at the moment her hair looked like a rat's nest with a rubber band hidden in there someplace.

He heard Rachel whisper to Maddie, just loud enough to be overheard by Landon, "What did your daddy do to your hair?"

Rachel glanced back at Landon, and he shook his head. That woman deserved better than Brent Benedict, he thought.

33

KERRI ARRIVED at Cipher's Manassas facility thirty minutes ahead of schedule and endured the same routine as before. The unsmiling guard at the gate popped her trunk and checked under the car with his mirror. He asked three new questions—this time about her childhood pet, her college major, and the name of her prom date.

The questions made her realize that Cipher Inc. wasn't just snooping around the Internet gathering publicly available information about her. Somebody was digging deep. Querying friends or former teachers or maybe even family. She felt like telling the guard it was none of his business, but she knew she would end up kicking herself all the way back to Virginia Beach.

She drove down the tree-lined asphalt road and waved at a few of the security cameras. She decided to leave her overnight bag in the car but took her iPhone and digital recorder into the building. The devices were promptly confiscated at the front desk, where the guards wanded her and then called Sean Phoenix's office. Fifteen minutes later, he stepped off the elevator.

They chatted on the way to his office about nothing in particular. He apologized for giving her such short notice for this adventure and asked how Landon was enjoying his work at McNaughten and Clay. When they arrived at Sean's office, he offered her a seat at the small table in the corner, closed the door, and took a seat across from her.

"Kerri, I've never done this before," he began. "We've never brought a journalist on the inside like this." His voice was soft and level, almost confessional, and his intense, steel-blue eyes never left hers. "There are things we do in the service of our country that nobody else knows about. Those operations must remain secret. There are lives at stake. Big national-security interests. Those types of things."

He paused, apparently searching for the right words. "Sometimes, we have to play a little fast and loose with the truth. We are, after all, an intelligence-gathering firm. You can't do that without inside sources, and those sources require some elaborate cover. Do you understand what I'm saying?"

Actually, Kerri wasn't sure, but she nodded anyway. Sean hadn't said anything of consequence, but the possibilities were tantalizing. She knew she had made the right call by coming here today.

"Everything you are about to see and hear from this point forward is confidential and off the record until and unless I say otherwise. Is that agreed?" Sean asked.

He knew the media lingo. And she knew she wouldn't get another word out of him without agreeing to the request. "Of course."

"The other executives in our company who know about this think I've lost my mind. No offense, but they've spent their entire lives not trusting people, and they don't like the idea of an embedded journalist—even one I believe we can trust."

"I've never burned a source," Kerri said. "Never violated a promise of confidentiality. Never broadcast something that a source said was off the record. You won't be the first."

"I know all that," Sean said. "That's why you're here."

He leaned forward and reminded her again of their terms. Everything she saw in the next few days had to remain confidential, even from her husband. She couldn't broadcast a story about these events or even allude to them in another story without Sean's express written permission. "There's a substantial chance you might never get to tell the world what you're going to see," Sean said.

"I understand that."

"But if something breaks bad down the line and we have to go public with the types of things we have been doing for the U.S. government, I want a fair and respected reporter to be able to say that she was there and witnessed this mission. That's why we called you."

"Because you couldn't find anybody fair and respected?"

Sean gave her a courtesy smile, which quickly vanished. He took himself, and his work, pretty seriously.

"In many respects, today will be pretty boring. We're going to be sitting around for hours, waiting and planning—all for thirty minutes of action. But that's what our company does. Plan for months, even years, so that thirty minutes of life-changing events will go exactly as scripted. And I can promise you this—what you see in those thirty minutes will be worth the wait. You won't be able to take any notes or record anything, but we'll have everything well documented so that if you ever do have to run this story, you'll be able to reproduce everything you see and hear today."

Sean's cell phone rang and he answered it. He said, "Excuse me," to Kerri and paced around his office as he talked cryptically on the phone about some internal logistical matter. When he finished the call, he apologized and sat back down. "We've got to get going in a few minutes, so let me give you a quick briefing."

He explained how Cipher Inc. had been contacted by a representative of the State Department to see if Cipher operatives could spring an Iranian pastor named Seyyed Hassan from prison so that he and his family could escape that country and be provided political asylum. Whether the operation succeeded or failed, the U.S. government wanted no ties to it.

Kerri knew that the president was taking a lot of heat for the situation. Hassan had been sentenced to death for apostasy based on his conversion from Islam to Christianity. People wanted the U.S. to act, and the president had issued some strong statements condemning Iran for its lack of adherence to "internationally recognized standards of human rights and religious freedom." But strong words had not silenced the president's critics.

"Our job is to extricate this pastor from prison so he can seek asylum in Great Britain," Sean explained. "If we fail and our operatives are captured, the U.S. will disavow any knowledge of the operation."

Kerri felt the type of adrenaline surge that made journalism so addictive. This was a reporter's dream! She had been speculating about some potentially explosive stories during her trip to D.C., but this story exceeded even her wildest expectations.

And yet, unless something changed, she might never be able to go public with the biggest story she would ever cover.

"You've probably got a thousand questions, but most of those will be answered in time," Sean said. "For now, we need to get down to the situation room."

34

IT WAS THE TYPE OF WAR ROOM Kerri had anticipated during her first trip to Cipher Inc., yet it was even more fantastic than she had imagined.

The centerpiece was an enormous round table whose surface was a gigantic computer screen. The screen could be navigated and changed by touch, using something akin to iPad technology. At the moment, it showed an aerial view of a prison complex and its surrounding environs. A label on the screen identified it as Evin Prison in Tehran. The war room's walls were covered with other monitors, each showing a visual image of a separate aspect of what Sean and his team had dubbed Operation Trojan Horse. The lead operative, Sean explained, was code-named Odysseus, after the mythological leader who hid inside the Trojan horse and led the Greeks to victory.

There were six people in the room besides Kerri and Sean, four men and two women, all high-level operatives of Cipher Inc. One of the men looked Persian, and one of the women had a European lilt to her voice. The rest seemed to be Americans, all dressed casually enough that they might have been at Sean's house to watch a football game on the big screens rather than conduct an international espionage operation.

"This is Kerri Reed, the embedded journalist I've been talking about," Sean said, speaking loud enough to get everyone's attention. Kerri smiled, but the people in the room did not step forward and introduce themselves. "It goes without saying," Sean continued, "that I need you totally focused on this mission as if Kerri is not even here."

Kerri had never served as an embedded journalist before, but many of her colleagues had. Most of the time, the journalist became part of the team and interacted with the others. But at Cipher Inc., the rules were apparently different. Being an embedded journalist meant that Kerri would be treated like wall plaster—part of the room but not worth talking to.

Morning and afternoon passed slowly, as the pieces of the operation started falling into place. Periodically, Sean pulled Kerri aside and explained various aspects of the mission.

"Part of our challenge is that this can't have the look and feel of a Navy SEAL operation," he explained. "We can't parachute a bunch of guys in with surgical precision and extract Seyyed Hassan, or everyone will assume it's a U.S. military op. We've got to make it look clunky. Local. Like an inside job. Use car bombs and the types of things that Iranians see every day."

"So what exactly are you going to do?" Kerri asked.

"You'll see."

Sean stepped over to the center table, and Kerri followed. "We have a contract with a group called Satellite Imaging Corporation. They provide high-resolution imagery from the world's most advanced satellites—GeoEye-1, WorldView-2, IKONOS, SPOT-5, and others. Our software combines the imagery with our database of terrain elevations and ongoing infrared heat-sensing data, and we can extrapolate a 3-D fly-through of almost any location on earth."

Sean touched part of the screen, and the image on the table became a horizontal 3-D view of the Evin Prison complex. Kerri felt as if she were on the ground, walking around the facility. Sean provided running commentary, pointing out where Seyyed was being held in isolation and the various layers of security that made Evin the Alcatraz of the Middle East. Most of the others in the room were either working at computer terminals or engaged in quiet conversation. One or two listened casually as Sean gave his tutorial.

The 3-D visualization was dark, with shadowy figures and barely discernible landmarks. "Is this real-time technology?" Kerri asked.

"That's the problem. Our best data is several hours old. The infrared input that allows us to map out people's locations is based on information from last evening."

He motioned for Kerri to follow him to another screen, hanging on one of the side walls. The camera feeding the input appeared to be traveling in a car somewhere in a city that Kerri presumed was Tehran. Again, the image was dark and grainy.

"We need to have someone inside the facility—thus the code name of this operation," Sean explained. "What you're looking at here is a real-time visual taken literally through the eyes of Odysseus, our lead operative. The camera is located in a contact lens Odysseus is wearing. Everything he sees, we'll see. Everything he hears, we'll hear."

Kerri stared at the screen in awe. She couldn't begin to imagine how much all this technology cost. Not to mention the millions of dollars Cipher must be paying to its various operatives in countries all over the world. How expansive was this company? Was there any part of the world they couldn't penetrate?

"How is he getting in?" Kerri asked.

"Always the journalist. So much curiosity."

A man came up to Sean and pulled him aside for a brief conversation. Kerri stared at the buildings Odysseus was riding by and then looked at the other wall-mounted monitors, trying to guess what each view represented.

When Sean returned, he picked up right where he had left off. "When the terrorists wanted to attack America, they found our Achilles' heel and used our cultural weaknesses against us. They exploited the openness of our society, our infatuation with freedom, our disdain for security measures. They waltzed onto our airplanes and turned them into bombs."

As he talked, Sean constantly glanced around the room, surveying each of the monitors. Kerri sensed a slight increase in tension and attentiveness, a hushing of conversations in other parts of the room.

"But every culture has its weaknesses," Sean said, his voice lower. "And now we will exploit one of theirs."

It was 8 p.m. on Saturday night in Washington, D.C. But more importantly, as a clock on the wall reminded them, it was four thirty Sunday morning in Tehran.

The vehicle in which Odysseus was riding stopped. Sean turned his attention to the monitor, his little guided tour over. Sean and the other Cipher employees put on headsets, and he handed one to Kerri. All eyes were on the wall monitor above Kerri's head.

The headphones picked up the live audio feed from Odysseus, and a voice provided real-time English translation. As Odysseus spoke to a few guards at the prison, Sean, never taking his eyes off the wall monitor, grabbed Kerri's elbow and led her to the round center table. He drew a circle with his finger, and they could see a 3D view of the front of the Evin facility from approximately two hours earlier.

Kerri watched and listened as the Evin guards checked Odysseus's ID, asked him a few questions, and frisked him. He was led through three sets of prison doors, each with bars, bulletproof glass, and magnetic locks. They eventually left him alone in a stark room with off-white concrete walls and a few bolted-down chairs. He took a seat and waited.

Kerri looked at Sean, knitting her brow in confusion, waiting for an explanation. But Sean just gave her a little shake of the head and waited.

It was probably five minutes, which seemed more like an hour, before the doors opened and three men entered Odysseus's room. Two of them wore guard uniforms. The third was dressed in a pin-striped business suit.

The guards checked Odysseus's ID again and compared it to a photograph on their clipboard. One of them fingerprinted Odysseus on some type of electronic fingerprint machine that, after a few seconds, flashed a green light. There was a sigh of relief in the war room, and Kerri could sense everyone relaxing just a little. She realized that she had been holding her breath along with the rest of them.

"We're in," Sean said quietly to Kerri. She felt a chill spiderweb down her spine. This was not the movies; it was real life! Odysseus was now walking down a tiled corridor into the guts of the infamous Evin Prison on the other side of the world, and Kerri was watching it in real time! It was a reporter's dream, an international story unfolding right before her eyes, even if she might never get to tell about it.

From this day forward, she would never look at the world the same way again. She was like Dorothy after Toto pulled the curtain back. She now knew things people like her were not supposed to know.

"Why did they let him in?" she asked Sean quietly.

Sean held out a palm as he watched Odysseus take his seat in a courtyard area. He was facing a wooden platform about twenty feet away. "Just a minute."

"Mr. Montazeri has passed his physical," one of the guards said to Odysseus. "Would you like to know what he ordered for breakfast?"

"The man's last meal is no concern of mine," Odysseus replied. His eyes turned to the gallows on the platform, the hangman's noose coming into focus on the wall-mounted monitor.

There was going to be some type of execution. And as far as Kerri could tell, Odysseus was in charge.

35

AS ODYSSEUS STARED at the hangman's noose, Sean Phoenix pulled Kerri aside and, in whispered tones, explained what was happening.

"Islamic law requires that executions occur at daybreak," Sean said. "In the case of murder, the condemned cannot be executed unless a member of the victim's family is present and calls for the execution. Our operative is disguised as the victim's father."

"What about the fingerprints?"

Sean snorted. "Fingerprints are 1970s science. With a few days' notice and a usable print from the real father, a good plastic surgeon can take care of that and do a decent job at face enhancements as well."

"Is Seyyed Hassan scheduled to die today?"

"No. That's the whole point. The prison break needs to look like it was designed to spring somebody else. Part of the reason we chose today is because there are two executions, and one of them—" Sean stopped midsentence as a prisoner approached the gallows. He focused on the monitor and slipped the headphones back on. "Later," he said to Kerri.

She put her headphones on as well and for the next few minutes witnessed a heart-wrenching scene. The accused man couldn't have been more than twenty-five years old. His hands were cuffed behind his back. Two guards shoved him onto the wooden platform in front of the hangman's noose. He had a five-o'clock shadow, and it looked like his hair hadn't been combed in days. His eyes were wild with fear.

According to Sean, the condemned man's name was Mehdi Montazeri. He looked directly at Odysseus, a look of stark terror Kerri would never forget, and began talking rapidly in Farsi. Pleading. After just a few sentences, the man in the pin-striped suit shouted something, and Mehdi stopped abruptly.

"He told him to shut up," the translator said. "He said it was not yet time to beg for his life."

Odysseus was now eyeing the man in the pin-striped suit, listening to an explanation of Islamic retribution law. "The right to retribution does not mean that the right must be exercised," the man said. From the way he was speaking, Kerri assumed he was some type of lawyer. "It is your choice. Just as you have the right of retribution, so you also have the right of forgiveness. According to the Holy Qur'an, the victim's family is king over the murderer. Whatever you decide will be righteous, and the peace and blessings of Allah will be upon you."

Kerri watched in amazement as the condemned man was led from the platform to a nearby table. The handcuffs were removed, and he was given a pen and a tablet to write on. Sean came a step closer, lifted one side of his headphones, and gave Kerri some running commentary.

"He's writing his last will and testament. If he's smart, he'll leave everything he owns to the victim and his family."

"Who's the guy in the suit?" Kerri asked.

"An imam."

After Mehdi finished his will, everyone performed a ceremonial washing. Next, the imam led them through the chants and incantations of the predawn *salat*. Even the guards knelt and prostrated themselves. Odysseus joined them, of course, and at times the camera showed nothing more than the ground in front of him.

The whole thing was a sight so strange that Kerri had to continuously remind herself it was real, that this man named Mehdi Montazeri was a murderer who was moments away from his own execution.

When the prayers were finished, the guards returned Montazeri to the platform and placed the noose around his neck. The imam gave him one last chance to talk.

Montazeri's pleas spilled out in a tearful and emotional monologue. He had a wife and three children. Who would provide for them? He was a changed man. He knew he deserved to die but he begged for mercy. Allah, he said, loved justice, but did he not also love mercy? Mehdi claimed he had only been trying to provide for his family. He had panicked when his victim resisted. He was wrong and he was making no excuses. He was sorry, so sorry. He rambled on as emotions overtook him, his bottom lip trembling, tears streaming down his cheeks. His whole body was shaking and his voice was now at a fever pitch.

With a word, the imam cut him off.

"It is time for you to decide," he said to Odysseus.

Odysseus rose and walked to the gallows. He looked down, and the camera zoomed in on a handle at the edge of the platform. It was obvious to Kerri that under Islamic law, a member of the victim's family was required to actually pull the lever that would drop the platform from under the feet of the condemned prisoner. She found herself holding her breath, wondering if Odysseus would look up at the condemned man as he plunged to his death, the rope breaking his neck. If Odysseus watched, the camera in his contact lens would record the action as well. Kerri didn't want to see it, but she couldn't look away.

Before pulling the lever, Odysseus looked at Montazeri one last time. Montazeri's face was twisted in fear, his eyes closed, his lips mumbling some kind of final prayer to Allah.

A few seconds passed before Odysseus looked back down. Kerri could see the big man's hand on the lever. He was going to pull it!

At that precise moment, a bright light flashed on a different wall monitor, and heads swiveled to watch it. A massive power line tower imploded and fell to the ground, snapping the huge electric lines connected to it. The lights in the prison yard on Odysseus's screen, which had provided only dim illumination in the first place, suddenly went dark.

Instantaneously, there was a second explosion lighting up another wall monitor, and Kerri lifted an earphone as Sean explained. "We cut the power line to the prison facility. The second explosion you saw was a car bomb at the site of the backup transformers. Keep your eye on the Odysseus monitor. He'll have on night goggles in a minute, and everything will come back into focus."

"Night goggles?"

"They look like regular glasses. That's how he got them past the guards."

Almost on cue, the Odysseus monitor showed an eerie green-black skeletal representation of the prison yard. Odysseus loosened the noose around Montazeri and told him to run. Odysseus then jumped one of the prison guards who was stumbling around in the darkness, beat the man, stripped him, and changed into his clothes, grabbing the man's gun and keys. He looked around the yard, this way and that, and then started running. The camera bounced around so much that it gave Kerri a headache.

Meanwhile, three other monitors came to life, ones that had been showing static shots of the outside walls of the prison. The cameras appeared to be mounted on three different Cipher operatives, all running toward the hole in the prison wall created by the car bomb's blast. When they reached the fence and barbed wire, the men cut their way through and eventually came to the cinder-block building that Kerri had been told housed Hassan.

Soon the Odysseus monitor was showing the same area from a reverse angle. Kerri realized that all four Cipher operatives had come together at a predetermined spot. She now had a chance to see Odysseus through the eyes of the other operatives as he unlocked the door of the building and led his team down a corridor.

It was hard to follow what happened next as the men made their way through the prison facility, avoiding the flashlights of the prison guards, and took out a few other unsuspecting guards along the way. Between the four operatives, they accumulated quite a collection of keys.

Eventually they came to the locked door of a pod where three of the operatives kept guard while Odysseus tried a number of keys. Inside the bars, about forty prisoners were cheering and clamoring to get out. When Odysseus finally found the right key and the door swung open, the men streamed out, heading off in a number of different directions, causing more chaos for the guards.

Next the Cipher team wound their way to a row of individual cells and began shining their stolen flashlights into each cell, opening one door after another. On about the fifth or sixth cell, they came on a man sitting in the back corner, hunched over as if in prayer. Sean nudged Kerri and nodded. *Pastor Hassan.* Kerri watched as Odysseus opened the cell, grabbed Hassan by the collar, and pulled him out. The pastor was small and frail. He looked scared to death.

Odysseus explained that he wasn't a guard. He was there to lead Hassan to freedom.

"Praise Jesus," Hassan said.

For the next thirty minutes, there was bedlam inside the prison facility as inmates ran for their lives and the guards shot to kill. The sun was just beginning to illuminate the scene. The Cipher agents worked quickly to herd Pastor Hassan through prison corridors and across the jail courtyards until they came back to the opening in the fence. Once they cleared the prison wall through the hole made by the car bomb, they jumped into a waiting vehicle that whisked the men away. Inside the war room, the headsets came off and the Cipher employees quietly congratulated each other.

The whole thing was over, as Sean had said it would be, in just about thirty minutes.

Ten minutes later, Kerri was in Sean Phoenix's office listening to him report on the raid to the State Department. Even the unflappable Phoenix couldn't hide the triumphant tone in his voice, though Kerri doubted he had as much of an adrenaline rush as she did. "Operation Trojan Horse was a complete success," he said. "The target is on his way to London."

He listened for a moment, then said, "Thank you, sir. Thank you very much."

///

At her hotel later that night, after the excitement had died down, Kerri had a chance to process things alone. She thought about the collateral damage Sean had shrugged off earlier that night in response to one of her questions. "There's no such thing as a clean war," he had said. "There will always be collateral damage."

But Kerri was left to wonder if it had all been worth it. Guilty prisoners had been set free. Innocent guards had been injured; some may have been killed. The sovereign rule of a foreign nation had been brushed aside as if it were of no consequence.

Christians around the world would undoubtedly rejoice and claim a miracle from God. Iran would probably blame it on Israel or that Western Satan, the United States. Kerri's own television station would still be running segments on the escape through the following week.

Yet Kerri was one of the few people privileged to know the truth, one of the few who had seen behind the curtain. Pastor Hassan and his friends around the world may have been praying for a miracle. But it was a phone call from the State Department and a group of brave men working for a reviled company named Cipher Inc. who had sprung the beloved pastor.

It was spectacular, just as Sean Phoenix had promised. But was it right?

36

FOR KERRI, DRIVING BACK HOME Sunday morning was like stepping out of the dream and back into reality. The thrill of being an embedded journalist watching an international rescue mission was hard to describe. Her journalistic instincts made her want to share the news with others. It was what she had been trained to do. Instead, she had this incredible story bubbling up inside her wanting to burst out, but nowhere for it to go. She was a thoroughbred locked in a slow trot, a Broadway actress doing used-car commercials.

Kerri took her professional obligations seriously, and paramount among them was the promise of confidentiality. But she had made another promise several years ago, one now at odds with her professional responsibilities. She and Landon had agreed they would harbor no secrets in their marriage. The two of them had become one flesh, and secrets could only cause distrust.

But this felt different. This wasn't the kind of secret that could damage her marriage. She had promised Sean Phoenix she would not say a word, even to her own husband. What she had witnessed was no trifling matter. It had international consequences. If word leaked out, people would be fired. People would be prosecuted. People might be killed.

She drove with the radio off, which gave her time to think. After what she had witnessed, her life somehow felt more trivial. The issues in the Reed family—Landon's work, balancing her obligations as a mother and journalist, even the ethical dilemmas posed by the Elias King case— were all dwarfed by what had just occurred.

She wondered if she would ever be able to tell the world about it. She also wondered if perhaps Sean Phoenix was evaluating her for a role in his company. Surely Cipher Inc. could use a spokesperson who better understood the world of journalism. She let her mind drift to a role where she wasn't just reporting the news but was right in the middle of it, part of an organization that was a significant player on the international stage. She bet that Cipher Inc. paid handsomely as well, though that wasn't a primary motivator.

By the time she got back to her condo in Virginia Beach, she had pretty much decompressed. Maddie charged her as soon as she walked in the door. Landon trailed closely behind and gave Kerri a kiss.

"How was your trip?" he asked.

"Interesting."

"Tell me about it."

"Later," she said. She turned to Maddie, always a welcome diversion. "Why don't you go get your brush and a few hair ties?" Kerri said. "Looks like Daddy hasn't brushed your hair all weekend."

When Maddie scampered off, Kerri grabbed Landon, pulled him next to her, and gave him a deep kiss. *This will take his mind off my trip.*

"I missed you," she said, pulling back as they heard Maddie coming down the hall.

He smiled and sneaked in another quick kiss. "I missed you, too," he said.

37

EXACTLY TWO WEEKS after Elias King's federal court indictment, on a blustery March day with overcast skies, Rachel Strach walked into Landon's office and plopped down in one of his client chairs. It was Friday, so she had on jeans and a button-down white blouse. She slouched back, kicked off her pumps, and propped her feet against the edge of Landon's desk. "Did you read about the indictments of that Texas lawyer and D.C. judge for insider trading?" she asked.

Landon had been buried in criminal case files all day. Harry spent most of his time on the Elias King files, which left Landon trying to do just about everything else. "I have no idea what you're talking about," he said. He liked the fact that he could be brutally honest around Rachel; she never judged him for not knowing something.

"Same deal as Elias King," Rachel said, "except this Texas guy suckered a judge into his little scheme. Here . . . let me show you."

She hopped up and moved behind Landon, leaning past him and taking over his mouse. A few clicks later she pulled up the article.

"How do you find out about this stuff?" Landon asked.

Rachel smiled—a broad white grin with perfect teeth. "You under-estimate me. Reese Witherspoon ruined my life. Everybody thinks I'm *Legally Blonde*."

Landon couldn't deny it. Rachel was pretty, came across as a little naive, and was a lock for Miss Congeniality at any gathering of lawyers. Subconscious comparisons to Witherspoon's character were unavoidable.

"I actually start each day reading about a dozen law blogs—not the snarky ones but the real law blogs that report on recent cases and on significant legal developments. Plus, I've got about fifty Google alerts programmed into my e-mail. When Elias got indicted two weeks ago, I added the phrase *insider trading* to my alert list."

"Impressive," Landon said. *Just when I thought I had her figured out.* "Can you show me how to set up an alert?"

After a brief tutorial, Rachel headed back to the first floor, and Landon read through the article on his screen.

John McBride, a notorious plaintiff's lawyer from Dallas, Texas, had sued just about every company in the Fortune 500. He had made most of his fortune on the mass tort cases, though he wasn't above a good share-holder derivative suit from time to time. He liked the high-profile stuff, and when Landon googled his name, the hits for Big John McBride went on for pages. Eventually Landon found the document he was looking for—the actual federal court indictment from the Northern District of Texas—and printed it out so he could highlight it for Harry.

Apparently Big John wasn't content to rake in millions just suing people. He also had to pad his pockets with a little illegal action on the side. According to the indictment, he had set up a number of off-shore companies in countries where it was impossible to determine the owner. Like Elias, McBride was accused of setting up a maze of off-shore accounts, and creating a spiderweb of interconnected companies and transactions that was nearly impossible to decipher. And just like Elias's case, the Feds' investigation had been initiated as a result of a confidential informant tipping them off.

The underlying scheme, however, was different from the one that had ensnared Elias. Big John's firm did exclusively civil litigation, so there were no mergers or acquisitions of clients that would provide inside information. Instead, Big John's offshore companies would short a company's stock, essentially betting against the company, just a few weeks before McBride filed a lawsuit against that company. If the suit was big enough—and most of McBride's were—the company's value would take a hit in the day or two after the suit became public. McBride would cash in on his options and use the funds to help finance his litigation against the company.

And he apparently wasn't in it alone. Some of the funds from the insider trading had gone into an account belonging to a Washington, D.C., federal judge named Rodney Zimmerman. And to make matters more interesting, McBride had a big case pending before Judge Zimmerman, scheduled to go to trial sometime within the year.

It was all fascinating stuff, but Landon didn't see how it could help Elias. Nevertheless, he took the highlighted indictment down the hall to Harry's office and left it on his chair.

Harry reviewed the document later that day when he returned from court, one of his rare appearances on a case other than Elias's. He called for Landon.

"Nice work," Harry said as soon as Landon set foot in his office. He was holding the McBride indictment in his right hand. "Seems pretty coincidental. Especially the part about the confidential informant."

"Thanks," Landon said. Harry wasn't big on attaboys, so even a small compliment like this one felt good. Landon probably should have credited Rachel for the research, but she didn't need brownie points with Harry.

"Not sure if this will actually help us in the long run," Harry continued. "It could work against us if we find out that McBride and Elias were buddies, which seems unlikely. On the other hand, it could provide for one heckuva red herring. I need you to find out if there are any links between McBride and Elias. Any common cases? Any phone calls between them? Did they have the same clients? The same friends? The same enemies?"

Landon jotted a few notes. He would need to check Elias's phone records and talk to him. But that wasn't enough for Harry.

"We'll need to see a list of McBride's clients," Harry said. "His billing records. A list of all the lawsuits he's filed in the last five years. I need you to prepare the subpoenas. Everybody at McBride's firm is going to scream bloody murder."

Landon could see the glint in Harry's eyes, anticipating the chaos and anger that the subpoenas would unleash. There was little chance a judge would give them access to the records, but that wouldn't stop Harry from trying.

"This is going to be fun," Harry said. "And while you're at it, you might as well subpoena Judge Zimmerman's financial records and phone records as well. No sense leaving him out of the party."

38

THE FOLLOWING WEEK Landon issued subpoenas for the McBride and Zimmerman documents, which were promptly opposed by their respective attorneys and by Mitchell Taylor, the assistant U.S. Attorney prosecuting Elias's federal case. A hearing was set up so Harry could explain to the court why the documents were necessary to Elias's defense.

Harry secluded himself in his office for long stretches to work on the two King cases, shuffling most other responsibilities Landon's way. As a result, Landon had to cancel his Tuesday night workouts with Jake and the other high school quarterbacks. During the first three nights of the week, he arrived home well after Maddie had gone to bed.

At five thirty Thursday evening, Rachel Strach came into his office looking like she had just seen a ghost. She sat down in one of his client chairs, and Landon could tell she was forcing back tears.

"Can we talk?" she asked.

She was wearing a tight red sweater and a short skirt. She crossed her legs and brushed her hair away from her face. For about the hundredth time, Landon found himself thinking that Rachel Strach could do way better than Brent Benedict. It wasn't just her looks. She was one of the few smart lawyers Landon knew who didn't have a huge ego. She loved life, had a quick and corny laugh, and never seemed to take herself too seriously.

"What's up?" Landon asked. Actually, he knew. Rachel's deposition was scheduled for the next day and she had been meeting with Brent Benedict's attorney, a stiff suit from the good-old-boy network named Allen Mattingly.

"I told Mr. Mattingly about your idea to take the Fifth," Rachel said. Landon had done some research for her. Adultery was still a misdemeanor under Georgia law, which meant that Rachel could technically plead the Fifth and not have to contradict Brent.

Rachel shook her head, regret lining her face. "He said it wouldn't work. He said anything less than unqualified support for Brent would force this thing to court. Stacy's attorneys would embarrass both me and Brent."

She stopped and sighed, clearly wishing she had never put herself in this position. "Only sexual intercourse is a misdemeanor in Georgia," she continued. "If I take the Fifth, Stacy's attorneys can probe all other kinds of sexual activities. . . ." Her voice dropped off; there was no good way out.

The law required Rachel to plead the Fifth Amendment question by question. It could make for a long deposition as they differentiated between sexual acts that constituted a misdemeanor under Georgia law and those that did not.

"What do you plan on doing?" Landon asked.

Rachel shrugged. Her shoulders slumped, the weight of the world pressing down.

"You can't lie," Landon said. It was, he knew, the reason Rachel had come to his office. She didn't want to lie, and she needed reinforcement.

"I know," she said, though Landon didn't hear much steel in her voice. "Sorry to drag you into this."

"I've got worse clients," Landon said.

This brought a small and fleeting smile. "Maybe we should go start our own firm," Rachel suggested.

The comment caught Landon off guard, and he couldn't tell if Rachel was serious. The idea actually had some merit. Rachel knew enough about the practice of law to mentor Landon. They could get rid of some of the dysfunctions that plagued McNaughten and Clay. But Kerri would never go for it. "Let's take things one step at a time."

They talked for a few minutes about the deposition, and Rachel nibbled at her fingernail. Landon did his best to calm her down, assuring her that everything happened for a reason. "No matter how this turns out, you'll be able to live with yourself if you tell the truth."

"That's what I keep telling myself," she said.

She perked up some, and Landon could tell their brief session had stiffened her backbone a little. "Are you hungry?" she asked.

He had skipped lunch. And he still had a few hours of work ahead of him. He was starving, but he didn't dare go home; Kerri would never let him head back to the office. "A little."

"I was supposed to meet some friends at the 501 City Grill. They've got five-dollar specials if we get there before six thirty," Rachel said. "Wanna grab something quick?"

A voice told him it wasn't a good idea. He had just finished talking with Rachel about her affair with Brent Benedict. Still, *his* relationship with Rachel was on a whole different level. They were friends. She needed some encouragement. He needed food. Male lawyers went to lunch or dinner with female lawyers all the time and nothing happened.

He checked his watch. "Five bucks?"

"Pizzas. Burgers. All kinds of healthy food."

He knew Kerri wasn't expecting him home anytime soon. What could it hurt? He had already done a few working lunches with Rachel in the office. This would be no different.

"Give me a few minutes to finish this e-mail," Landon said.

"Thanks," Rachel replied. "For everything."

///

The 501 City Grill was less than a mile from the office and packed out even though it was early in the evening. Rachel and Landon secured a booth in the bar area and ordered from the five-dollar menu. The background noise forced Landon to lean forward so he could hear Rachel. A few of the regulars in the bar stopped by their table to say hello to Rachel, and she introduced them to Landon. He started getting uneasy, wondering how he would explain this to Kerri if word got back to her.

Rachel's friends never showed.

Landon drank Diet Cokes even when Rachel tried to coax him into an imported draft beer. After her first beer, she relaxed. After her second, she became more talkative, almost giddy. It had been a long day. When the waitress asked if she needed another, Landon answered for her.

"We've got to get back to work," he said. "Two is probably her limit."

She gave him a little sideways glance. "He's right," she said. "I could never hold my liquor."

During the meal, Rachel opened up about her past. Her parents had divorced when she was in middle school. She had been abused by an uncle. She had been through several fractured relationships with men in the last five years. Two of them had cheated on her.

It was a tale of woe, but she told it with a half smile, as if even she couldn't believe her poor choices in men. "Seems like all the good ones are taken," she said.

Landon's own dating career had taken a different tack, so he kept his opinions to himself. Besides, he had learned from Kerri that sometimes women weren't asking for an opinion. Sometimes, they just wanted to talk things out.

While they were eating, a waiter who wasn't assigned to their table—a young guy who knew Rachel by name—noticed her empty glass and brought her another beer. That made Rachel smile. "Everything happens for a reason," she said, raising her glass in a toast.

Landon just shook his head.

"I was always attracted to the bad boys," Rachel confessed after the waiter left. "But Brent is different. He's the kind of man I could settle down with."

She took a drink and smiled at Landon. "But I didn't know that Prince Charming was married to the Wicked Witch of the West."

She was mixing up her fairy tales and her tongue was loose, her words a little slurred. She had been right about one thing—Rachel Strach was no good at holding her liquor.

By the end of the meal, Landon was determined she wasn't going to drive home. He offered her a ride but she turned him down. He insisted and she made a wisecrack about his motives. "It's a misdemeanor in Virginia, too, you know."

Landon was kicking himself for getting into this mess, but she was in no shape to drive. He paid the bill and grabbed her gently by the elbow. "Come on. You're going with me. If I have to, I'll come pick you up tomorrow morning."

On the way home she apologized profusely for putting Landon out. "I can get a ride to work with some friends tomorrow," she told him.

When they arrived in front of her house, they sat in the car for a few minutes. "Are you okay for tomorrow?" Landon asked, referring to her deposition.

"I really am. I owe you one."

"I didn't do anything."

"If you're not careful, you're going to restore my faith in men," Rachel said. "You're a good friend. I hope someday I can find somebody like you."

The comment made Landon blush, and he couldn't think of a thing to say in response. Always one step ahead, Rachel leaned over and gave him a quick kiss on the cheek. "Thanks again," she said and bounced out of the car.

He watched her walk up to the front door of her small home. He took a deep breath and a quick inventory of his emotions. She was beautiful, endearing, and smart. He had no business being here. He hoped she would find the right man. Perhaps it *was* Brent Benedict, though he doubted it.

Tonight Landon knew he had been playing with fire. He doubted that Rachel Strach felt anything toward him other than pure friendship. But she was flirtatious and more casual about drawing lines than he was. It would be up to him to keep this relationship within bounds.

He thought about Kerri and Maddie as he drove away from Rachel's house, lecturing himself for what he had done. Instead of heading back to the office, he went straight home.

ON FRIDAY MORNING, Landon rolled into the office after dropping Maddie off at day care. He carried his briefcase upstairs and went mindlessly through his morning routine. He plugged his laptop into his desk monitor (Harry insisted that Landon take his laptop home every night), hung his suit coat on the back of the door, and turned on the lights. He unpacked the documents from his briefcase and headed down to the conference room to brew a cup of coffee. Naturally, all the cups were dirty, so he took a few minutes to wash them out in the firm's bathroom. He wondered what Harry had done before Landon started working there.

When he returned to his office, coffee in hand, he was surprised to see Brent Benedict sitting in a client chair. White starched shirt, red tie, ramrod-straight posture. "Have a seat," Brent said, as if it were his office.

Landon settled in behind his desk and viewed Brent warily. He could sense an attempt at intimidation coming on, and he wasn't in the mood for it.

"I know you and Rachel spent some time together last night," Brent said. His voice wasn't accusatory, but the comment made Landon bristle. "Thanks for walking her through this."

Instead of responding, Landon took a sip of his coffee. He had no idea where this was headed.

"Allen Mattingly probably won't approve of what I'm going to say to you, but I really don't care. This thing between Rachel and me is more than just an office romance. I really do care about her, Landon, and I don't want anything to happen to her."

The conversation was making Landon uncomfortable. It was bad enough being Rachel's confidant. Now he had the firm's managing partner baring his soul. Landon wanted to be a lawyer, not a counselor.

"I need to ask you a favor," Brent continued, leaning forward. "I can't tell Rachel what to do or say in her deposition, because any conversations I have with her are subject to discovery by the other side. But any conversations she has with her lawyer are protected."

Brent gave the comment a moment to settle while Landon took another sip of coffee. Every lawyer knew how to play games with discovery battles. And Brent Benedict was a chess master.

"I want you to act as her lawyer for the purposes of preparing her for this deposition. I think you ought to tell her to take the Fifth Amendment when it comes to any questions about what happened in that Atlanta hotel room. That might make it look like I'm lying, but I can take the heat.

"The worst that can happen is that they file a motion to compel her testimony. They drag us into court and read parts of my deposition and then hers to the judge and make me look bad. I would tell her, if I could, that if the judge ever compelled her to answer the questions, she should tell the truth and let the chips fall where they will. I'm a big boy. I can take care of myself."

Landon didn't like getting dragged into the middle of a divorce proceeding, but he admired what Brent was trying to do. Yes, the man had lied in his deposition. And yes, those lies had caused this fiasco. But when push came to shove, he was trying to protect Rachel. *Maybe*, Landon thought, *I misjudged him a little.*

"I'll tell her," Landon said. He wanted to throw in a little lecture for free. He wanted to remind Brent that it was his out-of-control libido that had gotten them into this mess in the first place. But for the first time since he had joined the firm, Landon could see the faint outline of pain on the managing partner's face. Brent had enough lawyers after him. He didn't need one more piling on.

Brent pursed his lips for a minute, as if he wanted to say something more. Instead, he blew out a deep breath and stood. "You're doing a good job, Reed," he said. "It's not easy working with Harry McNaughten. You've already outlasted the last three associates."

Landon couldn't resist a small grin. "He's a little quirky," Landon admitted. "But he's starting to grow on me."

///

Landon not only counseled Rachel before the deposition started but decided to stay by her side throughout so he could interpose objections. Others in the conference room included the court reporter, Brent Benedict, Allen Mattingly, Brent's petite wife, Stacy, and Stacy's big-mouth lawyer, Carolyn Glaxon-Forrester.

Glaxon-Forrester was the lead partner in an all-female firm that represented only wives in divorce proceedings. To call her a pit bull would be to undersell her tenacity. She had put her own legal experience to good use, having successfully ground down three former husbands in her own divorce proceedings. According to the rumor mill, she was now living with a weight lifter she had met at the gym. He was ten years younger.

She liked to show up for court and depositions in sleeveless dresses that showcased her ripped arms—the result, Landon assumed, of both rigorous workouts and generous amounts of 'roids. Everything about the woman, including her long beak-like nose and square jaw, reminded Landon of some kind of Nordic warrior. She added to the effect by overdoing the blush, bright-red lipstick, and dark mascara. Men, with the possible exception of her live-in weight lifter, hated her, and the feeling was mutual.

She spit questions at Rachel for three hours in a condescending and patronizing tone. Following Landon's instructions, Rachel took the Fifth a total of seventy-four times, causing Glaxon-Forrester to snort and snicker and make snide comments under her breath. Halfway through the deposition, Landon grew tired of the abuse and started raising his voice when he objected. This typically generated a fierce argument between lawyers. The court reporter begged them to stop talking over each other so she could get it all down.

At the end of the deposition, Landon packed up his stuff and decided to take the high road. Even after fierce battles on the football field, he would shake his opponents' hands. He stuck out his hand toward Glaxon-Forrester and said, "Nice to meet you."

She stared at his hand and scoffed. Then she went back to packing her briefcase.

"C'mon, Rachel," Landon said. He put a hand gently on Rachel's back, and the two of them escaped the conference room, mindful of the hateful stares targeting their backs.

It was only midafternoon, but surviving the deposition called for a celebration. Rachel and Brent begged Landon to join them at a bar on the Virginia Beach boardwalk. Despite a pile of work waiting in his office, Landon eventually caved in.

It was a beautiful spring day, and they snagged a table in the outdoor section of the bar. The three of them kicked back, watching the waves break on the sand, the seagulls flying overhead. Landon stuck with Diet Coke, but Rachel and Brent needed something stronger. It didn't take long for everyone to start making fun of Glaxon-Forrester. By six o'clock, Landon realized he wasn't going to get any more work done at the office and decided to head home early and surprise Kerri.

Rachel stood up and gave him a hug before he left. Brent walked him to the front door.

"What you did for us today means a lot," Brent said.

Landon wanted to tell Brent he had done it for Rachel, not him. But he decided against it. "No problem."

Brent took a step closer and lowered his voice. "I know I've messed up a lot of things in my life," he said. "But this time I'm going to get it right."

Though Landon had worked hard to keep his feelings to himself, he figured that after slugging it out with Glaxon-Forrester for three hours, he had earned the right to say something. "Go slow with her," he said. "I don't want to see her hurt. If it's meant to be, you don't have to rush it."

Brent didn't blink. If he was offended, he was working hard not to show it. "It's meant to be," he said. The look of confidence was back, the same Brent Benedict who could stare down appellate judges and tell them they were dead wrong. "I wouldn't put myself through this for a one-night stand."

Landon took a quick look around. "They're probably following you right now," he warned.

"I know. I'm going to take her back to the office in a few minutes. And we'll leave in separate cars."

"Be careful," Landon said.

"I will."

Landon didn't believe him. But who was he to judge?

40

FOR THE NEXT THREE WEEKS Landon worked harder than he had since his training-camp days. In the morning, he took care of Simba, helped Maddie get ready, dropped Maddie off at day care, and still made it to work by eight. During those three weeks, he made it home a grand total of two times for dinner and, even on those nights, went back to the office as soon as Maddie fell asleep. One afternoon, Maddie's day-care director called, and Landon had to pick up his sick daughter. After Kerri got home from work, Landon went back to the office and stayed past midnight.

But he loved every minute of it.

Harry McNaughten continued to spend most of his time behind closed doors, working on the King file, trusting Landon to deal with the other clients. It was great experience for Landon—lots of courtroom hearings and trips to the jail to meet new clients. It was also a little overwhelming.

He only got a chance to watch Harry in court a few times, one of which involved the King case. Their subpoenas for the McBride and Zimmerman documents were quashed; the judge told Harry he hadn't proven any real connection between those cases and his. But that didn't seem to slow Harry down. He had Landon research every reported case that Big John McBride had handled as well as every ruling by Judge Zimmerman. Harry had charts cross-referencing the clients of McBride and Elias, the opposing parties for their cases, and the opposing lawyers. In addition, all of these were cross-referenced with the cases Judge Zimmerman had handled.

Harry also asked Landon to chase down any witness who would talk to him about Julia King. She had motive, and that was big. But Harry was troubled by two things. First, she must have had help disposing of the body. And second, where would she have gotten the date rape drugs?

"What's the first thing you do when you get a case ready for trial?" Harry asked Landon one day.

Landon had just reported on his phone interview of a potential witness. "Gather the facts. Interview as many people as possible. Develop a theme."

"Not bad," Harry said. "You know how I test my themes?"

Landon shrugged. He had learned not to guess with Harry. It never paid off.

"I construct my closing argument." He nodded toward a yellow legal pad with the top half of the pages folded back under the pad. Harry's chicken scratch filled the page in view. "That's the biggest mistake most lawyers make. They wait until the case is tried to put together their closing. Not me. I do it first. That way, I know what I have to prove. It keeps everything in the proper perspective."

He was chewing on the end of his reading glasses and was in one of his talkative moods. "It's like Clausen and his novels. Got to know the ending first. You ever read one of those things, by the way?"

"I glanced through one before I started working here," Landon admitted. "Never finished it."

Harry snorted. "I've never met anyone who did."

Landon had plenty of chances to apply Harry's advice. By the middle of April, he had already tried two misdemeanor appeals and one felony trial without a jury. Harry didn't even go to court with him—it was sink or swim at McNaughten and Clay.

But the longer he worked with Harry, the more Landon realized he wouldn't trade spots with anybody in the world. Landon Reed wanted to be a trial lawyer. You couldn't do that without getting into court and getting your hands dirty. Other lawyers liked to plead out their cases, throwing their clients on the mercy of the prosecutors. They called themselves trial lawyers, but they were really negotiators.

Not Harry. He trusted juries. He relished the courtroom. He loved to poke prosecutors in the eye and ridicule witnesses on cross-examination and generally wreak havoc. It was, Landon decided, a lot like learning to play quarterback as the understudy to Brett Favre, the NFL's all-time leader in both touchdown passes and interceptions.

Nobody would ever accuse you of being afraid of making mistakes.

///

The assassin was a careful man, a control freak, an obsessive nut about the details of a hit. He checked and rechecked his final punch list. He was a professional killer; he couldn't operate on emotion or instinct. He planned. And he performed every task himself, no matter how menial or insignificant.

Otherwise, he wouldn't have survived this long.

Tonight he was dressed like a common street thug. Big, baggy jeans that hung halfway down his rear. A baseball cap with a large brim still bearing the store sticker—he wore it low on his forehead, dreadlocks sticking out the back. Lots of jewelry. A puffy winter coat, though it was late spring.

He entered the parking garage and waited. The old man made it easy. He was a creature of habit. He would leave the office at eight. Head down to the oceanfront for a drink. Leave the bar around ten.

The assassin would be waiting. He hoped that the beer was cold tonight, that the music was just right, that the old man would enjoy himself immensely.

Even death row inmates were entitled to a nice final meal.

41

HARRY McNAUGHTEN HAD A LOT on his mind as he left Mahi Mah's on Monday night, April 15. It was tax day, so he had spent most of the past hour complaining about the federal government to the bartender. "Did you know half the people in this country don't pay a dime in taxes?" And then there were people like Harry, an honest working stiff who made a living by the sweat of his brow and had to carry the entire country on his back.

"Wait a minute—I thought you were a lawyer," the bartender had said.

"Very funny."

As he rounded the corner toward the parking garage, he thought about the new theory he had developed for the King trial. Brent Benedict wasn't going to like it. In fact, Brent would probably vote in favor of withdrawing from the King case altogether after Harry explained his theory at the partners' meeting the next day. But Harry didn't care. He had pulled Parker Clausen off to the side earlier in the day, sworn him to secrecy, and then finagled a promise from Parker that he would vote with Harry on this one.

He climbed the stairwell to the third floor of the garage, getting winded from the effort, and started walking down the ramp toward his car. The garage was well lit and pretty much deserted. Harry thought about the arrival of the tourists in a little over a month. Parking would be miserable. The oceanfront would be crawling with people. Harry would start heading inland for his nightly drink.

He unlocked the car using his remote and saw the headlights flash obediently. He reminded himself to be careful driving home. The cops would love nothing better than to bust Harry McNaughten for a DUI.

He thought he heard someone shuffle behind him, but before he could turn and look, he felt the cold steel on the nape of his neck.

"Don't move," a hoarse voice said.

Harry stopped midstep and his mind started racing. *One man. Probably just wants my wallet. No need to panic.*

"Hands in the air," the man said.

Harry did as he was told, slowly lifting his hands just above his shoulders. He extended his fingers to show he had no weapons.

The man reached into Harry's back pocket and pulled out his wallet, keeping the barrel of the gun jammed against Harry's neck. They were behind the trunk of a vehicle, just a few cars down from Harry's.

The man rifled through the wallet, and Harry heard something hit the ground. The mugger had probably pocketed the credit cards and thrown down the rest. Harry didn't carry cash in his wallet.

"I've got some cash in my front pocket," Harry said. Maybe this would satisfy the guy. Maybe he could get a glimpse of the man's face, a reflection from the nearby cars. He would make sure this thug got every day of jail time he deserved. But for now, Harry just needed to survive.

"It's not about your cash," the voice said. "It's about keeping your nose out of other people's business."

Harry had only a split second. His eyes shifted to the right, catching the reflection from a rear window. He couldn't make out the man's features, but he could see one thing. The barrel of the gun. Extended. A silencer.

This wasn't a mugging. It was an execution!

But Harry McNaughten was not going down without a fight.

He spun, swinging his left elbow back, hoping for the element of surprise. The approach had served him well for so many years in court—drastic action that nobody anticipated.

But this time, even before he connected, he felt a flash of pain at the base of his skull. The world went white. And Harry McNaughten crumpled to the ground.

He was dead before he hit the concrete.

///

The assassin checked Harry's pockets and took his cash. He looked around—the coast was still clear—and slid the gun into a chest holster hidden under his jacket. He walked to a stairwell and a few minutes later was at the side street where he had parked.

Before pulling away, he sent a text.

Finished assignment. No glitches. 50% courtesy discount. Subject was a lawyer.

///

Landon learned about the shooting at ten thirty that night. He was still at his desk, the only lawyer in the office, trying to make up for the fact that he hadn't worked at all on Sunday.

Rachel was the one who called, and Landon could tell she had been crying.

"I've got some bad news," she said, her voice breaking.

Landon waited a moment for her to continue, his stomach in his throat. He assumed it was something to do with her and Brent. "What's wrong?" he asked softly.

"Harry's been shot," Rachel managed. She sniffled, and it sounded like she was hyperventilating. "He's dead, Landon. Somebody killed him."

The news stunned Landon—a gut punch—and the rest of the phone call was a blur. He asked Rachel if she was sure. She struggled to hold it together as she gave him what few details she knew. Harry had been shot in a parking garage; whoever did it took his cash and credit cards. The police were investigating. It looked like a random mugging.

Landon still couldn't believe it. *There had to be some mistake!* He felt like he had stepped into another dimension.

Numb, he hung up the phone and stared at it. The office suddenly seemed suffocating. The silence deafening. He was very much alone.

Strangely, he wished he could be with Rachel. Or even Brent Benedict or Parker Clausen. Someone who could understand what he was feeling right now.

Harry McNaughten was dead.

After a few minutes, he got up and walked down the hallway. He turned on the lights to Harry's office and stepped inside. He sat down at his mentor's desk and smelled that musty old-man smell that seemed to follow Harry around. He let his mind wander to the Character and Fitness Committee, to the General District Court trial, to the gruff calls from this office to his own. *"Landon! Come here a minute!"*

He would give anything to hear that voice right now.

He picked up a pair of Harry's reading glasses, held them the way Harry would have—between his thumb and index finger, twirling them a bit—then put them down.

Harry McNaughten was dead.

Landon leaned back in the chair and closed his eyes. He thought about Harry, realized how much the man had become like a father to him, and wept. Fifteen minutes later, his heart still aching, he left the office.

"Thanks for believing in me," he said.

42

DETECTIVE ANGELA FREEMAN was waiting for Landon when he arrived at work on Tuesday morning. The officer was short and thin with long, straight dark hair. She wore a blue blouse tucked into black slacks and appeared to be in pretty good shape. Her most striking features were big dark eyes that seemed to bug out a little and slightly oversized ears. She was pretty and probably would have been prettier if she smiled. But homicide detectives seldom allowed themselves that luxury.

"Detective Freeman is investigating Harry's death," Brent Benedict explained. "She wants to ask us each a few questions."

She ushered Landon into the firm's main conference room and closed the door. It felt awkward—just the two of them sitting at the massive slate table. Landon took a seat on the end. Freeman chose the nearest chair on the side and slid it closer. She took out a tablet and made a few notes, pretty much right under Landon's nose so he could read every word. She pulled out a Dictaphone and placed it on the table.

"Is it okay if I record this?" she asked.

"Sure."

After a few preliminary questions, she asked Landon whether Harry McNaughten had any enemies, anybody who might want him dead. She stared at Landon as he processed the implications of the question.

"I thought this was a random mugging," he said.

"It probably was. But a few things have me concerned. The suspect shot out the security cameras in the garage before the event. Nobody heard any gunshots, indicating he may have used a silencer. The kill shot went through the occipital lobe in the back of the head. It's a very efficient way to kill someone. He left a wallet behind, but the only fingerprints on it belonged to Mr. McNaughten. Either this mugger knew what he was doing or he got very lucky. So we need to look at every angle. Were you aware of any enemies?"

"He was a criminal-defense lawyer. He had lots of enemies."

"Does anybody in particular come to mind? Any recent death threats, for example?"

Landon thought for a moment. Even Harry's enemies seemed to have a grudging respect for the man. He couldn't imagine why anyone would want Harry dead.

"No. Nothing stands out."

"I understand that you were Harry's associate."

"That's correct."

"I'll need a list of all his active cases. I need to know names of defendants that he was representing as well as the victims of their crimes. Also, if you recently lost any cases, I'll need to know the names of those clients and the types of cases."

"I need to check with Mr. Benedict on that," Landon said. "But I'll give you what I can."

"I already spoke to Mr. Benedict this morning, while we were in Mr. McNaughten's office," Freeman said tersely. She had been too close for comfort throughout the entire conversation, and the space seemed to shrink now. "He said the firm would cooperate fully. I'll set up a firewall in our department so that anything you tell me will never be used against any of your clients. It may just be a random shooting from a mugging gone bad, but I'm not taking any chances."

"Okay," Landon said. "I'll do anything I can to help you catch this guy."

But even as he said it, Landon was already drawing battle lines in his mind. He would give Freeman the names of Harry's clients. That couldn't hurt. The names of the victims and the cases Harry lost were matters of public record. He would just be saving the police time on those issues.

But Landon wasn't about to share any details from the case files, and he knew Brent Benedict would back him. There was nothing that Landon wanted more than for Harry's killer to be brought to justice. Yet that didn't mean he could violate the attorney-client privilege.

Nor could he forget the number one rule that Harry had always taught him: never trust the cops.

43

HARRY McNAUGHTEN'S MEMORIAL service took place at the largest funeral home in Virginia Beach, and there still wasn't enough room for everyone. In keeping with his wishes, Harry had been cremated, so there was no casket. Instead, there were pictures of Harry scattered across the front of the auditorium. Landon and Kerri got a kick out of seeing what Harry looked like in his younger days. Even then he had the round shoulders and drawn face that resembled a vulture, but his hair was dark and long. He had been handsome by the standards of the day.

Harry had been married three times. There were pictures of wives one and two but not a mention of wife three. He had four kids and a half-dozen grandkids who all lived out of town. They were all accounted for at the funeral, each undoubtedly hoping for a piece of Grandpa's estate.

A minister from some local church presided over the service, but there was really nothing spiritual about it. The speakers were Harry's friends and partners and a Virginia Beach Circuit Court judge. They all told stories about Harry, and most of them started by saying, "I probably shouldn't tell you this, but . . ."

Brent Benedict performed the main eulogy and gave a stirring tribute. Harry McNaughten was, according to Brent, the greatest trial lawyer in Virginia, perhaps on the entire East Coast. If Brent had his life on the line, he would want Harry to defend him. The man had a heart for the underdog, and he loved a good fight. Just to emphasize the point, Brent told a few war stories about some of Harry's most famous fights. Landon found himself laughing and missing Harry more than ever.

Before he sat down, Brent turned serious. "Harry was like a father to me," he said. "He would give you the shirt off his back. And he was a tough old codger.

"In fact, I remember one case where his appendix burst in the middle of the trial. It was a three-day case, and after the second day, Harry complained about a stomachache. The next day, he gave one of the best closing arguments I'd ever heard and then checked himself into the hospital while I waited for the verdict. The doctor said Harry might have died if he had waited a few hours longer. But I knew he wouldn't have. It always seemed to me that Harry McNaughten was indestructible.

"In life, there are people who get heart attacks and people who give them to others." Brent smiled wryly. "No doubt about it. Harry was in the heart-attack-giver category. That's why I thought for certain that he would outlive me. Even when he was diagnosed with cirrhosis, I was sure of it."

Brent paused for a moment and collected himself. He swallowed hard and surveyed the crowd. "Frankly, it just never occurred to me that Harry might be the first to die. I may be the managing partner at McNaughten and Clay, but Harry was our heart and soul. I never thought about the practice of law without him, and I can't imagine it now."

Brent paused and turned his attention to the family members in the front row. "Your father was a good man," he said. "Your granddaddy was a great man." He then looked at Harry's ex-wives. "Admittedly, your ex-husband had a few flaws, but we loved him anyway."

The room chuckled. Brent Benedict smiled. He looked toward the ceiling.

"Rest in peace, Harry," he said.

///

That night, Landon and Kerri got a babysitter for Maddie, donned windbreakers, and went for a walk on the beach. They took off their shoes and felt the cold sand between their toes. They stayed just out of reach of the lapping waves. For long stretches, they didn't say a word.

In the last few days, they had replayed their own Harry McNaughten stories. If it weren't for Harry, Landon wouldn't be a lawyer at all. Kerri had harbored mixed emotions about the man while he was alive because he made Landon work unreasonable hours and didn't seem to care much about family. But now that he was dead, she was coming around to Landon's way of thinking. Harry had believed in her husband just like she did. He'd given Landon opportunities that most fifth-year lawyers didn't get. And nobody would dispute that he was one heck of a mentor and trial lawyer.

But something had been eating at Landon, and he chose this moment, walking hand in hand with Kerri on a chilly April evening at the beach, to talk about it.

"You notice what was missing from the memorial service today?"

"They should have had you speak."

"No, I'm talking about the whole tone of the thing. The absence of any spiritual dimension. It was all about Harry as a lawyer and a friend and a partner at the firm."

"I noticed that too," Kerri said, softening her voice. "Do you think he was a Christian?"

It was the question that had been haunting Landon since Harry's death. All of those weeks they spent together and they had never once discussed anything spiritual. After his conversion in jail, Landon had become a serious follower of Christ. For him, it was as natural as breathing.

Yet for some reason, he had turned it off at the office. Maybe Harry had intimidated him. Maybe he was just glad to have a job and didn't want to push the issue. But now he was filled with regret that he had never once shared with Harry how important faith was in his life.

"I saw a Bible in his office once," Landon said hopefully. "But I never saw him read it. He may have been one of those guys who just kept his faith private. That's his generation, you know."

"He obviously didn't go to church," Kerri said. "That minister didn't know a thing about him."

"Yeah, it was pretty obvious."

"You can't blame yourself, Landon. He knew where you stood. Don't forget that hearing before the Character and Fitness Committee. Plus, he saw the way you lived. You've just got to trust that God gave him the opportunities to hear what he needed to hear."

"Thanks," Landon said. But he knew she was just saying it to make him feel better.

Kerri edged closer to him, and he put his arm around her as they walked. He wouldn't forget this night—the crisp wind, the smell of salt water, the incessant breaking of the waves as they approached the shore—or the moment of clarity that Harry's memorial service had provided. People had talked about what a great trial lawyer Harry was, but his family life had been a disaster. And the last few months, Landon had been so consumed with becoming a great lawyer himself that he had lost all sense of perspective.

"I'm sorry I haven't been much of a husband or father lately," he said to Kerri. "I don't want people talking about what a great lawyer I am at my funeral. There are a lot of other things more important."

Kerri stopped, and Landon turned to her. She wrapped her arms around his body and leaned in, pressing the side of her face against his chest. He placed his cheek gently on top of her head, the way he had so many times in the past. Neither of them spoke. Not during that embrace, not after the kiss, and not for several more minutes as they walked back in the same direction they had come.

Kerri was the one who finally broke the silence. "You're the best husband ever," she said softly.

44

ON MONDAY MORNING, two days after Harry's memorial service, Landon sat in his truck for a few minutes before he mustered the strength to walk into the building and head upstairs to his office. Something about the memorial service had made it final. Harry was gone, and he wasn't coming back.

Landon would not only be alone on the second floor again today, but his job was to go through every one of Harry's files so he could give Brent Benedict a status report. He'd also been charged with cleaning out Harry's office and boxing stuff up for storage.

Landon climbed the steps, put his briefcase down in his office, plugged in his laptop, and eventually made his way to Harry's office. He took a seat in one of Harry's client chairs and stared at the old man's desk.

There were pieces of Harry everywhere. Pictures of the grandchildren. A United Way pledge card with a box checked for two thousand dollars. Behind the desk were a few mementos from prior cases. Harry had lined them up on his credenza like little soldiers in formation. A spent bullet casing. A lab report with DNA evidence. A phone log. A small square of carpeting with dried blood. A small cloth doll with needles stuck in it, a relic from an insanity case. Each one had a story.

"You want some help?"

The voice startled Landon. He turned and saw Rachel, standing in the doorway, holding two cups of coffee.

"Sure." If nothing else, he wanted the company.

Compiling a status report on each of Harry's cases would be a daunting task. Before he could do that, Landon had to make sure the case files were not missing anything, meaning he had to find a home for the reams of paper and pleadings and exhibits scattered around Harry's office.

A couple of months ago, Landon had been determined to get every file on the second floor organized so they could find stuff they needed and know the status of each file in a heartbeat. But he had been overwhelmed with other work and had procrastinated on the clerical tasks. It was probably just as well, because it gave him something to focus on now—something to take his mind off how much he missed Harry.

Landon and Rachel rolled up their sleeves and began the tedious process of putting every scrap of paper where it belonged. It was like somebody had taken eighty different puzzles and dumped all the pieces into Harry's office, then shaken it up. Before you could put any of the puzzles together, you first had to separate the pieces box by box. It was a frustrating task, but neither of the two young lawyers wanted to be too critical of a man whose ashes were not yet cold.

45

THE DAY ENDED with an hour-long meeting of the four lawyers in the main conference room. They went over each of Harry's files and made decisions about whether they should try to keep the clients. Brent Benedict was in a foul mood because Harry hadn't gotten a big enough retainer on several of the cases, so if the firm kept those clients, they would essentially be working for free. Plus, Brent was worried about Landon getting in over his head if they kept any of the more complicated felony files.

"How many felony jury trials have you had?" he asked Landon when they were discussing one of the cases Landon wanted to keep.

"I've done a few bench trials, but no juries," Landon admitted.

Brent frowned and made a check on his list. "Let's refer this one out," he said.

They also filtered out any defendants who had serious gang connections. Though they continued to believe that Harry's death was just a mugging gone bad, Detective Freeman's questions had them all a little spooked. No sense taking any chances.

Landon fought to keep as many files as possible. "How am I supposed to get trial experience if we refer out the ones that might get tried?" he asked. He was supposed to be Harry's heir apparent. In their short months together, Harry had trained Landon for this type of moment. If Harry had been in the conference room, he would have said Landon was ready to try all the cases.

When they came to Elias King's cases, Brent didn't see much need for discussion. "There's no way we're equipped to handle these," he said. "And knowing Elias, he's probably already interviewed other firms."

To Landon's surprise, Parker Clausen spoke up, one of the few things he had contributed the entire meeting. "Doesn't mean we shouldn't try," he said, eyes glued to his iPad.

"You want to take responsibility for them?" Brent asked.

Clausen looked up. He stroked his gray beard for a second, and Landon thought about what a disaster it would be serving as Clausen's second chair. "I could quarterback it," Clausen said. "I haven't actually tried a case in years."

"That's my point," Brent said in a satisfied tone. "Landon, let's contact Elias and get that file boxed up. The trial date is coming fast." He looked back down at his sheet. "*Commonwealth v. Bronson.*"

"Going back to King," Landon interjected, "what if you and I handled it together? You've done plenty of criminal work, and we've got a lot of retainer money left."

Clausen grunted his approval. "Makes sense to me."

But Brent had other thoughts. "I don't have time to get up to speed on that file," he said. "And I haven't tried a criminal case in a few years."

"Maybe Landon could stay in the case and help whatever new firm takes over," Rachel suggested. She had been quiet most of the morning, but she seemed to sense that Landon wanted to stay involved in this one. "I know Elias really likes Landon."

"I understand that. But Landon's going to have his hands full with these other cases that he'll be handling on his own," Brent said.

Parker and Landon both started to respond, but Brent cut them off.

"Look, I don't like this any better than you guys. But the truth is that Harry's gone and Landon's not yet ready to take his place. So let's keep some cases that are appropriate for a first-year lawyer and not worry about the rest."

He spoke with the authority of the managing partner, one who had grown accustomed in the military to never having his orders questioned.

But Clausen had never served in the military. And he had a stubborn streak. "I'll handle it," he said. "I'll tutor Landon, and we'll figure out how to split the trial when we get there."

"That's not your call to make." Brent's voice was emphatic, a parent getting the last word. *Because I said so.* "You and I have other fish to fry."

"I'm a partner. And I'm taking it."

The ultimatum surprised Landon. He had never seen Parker Clausen stand up to Brent like this. For a few moments, there was an icy silence, finally broken by Brent's calm and dispassionate voice. "Can we have a minute?" he asked, dismissing Landon and Rachel.

The two associates stepped out of the conference room and took bets on who would prevail. They both agreed that the smart money was on Benedict, though Landon said they shouldn't rule Clausen out. Technically, Clausen was right. He was a partner. He could take cases if he wanted them.

"Would you really want to try those cases with him?" Rachel asked.

"Good question," Landon conceded.

They stopped talking so they could hear what was being said behind closed doors.

When the associates were allowed back in the room, the partners acted as if there had never been a disagreement. Brent announced the decision. Parker and Landon would meet with Elias King. If Elias wanted them to stay on the case, they would. Parker would be the brains behind the operation, and he and Elias would have Landon ready to handle most of the courtroom duties.

"Now," Brent said, his voice still authoritative, as if his view had carried the day, "*Commonwealth v. Bronson.*"

Landon and Rachel stole a quick glance. Parker Clausen had more backbone than they had thought.

///

The firm could have saved a lot of angst. The next day, Elias King came by and listened to their sales pitch. He told Parker and Landon how much he appreciated their willingness to stay on the case. He believed that Landon would someday be one of the best trial lawyers in town. But he needed someone who already had big-time experience. He had been in contact with a few other firms. They were good, even if they weren't the same caliber as Harry.

Landon promised he would have a complete copy of the files ready the next day. He wished Elias luck and asked about Jake.

"He's hanging in there," Elias said. "But it's been a rough few months."

"He's a tough kid. He'll be all right."

Elias thought about it for a moment, perhaps trying to convince himself that Landon was right. "When all this gets behind us, I'll send you a copy of the fall football schedule. Maybe you could come to a game."

"I'd like that," Landon said.

After Elias left, Landon returned to the conference room to thank Parker Clausen for trying.

"It would have been an interesting case," Clausen said. "Just let me know if you need any help on your other ones."

Landon left the conference room feeling a little ashamed. Maybe Parker Clausen wasn't such a bad guy. *Maybe,* thought Landon, *I should be a little more careful before I rush to judgment.*

46

FRIDAY MORNINGS were always chaotic in Virginia Beach Circuit Court. The day was reserved for hearing motions, and the judges in all nine courtrooms spent their time listening to the bickering lawyers and ruling on their cases. It wouldn't be unusual for a single judge to hear twenty or thirty motions. The lawyers argued about custody matters or support agreements or motions to compel in civil cases. For the most part, it resembled a long family road trip with the kids in the backseat squabbling about who put whose foot over the line. The judges, like parents, would chew out both sides. *"Don't make me stop this car!"*

On Friday, April 26, just six days after Harry's memorial, three lawyers from the McNaughten and Clay firm were camped out in Courtroom 5, Virginia Beach Circuit Court, because Carolyn Glaxon-Forrester had hauled them in there to respond to her motion to compel.

She had already filed a ten-page brief, complaining about the shenanigans that had taken place during the depositions of Brent Benedict and Rachel Strach. Glaxon-Forrester wanted Brent held in contempt of court for lying under oath during his deposition. She wanted to compel Rachel to answer questions about her sexual escapades in Atlanta. She wanted blood, and she wanted a chance to strut around the courtroom for fifteen or twenty minutes and, quite literally, flex her muscles while she made her salacious accusations.

Because Glaxon-Forrester's motions would take a good deal of time to resolve, Judge Samantha Traynor, a former prosecutor with a reputation for fairness, made the lawyer wait until all other motions had been heard. Glaxon-Forrester did a slow boil, stewing for three hours while her client, Stacy Benedict, shot menacing glances at her husband.

At eleven thirty, when their case was finally called, Rachel and Landon took their places at the defense counsel table, alongside Brent Benedict and his high-priced lawyer, Allen Mattingly.

Mattingly seemed unperturbed by the coming storm. The word on Mattingly was that he was seriously smart and had lots of useful connections. But Landon wasn't sold on the guy. For starters, if Mattingly was as brilliant as people said, Landon wondered why he wore a toupee that made him look like a sixty-year-old with the hair of one of the Beatles. It didn't seem to Landon like any lawyer with a toupee would be much of a match for Glaxon-Forrester. Landon hoped he was underestimating the man, that maybe Glaxon-Forrester was fire but Mattingly was ice.

It would sure make Landon's job a lot easier if Mattingly stepped up and earned his hourly rate.

"I understand we are here on your motions, Ms. Forrester," Judge Traynor said.

"*Glaxon*-Forrester." The lawyer's correction carried a healthy dose of disdain.

"Excuse me," Judge Traynor said pleasantly. "Ms. Glaxon-Forrester." Traynor reviewed the pleadings in the file for a moment. "It's been a long morning, so I would appreciate it if you would keep your argument concise."

"It *has* been a long morning," Glaxon-Forrester said. "And I'll do the best I can."

She stepped out from behind her counsel table and jumped right into the juiciest allegations. "I'd like to hand the court some photographs taken at a hotel in Atlanta, Georgia, where Mr. Benedict and Ms. Strach spent the night together. We have photos of them going into the room that night and coming out the next morning. We also have deposition testimony from Mr. Benedict denying that he had sex with Ms. Strach. When we tried to depose Ms. Strach, she hid behind the Fifth Amendment."

As she spoke, Glaxon-Forrester took the photographs and excerpts from the depositions to the bench and handed them to the judge. It seemed like she struck a pose in her sleeveless blouse as she did so, flexing her biceps, triceps, and lats all in one smooth motion. On her way back to the counsel table, she slapped a copy of the exhibits in front of Allen Mattingly. He ignored them.

"My motion is basically twofold," Glaxon-Forrester continued. "First, I want Ms. Strach compelled to answer my questions. Invoking the Fifth Amendment was improper. Adultery might be a misdemeanor in Georgia and Virginia, but nobody's been prosecuted under those statutes for half a century, and she won't be the first. A Fairfax judge, who compelled testimony about adultery in a similar case despite a Fifth Amendment claim, called prosecution under the Virginia statute a 'matter of historical curiosity' rather than a real-life threat. More importantly, sexual conduct between consenting adults apart from adultery is not a crime at all in Georgia, which is where the conduct occurred. So I should be able to ask Ms. Strach about anything short of intercourse.

"And second, I'm asking for sanctions against Mr. Benedict for lying under oath about whether he had sex with Ms. Strach. He should know that I'm also going to turn his deposition transcript over to the Commonwealth's Attorney for possible perjury charges. Now, maybe Mr. Mattingly is going to argue that his client and Ms. Strach were just preparing for an appellate argument the next day, studying their briefs all night. But I think we all know the truth. Those legal briefs weren't the only ones being studied."

The remark brought some snickers from the lawyers in the audience who had stayed to watch the action. Traynor didn't find it funny. "Stick to your argument, Ms. Glaxon-Forrester."

"Sorry, Judge."

But she wasn't really. Within seconds, she was rolling again, jabbing her finger in the direction of Brent Benedict and the others at the defense table. She called Benedict a liar, Mattingly an obstructionist, and Rachel . . . "Well," Glaxon-Forrester said, "I can't say what she is in polite company."

This brought Landon to his feet. "That's ridiculous, Judge."

Glaxon-Forrester swiveled toward him.

"Are we back in middle school here?" Landon asked. "This is name-calling, not argument."

From there, the battle was on. Glaxon-Forrester suggested that Landon should have paid better attention in civil procedure class, since he obviously didn't know the first thing about courtroom etiquette. He called her a bully who used sleazy detectives to satisfy her client's obsessive desire for revenge. Judge Traynor chewed them both out and told them to show a little professionalism. "Is that asking too much?"

"No, ma'am," Landon said.

Glaxon-Forrester didn't respond.

After things calmed down, Glaxon-Forrester finished her argument. Adultery could be considered under the equitable distribution process of Virginia law. It was one of the factors the court was entitled to weigh when divvying up the assets. Therefore, Glaxon-Forrester and the court should know what happened in that hotel room. Brent Benedict could sleep with anybody he wanted, as far as Glaxon-Forrester and her client were concerned. But when he did it while married, and when he denied it under oath, then it became the court's business.

"Hold him accountable, Judge," Glaxon-Forrester urged. "Just because he's a lawyer doesn't mean he should get away with it."

Landon was next and responded with some passion of his own, though the judge limited him to just five minutes.

"If the Fifth Amendment means anything, it means that a witness like

Ms. Strach cannot be forced to answer questions that would implicate her in a crime in either Virginia *or* Georgia. It doesn't matter whether it's a misdemeanor or a felony. And it doesn't matter whether the prosecutor has chosen to prosecute for this particular crime or not in the last ten years or even the last century."

"May I ask you a question?" Judge Traynor interjected as soon as Landon paused to draw a breath.

"Of course."

"As I understand it, only the act of sexual intercourse is defined as adultery in the state of Georgia; is that correct?"

"Yes."

"Well, since that's the scene of the crime, so to speak, then what about all these other questions that Ms. Glaxon-Forrester asked in the deposition? There are a lot of activities short of sexual intercourse where your client also asserted the Fifth. How do you justify that?"

Out of the corner of his eye, Landon noticed a smug little grin on Glaxon-Forrester's face.

"The test is whether my client's answer to the question would tend to incriminate her in any way," Landon explained. "If my client is asked about a bank robbery, she doesn't have to answer questions about whether she purchased a gun on the black market, or whether she drove a car to the bank, or whether she had scoped out the bank three days earlier. It's not just answers about the crime itself that are shielded by the Fifth Amendment, but answers about any acts that tend to incriminate."

Landon's argument was followed by the unflappable Allen Mattingly. He took a different approach than Landon, refusing to get involved in the mudslinging. "When you wrestle with a pig, you both get dirty, but only one of you likes it," he said. Instead, he treated the whole matter as an academic exercise, citing cases that supported his proposition and giving the court a lecture on the history of the Fifth Amendment. His argument was effective, Landon thought, and especially so because Glaxon-Forrester made every grunting sound and *tsk-tsk* noise possible to show her displeasure.

Glaxon-Forrester insisted on having the last word, and Judge Traynor heard her out. When the lawyer finally sat down after repeating much of what she had said earlier, Traynor took a few minutes to jot down some notes.

When she finished, Judge Traynor looked up and sighed. "Mr. Benedict, your wife's attorney is right about one thing. You would think that you'd be able to exercise enough restraint to forestall your affairs until the divorce decree is final. But you apparently didn't, and so I'm forced to rule.

"Did Mr. Benedict exercise good judgment and demonstrate great moral character? It appears he didn't, although nobody really knows for sure except Mr. Benedict and Ms. Strach. But under the law as it now stands, Ms. Strach is within her rights to assert the Fifth Amendment as she did. Ms. Glaxon-Forrester, you might not like it, and that's okay. The Fifth Amendment has never been our most popular amendment. Yet as long as it's part of the Constitution, I'm going to honor it. Accordingly, your motion to compel and motion for sanctions are both overruled."

She paused for a moment and surveyed both sides. The other lawyers in the courtroom had gotten what they came to see—some good fireworks and a few scandalous accusations by the attorneys. But Traynor wasn't done lecturing the participants. She closed the file and shook her head.

"You didn't ask for my advice, but I've seen this scenario unfold too many times. The parties need to get together and resolve this matter so you can both get on with your lives. Nobody's going to be happy if this case goes to trial, and it's going to cost you both thousands of dollars in legal fees and days and days of your lives fighting each other. Settle the case and move on."

No lawyers responded, and Landon knew they weren't expected to. It was a good ruling by Traynor, and the parties deserved their little dressing-down. But this whole affair also reminded Landon why he never wanted to practice domestic-relations law. He couldn't wait to get back to the felons and miscreants who needed his help on criminal matters. Anything would be better than this.

47

KERRI WAS SURPRISED they were meeting at Kincaid's Fish, Chop & Steakhouse at the MacArthur mall. She thought the great Sean Phoenix would have preferred a more private location, or at least something more exotic. He had promised her the scoop on a story that was volatile and said they couldn't talk about it over the phone. They had to meet, according to Sean. They might as well do lunch.

She had obsessed over what she should wear. Her wardrobe was a television reporter's wardrobe. Loud colors looked better under bright TV lights—large print patterns so they didn't blur together. Form-fitting skirts and V-neck blouses. Avoid black; it adds extra pounds on TV.

But today, she wasn't dressing for the cameras. She had pinned her hair back into a messy bun. She put on a straight black skirt, heels, and an aqua blouse with a wide collar and matching necklace. It was conservative and classy; she wanted to let Mr. Phoenix know she could play in the big leagues too. Today was all about impressing a confidential source, a source who had access to top-level information, a source who had promised a big scoop. Maybe, Kerri hoped, he was going to tell her to run with the story about the rescue of Pastor Seyyed Hassan.

When she saw him, she realized that Sean had apparently spent a lot less time worrying about what he was going to wear. He met her at the door of Kincaid's wearing khakis, a black T-shirt, and flip-flops. He flashed a big white smile, carving dimples into the chiseled face, and shook her hand.

"I've got a place in the last booth in the back," he said.

The restaurant had a classic feel with a dark-mahogany bar, chandeliers, and a spacious seating area. It seemed like they had stepped into a New York City restaurant in the 1930s.

They settled into their booth, and Sean was in no hurry to get down to business. Kerri didn't push him. She had cultivated sources before. She knew the rules—keep them talking; get them to relax; build trust. When a source calls a meeting, they want to spill the information. Don't push them or they might get spooked.

She followed her rules all the way through lunch. The only business they discussed was when Kerri lowered her voice and thanked Sean again for letting her see the Hassan rescue. She still couldn't believe what had actually happened. Sean brushed it off, and her hopes about getting a green light to run the story faded.

When the bill came, Sean insisted on paying, and Kerri let him. She was still playing cat and mouse, waiting for him to glance around the restaurant, make sure the coast was clear, and give her the tip he had promised. Instead, he kept asking questions, just like he had during lunch, and seemed more fascinated with her life's story than with sharing his confidential info. Had this all been just a ruse to get her to lunch?

"Are you doing reconnaissance on me?" she asked.

Sean smiled. The dimples again. "If I were, I would have had you drinking by now."

"Not this girl."

"Regardless, I already know everything I need to know."

"I doubt that."

Sean sat back with a smug look, his head tilted a little to the side, as if he were sizing her up. "Try me," he challenged. "Ask me a question about you."

Kerri wasn't sure she wanted to play this game, yet she *was* curious. How much did he *really* know?

"What sports did I play in high school?"

He laughed, as if the question were too easy. "Basketball and soccer. You ran track until your senior year."

She forced a smile, but the answer unnerved her a little. Why did he know these things?

"What was my nickname?"

This time the great Sean Phoenix hesitated. He put an elbow on the table, resting his cheek on his fist. He waited and stared, as if he could detect the answer in her brain waves.

"They called you Petro," he eventually said, and Kerri felt her jaw drop. "But I'm not sure if that's because of your nonstop motor on the soccer field or because you were smokin' hot."

Her face flushed. Enough of that game. "Why do you have all this information on me?"

The smug grin left Sean's face, and the intensity Kerri had seen a few weeks ago in Manassas returned. He used his napkin to wipe the table in front of him, then carefully folded it and placed it off to the side.

"We wanted to make sure we could trust you, Kerri. So we did a little checking. I'm sorry if we went too far. Our guys are pretty compulsive."

Sean paused, a cue for Kerri to tell him it was okay. Fat chance. She wanted the story, but she didn't like the way Cipher Inc. pried into her life.

He was quick to pick up on her mood and began laying on the charm. He and his executives had vetted at least twenty different reporters. Kerri was head and shoulders above everyone else. Her integrity. The quality of her reports. Her commitment to her sources.

"You waited for Landon for two years," Sean said. "A lot of women would have moved on."

"And that's relevant because . . . ?"

"Because we believe in loyalty. You've seen what's at stake with some of our operations. We need people we can trust."

Sean's phone rang and he pulled it out, looked at the number, and hit Ignore. Nothing was more important than this, it seemed.

He pulled out a business card and wrote a name on the back. He checked his cell phone and added a phone number.

"This man is middle management at Universal Labs," Sean said. "He learned that his company has been bribing doctors to prescribe one of their premier drugs for an off-label use. It added about two hundred million to the bottom line last year, and he's given us the documents to prove it."

Sean slid the card across the table to Kerri. "He wants to remain confidential, of course."

"Of course," Kerri said. *Don't they all?*

She thought Sean was done, but there was more. "The number two guy at the FDA knew about this," Sean said. "Turned his head. This source has the smoking-gun e-mail."

Kerri was trying to play it cool, but he definitely had her attention. The background checks prying into her personal life suddenly seemed like a small price to pay. Her bosses would be drooling. They would want to run this story during sweeps.

"What do you want out of this?" she asked Sean.

He pointed to his chest and feigned surprise. *Moi?*

"Yes, you," said Kerri.

"Our client is a competitor of Universal Labs. He's trying to do things the right way. We just want this stuff to be exposed, to make sure everyone is playing by the same rules."

Kerri could live with that. Confidential sources seldom came without their agendas. Sean's motive was to help his client by exposing an unethical competitor. As long as Kerri knew the motivation, she could weigh that in judging the reliability of the information.

They talked for a few minutes about the source. How had Sean located him? Did the source have any axes to grind? That type of thing.

She thanked Sean for lunch. She promised him that both the source and Sean's role in being the liaison would be protected. She couldn't make any promises about when the story would run, and Sean said he understood.

But in her mind, she was already envisioning the teaser.

They were outside the mall, in the first floor of the parking garage, before Sean dropped the real bombshell. "I've got a friend at the NBC affiliate in D.C.," he said. "I've talked to him about you. They've got an opening for an investigative reporter, and he thinks you might be the perfect fit. The salary's 50 percent more than what you're making now."

Was he serious? D.C. was one of Kerri's dream markets! Sean Phoenix was making her head spin. How did he know her salary?

"What are you saying?" she asked.

"You'd have to go through the interview process. But basically, if you want the job, you'd have a great chance. My friend is the station manager."

Kerri suspected there was more to it than that. Perhaps Sean had hinted to the station manager that Kerri would be fed juicy stories by Cipher Inc. Perhaps Sean had something on the man. There were lots of red flags, including the thought of moving her family, but they were talking about one of the Big Four network affiliates in one of the most sought-after media markets on earth.

"I would need to talk to Landon."

"Of course. But let me know something within the next week or so. Jobs like this don't stay open very long."

48

AFTER THE COURT HEARING on Friday morning, Landon went home and changed into jeans and a T-shirt. He made a peanut butter and jelly sandwich and stopped by a 7-Eleven on the way to the office to grab an ice cream bar for dessert.

He was feeling good about the hearing but not looking forward to an afternoon of drudgery—boxing up files the firm had closed out in the wake of Harry's death and taking them to the firm's storage unit. He put the earbuds in for his iPhone, fired up the firm shredder, got out the boxes and packing tape, and started working.

For two hours, lost in his thoughts, Landon waded through files, boxed them up, and labeled them for closure. He made copies of the case files he had to send to other law firms—new lawyers hired by clients who had originally chosen Harry, not the firm.

With each file Landon prepared to close, he asked a single question: "Is there anybody in this case who wanted to kill Harry McNaughten?" By four o'clock, he had jotted down a dozen candidates on a yellow legal pad. He didn't send those files to storage but kept them in Harry's office until he could show the list to Detective Freeman sometime next week.

At four, he was joined by Rachel, wearing tight shorts, a tank top, and flip-flops. Her hair was pulled back in a ponytail, and she wore sunglasses propped on her head. The conservative businesswoman who had appeared in court that morning was gone, and Beach Rachel had taken her place.

"Need some help?" she asked. "Brent and Parker are gone for the afternoon, and after what you did for me in court, I feel like I owe you one."

Landon popped out an earbud. "You don't owe me anything, but I could use the help. What's Janaya doing?"

Rachel started picking up files. "Brent sent her home for the day. After this morning, he's feeling pretty generous."

Landon explained his system and set down his iPhone while he and Rachel continued packing the files they had organized earlier that week. The conversation flowed easily—first about the court hearing, then about Maddie, and finally about Rachel's personal life. It was, according to Rachel, "pretty much a hot mess."

The sun was streaming through the windows of Harry's office, illuminating trails of dust floating around the room. Landon found himself studying Rachel, fascinated by her easy self-confidence. She had the kind of carefree attitude that Landon and Kerri had lost a long time ago. None of her personal problems seemed to affect her bubbly self-image. Landon's DNA was wired for intensity; Rachel's for enjoyment. And right now, Landon had to admit, she was making the mundane task of boxing up old files seem surprisingly like fun.

He found another case with a potential Harry-hater and wrote it down.

"What's that?" Rachel asked.

"I'm putting together a list. Folks who might have wanted Harry dead."

Rachel walked over and picked up the legal pad. She studied it for a moment, and her pretty face twisted into a perplexed look. "This guy gave me the creeps," she said, pointing, "but I think he's serving something like twenty years."

"Maybe he's got contacts on the outside."

Rachel shrugged. She nibbled at a fingernail and studied the list some more. Deep in thought, she put the list back on the desk.

She picked up her water bottle and slouched in one of Harry's office chairs. Landon continued to stuff files into boxes.

"Do you really think somebody wanted Harry dead?" Rachel asked.

"We've been through this. I don't know."

"Have you ever thought that maybe Harry knew something he wasn't supposed to know? That maybe somebody wanted him dead not because they were mad at Harry but because they wanted to silence him?"

It seemed like a stretch to Landon. "Not really. Most of Harry's files weren't that interesting. It's not like he was working the JFK assassination."

Rachel took another swig of water and stood up. She walked over to where Landon was organizing files and hopped up on the desk, sitting a little sideways, a few feet away. "I think you need to be careful," she said. The carefree lilt to her voice was gone. "If it was something he knew, and you take over that file . . ."

She stopped, her point made.

"If you're not living on the edge, you're taking up too much room," Landon quipped.

She reached out and touched his arm. It made him stop and look at her.

"I'm serious, Landon. I don't want to see anything happen to you."

For a few seconds, maybe longer, neither of them said a word. Maybe it was the way Rachel had said it, the twinge of desperation in her voice. Maybe it was the sudden seriousness on a lighthearted afternoon. For whatever reason, Landon just stood there.

"I'll be careful," he said.

The moment passed, and Rachel dropped her hand. She got down from the desk and got back to work.

"You sure you don't want to start Strach and Reed?"

"You mean Reed and Strach?"

"If that's what it takes." Rachel said it while leafing through a file, not even looking at Landon. He had a hard time telling if she was serious about the idea or not.

"I've often felt like I wanted to just start over," Rachel said. "My career. My personal life. Everything."

For Landon, the idea of a new firm had some merit. Yes, much of Rachel Strach's personal life was a disaster. But she was also smart and a hard worker. Professionally, she and Landon got along well.

But the plan had a serious flaw. There was no way Kerri would agree to it. And days like this were precisely the reason why.

"Harry brought me to this firm," Landon said. "I'd feel like a traitor if I left it."

"I get that," Rachel said. "I really do."

///

His first mistake was agreeing to stop at Starbucks for coffee. They were on their way back from the storage unit, a few blocks away from Thirty-First Street, when Rachel asked if she could buy Landon a latte to thank him for being her lawyer that morning.

"I don't drink that stuff," he said.

"But I do," Rachel responded. "So you can stop anyway to thank me for helping you pack boxes all afternoon."

He didn't put up much of a fight, certainly not the kind of fight that hindsight would later suggest he should have. He detoured a few blocks and parked his truck in the parking garage across from the Hilton. When they got to Starbucks, there was a line nearly out the door, and Rachel suggested an alternative. They walked another block toward the ocean and ended up in the bar area of the Catch 31 restaurant, surrounded by big-screen TVs and the bustling activity of a Friday night happy hour just getting started. They commandeered a booth from which they could see the ocean on one side and the outdoor fire pits on the patio on the other. Within earshot was a small gazebo where a band was unpacking and tuning their instruments.

Rachel's latte turned into a light beer, and she tightened her ponytail holder. Landon noticed the muscles in her arms that she had put to good use all afternoon carrying boxes. She had held her own and refused to be treated like a girl. She was, thought Landon, tougher than she looked.

They talked naturally and good-naturedly. They made fun of tourists, and Rachel went on a roll about Parker Clausen's books. They were over-the-top and cheesy, according to Rachel. The love scenes were especially ham-handed. Clausen had asked for Rachel's feedback once, and after reading a few of his scenes, Rachel had brought in three Nora Roberts books and suggested that Parker read them. She spent the next three days trying to avoid getting cornered by Parker so she wouldn't have to debrief the details of Nora's romance scenes. "I think he even went to a romance writers' convention one year," Rachel said.

Landon was enjoying the banter but had the good sense to cut Rachel off at one beer.

"No ride home tonight?" she asked.

"You're a quick study," he said.

A waitress brought the bill, and Rachel handed her a credit card. When the waitress left, Rachel's blue eyes turned soft. "Can I ask you a question?"

"Sure."

"Do you think Brent and I have a chance at making it work? I mean, how do you and Kerri do it? You guys seem so committed to each other, and the whole thing about her waiting for you while you were in jail . . . It's just so—" Rachel seemed at a loss for the right words, unusual for her—"so romantic. It's a little like a twenty-first-century fairy tale."

Landon had been getting restless. He was feeling guilty for being there, in a bar with a beautiful woman, much longer than he had planned. He loved being around Rachel because they were good friends and the conversation was easy. Still, there were boundaries he had promised he wouldn't cross. Yet the question gave him an opening to talk with Rachel about Brent.

"I like Brent," Landon said. "He's a good lawyer and I respect him." He hesitated. Comments like this next one had a way of backfiring. "But I think you can do better. A lot better."

Rachel blushed. "You can't prove it by my track record."

Landon wanted to tell her she was selling herself short. She was smart. She was beautiful. She was fun to be around. But he didn't say any of those things. She might take them wrong.

"If he's really the one—you'll know," Landon said. "I know it sounds clichéd, but it was true for me and Kerri."

"I don't think it sounds clichéd at all. To me, it makes perfect sense."

Rachel ran her finger along the lip of her glass. She studied the drink in silence, as if even looking at him would spark more electricity than either of them could handle.

After a few seconds, she looked up—less pensive, her voice lighter. "Tell me how you and Kerri met."

///

Later that evening, after they had left Catch 31 and were walking on the boardwalk toward the parking garage, the conversation turned back to Rachel and Brent. Rachel claimed she needed Landon's help to understand things from a man's perspective. A few blocks from the truck, she took a step closer and placed a hand on Landon's arm. "Thanks for not judging me for who I am," she said. "I don't have many people I can talk to like this."

He gave her a ride back to the office and pulled up next to her car. He thanked her for helping with Harry's files.

"You really do love Kerri, don't you?" Rachel asked.

"Yes," Landon said, without hesitation.

"She's lucky to have you," Rachel said. She sat there for a moment, looking at him, her blue eyes reading his thoughts. "I'd better go," she said at last.

"Yeah," Landon said. "You'd better go."

///

The photos were perfect. Landon and Rachel approaching the Hilton. Landon and Rachel at the bar. Landon and Rachel on the boardwalk. Rachel moving closer, her hand on his arm.

He already had a photo of the kiss from the last time they were together.

It wouldn't take a genius at Photoshopping to put together the most damning photo of all. Rachel and Brent Benedict had been caught coming out of a hotel room. Now it would be Landon's turn.

49

FOR KERRI, THE TIME NEVER SEEMED quite right. Landon spent most of Saturday at the office, and when he arrived home Saturday night, Maddie was sick. Sunday was church and family day, but Maddie, who had rebounded with a vengeance, was with them the entire time. Kerri really did want to talk with her husband about the job opening in D.C., but she couldn't just blurt it out in the middle of the chaos that seemed to swirl around their lives. She had envisioned a long walk on the beach or dinner alone in a restaurant. None of that was going to happen.

She had paid extra attention to Landon all day Sunday. A touch on the arm during church. A hug when they were changing from church clothes into shorts and T-shirts. A back rub after lunch. Landon interpreted the overtures as an invitation for romance, and Kerri finally got her opening to talk when it was nearly midnight, her exhausted husband lying beside her.

She turned toward him and propped her head on an elbow. "Can we talk about something?"

"Sure."

He still had the glow, and it was almost unfair, taking advantage like this. She went ahead anyway. "There's something I've wanted to talk to you about for a couple of days, but the time just didn't seem right." Kerri watched as her husband's face turned from that satisfied I-don't-have-a-care-in-the-world look to one of concern.

"It's nothing bad," she added quickly. "In fact, I'm pretty excited about it."

"What's up?" he prompted, placing a hand on her side.

She hesitated—*How do I phrase this?*—then decided to just jump right in. "There's an opening for an investigative reporter at the NBC affiliate in D.C. The salary alone is half again what I'm making now. Sean Phoenix knows the station manager and has talked to him about me. He says I could probably get the job if I wanted it."

She watched the news register on his face. He chose his words carefully.

"Would we have to move?"

Kerri chuckled. "Last I checked, most stations like their investigative reporters to show up at the station every day. Of course we'd have to move."

Landon pulled back his hand. He frowned.

His expression made her heart sink.

"I don't know, Kerri. I mean, D.C. is a great market. But I thought we were digging in here, making this our home. Can't you just use this to negotiate a raise at WTRT?"

"Not really. That's not the way it works. And even if it did, Hampton Roads will always be a small-time market."

She twisted around so that she was lying on her stomach, her arms under her pillow, still propped up on her elbows. They were no longer face-to-face. The romance, which had been so perfect thirty minutes ago, had quickly left the bedroom.

Landon must have sensed her frustration and put a hand on her back. He cheated, starting a back rub while making his case. "It's a bad time to leave McNaughten and Clay," he said, his voice soft. "I know it's not the world's greatest firm, but they gave me a chance when nobody else would. And now, with Harry's death, I feel like it's somehow my legacy to take care of his clients and build this criminal practice that he had. It's not perfect—heck, it's totally dysfunctional—but it seems like family. If I left now I'd feel like I was quitting again, turning my back on my team. I promised myself in prison that I would never do that again."

On some level, what he said made sense, and the back rub was definitely hitting the spot. She turned again toward him, ending the contact and evening the tables.

"I'm tired of hearing about Harry. I know he was a great lawyer and all that, but this isn't about Harry. That firm doesn't own you, Landon. You've given them everything they could ask for."

Like many of their disagreements, the words being left unsaid were more important than the ones they were saying. Whose career was more important? Could Landon handle it if Kerri became the primary bread-winner? And did Kerri really want that? In some ways, she was hoping Landon would say no. The demands of her current job were enough to cause a never-ending stream of guilt in her life. If she took the D.C. job and Cipher Inc. became a constant source of high-profile stories, she'd have to spend even more time away from Maddie.

Maybe it would be best if they just stayed here.

But it bothered her that Landon couldn't see how illogical he was being. He was putting his job at a small-time firm—the kind of firm that was on every street corner—above a career opportunity that very few journalists ever even sniffed.

"I just thought you'd be more excited for me," Kerri said. "I'm not saying I think we should make the move. But I thought you'd at least be proud."

Landon edged closer and put his arm around Kerri's shoulder. "I am proud," he said. He leaned toward her and gave her a kiss on the cheek. "And we'll figure this out later. Tonight, we ought to just celebrate the fact that somebody's finally recognized true talent when they see it."

"We already celebrated," Kerri said.

"But that didn't count. We didn't know why."

Kerri snuggled into her pillow. "Let's just talk about it tomorrow," she suggested.

///

Landon lay awake for an hour trying to navigate this new challenge. On the one hand, he felt selfish for raining on Kerri's parade. A good husband would have suggested she call the station the next day. A good husband would have been excited for his wife.

On the other hand, Landon felt manipulated by the way Kerri had played this out. She had waited forty-eight hours until she thought the moment was just right to spring it on him. And as much as she had supported him the last several years, she didn't seem to value his work at McNaughten and Clay. She certainly didn't understand the impact Harry had made on his life.

He hated to admit it, but he had always been more comfortable when he was the star. He wanted to be the guy on the field, not the one carrying the clipboard. Yes, he wanted Kerri to do well—he really did. He always swelled with pride when people talked about what a great reporter she was. But he wasn't excited about playing Mr. Mom.

In his dreams, he had already figured life out. He would be a big-shot lawyer; she would be a big-time reporter. Their stars would shine equally. They would share duties with Maddie, the child genius.

But what if Kerri's star shone brighter? Could he handle that?

He turned to Kerri and watched her sleep. This was what it meant to love your wife sacrificially. She deserved this. If God had opened this door, who was he to slam it shut?

He stroked her hair and she stirred, then turned her back and curled up on her side. He fell asleep facing her.

Nobody ever said that marriage would be easy.

50

KERRI WOKE UP EARLY and got ready for work while Landon slept. Normally he would get up too, but this morning, even though she did some extra clanging around, he just grunted, stirred, and slept right through it.

She didn't like the way they had left things last night. And when she kissed Maddie good-bye that morning, she realized that she didn't want to get so busy breaking the latest national scoop that she missed the best days of her sweet daughter's life. She wasn't going to be that type of mom, the one whose day-care providers knew more about her kids than she did.

As she drove to work, she admitted to herself that what she really wanted was for Landon to support the move to D.C. so that she could turn it down and be the martyr. She also realized that wasn't fair to Landon. Even though she didn't quite understand the intensity of his commitment to McNaughten and Clay, she was glad to see him happy. They had sacrificed for years for an opportunity just like this.

After the newscast—another typical day in the South Hampton Roads market that nobody in the nation's capital would notice—she made a call to Sean Phoenix.

"I really appreciate your willingness to put in a word for me, but I think I need to stay here."

He spent ten minutes trying to talk her out of her decision but eventually conceded defeat. "That's one of the things I like about you," Sean said. "Once you make up your mind, nobody's going to change it."

She gave him an update on the Universal Labs story. Kerri had already spoken to the source. He was bringing the documents later that day. If everything checked out, this thing could be huge.

"That story's in good hands," Sean said. "I knew it would be."

///

That same afternoon, Kerri received the photographs.

They came in a plain manila folder. There was no note or letter enclosed. Just photos of Landon and Rachel, 11.5 by 14, looking like the world's happiest couple.

They were inches apart in a booth, staring at each other across the table. They were walking down the boardwalk together. She was hanging on to him, and they were both smiling. She was kissing him in the car. They were leaving a hotel room together.

Kerri was stunned. She flipped through the photos once. Twice. She placed them down on the counter as if they were a snake. Landon would never do something like this.

Disbelief turned to anger. Maybe this was the reason that Landon so desperately wanted to stay at McNaughten and Clay. Kerri had not trusted Rachel from day one. Now she wanted to rip the woman's heart out with her bare hands.

But her real fury was reserved for Landon. They had so much to live for and he was going to throw it away for *this*? She had waited for him when he was in prison. Endured the endless recriminations that came his way. Defended him to her friends and even her own family.

Was this man in the photographs the real Landon? The one that love had blinded her to?

Now she knew how his teammates felt.

She thought about Maddie, their little family unit, and her anger turned to a gut-wrenching grief. The room started closing in, suffocating her, and tears streamed down her face. The photos scattered on the counter stared up at her, mocking her, making her question everything she thought was solid. Her love for Landon. His love for her. Was it all just a mirage?

She found her way to the kitchen table and sat down. The room, like her entire world, was spinning out of control.

How could he do this? Why would he throw away everything they had? What did she do wrong to cause this?

And the ultimate question, the one she was almost afraid to ask. But she asked it anyway. For the sake of Maddie. For her own integrity. Because she had never once in her life run away from the hard truths of reality.

How could she live without him?

51

LANDON WAS NOT A TOTAL IDIOT, and even if he had been, Kerri was making no effort to hide her feelings on Monday night. There wasn't just a chill in the air; it was more like the North Pole. Kerri spoke to him in clipped, one-word answers. She put the dishes in the dishwasher with the ferocity of a middle linebacker. The lines on her face were tight, the edges of her mouth turned down in a serious scowl.

"You okay?"

"I'm fine."

"Are you sure?"

"I said I'm fine."

A few minutes later she snapped at Maddie, and Maddie went crying to her room. Landon shot Kerri a look—*You don't have to take it out on her!*

"I don't know what's wrong with you," he said, as he took off after Maddie. He noticed that even Simba seemed to be keeping his distance from the matron of the condo.

It took less than ten minutes to get Maddie straightened out. But now Landon was determined to get to the bottom of what was bugging his wife. He had tried to give her some space, but she had no right to vent her anger—probably from work—on the other members of the Reed household.

He cornered her in the bedroom. She had her back to him, stuffing clothes she had just folded into the dresser drawers.

"Look, I don't know what's eating you, but it's not fair for you to take it out on me and Maddie. If you don't want to talk about it, that's fine. But we can't walk around on eggshells all night just because you're in a bad mood."

"A bad mood?" she asked.

"Yeah. A bad mood."

She continued stuffing clothes in the drawers with the same level of intensity she had demonstrated with the dishes. Landon caught a glimpse of her face in the mirror, eyes red and puffy, her bottom lip trembling. This was more serious than he thought.

He walked over and put a hand on her shoulder. "You okay?" he asked. His voice was conciliatory, comforting.

"*Don't* touch me," she said, jerking her shoulder free.

What was that all about? Landon was ready to fire back but got pre-empted by Maddie, who had picked that precise moment to enter the room.

"I'm sorry, Mommy," she said.

Kerri stopped what she was doing, left a small pile of clothes on top of the dresser, and turned toward Maddie. Kerri had big tears in her eyes when she knelt down in front of her daughter. "Mommy's sorry too."

As she hugged Maddie, she looked up at Landon. "Later," she mouthed.

Landon nodded. Whatever was bothering his wife would have to wait until after Maddie went to sleep.

///

An hour later, after Landon had read Maddie a bedtime story and tucked her in, he walked back into the bedroom, anxious to find out what was eating at his wife. There on the bed, she had spread out several large photographs, each prominently featuring Landon and Rachel. Kerri stood in the doorway to their walk-in closet, leaning against the doorjamb, her arms crossed, her eyes still bloodshot and puffy. Landon's heart dropped to his ankles.

He took a few steps toward the bed to get a better look, desperately trying to think of something to say. He literally felt sick, an internal bleeding, as if somebody had cut him and ripped out a piece of his insides.

He noticed the picture of him and Rachel coming out of a hotel room and picked it up. He examined it under the watchful eye of his wife. "This isn't what it seems," he managed.

"Spare me."

"No, I mean it. Some of these photographs aren't right."

"Some?"

"None of it is the way it looks," Landon said. He had regained his balance a little and was starting to think clearly again. Yes, he had gotten too close to Rachel. But somebody was trying to make it look much worse.

"This photo here—it never happened. In fact, nothing has happened between me and Rachel. Where did you get these?"

Kerri's eyes were red, but her voice was calm and unwavering. "Why does it matter? What are you doing at a bar with Rachel? Why are you walking down the street with her as if she's your wife? How do you explain *any of this*?"

Landon picked up the photos and began stacking them so they weren't just sitting there staring back at him.

"Rachel and I are friends. That's all it is—all it's ever been. I represented her in court last week, and she needed some advice. That's all."

He looked directly at Kerri. He knew she could see the truth in his eyes. "There's *nothing* between us, Kerri. *Nothing.*"

"Did she kiss you? Did you kiss her? Did you walk down the street with her hanging on to you like that?"

"No. I mean . . . yes. But, Kerri, just listen—"

"No," Kerri snapped. "You listen. From day one I worried about Rachel. You knew she was having an affair with another lawyer in the firm and you still cozied up to her. And now you're trying to tell me that maybe she kisses you and maybe you walk with her on the beach, but you don't go to hotel rooms together?" Kerri was talking with her hands now, fully animated, her voice rising. "How could you do this to us?"

Landon had seen this side of her before. She was on the verge of crying, not so much from sadness but from anger. He walked toward her.

"Don't. Come. Near. Me."

Her tone stopped Landon in his tracks. "What do you want me to do?" When Kerri didn't answer, he continued. "Yes, I should have been more careful. And yes, Rachel is too touchy. But that doesn't mean I had an affair." He picked up the picture of him and Rachel leaving the hotel room. "Send this to an expert. He'll tell you. This whole thing is just Photoshopped."

Kerri snorted at the response. "What do I want you to do?" she asked caustically. "I want you to be my husband. I want you to tell me the truth. And right now, to be honest, I don't want to be around you."

The words stung Landon. They were supposed to. A smart husband would have let the words bounce off his chest. She needed to vent. The least he could do was listen. But Landon had never been one to run from a fight, especially when someone was challenging his integrity. "I thought we were all about trust," he said, his tone now matching hers. "Somebody sent these pictures to try and destroy our relationship, and you're believing that person rather than me."

He saw the tears start and lowered his voice. "All I'm asking is that based on our years together and everything you know about me, that you would give *me* the benefit of the doubt."

Kerri shook her head. "I knew you were going to do this. That somehow, you'd twist this so that it's all my fault."

She walked over to the bed and picked up the pictures. She tore the one that showed Landon and Rachel coming out of the hotel room. In half. In quarters. Then in small pieces that she dropped on the bed. She took the other pictures and spread them out.

"There. I believe you. No hotel room." She stood back and surveyed what was left. It was, Landon had to admit, still a damning montage.

"So where does that leave our marriage?" she asked.

"No different than it was before."

At this, she scoffed. There would be no satisfying her now.

"What do you want me to say?"

"How about that you're sorry? How about that you're ready to leave the firm if that's what it takes to keep our marriage together? How about that you understand why I would be so upset?"

Landon spread his arms. "Kerri, I *am* sorry. And I'll do anything it takes to keep our marriage together. But you've got to believe me—there's nothing between me and Rachel."

Kerri stood there for a moment and then sighed. "You have no idea how deeply this hurts, do you?"

Landon didn't answer. What could he say that he hadn't already said? He wanted to hold her. He wanted to tell her it would be all right, that their marriage was strong enough to survive. He wanted to tell her that he loved her.

But right now, she wasn't ready for any of that.

Her shoulders sagged, and she went into the closet and brought out a small gym bag.

"Where are you going?"

"I don't know. I just need you to take care of Maddie tonight. I'll pick her up after day care tomorrow. I need some time alone."

Landon tried to talk her out of it, but he knew it was a losing cause. She packed her stuff, went back and kissed Maddie, and walked out the door. She shut it behind her—not hard, because she didn't want to wake Maddie. But there was an unmistakable finality to it.

"I love you," Landon said.

He tried to call a few times that night, but she wouldn't answer. He sat in the family room with the TV on until three in the morning.

Simba stayed with him, sprawled out on the family room floor, breathing deeply, not a care in the world. Landon envied him.

When did life get so complicated?

52

THE NEXT DAY, Landon couldn't concentrate at work. He didn't eat breakfast or lunch. Guilt weighed him down, smothering every emotion except regret and despondency. In truth, he had grown close to Rachel and had loved being around her. Kerri was right. Landon had blurred the lines and then stepped over them. Now he would have to re-earn Kerri's trust.

But he was also blistering mad. Somebody was trying to sabotage his marriage. His prime suspect was Carolyn Glaxon-Forrester. Her investigator would have been following Rachel around. Glaxon-Forrester had lost in court last week, so maybe this was her sick way of getting revenge.

Landon called the divorce lawyer three times during the day and left increasingly irate messages. When she finally called back, late in the afternoon, she denied having an investigator trail Landon and Rachel. She denied Photoshopping any images.

"Thou doth protest too much, if you ask me," she said.

Landon reamed her out and hung up the phone.

He left work early that night and brought home a dozen roses. He pulled Kerri away from Maddie and tried to apologize.

"I just need time," she said. "Can we not talk about this right now?"

Kerri had stayed at a hotel on Monday night, and on Tuesday, after Maddie went to bed, she started packing again. Landon insisted that she stay so they could talk it through. But Kerri said she didn't have the emotional energy.

"I've cried about this. I've gotten mad at you. I've beat myself up. I just can't deal with it right now with everything going on at work and the thought that maybe our marriage isn't what I thought it was."

"But that's what I'm trying to tell you," Landon insisted. "Our marriage *is* everything you thought."

She wouldn't hear any of it. So instead of watching her leave again, Landon said it was his turn. He took Simba and an air mattress to the office and tried to sleep there. The building had more moans and creaks than he had noticed during the day.

He tossed and turned and couldn't get comfortable. He told himself that it was just a matter of time. Kerri would come to her senses and feel sorry for him. They would kiss and make up, and Landon would be more careful with Rachel. Someday, Kerri and Rachel might even become friends.

In the meantime, Landon wanted to kill Carolyn Glaxon-Forrester.

///

The flight plan would be perfect. On his approach to the Norfolk International Airport, Brent Benedict would have to spend a good twenty minutes over the expansive Chesapeake Bay, just a few miles from the Atlantic Ocean, looping around before he merged into the approach vector. The plane would be close enough to shore that the explosion would be seen. Far enough out that most of the pieces would never be found.

The Chesapeake Bay. What could be better?

The NTSB, of course, would conduct a comprehensive investigation. It would be the agency's job to determine the cause of the accident and to issue safety recommendations based on its findings. But they were only as good as the evidence they had to work with. And when a plane explodes into ten thousand tiny pieces over the Chesapeake Bay, most of the evidence is lost forever.

The mastermind congratulated himself. It was a near-perfect plan.

There was still work to do. The explosives couldn't be attached to the plane until Thursday night, the night before Benedict's return trip. But that should be no problem. The Cessna Citation would be sitting on the tarmac at the Allegheny County Airport. Ironically, even with all the elaborate security surrounding commercial flights—the invasive searches at the TSA checkpoints, the elaborate background checks on everyone working in aviation, the guards constantly patrolling the premises— private aircraft still had very few protections.

He had already scoped out the facility. The airport closed at nine. Only one security guard roamed the premises at night, and he liked to watch TV. Sneaking onto the tarmac in the middle of the night and planting the explosives would be child's play. The mastermind would use a plastic C-4 explosive, which could be molded into any shape and could be fastened securely into a hollow spot in the wheel well. He believed in overkill. He would have enough explosive power on board to blow up a small warship.

He would need an accomplice, of course, because he couldn't be in two places at once. For this, he enlisted an old friend with plenty of combat experience. The man would be well paid to drive the boat to the precise latitude and longitude on the bay, just under the flight path, close enough to detonate the explosives.

The man could be trusted to keep his mouth shut.

The deposition Brent Benedict would be taking was scheduled to start at 10 a.m. Friday. It was supposed to take at least six hours, so Benedict had filed a flight plan that had him leaving Allegheny County at six. By the time he flew out over the bay and radioed Norfolk air traffic control to get his final entry vector, it would be dark. The explosion would be even more spectacular in the nighttime sky.

It was only May 3. But it would seem like the Fourth of July.

53

WEDNESDAY NIGHT Landon was facing his second night on the air mattress, and guilt was giving way to frustration. He hadn't actually *done* anything. Yet Kerri was treating him like a serial adulterer. She had been jealous of Rachel before she ever met the woman. There were moments when Landon thought Kerri was blowing the whole thing out of proportion, and then other moments when he couldn't believe how stupid he had been.

He fell asleep that night sitting at his computer, wearing workout shorts and a T-shirt, his head tilted back, mouth wide open sucking in air. He was startled awake by Simba's loud barking. It took Landon a few seconds to get his bearings before he realized that Simba was out in the hallway by the steps. He thought he heard a voice talking to his puppy. It was a female voice speaking in baby talk, and Simba had stopped barking. He was probably getting his stomach scratched. He would make the world's worst watchdog.

When Landon turned the corner in the hallway, he saw Rachel squatting down, giving Simba a belly rub. The dog was sprawled out on his back and twisted his head to look at his master. *This is the life.*

"What are *you* doing here?" Landon asked. It was nearly eleven, and he'd been asleep for an hour.

"I work here, remember?" Rachel said, standing up. She was still perky, as if her motor was just getting started this time of night.

"I didn't mean that. I meant what are you doing here at eleven at night?"

"Brent and I have a deposition Friday in Pittsburgh," Rachel said. "I had to stop by and grab some files for our trip tomorrow. I saw your light on."

"Yeah, I'm practically living here these days," Landon said.

The whole conversation was making him nervous. It would be just his luck to have Kerri stop by the office to make amends and find him here with Rachel. On the other hand, he would feel like a jerk if he just asked her to leave.

"I was actually just packing up," he lied.

"What are you working on?" Rachel asked.

"The usual stuff—finding loopholes for serial murderers and terrorists. You know, criminal-defense work."

Rachel stood there for a moment and studied him. Landon knew her well enough to interpret the look. She had something on her mind, and she needed to talk. But he couldn't go down that road again. Plus, he couldn't let her wander back to his office and see the air mattress. She would ask questions he wasn't ready to answer.

"Have you got a minute?" she asked.

He bit his lip. He wanted to help. Yes, she was gorgeous. It was only the first day of May, but her tan was already in midsummer form and her hair was more blonde than ever. Plus, the blue eyes and pouty lips knew how to beg. But this was how bad things started, things he would regret.

"Actually, I've got to get going. Can it wait until tomorrow?"

Rachel didn't try to hide her disappointment. "We can talk when I get back," she said, trying to sound upbeat. She brushed some hair back and smiled. "See ya, buddy," she said to Simba. And then to Landon, "You sure you don't need help with anything?"

He hesitated for a moment. He wanted to tell her about Kerri. He wanted to get her advice. He'd only been working with her for a few months, but sometimes he felt like Rachel understood him better than his own wife. And he sure could use a woman's perspective.

But office friendships became office romances. That's why he was sleeping here in the first place.

"I'm good," he said.

"Okay," Rachel said. She headed for the stairs but stopped and turned with one arm on the handrail.

"Things are going great between me and Brent," she said. "You're a big part of the reason that's even possible."

"Thanks," Landon said, hoping she would come to her senses and dump the guy. "Good luck on Friday."

"I'll need it," Rachel said and then bounded down the steps.

54

THE WITNESS at the Pittsburgh deposition was an engineering expert in a complicated product liability case. Brent Benedict asked the questions, while Rachel fed him documents and huddled with him during breaks, suggesting additional questions that might have otherwise slipped through the cracks.

One lawyer could have easily done the job, but it gave the two of them a chance to take another trip in the firm's leased Cessna Citation Mustang. The day before, they had flown over the Blue Ridge Mountains on a cloudless spring day. Brent Benedict had opened up and shared a piece of his soul.

Rachel was glad Parker Clausen wasn't with them this trip. It was just the two of them. Alone. It was times like these when Brent confided in her. She already knew things about his past that Stacy never knew. But this trip was also about the future. It was a chance to bond and dream together and celebrate the fact that Glaxon-Forrester's investigators could no longer do them any damage. Their secret was out. If somebody snapped a few more pictures of them entering or leaving a hotel room—who cared?

The deposition was contentious, and the witness didn't want to cooperate, so it took longer than expected. As soon as it was finished, Brent took a cab to the airport to log in and prepare the Cessna for take-off. He filed a revised flight plan that would get them to Norfolk before the airport closed.

Rachel stayed behind after the deposition, cleaned up the exhibits, made copies of some documents, and headed for the airport in a rented limo. She carried the briefcases onto the plane while Brent completed his preflight.

He received their clearances at 7:40. With a good tail wind, he could make it to Norfolk by ten.

///

Two hours and ten minutes later, shortly after Brent had given his final approach vector, the explosion lit the sky over the Chesapeake Bay. Witnesses walking on the beach almost two miles away claimed to have felt the vibrations. A commercial jetliner, scheduled to land just after the Cessna Citation, actually had the best view.

"It turned into this huge fireball for a split second," the pilot said. "And then it just blew into a million pieces in every possible direction."

Tiny shards of the Citation rained like confetti into the bay.

It would undoubtedly take the NTSB months to complete its investigation. But given the destructive power of the explosives and the location of the plane at the time, experts were already predicting that the report would be inconclusive.

One thing, however, seemed certain. The plane had been deliberately sabotaged. Somebody wanted the lawyers dead.

55

A KNOCK ON THE DOOR at two in the morning is never a good thing. This one was insistent and loud. Kerri instinctively reached over and patted the other side of the bed, but Landon wasn't there. Recently she had become accustomed to Simba going nuts when anybody came to the condo, but he wasn't there either.

Everything was working together to disorient her.

She swung her legs over the side of the bed, turned on the lamp on the nightstand, and thought about Maddie. Whoever was at the door knocked again, just as loud and insistent as the first time.

Kerri ran her hands through her hair, pushing it back and out of her face. She grabbed one of Landon's T-shirts and threw it on over her pajamas. She hustled down the hall to get to the door before the person knocked again. She flipped on the hall light and peered through the peephole.

The woman standing there was in her midforties with dark hair, wearing khakis and a dark polo shirt. She was staring at the door with intense brown eyes that seemed to pop out of her head. Her hair, shoulder length, was pushed back behind her ears. She was plain and nondescript, as if her goal in life was to fit into every crowd. She frowned and shifted her weight from one foot to the other, very antsy. She reached out to knock again.

Kerri cracked the door but left the chain lock in place. The woman flashed a badge. "Angela Freeman, Virginia Beach Police Department. May I come in?"

The words made Kerri's heart stop. Her first thought was of Landon. Maybe he hadn't been staying at the office. Maybe he'd been in an accident. But suddenly the name registered. This was the detective who had interviewed Landon after Harry McNaughten's death.

That connection sent chills down her spine again. "Is Landon okay?"

The question seemed to confuse Detective Freeman. She twisted her head as a look of concern flashed across her face. "Can I come in?" she asked again, nodding down at the chain.

"Of course."

Kerri pushed the door closed and dropped the chain. She led Detective Freeman through the kitchen and saw Maddie standing in the hallway, thumb in her mouth, holding her worn blankie with the opposite hand. She looked like she was ready to cry.

"Where's Daddy?" Maddie asked. Her eyes were sleepy and confused.

Kerri took a few steps and picked up Maddie. "Why don't you just have a seat?" she said over her shoulder to Detective Freeman. "I'll be right back."

She carried Maddie into her room and told her that everything was fine. Mommy had to talk to their guest for a few minutes. She explained that Daddy and Simba were at the office and would be back soon. She tucked Maddie in, gave her a kiss, and turned off the light.

She sat down opposite Detective Freeman in the family room. Freeman was on the edge of the couch, hunched forward, increasing Kerri's anxiety.

"Has something happened to Landon?" Kerri asked again, bracing herself.

"He's not here?" Freeman asked.

Kerri felt her face flush. "He's still at the office."

"At two in the morning?"

Kerri shifted in her seat and looked down. She crossed one leg over the other and realized that Detective Freeman could read her every emotion. She was slowly waking up, and her reporter instincts were kicking in. "Can I ask what this is about?"

Freeman leveled her gaze. "There was an accident last night," she said calmly, measuring Kerri for any reaction. "The firm's private plane went down. Brent Benedict and Rachel Strach were on board and did not survive."

The words carried a tsunami of emotion across the room, overwhelming Kerri. Landon was okay, but his colleagues were dead! It was a feeling of exhilarating relief meshed with horrifying sadness. Landon could have been on that plane.

"Landon doesn't know?" Kerri asked.

Detective Freeman shook her head. "That's why I'm here. To tell him." She hesitated, but added, "And to warn him."

"Why? Did somebody sabotage the plane?"

"We won't know that for sure until the NTSB investigation is complete. But there was an explosion. And with three lawyers from the same firm killed within three weeks of each other, we have to assume the worst."

"An explosion?"

Freeman nodded. "It blew up over the Chesapeake Bay, about ten minutes before touchdown."

Kerri asked a number of questions about the plane crash, none of which Detective Freeman could answer. Then the detective turned the tables, boring into Kerri with her icy stare. "Why is Landon working at two in the morning?"

Kerri weighed her options. There had been three deaths, possibly all connected. This was no time for lies.

"We haven't been getting along," she confessed. "He's been sleeping at the office the last few nights."

Freeman waited for more, but Kerri knew that game. Hard as it was, she stayed quiet.

"What are you fighting about?" Freeman asked.

"I'd rather not say."

"Look, Kerri, I'm not here out of idle curiosity. If somebody is killing the lawyers in your husband's firm, secrets can be deadly. Frankly, I don't like prying into people's marriages. But until we can figure out what happened to Ms. Strach and Mr. Benedict, I need to know every detail about your life and Landon's. Now, let's try this again—why aren't you guys getting along?"

Bullying had never worked with Kerri, and it wasn't going to work now. "Am I some kind of suspect?"

"There are no suspects. There are no persons of interest. Right now, you're a cooperating witness, and I hope you will stay that way."

"I want to talk with Landon about this."

"We'll do that soon enough. But first, I need you to answer my question."

"Like I said, I'd like to do this with Landon present."

The two women stared at each other, and Kerri sensed the detective was sizing her up.

"Okay," Freeman said, "have it your way. Let's go see Landon."

///

Simba was lying on Landon's legs and went absolutely bananas when he heard the distant knock on the downstairs door. Landon bolted upright on the air mattress and tried to calm Simba down. "Take it easy, big guy."

But Simba was working himself into a *Yippee! We've got company!* lather. He was barking and jumping in circles, anxious to get out the closed door of Landon's office. A second knock while Landon was pulling on a T-shirt gave Simba another shot of adrenaline, catapulting him from bananas to totally out of control.

Landon opened the office door and Simba went flying down the hall and screeched down the steps like they were a NASCAR track, almost wiping out as he negotiated the landing.

Landon's own heart was picking up speed. He assumed it was Kerri, and that could only be good news. She wanted to talk. It would be his chance to set things straight.

He checked his watch. Two fifteen in the morning. Maybe it wasn't Kerri. If she wanted to talk in the middle of the night, she would have called. She wouldn't have left Maddie at home alone.

When he reached the bottom of the steps and saw the two women standing outside, his stomach dropped. He knew from the look on Kerri's face that something terrible had happened.

He opened the door and Simba ran circles around the legs of the women, nuzzling up for some love. Kerri instinctively reached down to pet him and to hold him away from Detective Freeman.

"What's going on?" Landon asked.

"Maddie's in the car, so we need to talk out here for a few minutes if that's okay," Kerri said softly. The night air had a nip to it, and there was rain in the forecast. She was struggling to keep Simba in check.

"Why don't we put him inside?" Kerri said.

"Good idea."

Landon dragged Simba back inside the door, and the puppy immediately started clawing at the glass. The three adults moved to another spot in the parking lot where Simba couldn't see them.

Kerri stood next to Landon and slipped her arm around Landon's back. He placed a hand around her shoulder.

"There's no easy way to say this," Detective Freeman began. "Brent Benedict and Rachel Strach are dead. Their plane crashed over the Chesapeake Bay earlier tonight."

Landon felt his knees buckle and he leaned into Kerri. It felt like some-body had reached into his chest and squeezed the life out of his heart.

"Are you sure?"

"The plane went down just before 10 p.m. The NTSB is already at the scene. We're sure."

Landon couldn't speak. His thoughts immediately turned to Rachel. Just two nights ago she had stopped by with something on her mind, something she needed to talk about. But Landon had blown her off. He felt the ache of losing a close friend compounded by regret at the way he had treated her the last time they spoke. Her beautiful smile flashed in front of him, playful and full of life. He felt a twinge of resentment at Kerri for the way she had reacted when she had seen the photos.

Rachel was gone.

He couldn't deal with it, couldn't process it. His mind was numb with pain.

"Detective Freeman said there was an explosion on the plane," Kerri said.

Landon absorbed this second blow and looked at Freeman for confir-mation.

"Everything's preliminary," the detective said. "But we're not treating it as an accident. I'm going to need you to come down to the station for questioning. And we're placing you and Parker Clausen on around-the-clock protection."

"What about Kerri and Maddie?"

"Them, too. We'll station someone outside your condo tonight."

Landon requested a few minutes alone with Kerri before he headed to the station. Freeman walked to the other side of the parking lot as Landon and Kerri embraced.

"I'm sorry," Kerri said. "I'm so very sorry."

"There's nothing you could have done," Landon said. "There's no reason for you to be sorry."

"Can we just go back to the way it was before?" Kerri asked. "I don't care about D.C. or anything else. I just want you to leave this firm so we can get our family back together."

But Landon's emotions were running the other way. His mentor was dead. Now his good friend was dead too. How could he just turn his back and run?

He knew that he and Kerri couldn't have that conversation right now. The shock was quickly turning into the kind of heart-searing grief that weakens every bone in your body, the pain of a good friend struck down in her youth. The tragedy of unrealized potential. The sadness and mystery of why the good die young. "Let's talk about that later," Landon said.

Kerri didn't argue. "Why would anybody want Rachel and Brent dead?" she asked.

Landon was asking himself the same question. It was impossible for him to imagine anyone having a vendetta against Rachel. Maybe Glaxon-Forrester and her small-minded client did. But for all their pettiness, those two weren't killers.

"I don't know," Landon said. "But I intend to find out."

56

LANDON MET PARKER CLAUSEN at the police station. The man looked stricken, the blood drained from his face, his hair matted from half a night sleeping. He hadn't brushed his teeth, and his breath could have killed a moose. His body seemed to sag under the weight of the moment, a mountain of flesh folded into a chair, spilling over the edges.

His red eyes and body language bespoke the same kind of shock that Landon felt. When the two first saw each other, Parker stood and they exchanged an awkward hug. Landon realized how little he had in common with the firm's remaining lawyer.

The two men took turns in the interview room with Detective Freeman. She was incredibly intense, her foot bouncing with nervous energy, her frustration palpable. But she tried to be as sensitive as possible under the circumstances. Her voice was softer, less accusatory, her iron-cutting stare less direct.

"I know this is hard," she said numerous times, "but I need you to stay focused."

They went through a pot of coffee as the lawyers fielded questions about the cases that both Harry McNaughten and Brent Benedict had worked on. Somebody had it out for the lawyers at McNaughten and Clay, or somebody believed the lawyers knew something they shouldn't. As far as Freeman was concerned, the answer lay hidden in the files of the embattled firm.

This time around, the lawyers played no cat-and-mouse games with the attorney-client privilege. Freeman had already pledged confidentiality and a firewall at the police department that would protect anything they told her about their clients from other investigators or prosecutors, and she renewed that commitment now. They had no choice but to trust her.

After the questioning, Landon and Parker had a chance to talk alone for a few minutes. Parker was downcast, his speech hesitant.

"If you want to leave the firm, I wouldn't blame you," he told Landon. "But I'm not sure that solves anything. If somebody is after us, leaving the firm won't make any difference."

Parker sighed and rubbed his face. If ever there was a man who didn't seem quite up to the challenge, Parker was that man. But what choice did he have? He was now managing partner by default.

"If I wrote this in a novel," he said, "nobody would believe it."

His novels were the furthest thing from Landon's mind.

Parker looked down and shuffled his feet. "If you choose to stay," he said, "I'll make you a full partner." He paused, looking Landon in the eye. "I mean, we could work through the details later, but I just want you to know that I'm not going anywhere. If you're up for it, I'd like to have you stick around as well."

It wasn't exactly a win-one-for-the-Gipper speech, but Landon had heard worse. He knew that there were no great choices here. It was foolish to think he could somehow outrun this danger. Somebody apparently believed the lawyers at McNaughten and Clay knew something they shouldn't know. If Landon left the firm, that supposed knowledge would go with him, and the danger would follow.

"I'm not going anywhere," Landon said.

By the time Landon got back to his condo at 7 a.m. on Saturday, he was numb with grief and bone-tired from Freeman's questioning. Kerri asked if he wanted to talk, but Landon put her off.

He went back to the bedroom and lay down on top of the covers, still wearing the same shorts and T-shirt he had worn the prior night at the office. Kerri came back, kissed him on the cheek, and gently placed a blanket over him. She kept Maddie and Simba out of the room and turned off the lights.

Not surprisingly, Landon's caffeine-laced body was not cooperating. He had gulped down at least two cups of coffee and one or two Diet Cokes during the long night. He slept fitfully, his body wired for action and his mind reeling with the pain of lost friends.

His life had become a nightmare, and he couldn't even fall asleep.

///

When news of the explosion made it to Manassas, Sean Phoenix double-checked his sources and took immediate action. Sean was a man who hated surprises. He called his best agent into his office, briefed him on the situation, and gave Daken Antonov—aka the Wolfman—two explicit orders.

"Find out who planted that bomb," he said. "And make sure nothing happens to Kerri Reed."

The Wolfman reminded Sean that he had several other high-priority projects dominating his time.

"We've got other agents who can handle those," Sean told Antonov. "I need you on this one."

Sean made the arrangements through Parker Clausen. The police were providing 24-7 protection for the remaining McNaughten and Clay lawyers for the immediate future, but they couldn't guarantee how long it would last. Sean told Parker that Antonov was available to look after the Reed family and offered another of his best agents to Parker. Sean's men would be assigned indefinitely.

Parker thanked him and promised to convey the offer to Landon.

57

BRENT BENEDICT'S MEMORIAL SERVICE took place on Tuesday, but it had none of the folksy charm that had made Harry's special. Stacy Benedict attended and nearly made Landon gag. She sat in the front row, dabbing at her eyes, and Landon didn't doubt that the tears were real. Her exorbitant demands for spousal support and her consuming desire to make her ex-husband's life miserable had been blown to pieces late Friday night. That, and thinking about Glaxon-Forrester's reaction, was the only thing about the service that brought Landon even a modicum of comfort.

The service was held in a church, but the ceremony was cold and formal. The minister spoke in vague generalities about what a good man Brent had been. The homily reminded people that God "works in mysterious ways" and seemed to Landon like a patchwork of clichés that did nothing to lessen the grief of anyone attending. Or to lessen Landon's desire for vengeance against the killers, for that matter. He found himself glancing around at those in attendance, wondering who might have secretly wanted Brent dead.

The biggest surprise of the day was the revelation that Brent had once been a member of SEAL Team Eight stationed at the Little Creek Amphibious Base in Virginia Beach. Like many former SEALs, he had never bragged about serving on a special-ops team. On the contrary, he had downplayed it, describing his military service in much less flamboyant terms and telling everyone he had been a Navy pilot.

But his former team members showed up in force at the memorial service, and they all followed the hearse to the graveside. As a former service member, Brent received a full twenty-one-gun salute and a flag-folding ceremony. When that was finished, at the prompting of the former SEAL Team Eight commander, the team members all shouted in unison, "Hooyah Brent Benedict!" followed by a moment of silence. It gave Landon chills even before the lone bugler started playing taps. He walked away with a greater sense of admiration for his former managing partner.

Rachel Strach's memorial service took place on Wednesday, but it was held in her hometown in Mississippi and Landon knew he couldn't attend. Kerri would never understand. Besides, he wasn't sure a fellow lawyer from the firm that had apparently been the reason for Rachel's death would be warmly welcomed by her family and friends.

Landon and Kerri were grateful for the 24-7 police protection and the backup protection provided by Daken Antonov. At first, Landon had been skeptical. "He's the guy who blew away that Sudanese official," Landon said.

But Kerri had a different take. She knew enough about Cipher Inc. to trust Sean Phoenix on this. "Isn't this Antonov exactly the kind of man we need on our side right now?" She reminded Landon that the police were primarily charged with watching *him*. "What about me?" she asked. "What about Maddie?"

After a long phone conversation with Sean Phoenix, and after meeting the no-nonsense Antonov in person and learning a few things about his training, Landon agreed to add him to the mix. The police seemed less than enthusiastic about the additional hired help, but Landon had a right to protect his family however he wanted.

For the most part, the media reports were surprisingly subdued and responsible. Nobody could be sure that the deaths of Harry McNaughten, Rachel Strach, and Brent Benedict were related, but the police acknowledged they were working on the assumption that it was not a coincidence. Speculation about the reasons for the murders became a hot topic on the cable news. The striking glamour shot of Rachel peering over her shoulder, downloaded from the website, helped spark even greater interest in the case.

For the first few days after the Cessna exploded, a handful of reporters camped out in the McNaughten and Clay parking lot, politely asking questions of Landon and Parker Clausen whenever they emerged. But this wasn't the O. J. Simpson case, and by Wednesday, the reporters had better things to do.

On Wednesday night, just as the publicity was starting to wane, Kerri went public with her story about the bribes-for-drugs scandal at Universal Labs. Based on credible confidential sources, she named names at Universal and even called out the number two man at the FDA, who allegedly knew what was going on and had turned a blind eye. The report was first carried on the 6 p.m. news. By eleven that night, it had gone viral.

In any other week, this would have been cause for a big celebration in the Reed household. But truthfully, Landon had no interest in the story. He watched it, of course, and told Kerri how proud he was of her work. But anything that didn't help him find Rachel's killer was not a top priority in his life.

One lawyer who *was* interested in Kerri's story was the assistant U.S. Attorney for the Eastern District of Virginia. He issued a subpoena to Kerri within twenty-four hours, requesting the names of her sources. It would be the kind of case every prosecutor longed for—a high-profile affair against a government bureaucrat and the executives of an unpopular pharmaceutical company. But the case couldn't go forward without the names of Kerri's sources. Accordingly, Kerri was called into the station on Thursday for a crisis meeting with the station manager and the station's lawyers to resolve the situation.

She didn't get home until late in the evening, and she was fuming mad. The station manager and lawyers were not backing her up. Under Virginia law, a reporter had a qualified privilege to protect sources, but that privilege could be overcome if a prosecutor had no equivalent means of obtaining the same information. The lawyers had suggested that they didn't stand much of a chance under that test.

"This is why you can't break stories like this in a small market," Kerri said, as she and Landon discussed the matter. "Nobody has the guts to protect their sources. You spend four years in journalism school talking about ethics and how important it is to fulfill your promises of confidentiality, and then in the real world, your employer caves as soon as the first e-mail arrives."

Landon watched her pace back and forth in the kitchen. He was leaning against the counter and munching on fish crackers. He ate when he got nervous. Kerri didn't. He had already seen, just in the past few weeks, that her face was looking more drawn and her eyes more hollow.

"What do you want to do?" he asked.

"I'm not going to burn my sources, that's for sure."

"Do your editors know who your sources are?"

"Of course not."

"Are the lawyers willing to defend you in court if you refuse to divulge your sources?"

Kerri shook her head and snorted. "I don't think these guys ever go to court. They just sit around and fret about what would happen if we did."

Landon loved Kerri, but the woman was stubborn. "You can't represent yourself, honey." It was obvious, but somebody had to say it.

"I know. That's why I married you."

"Very funny."

"I'm not kidding."

Landon leaned back and shot her a glance. *Is she serious?* "I don't know anything about this. It would be federal court and the First Amendment—"

"I could teach you the First Amendment stuff about confidential sources." She stopped walking and stood next to him. "It seems to me that court is court."

He frowned. Representing yourself was always a bad idea. The only thing worse would be representing your wife.

"Kerri, this is a big deal. I can't just walk in there and—"

"Fine," she cut him off. "I'll do it myself."

"You can't—"

"Landon," she said, interrupting again, "you said you didn't want to do it. The station's lawyers are too scared to do it. So I guess that means I just do it myself."

"Don't be ridiculous. We'll hire a lawyer out of our own personal funds."

She groaned. "Have you seen our funds lately?"

Landon sighed. He blew out a breath. He didn't need this. But he also didn't need his wife in jail. He had heard the stories about other reporters who refused to divulge sources. Some of them were locked up for months. Knowing how stubborn Kerri could be, she had the potential for setting a world record.

"Who are your sources?" Landon asked.

Kerri eyed him with curiosity. He had taken his first nibble. "I can't tell anyone," she said. "That's the whole point."

"Do you want me to be your lawyer or not?"

"I think we established that."

"Then tell me who your sources are."

"If I do that, and they send me to jail, how do I know you wouldn't divulge them?"

"Fair question. But you've got to trust me."

He had said it largely without thinking. But as soon as the words were out of his mouth, he understood the implications. *Trust me.* He hadn't spoken those words since the night Kerri had laid out the pictures.

She came over and placed her hands on his arms. "I trust you," she said softly. She had that look, the same one she had used when they said their vows. "But I can't put you in that position. I don't want you to have to choose between your loyalty to my principles and having me locked up in jail. I need you to help me out on this, Landon, but I'm not going to beg. And I can't reveal my sources."

His lawyer instincts were telling him this was a terrible idea. There were so many things that could go wrong. He could lose and look like a fool in the process. Kerri could end up behind bars, and it would all be on his shoulders.

But his husband instincts were telling him something else entirely. He *needed* to do this. They had always been there for each other. Crisis brought them together. How many times had she covered his back? Now it was his turn to cover hers.

"Let me do a little research," Landon said. "And then, if I decide to take the case, we can discuss my retainer."

She stood on her tiptoes and kissed him. A down payment?

"If you expect that kiss to turn this frog into a First Amendment lawyer, I hope you've got a backup plan."

Kerri smiled, and it dawned on Landon that it was the first time he had seen her do that since she had seen the pictures of him and Rachel.

"You *are* the backup plan," she said.

58

ON THE MORNING of the subpoena hearing, Landon took Maddie
to day care just like any other day. But today, Kerri tagged along. She
hugged Maddie at the door and held on until Maddie started squirming.
Grudgingly, Kerri let her go.

"Have fun," Kerri called out as Maddie turned to attack the day. "Be
a good girl."

Maddie turned around—one last backward glance. "Don't worry,"
she said. Then she disappeared around the corner.

Kerri stood up and walked back to the car. Her eyes were wet, and she
held Landon's hand. He wanted to comfort her but really couldn't think of
anything to say. Besides, he was probably more anxious than she was.

///

Like the nervous rookies they were, Landon and Kerri arrived at federal court thirty minutes early. Media trucks lined the front of the large
stonemasonry building, but there was none of the usual shoving of

microphones under the noses of the litigants and asking of obnoxious questions. Kerri was, after all, one of them—fighting for their right to protect confidential sources.

"Any statements, Kerri?"

She shook her head.

"Good luck," someone said.

The courtroom was a massive space, designed to intimidate, with vaulted ceilings and carved marble and fifteen rows of wooden pews on each side. Landon sat in the front row, next to Kerri, and reviewed his notes.

The waiting was always the hard part.

Ten minutes before the hearing, the assistant U.S. Attorney entered the courtroom. He set up shop at the prosecution table and came over to give Landon a firm handshake.

"Mitchell Taylor," he said.

"Landon Reed. Good to meet you."

Mitchell had a reputation as a straight-shooting and talented attorney who had cut his teeth on state-court murder trials. He looked like a Marine in a dark-blue business suit. His hair was short—not quite a jarhead but close. He had that stiff Marine posture—the head held unnaturally high—and a jutting jaw. Landon could tell that the man had law enforcement in his veins. Everything was black-and-white, good guys and bad guys.

"I'm sorry to put your wife through this," Mitchell said, surprising Landon with the comment. "But if her report is true, we're looking at some serious crimes by these executives. My job is to make sure they pay for them."

"And my job," Landon said, "is to make sure my wife goes home today."

///

Judge Lincoln Greer normally sat as a federal court judge in the Richmond division but had been assigned to this hearing in Norfolk because the local judges either had conflicts of interest or previously scheduled hearings. Judge Greer had been appointed by President Carter in 1981, had taken senior status in 2008, and showed no signs of slowing down.

He was a short man with an eggshell skull, mostly bald with a few tufts of gray. He had been wearing the same pair of wire-rimmed bifocals for the past fifteen years, and his frame was as wiry as the glasses. His spinal column had been permanently molded into the shape of a question mark from his hunched posture on the bench. He was everything you could ever want in a federal court judge—patient, firm, fair, and decisive.

"I've read Mr. Taylor's motion and his accompanying brief. Mr. Reed, I don't believe I've had the pleasure of meeting you before."

Landon stood. "That's probably because I've never been in federal court before."

"Well, we don't bite," Judge Greer said. "But we do like to run things efficiently and get right to the point."

"Point taken," Landon said, and he sat down.

Mitchell Taylor took his place behind the podium, and his argument was as crisp as his suit. If Ms. Reed could be believed—and Mitchell had no reason to doubt her veracity—then she had uncovered corruption at a very high level in both a major pharmaceutical corporation and the federal government. She had unearthed a wide-ranging conspiracy involving drug companies and doctors, a conspiracy that was undoubtedly harming patients even as he spoke. It was, he said, a jaw-dropping piece of journalism.

It was also his job to see if those allegations were true. And for that, he needed the names of her confidential sources.

"As you know, Your Honor, witnesses can be intimidated. Their memories suddenly fade or their minds change or they become confused about facts that once seemed so clear. If the allegations made by Ms. Reed are true, then some very powerful men and women could be facing a long time behind bars. They may be working on her sources right now to get them to change or conveniently forget their stories. My greatest fear, and something that weighs heavy on the court as well, is that some of the confidential sources may 'disappear'—" Mitchell put air quotes around the word—"without federal protection in place. We see it happen all the time."

"It happens in narcotics cases and gang wars," Judge Greer interrupted. "But do you have any evidence that executives of Universal Labs or the FDA have intimidated or pressured witnesses?"

Landon loved the question. But Mitchell didn't blink.

"Before this journalistic report, we had no evidence that executives at Universal Labs or the FDA were involved in conspiracies to illegally market drugs and bribe doctors. My experience is that desperate men and women do desperate things. But even if the witnesses are not in danger, it's still my job to prosecute crimes. The law says that we're entitled to know Ms. Reed's sources if there are no alternative ways to find out the same information. Trust me, Your Honor, if there were another way to go about this I would be using it."

Mitchell went through a list of cases supporting his position and answered questions from the judge for about thirty minutes. It was clear to Landon that he was now in the big leagues. The judge had read every case cited in Mitchell's brief and asked him detailed questions about them.

Mitchell more than held his own. He had all the cases neatly organized in a black three-ring binder and seemed to know them by heart. He even corrected the judge a couple of times on the intricacies of First Amendment law.

They had lost Landon about fifteen minutes into the argument.

59

WHEN IT CAME HIS TURN to approach the podium, Landon took his yellow legal pad full of handwritten notes and his iPad, which contained copies of the five most important cases he had studied the prior night. He suddenly felt woefully unprepared.

He began his argument with a little speech about the importance of the First Amendment, but Judge Greer cut him off.

"What if your client talked to the only witness in the rape of a ten-year-old girl and reported that story on the air? What if that witness didn't want to get involved and your client promised him or her confidentiality? Would you be making this same argument?"

Landon thought about it for a moment. "No, because my client wouldn't do that. We've got a five-year-old daughter."

Greer gave him a lopsided smile. "But in principle, it's the same thing, isn't it? Doesn't a reporter's First Amendment right to protect confidential sources have to yield to the government's ability to prose-cute serious crimes?"

In a nutshell, Landon knew, that was the law. And whether he had five cases with him or fifty, they all seemed to say the same thing—a reporter had only a *qualified* right to protect her sources. She lost that protection if those sources were witnesses to a crime and the government couldn't prove that crime without their cooperation.

"In certain situations, Judge, that's correct. But only if the prosecutors have exhausted all other means of getting the same information. And with all due respect for Mr. Taylor, he hasn't even tried any other sources. I mean, he has all the firepower of the federal government at his disposal. Subpoenas. Search warrants. Wiretaps. He knows the exact company and the FDA officials who are being accused. But instead of doing his own exhaustive investigation, he just wants to piggyback on my wife's investigation.

"Judge, that's bad policy for a number of reasons. It would make prosecutors lazy. It would also dry up sources for investigative journalists. Let's at least have Mr. Taylor make a good-faith effort to conduct an investigation on his own before he deputizes my wife.

"The only thing she knows about law enforcement is what she learned from visiting me in jail. If she can break this story with that limited knowledge, certainly Mr. Taylor can nail down the same information if he takes a few weeks and really tries."

The back-and-forth with Judge Greer would go on for another forty-five minutes, but the money line had already been delivered. *"The only thing she knows about law enforcement is what she learned from visiting me in jail."* It was jotted down almost verbatim by every reporter at the hearing.

Judge Greer found Landon's argument compelling enough. He quashed the subpoena. He told Kerri that he didn't agree with her decision to run a story based on confidential and unnamed sources but that the Constitution and case law gave him no real say in the matter. "Mr. Taylor, you'll have to conduct your initial investigation without Ms. Reed's help. If you hit a stone wall and come back to court with a subpoena for her sources as a last resort, rather than a first resort, we might get to a different result."

On a slow news day, the story was too juicy for the media to resist. Even though Kerri and Landon had no comment after the hearing, the video of the two of them walking hand in hand away from the courthouse made for interesting B-roll. The story had so many angles! Landon's firm was under siege. His wife had put her future in the hands of her husband, a first-year lawyer. Here was a budding legal star and a budding media darling all rolled into one happy little family. And not only that, but this lawyer was a one-time felon who had found religion and gone straight!

The talking heads on cable loved it. Conservatives denounced Judge Greer's opinion. He had caved to Kerri Reed, a member of the hated mainstream media, and now a bunch of corporate criminals would get away with the equivalent of murder! On the other side, the media protected one of their own. She was a courageous investigative reporter. Freedom of the press was what made this country great. If she could find these sources, why couldn't Mitchell Taylor?

As their names were bandied around the airwaves, Landon and Kerri retreated to their condo and unhooked the umbilical cords to the outside world. No Internet. No television. No phone calls. They put Maddie to bed early and hunkered down for the night, secretly hoping that something more explosive would happen in the nation's capital or the Mideast or in Hollywood that would redirect the collective curiosity of the American people to a new set of victims.

60

ON SATURDAY NIGHT, Landon fell asleep reading Maddie a story. It was almost midnight when Kerri, who had been asleep herself on the couch, staggered into Maddie's room and woke Landon up. "Let's go to bed," she suggested.

It took Landon a second to respond. He had been sleeping so hard that there was drool on the pillow. He felt like his body weighed a thousand pounds.

"Okay."

But Simba had other plans. He was doing his little *I've got to go this very minute!* dance, and Landon wanted to drop-kick him.

"When's the last time he went out?" Landon asked.

"Right after dinner." Kerri was rubbing her eyes, sending every possible message that she wanted Landon to take out the dog. But he wasn't going down without a fight.

"It's part of my legal fees," he said.

"I paid your fees last night."

"Odds or evens?" Landon asked.

"It's your turn."

Landon finally gave in, put Simba on a leash, grabbed a plastic bag, and took one last shot over his shoulder. "This dog wasn't my idea."

Kerri didn't respond.

As usual, Simba had to find exactly the right spot to do his business, and that process couldn't be rushed. The cool night air woke Landon up a little and made him shiver. He waved at the police officer sitting in his car a few spots down from the condo entrance. It had been eight days since Brent's and Rachel's deaths. Landon wondered how long it would be before the city reassigned its officers and he and Kerri were on their own.

By the time he got back into the condo and brushed his teeth, Kerri was sound asleep. But having slept a few hours already, Landon had a harder time dozing off. He stared at the ceiling for about twenty minutes and then decided to get up and sneak a look at his iPad. He sat at the kitchen table and read yesterday's stories about the hearing in federal court. Most of the press coverage was positive, but the haters were filling up the comments pages. They slammed lawyers and slammed reporters and complained about the fact that a convicted felon was allowed to practice law.

Simba heard the commotion first and started barking immediately, running in circles. There was shouting in the hallway outside the front door and a few thuds. Simba was at the door in a flash, as if he wanted in on the fight. Landon hurried to the door, and Kerri came stumbling out of the bedroom, groggy-eyed, with a gun she had purchased the previous week.

"Is it loaded?" Landon asked. With Maddie in the house, they had agreed to keep the bullets stored separately in a sock drawer.

"I don't know."

There was a loud bang on the front door accompanied by cursing, and Landon looked through the peephole. Kerri was right behind him and handed Landon the gun. Maddie was awake now and calling for her mommy.

The cop Landon had seen earlier was a few steps away from the door, his gun drawn and pointed at two men on the ground.

"What's going on out there?" Landon called.

"Hands in the air, now!" the officer yelled.

Maddie was at the end of the hallway, crying. "Take care of Maddie," Landon said to Kerri. He shouted at Simba, but the dog kept barking wildly.

Eventually the officer shouted that the coast was clear and Landon could come out. Landon opened the door just a crack, the chain lock still in place, and stared at the scene in front of him.

He dropped the gun to his right side, shut the door quickly, and unhooked the chain. He reopened the door and couldn't believe his eyes.

"Tell Chuck Norris here to get off my neck," the big man on the ground said. His hands were cuffed behind him, and his voice was hoarse. The lithe and muscular man on top of him—the man with the bushy eyebrows, long sideburns, and deep-set eyes—was Daken Antonov. He had his knee on the other man's neck. The cop had his gun trained on the big man as well.

"This right here," said Landon, "is why I had so many sacks in college football. Officer, I want you to meet the starting center for the Green Bay Packers, Mr. Billy Thurston."

The cop looked surprised, and Antonov released his hold.

"He always got manhandled like that in college, too," Landon said.

"Very funny," Billy said. "That dude just about killed me."

The Wolfman stood up. "So you know this guy?" he asked Landon.

It took about ten minutes to straighten everything out. Billy Thurston had been watching the news at his home in Green Bay and decided his buddy was in danger and needed help. He was going to surprise Landon and arrive at his condo unannounced. When he saw the police officer parked by the curb, he foolishly decided to prove a point and sneak past him, up to the condo door. Before he could knock, "this guy came out of nowhere and blindsided me."

The Wolfman said he saw Billy sneaking around and didn't have time to ask questions.

Listening to what happened, Kerri couldn't resist giving Landon a little nudge in the back. *See, I told you he was good.*

Landon invited everyone in, but the police officer and the Wolfman declined. They both had a job to do.

"Thanks for keeping an eye out," Landon said.

"No problem," the police officer responded, as if he had been the one to stop Billy Thurston.

Landon couldn't be sure, but it looked like the Wolfman flashed a brief little smile.

///

Billy, Landon, and Kerri stayed up almost the entire night. Billy spent the first hour eating and the next few catching up on Kerri's and Landon's escapades. He wanted to take Kerri and Maddie back to Green Bay until the cops figured out who was killing the lawyers in Landon's firm. But Kerri wasn't buying it.

"We got into this together," she said, referring to Landon and herself. "We're going to get through it together."

"Then you better go to the grocery store," Billy said. "Because I ain't leaving until it's over."

"You don't have to do that," Landon said. "We've got plenty of security."

Billy snorted. "Yeah, one cop who I snuck right by and some secret-agent bozo who got lucky 'cause I didn't see him. And besides, who's watching Maddie and Kerri during the day when you three are split up?"

They had that covered at the moment, between two Virginia Beach police officers and the Wolfman. But Landon didn't know how much longer the police could keep an eye on his entire family. It wouldn't hurt to have a three-hundred-pound NFL lineman hanging around. And this *was* the off-season.

"We could get an air mattress for my home office," Landon said. "Or that couch in our family room could probably hold you."

Billy smiled. "I've got your back," he said. "Just like the old days."

"That's what I'm worried about," Landon said.

61

LANDON JUST WANTED LIFE to get back to some semblance of normalcy, but the week of May 13 was not cooperating. The firm's only assistant, sweet Janaya Young, tearfully resigned on Monday. She thanked both Parker and Landon profusely. Through tears, she told them how much the firm had meant to her. But she had twin boys whose daddy was nowhere to be found, and Janaya had to take care of her family.

Parker and Landon both said they understood. Parker even offered six months' severance pay. "We can't do it all in one check," he said apologetically, "because our cash flow is too tight. But I'll keep you on payroll so you get a check every other week for the next six months, as if you'd never left."

Landon had never been more proud of his partner.

The investigation into the deaths of the firm's lawyers continued to hit brick walls. The Feds were taking the lead in the investigation of the Cessna explosion. But Detective Freeman was still the lead on

Harry's death, and she had practically taken up residence in the offices of McNaughten and Clay. The court had appointed a special prosecutor from another jurisdiction to work with Freeman, thus keeping any privileged information out of the hands of the Virginia Beach Commonwealth's Attorney's office.

Freeman had turned the second-floor conference room into her own private war room, as she shuffled through files and yelled questions down the hall at Landon. The whole thing had an *Alice in Wonderland* feel. A Virginia Beach detective setting up shop in Landon's office, freely accessing the firm's files, shouting down the hall to Landon the same way Harry had done. What other criminal-defense lawyer operated like this?

Things had changed dramatically at the condo as well. Billy Thurston made himself at home, sleeping on the couch most of the night. When Landon woke up, he would nudge Billy, who would traipse back to Landon's home office and sleep for a few more hours on the air mattress. Kerri was feuding with her bosses about their lack of support for her refusal to reveal her sources in the Universal Labs story and had requested two weeks off to sort stuff out. Landon suspected she really just wanted to stay home with Maddie so they wouldn't have to drop their daughter off at day care.

On Wednesday, Detective Freeman told Landon that the VBPD could no longer afford to keep his family under twenty-four-hour watch. They would drive by the condo frequently at night and make their presence known. Freeman had gone to the mat for both Landon and Parker, threatening to resign if anything happened to them, but she had lost the battle. Budgets were tight, and lots of people received death threats. Though she never said it, Landon could guess the dynamics in the upper echelons of the police department. *"Let's see, we can keep our streets safe or we can provide around-the-clock protection for a couple of small-time lawyers. Next question."*

Billy Thurston decided he would pick up the slack and stick to the Reed girls like glue. Except for the three hours a day when he worked out at a local gym, he shadowed them most everywhere they went. The Wolfman, of course, continued to lurk around as well and said he wasn't going away anytime soon. He wasn't very talkative, but Kerri and Landon weren't complaining. If you were in a football game, you wanted Billy Thurston on your side. But if you were trying to catch a serial murderer, the Wolfman was your guy.

According to the Wolfman, Cipher Inc. was conducting its own below-the-radar investigation into who was after the McNaughten and Clay lawyers. It wasn't just that McNaughten and Clay was their firm and that Sean Phoenix took it personally when somebody killed his longtime attorneys. He also appreciated Kerri's reporting and wanted to keep her family safe. Though Kerri never admitted it, Landon suspected that Sean Phoenix was one of the confidential sources she had gone to court to protect.

By Thursday, Landon just needed a break. He was tired of living life like a zebra on a lion preserve, constantly glancing over his shoulder or studying people's faces for the slightest hint of guilt or deception. He was tired of worrying about Maddie and Kerri every second of the day, finding makeshift reasons to text Kerri every few minutes just to make sure his family was okay. He was tired of everyone lowering their eyes when they met him and passing on their condolences, keeping their voices low as if by talking normally they might somehow shatter his fragile psyche. He hadn't been sleeping. He hadn't been exercising. And he still couldn't figure out who was killing his partners or why.

On a whim, he called the three high school quarterbacks he had been mentoring and told them to show up that night at a local football field. They were to bring as many of their offensive linemen as they could. And everyone should be prepared to work out.

That evening, Landon and Billy climbed in Landon's truck and picked up Jake King at his house in Chesapeake. The poor kid was so intimidated by the presence of the Green Bay Packers starting center that he hardly spoke a word on the way to the practice field. When the players all gathered, introductions were made, and the linemen who came looked at Billy wide-eyed. The guy was way bigger than he looked on TV!

They divided up into two groups—quarterbacks and linemen. Before long, most of the linemen were wishing they had never met Billy Thurston. Landon and his quarterbacks fell into a comfortable routine. Passing drills, footwork, pop quizzes about check-down progressions for certain types of coverage. But the linemen were another story.

Billy Thurston had always been an emotional player—one of those guys who was a teddy bear off the field but a vicious animal on it. He started with one-on-one blocking drills and was yelling at the kids almost immediately, forcing them to keep their pads down and get better leverage. When he would get really frustrated, he'd step in and show them how to do it himself, knocking some hapless two-hundred-pound high school lineman flat on his back.

"You can't stand straight up like that!" he'd yell. "You're going to get your quarterback killed!"

Landon smiled to himself from fifty yards away. It had always been, in Billy Thurston's world, the greatest transgression of all—letting a defensive lineman get to your quarterback.

"Doggonit!" Billy was yelling. "You've got to take more pride in yourself than that!"

Before long, the high school kids started catching on, and the intensity of the workout picked up. They began yelling and grunting and egging each other on. "That's more like it!" Billy hollered. "Now you're talking!"

When the linemen were so worn out that they could hardly move, much less block with the technique that Billy insisted on, Landon and Billy brought the players over to the bleachers and sat them down. Billy talked to them first. Discipline. Humility. Take care of your body. And remember, the ability to play football is a gift. Don't take it for granted.

At the end of his bleacher speech, Billy parceled out a few compliments. He told the guys that they had worked hard and that he saw real potential. He loved their attitude. But to be honest, their blocking techniques were pitiful. He wondered if they could work out again in a few days, and the heads started nodding. "Yes, sir," a few of them said.

"All right," Billy said. "I'll see you out here Saturday morning at seven."

It was a tough act to follow, but Landon had to say *something*. He mainly lectured the quarterbacks, telling them that they were only as good as their offensive line. When they got credit for a win, they should deflect it to the guys in the trenches. "We get all the glory, but they do all the work."

Most of them already knew about the personal challenges Landon was facing, but he gave them a few additional details. Somebody was apparently targeting all the lawyers in his firm. And when Landon needed help, Billy had shown up uninvited on Landon's doorstep.

Landon had intended to tell the guys about Billy getting face-planted by one of the other men already guarding the Reed family. He wanted to get the guys laughing. But when he got to that part, he couldn't do it. Instead, he swallowed hard and lost the ability to say much of anything at all. They all waited for a few awkward moments as he struggled to regain his composure.

He decided he'd said enough. "Listen to what this man says," Landon concluded, motioning toward Billy. "Because there are some things in life more important than football."

62

JAKE WAS UBERTALKATIVE on the way home. Three of the linemen on his team had shown up for the workout. They were younger than the others and gave up about fifty pounds to the older guys, but Jake's friends had fought hard and Billy was proud of them. With his dad's trial looming, it must have felt good for Jake to just focus on football for a night.

When they pulled into Jake's driveway, Elias came out and thanked Landon and Billy for what they were doing with the kids. He asked Landon if he could have a word with him in private.

Landon turned to Billy, who shrugged. "I'll hang with Jake," he said.

A few minutes later, Landon was sitting in Elias King's study. He had asked Elias for a towel to sit on so he wouldn't get sweat all over the leather chair, but Elias told him it was the least of his worries. Elias was dressed in khakis and a crisp button-down shirt. He wasn't wearing shoes, but otherwise he could have been at the office on a business-casual day.

The pictures in the office reminded Landon that the King family had seen better days. Mixed among the obligatory pictures of Elias hobnobbing with legal big shots, including a sitting justice of the U.S. Supreme Court, were pictures of Elias and his family. The three of them vacationing together at the beach. A casual shot of Elias with his arm around Julia. A stiff pose of the three of them in the photographer's studio, all wearing blue jeans and white shirts. Jake was the spittin' image of his dad.

"I'm sorry about Brent and Rachel," Elias said. "I never got a chance to express my condolences."

"Thanks," Landon said.

Elias fidgeted with a pen. "I really miss Harry," he said, not looking up. "I miss him for a lot of reasons, not the least of which is that he was in a different league than my current lawyers."

Elias followed with a laundry list of problems with his new attorneys. They had recently completed a mock trial exercise to see how the case would play out. Both mock juries had returned a guilty verdict. Elias's lead lawyer had represented him, and a few other firm lawyers had played the part of the prosecution.

"I learned two things from that," Elias explained. "First, I need to change lawyers. Landon, these guys have no idea how to try a case. They've built a reputation representing high-profile clients, but they almost always plead them out. My case is going to trial."

Elias shifted in his chair, narrowing his eyes. "Second, I learned that I make a terrible witness. As a prosecutor, I always hoped the defendant would take the stand. They generally make an easy target. But as a defendant—" Elias grinned a little to himself—"I knew I was smarter than everybody else. I figured I would make a darned good witness. Plus, I had truth on my side." Elias shook his head and frowned. "But there are too many questions I can't answer. Even the young partner who played the prosecutor made me look like a liar, and he wasn't even very good. In postverdict polling, my credibility was about zero. Cheating on your wife has a way of doing that, you know."

"I don't think Harry was planning on putting you on the stand," Landon said.

"Precisely. But if I don't take the stand, the jury's going to think I'm hiding behind the Fifth Amendment. They'll expect better from a former prosecutor."

It was déjà vu for Landon, the same problems he and Harry had discussed at length. In a way, it made him thankful that they were some other firm's challenges now.

But then Elias looked at him and said the last thing Landon ever expected to hear. "I'd like for you to consider taking my case."

Landon did a double take, as if somebody had just taken a swing at him.

"Hear me out," Elias said quickly, reading the expression on Landon's face. "I've been thinking about this a lot. We could actually work together as cocounsel. I would do the opening, which would give me a chance to speak directly to the jury without having to take the stand. You could do a lot of the witness examination."

It took Landon a moment to realize that the man was serious. He was actually asking a first-year lawyer to help him try his case! The pressure must have been getting to him.

"Harry thought highly of you, and that's saying something. Sure, you lack experience, but I've got experience in spades. Plus, right now you've got a lot of goodwill with the press. I know this sounds pretty Machiavellian, but I could use some of that."

Landon hadn't thought about Elias acting as his own lawyer. As he suggested, this would give him a way to speak to the jury without being cross-examined. But he could use that same strategy with his current lawyers. Why change to a first-year attorney?

"Lately, I've been asking myself what Harry would do," Elias continued. "And that's what led me to this. Harry would try something totally out of the box. Harry would use you to help. He believed in you, Landon."

It sounded crazy, but maybe the idea had some merit. Harry had made a pretty good living off crazy, or at least unconventional. Plus, the approach was bound to create a national media frenzy—publicity the firm could parlay into other cases.

"There's one other thing," Elias said. "And this is nonnegotiable. My current lawyers have hinted that the best way to plant reasonable doubt is to point a finger at Julia." Elias set his jaw. "I'm not willing to do that, Landon. Not under any circumstances. If you take the case, I need you to understand that."

That part didn't bother Landon. In fact, he admired it. "I never liked that strategy anyway," he said.

"Does that mean you'll think about it?"

"I'll think about it," Landon said. "And I'll give you my answer by Monday."

63

"THIS IS WHY I BECAME A LAWYER," Landon said. But Kerri was shaking her head. They had been discussing the matter at the kitchen table for thirty minutes. It was nearly midnight, and neither Landon nor Kerri was giving an inch. Not only was Kerri against taking on the case; she was still proposing that Landon leave the firm altogether. Billy Thurston was within earshot, sitting in the family room, working on his second bowl of cereal and watching *SportsCenter*.

"Billy, what do you think?" Kerri asked.

"My friends are for it. My friends are against it. I'm for my friends." Billy's eyes never left the television.

"This is the firm that gave me a chance. This is what it means to be loyal," Landon said. "I can't turn my back on this."

"What would it hurt to at least call the station in D.C.?" Kerri asked. "Just to see if the job's still open?"

"For me, moving to D.C. is not an option."

Kerri was picking at a loose thread on the place mat. "What about our family, Landon? I can't sleep at night because I'm worried about what I would do without you. Every jet that flies over reminds me that it might have been you on that Cessna. I know you feel like you owe the firm, but that firm is cursed."

She shot a glance at Billy. "I mean, look at us. We can't even leave the condo without some kind of protection. We need a new start."

Landon was tired of new starts. He was tired of acknowledging to a whole new set of folks that he was the guy who had cheated on his teammates. Of trying to convince them that he had changed.

He couldn't keep running. There was an old saying in Alcoholics Anonymous: "Wherever you go, there you are." He knew it was true of him as well. Wherever he went, the point-shaving scandal followed. At some point, he had to just hunker down and *prove* to people that he could be trusted.

"Kerri, we can't outrun this. Just like we've never been able to outrun what I did in college—"

"I'm not saying we can outrun it," Kerri interrupted.

"Let me finish, okay?"

"I'm just saying, if this were about running, I wouldn't have waited two years for you to get out of jail. This is about our family."

Landon blew out a breath. "Is it my turn?"

"Yes." She didn't sound convinced.

"The only way we get out of danger is by finding out who's killing the firm's lawyers and why. And we're not going to get that done by moving to D.C."

"Whoa!" Billy said from the family room couch. It was a top-ten play on *SportsCenter*, an in-your-face-dunk by some NBA rookie sensation. "He posterized that dude!"

Landon shook his head. His life was like a bad sitcom. "Turn that thing off," he said. "Get out here and join us."

"I'm trying to be the Swiss," Billy shot back. "The Swiss don't take sides."

"Get your fat Swiss tail out here!" Kerri said. "We need your help."

Billy mumbled under his breath but lumbered to the table. If he was going to be the mediator, he said, he needed some paper and a pen. He drew two lines, dividing the page into thirds, and told Landon and Kerri to give him a list of the pros and cons for each of three options—moving to D.C., staying in Virginia Beach and taking the King case, or staying in Virginia Beach and not taking the case.

"A pro for moving to D.C. is that maybe Landon wouldn't get killed," Kerri said.

"Okay," Billy said. He wrote down *Landon stays alive*. "You sure that should go in the *pro* column?"

Kerri didn't smile, so he batted his eyes at her. "I'm just sayin', with Junior here out of the way—maybe you and me?"

Billy's offbeat sense of humor managed to lighten the mood a little and got Kerri and Landon talking in less threatening tones. The list grew lopsided in favor of D.C. even though Landon did his best to come up with alternative ways of making the same arguments against it. He believed in Elias King's innocence. He wanted to help Jacob. And he wanted to prove that he was the kind of lawyer who would never turn his back on a firm or a client. "Plus, we've got the ocean here," he said.

"When's the last time we went to the ocean?" Kerri asked.

When Billy was done writing, most of the factors weighed in favor of moving. None of them knew for sure that moving to D.C. would make things safer for Landon, but their instincts told them that disentangling from the firm would help. Kerri could be a rock-star journalist on a big stage in D.C. With everything Landon had learned under the tutelage of Harry McNaughton, he could start his own firm. In fact, it might be easier to open his own shop than it would be to pick up the pieces at McNaughton and Clay.

Billy turned the page around so they could both see the list. The choice was obvious. It was time to bail.

"You want my advice?" Billy asked.

"Sure," Kerri and Landon said in unison.

"You guys are both people of faith, and I respect that about you. So here's what I'm thinking. Kerri calls this station in D.C. If the job's still open and she gets it, then God wants you to move to D.C. If not, you stay here." He looked down at the list. The column for taking Elias's case was far longer than the one for not taking it. "And if you stay, you take the case."

It felt like a cop-out to Landon—let the circumstances dictate what God wants. But Kerri liked the approach.

"Makes sense to me," she said. "I think it leaves room for God to do his thing."

She reached under the table and took Landon's hand. He swallowed a lump in his throat and nodded his head. Billy was right about one thing—if God didn't want them moving to D.C., he would close that door. But this took it out of Landon's hands, and that was hard.

"I guess that works," Landon said. He turned to Kerri. "I'd like to finish Elias's case first, but if you're not okay with that, then I won't."

"I don't think it's a good idea. Not with everything else that's been happening."

"Well then," Billy announced. "I see my work here is done." He stood from the table and headed back to *SportsCenter*.

///

The next morning, after Kerri had left, Landon came out and shook Billy awake on the couch. The big man grunted and rolled over. Landon shook his shoulder again, and Billy squinted, opened an eye, and muttered something like "lea' me 'lone."

"Kerri said she wants to stay in Virginia Beach," Landon said. "She woke up this morning and said that she had prayed about it half the night. She said this was our home; that I needed to take that case; that God wouldn't let anything happen to me."

Billy sat up, rubbing his eyes. He had a serious case of bed hair.

"Did you hear what I said?" Landon asked.

"Reverse psychology," Billy said. "It works every time."

///

The trial was scheduled to begin exactly six weeks from the day Landon was rehired as Elias King's attorney. He worked fourteen-hour days. Seven days a week. Billy Thurston saw more of Kerri and Maddie than Landon did.

The only thing Elias King had in common with Harry McNaughten was his superb ability as a trial lawyer. His style couldn't have been more different from that of Landon's mentor. Elias was a control freak. He and Landon scrutinized every detail of the case. They wrote out their witness examinations question by question. They brought in witnesses and grilled them for hours, preparing them for cross-examination by Franklin Sherman. They took turns playing an adverse witness while the other one worked on his cross-examination. For Landon, it was a month of trial-advocacy boot camp with a drill sergeant who was pumping caffeine by the gallon and had his own freedom at stake. All of this while answering occasional questions from Detective Freeman and worrying about cash flow in his role as a new firm partner.

As the trial approached, Landon also worried about Parker Clausen. The man was becoming more unkempt, wearing the same faded jeans and T-shirts every day. A few times, Landon smelled liquor on Parker's breath by midafternoon. His office, which used to be relatively clean, was starting to look like a scene from *Hoarders*.

But Landon didn't have time for those problems now. There was so much to be done on the King case and so little time to do it.

On the bright side, each new day that passed seemed to lessen the threat of further violence against firm members. Billy Thurston was sticking with Maddie and Kerri. The Wolfman—or occasionally another operative from Cipher Inc.—was always hanging around someplace. Detective Freeman finally finished her analysis of the firm files and now only occasionally stopped by or called with another question.

"Any leads?" Landon would ask.

"I'm working on it."

Two weeks before trial, Landon still didn't know who had killed Erica Jensen. He had learned that Julia King had wrestled with depression her entire life and had been diagnosed as bipolar. But that didn't make her a killer. Even if she was, that defense was off-limits.

The net result was that Landon and Elias were preparing a case of counterpunches—the precise strategy that Harry had once eschewed. *"The jury will want to know who did it,"* Harry had said, and those words kept ringing in Landon's ears, haunting him.

Elias, on the other hand, clung to the presumption of innocence. "All we have to do is create reasonable doubt," he reminded Landon on numerous occasions.

Landon didn't argue—since they had no alternative suspect, what was the point? But deep down, he suspected that Elias was wrong and Harry was right. If they couldn't prove who murdered Erica Jensen, the jury would pin it on Elias.

"Reasonable doubt" was lawyer-speak. The jury just wanted to know who did it.

64

FOR A WEEK, the weather was hot and humid with highs reaching one hundred degrees, making global warming seem immediate and real. The forecast for Saturday, June 15, was no different. Possible afternoon thunderstorms. Light wind. Lots of sun and dripping with humidity.

Kerri wondered why anybody in their right mind would go to Busch Gardens on a day like this.

As it turned out, the park was jammed with thousands of people who could think of no better way to spend their Saturday than walking around on asphalt and standing in line with hundreds of other sweaty park guests, crushed together, winding their way to the front of the line, all to enjoy two or three minutes of bliss on one of the park's big roller coasters.

As Kerri hustled through the park, heading toward the Festhaus at the far end, she looked with envy at the "normal" families. There were moms and dads with kids Maddie's age, studying their maps and trying to decide what ride to go on. Eating cotton candy. Waiting in line at the water fountain. Watching the Clydesdales. Laughing together. Even arguing with each other.

Is this the way normal families spend a Saturday afternoon?

She and Landon were burning the candle at both ends, and Kerri was worried that Maddie was paying the price. The Elias King trial seemed to have Landon handcuffed to the office. Kerri's job had its own set of unreasonable demands. Add to that their 315-pound live-in guest and a mysterious man in a black T-shirt from Cipher Inc. following them around all day, and you had the ingredients for an extremely dysfunctional childhood.

Since the deaths of Brent Benedict and Rachel Strach, Kerri had been feeling separation anxiety whenever she was away from her daughter. Even on days like today, when she knew that Maddie would be safe with Billy, Kerri couldn't help thinking about the what-ifs. There was still a serial killer on the loose and no serious leads to find him, and Landon had been letting his guard down lately. "God will take care of us," he would tell Kerri. She agreed with that, of course, but she didn't think God wanted them to be stupid.

She was at Busch Gardens today because Sean Phoenix had called and requested a meeting. For reasons he didn't share, the meeting couldn't take place at the Cipher headquarters in northern Virginia. Instead, on the theory that the safest place to meet was in the middle of a crowd, he had set up this meeting at the theme park on a busy Saturday afternoon.

Landon and Billy knew that Kerri had to meet with a source, but she couldn't tell them who. Landon didn't like Kerri running off on her own like this, but he knew the Wolfman would be trailing at a distance. Given the amount of time Landon had been spending at the office, he wasn't winning many arguments lately anyway.

The Festhaus was a two-thousand-seat festival hall where guests were entertained by dancers and enjoyed traditional German food. While the crowd ate, the dancers taught the polka and re-created a bit of authentic

German Oktoberfest spirit. In other words, it was like a big German tailgate party.

The building had a Bavarian feel to it. When Kerri stepped inside, a wave of cool air hit her face as her eyes adjusted to the semidarkness. There were picnic tables scattered throughout the hall and a big stage in the middle. Kerri placed her sunglasses on top of her head and scanned the place. She was fifteen minutes late and didn't see Sean Phoenix anywhere. She pulled out her phone and dialed his number.

"May I help you?" a deep voice said behind her.

Startled, she turned around quickly. "You about gave me a heart attack."

"Sorry about that," Sean said, flashing a big grin and working the dimples. He looked relaxed in his shorts, T-shirt, dockside shoes, and baseball cap with his sunglasses propped on the bill. "You looked lost."

Kerri hadn't eaten since breakfast, and Sean talked her into going through the line with him. She grabbed some German bratwurst, a huge piece of chocolate cake, and a drink. She followed Sean to a picnic table at the far end of the hall. He placed his tray at the end of the long table, a good distance from the family of six at the other end who all looked exhausted.

Kerri sat facing the middle of the hall, and Sean squeezed in next to her, rather than on the opposite side. She looked askance at him, but he shrugged it off. "I never put my back to the crowd," he said.

She thought about moving to the other side of the table but decided to slide down a little instead.

"I don't bite," he said.

"That's what they all say."

She thought about the fuss she had made over the pictures of Rachel and Landon and knew she would have a hard time explaining things if that same photographer was lurking about. But it was different, she told herself. There would be no touching or kissing or dropping somebody off at their apartment because they had been drinking too much.

Unlike Landon's meetings with Rachel, this one was strictly business.

Yet Sean seemed determined to lighten things up and suggested a game where they would pick out a family and tell that family's story. Sean was a gifted people-watcher, and he picked up on little hints that Kerri hadn't noticed before. As they ate, he gave her an informal clinic on facial expressions and body language and even pointed out a few men who were stealing glances at other women when their wives weren't looking. Including, to Kerri's embarrassment, a guy they caught staring at her on two separate occasions. The man tried to pass it off like maybe he was just surveying the picnic tables, looking for a friend. But when his gaze lingered on Kerri, Sean lifted his beer in a mock toast, and the man looked quickly away.

Just when they had taken their first bite of German chocolate cake, having finished off the bratwurst, the music started. A band was lowered in a gazebo from the ceiling onto the stage, and brightly clad dancers, the boys in knickers and the girls in frilly dresses, came waltzing arm in arm down the middle aisle. They smiled and chanted and taught the crowd a few German beer songs. The audience, including Sean and Kerri, raised their glasses for a traditional German toast.

The second time the dancers scoured the crowd for volunteers, Kerri saw it coming. One of the guys eyed her and started weaving his way back to their table. She tried to shrink into her seat and duck her head, but it didn't work. He bowed politely in front of her and asked her for a dance.

"No thanks," she said. She scowled in case the guy was a slow learner.

"Nonsense!" Sean said. He took her by one elbow, and the persistent little German dancer took her by the other. Before Kerri knew what was happening, one of the female dancers had latched on to Sean as well, and the two couples were on their way to the dance floor to join in a German polka.

Sometime during that song, Kerri's perception of Sean began to change. He was no longer just a sophisticated spy; he acted like a little kid, smiling and singing and twirling the girls around. He puffed out his chest, tilted his head back, and laughed. He was a terrible dancer, but he didn't seem to care. Kerri, by contrast, felt stiff as a board and self-conscious, counting down the seconds until she could get back to her seat.

Toward the end of the song, Sean managed to extricate himself from his dance partner and grabbed Kerri's hand, turning her around in a rough approximation of what the other dancers were doing. She had to smile in spite of herself, and she somehow managed to keep from tripping.

The German dancers smiled and thanked them when the song was over, and Sean let go of Kerri's hand. Like a perfect gentleman, he escorted her back to her seat while the dancers started prowling around for their next set of victims.

"If you ever do that to me again, you're dead," Kerri said.

Sean grinned, his eyes sparkling. "I've been threatened by less beautiful women."

She ignored the comment but this time stayed on the opposite side of the picnic table.

65

WHEN THEY FINISHED THE CAKE, Sean leaned forward and lowered his voice. The smile was gone, the eyes serious. Because the band was still playing, Kerri found herself leaning forward as well, making sure she heard every word.

"Her name was Fatinah Najar," Sean said. "She was a beautiful Syrian woman who was once part of the Hezbollah. I flipped her and she became one of my assets, which is a nice way of saying that we used her to get inside information from the terrorist organization and some high-ranking Syrian officials. Do you know what the name Fatinah means?"

Kerri shrugged. She was thrown off by this new direction. But her source was talking now, and she knew the number one rule: keep him talking.

"I don't have a clue," she said.

"It means 'fascinating, alluring, or enchanting.'" Sean paused for a moment and looked down at the table. "She was all of that," he said, lifting his eyes back to Kerri. "She had these beautiful almond eyes and this laid-back Mediterranean personality. As a little girl, she lost her dad during an Israeli bombing raid. One year later, on the anniversary, her mom died as a suicide bomber. Fatinah bought the Hezbollah party line until she turned twenty-five. That's when I met her. We fell in love. Eventually she became one of us."

This was, Kerri knew, the woman she had heard the rumors about. The reason Sean had left the CIA and started Cipher Inc. Sean did a quick visual sweep of the room before continuing, pain pulling at the edges of his mouth.

"A year later, the Syrians arrested us and put her in the cell next to mine. They released me unharmed but not until after they had interrogated me and made me listen to Fatinah being tortured and raped. After my release, we could have rescued her. We had enough agents and firepower to break her out of that place. But the guys in suits decided we couldn't risk it politically."

Sean seemed to be in another place now. He had a faraway look, describing what had happened in a calm and detached tone devoid of feeling. It was almost as if he wouldn't allow his emotions to be part of the equation anymore, for fear that he wouldn't be able to handle where they might take him.

He told Kerri about his short-lived attempt to rescue his lover, cut off by his own fellow agents.

"The Syrians killed her, Kerri, because she wouldn't talk. They cut out her tongue and let her bleed to death. She probably choked on her own blood."

The thought was appalling to Kerri, but she didn't flinch. She had her hands folded together, forearms resting on the table, leaning forward. She kept her eyes on his. "I'm sorry," she said. It occurred to her that the average American, the average Busch Gardens guest on this hot summer day, had no idea how much people like Sean Phoenix and Fatinah Najar had sacrificed to protect their freedom, to make days like this possible.

"Victor Carson made the call," Sean continued, referring to the head of the CIA. Kerri saw a flash of flint in the blue eyes, the same look she remembered from their first meeting. "He consulted his top lawyer, a midlevel bureaucrat from the State Department, and the two of them decided to just let her die. They probably discussed it over a Scotch and martini."

Sean clenched his jaw, and Kerri could tell that time had not healed the wounds. She wondered if Sean had ever truly loved anyone again.

"For the past three years, I've had some folks investigating Mr. Carson. I've now got sources and documents for everything I'm about to tell you."

He paused so the magnitude of what he was saying could sink in. He had dirt on the head of the CIA, and he was about to entrust Kerri with the story! It might not be Watergate, but it was bigger than anything she had done before. Even the Universal Labs story was child's play compared to this.

"Carson has files on D.C.'s top politicians," Sean continued. "Democrats *and* Republicans. And we've got copies. He's used the information in those files for blackmail. There's a reason the CIA's budget never gets cut. A reason that Carson is never called to the Hill for a congressional investigation.

"I'm big on loyalty, Kerri. You proved yours when you protected our sources in the Universal Labs story. Later, when we leave the park and you get in your car, reach under the front seat, and you'll find a copy of my entire Carson file. You can take it from there."

Kerri nodded. She had stepped through the looking glass again, into the Cipher Inc. dreamworld where stories fell from trees. Sean could have planted this story with any one of a thousand other journalists, many of whom had more experience and credibility than she did. "I appreciate your trust," was all she could think to say.

Sean reached out and touched her hand. It wasn't a romantic touch—more like a point of emphasis.

"I know that I'm emotionally involved with this," he said. "And I want you to verify everything. I would like nothing more than for Mr.

Carson to get what he's got coming. But that's why I'm taking myself out of the equation. It's got to be evaluated by somebody whose judgment isn't clouded by revenge."

"I understand," Kerri said.

At some point, the Festhaus band had stopped playing and the dancers had retreated to their break room, where they would wait for the next show. The family of six had left as well. But Kerri hardly noticed. Her life, already a chaotic mess, was about to go to the next level of stress. She could already feel the pressure.

"We'd better get going," Sean said.

"Yeah," Kerri agreed. "We'd better get going."

///

Sean walked with Kerri toward the main gate, keeping one eye on the other guests. He glanced a few times at her profile, struck by how beautiful she was.

On the way, the conversation turned to Landon's upcoming trial. Sean listened intently as Kerri shared her fears about her husband's safety and her concerns that Landon was defending a guilty man.

"Who does Landon think killed Erica Jensen?" Sean asked.

"That's the whole problem. He has no idea."

They were walking by the pasture where the Clydesdale horses were grazing. "They're beautiful animals, aren't they?" Sean asked.

"Yeah," Kerri said, though she sounded distracted.

"That was enthusiastic."

"Sorry, I've just got a lot on my mind."

"Why don't I put our folks on it?" Sean suggested. "We can work behind the scenes so nobody knows. If we figure something out, I can tell you, and you can decide whether to share it with Landon."

Kerri seemed to straighten her shoulders a little. "That would be tremendous," she said.

They rode the tram together to Kerri's car. Sean was parked in a different lot but had insisted on accompanying her. A few rows away, they saw the Wolfman milling around.

"One last thing," Sean said, as they approached her vehicle. "Before the King trial starts, I'm going to have the Wolfman deliver four Kevlar vests—one for you, one for Elias, one for Landon, and one for Billy Thurston. Do me a favor and wear them to and from court. And buy Thurston a suit coat, so everybody won't know you've got them on."

"Do you know something I don't?" Kerri asked.

"No. I just need my prized reporter safe."

He opened her car door and had her check under the seat before he closed it. She held out the file for him to see.

"How'd they get in?" she asked.

Sean smiled. "It's what we do."

He told her to be safe, closed the door, and stood in the parking lot as she drove away.

She reminded him so much of Fatinah. He could tell, though he knew Kerri wouldn't admit it even to herself, that she felt the chemistry too.

Landon Reed was a lucky man. He had married way over his head, way out of his league, and he would probably be the first one to tell you so.

Sean liked Landon. The kid had guts. But still, Sean had to wonder: What kind of chemistry would exist between him and Kerri if Landon Reed weren't in the picture?

///

On the way home, Kerri's head was buzzing with the reality that she and Landon, just another young couple trying to make ends meet, were now in the vortex of some pretty big stuff. Even the Elias King trial, which had seemed all-important just a few days ago, would be dwarfed by the potential story about the director of the CIA. That story would dominate network news for months. First the director. Then every politician who had yielded to his threats. Her mind raced with the implications of what was coming. Assuming, of course, that everything checked out.

She got off at an exit in Newport News, found a hotel parking lot, and pulled out the file. She spent forty-five minutes glancing through every piece of paper.

It checked out, all right. Not surprisingly, Cipher Inc. had done its homework.

The next few weeks were going to get very interesting.

66

JUDGE TAJ DEEGAN, a former prosecutor, had been on the Chesapeake Circuit Court bench for less than a year. At forty-one, she was the youngest judge in the city. She had a big frame and carried around a few extra pounds, which rounded out her face and made her look more imposing. She wore small black reading glasses that she propped on the end of her nose. She had a quick wit and a dry sense of humor. Nobody outworked her.

The woman had a Horatio Alger story, a single mom who had taken college and law school classes at night while working for a private security firm during the day. She had gained notoriety as the lead prosecutor against a Muslim imam accused of honor killings. During that case, she survived a courtroom shoot-out in Virginia Beach Circuit Court and became a legend. One year later, when an opening came up on the Chesapeake bench, Deegan changed her residence and was immediately appointed by the politicians. She was a local hero who would bring diversity to the bench and believed in law and order. Who could vote against that?

On Monday afternoon, one week before the scheduled start of the Elias King trial, Landon found himself in Deegan's courtroom, arguing a number of pretrial motions.

The most important issue was the role of Elias King at trial. Landon and Elias had filed a motion informing the court that Elias intended to participate in his own defense. Franklin Sherman had objected, claiming that the defense was simply gaming the system by trying to find a way for King to testify without having to endure cross-examination.

"Judge, we're dealing with constitutional rights here," Landon argued. "Mr. King is entitled to participate in his own defense, and he's also entitled to assert his Fifth Amendment rights. I'm sure in your days as a prosecutor you had numerous defendants represent themselves and never take the stand. If a defendant can handle the entire case, he can certainly handle just a portion of it."

After she had heard from both lawyers, Judge Deegan removed her reading glasses and hunched forward a little, rounding her shoulders. "You're right, Mr. Reed. I've seen many defendants represent them-selves." She paused and looked at Elias. "It's generally not a good idea. In fact, I can't remember a single one of them winning."

She sighed and sat back in her chair. "But Mr. Reed is correct—the defendant has a constitutional right to do so. However, Mr. Sherman is also correct in that this is not an unqualified right. It can be revoked by the court for misconduct. And if this court suspects that Mr. King is doing what the prosecution suggests and using this as a ploy to tes-tify without taking the stand, the court will not hesitate to revoke that right."

She fixed her no-nonsense gaze on Landon and Elias again. "I think it becomes especially problematic if Mr. King gives an opening state-ment, which would, by necessity, address factual matters in the case. So I'm putting both of you on notice right now. If Mr. King decides to give his own opening statement, despite the fact that he's represented by very capable legal counsel, I will be inclined to rule that he has waived his Fifth Amendment privilege on any factual matters addressed in that opening statement of which he has personal knowledge. The same will be true if he examines witnesses using questions that sound more like narratives than questions. Is that clear?"

"Yes, Your Honor," Landon said.

Deegan flashed a quick grin showing straight white teeth. "Good. What's the next issue?"

Forty-five minutes later, in the parking lot, Elias took an optimistic view of things. "I was going to let you do the opening anyway," he said. "I'll do the closing, because by then it won't matter if I waive my Fifth Amendment right. They can't force me to take the stand at that stage."

It was an interesting strategy, one that Harry McNaughten would have liked. It would be one more reason why the press, already focused on the case, would be tracking their every move.

"We've got a lot of work to do," Landon said.

67

THE DAYS BLURRED TOGETHER in the final week before trial. Landon spent nearly every waking moment at the office, and most of the time, Elias King was there with him. Detective Freeman breezed through once in a while to inform Landon and Parker Clausen that she still didn't know who wanted them dead.

Elias had commandeered one of the empty offices on the second floor. The conference room became the Elias King war room, used to store most of the case files. When she came, Freeman set up shop in yet another empty office. If there was one thing McNaughten and Clay had, it was plenty of space.

Out of respect, nobody did an ounce of work in Harry's old office. In the back of his mind, Landon had plans to move into that office if he won the King case. Harry would have wanted it that way. But if he lost, Landon would stay in the first-year associate's office that he had been occupying since the day he walked in the door. For that matter, if he lost, Landon would probably vacate the firm altogether.

But he didn't have time to think about the future right now. Every morning he wrote out a two-page list of things to do, and by the end of the day he had added more items than he had crossed off. He wondered how any lawyer ever got ready for a big felony case.

That was one of many reasons it surprised him late Friday morning when Elias King stuck his head in Landon's office and asked if he needed a break.

"What I need is about four more weeks," Landon said.

"Jake's in his last day at an Old Dominion football camp," Elias said. "I was thinking about going over and catching the seven-on-seven scrimmage. Want to come?"

Landon looked at the man as if he'd just suggested they go rob a bank. They had a trial coming up in three days! A murder trial. *Elias's* murder trial.

"Are you serious?"

"Look, we haven't taken a break in about four weeks. We're as ready to go as we're going to be." Elias paused and swallowed. "This might be my last chance to see him play."

"Why don't you go on over? I've still got a ton of stuff to do before Monday."

Elias hung his head, as if his last friend in the world had just betrayed him. "The terms of my bail only allow me to leave the house for meetings with my lawyers. If you go with me, we would probably be covered. Plus, it would mean a lot to Jake. To be honest, if I show up with you, he would think it was cool. If I show up on my own, he'd probably be annoyed."

Against his better judgment, Landon agreed to take a few hours off. He called Billy Thurston, who decided to ride over with them.

///

When they got to the field, the shaded spots on the bleachers were already taken, so the three men picked an isolated spot about halfway up where the sun could beat down on them. Elias still had on the white starched shirt and striped red tie that he had worn to the office. He loosened the tie and rolled up his sleeves. He didn't have any sunglasses, so he squinted at the field. Landon wondered if the man had ever been to one of Jake's games.

Landon was more comfortable. The past three days, he had rolled out of bed, taken a quick shower, and thrown on shorts and a T-shirt before heading to the office. No sense shaving—that took time.

Billy Thurston had on a pair of gym shorts, a Packers workout shirt, and an old Packers cap that he wore backward. The cap was frayed around the edges, and the white trim had turned brown. It looked like it had been around since the Vince Lombardi days.

When Jake noticed them, he broke into a smile, and Landon gave him a thumbs-up. When his team got the ball, Jake threw an incomplete pass on the first play and an interception on the second. He jogged back to the sidelines, head down. He avoided eye contact with the three men in the bleachers.

"I think that receiver ran the wrong route," Billy said. "That one's not on Jake."

The next series was a little better, and Jake's team marched down the field until the drive stalled at the other team's twenty. But on the third series, Jake threw another pick, and Billy Thurston had seen enough. He stood up.

"What are you doing?" Landon asked.

"I can't watch this anymore," Billy said. He had his hands on his hips. "Those receivers are terrible. I'm going down to talk to Jake's linemen."

Billy marched down to the sidelines, and, within minutes, he was coaching. He shouted encouragement to the kids and demonstrated techniques when they came to the sidelines. The camp coaches took a backseat and let Billy do his thing.

Landon took a quick glance around. If a sniper wanted to take him out, this would be a good opportunity. He and Elias King were sitting ducks. If Kerri were here, she might be having second thoughts about Billy's expertise as a bodyguard.

"Don't let that daughter of yours grow up without knowing her daddy," Elias said. He was squinting at the field, and the comment came out of the blue.

"She won't."

"All those hours at the office. Running around prosecuting big-time criminals. Literally putting my life on the line to put those thugs behind bars. And where am I now?" Elias looked at Landon briefly, as if his lawyer might actually have an answer. Landon kept his eyes glued to the field.

"My kid's a teenager, and he hardly knows me," Elias continued. "Let's face it; there's a good chance I won't be there for his high school graduation or to take him to college or to see him get married."

It was the first time Elias had talked this frankly about losing the case. He said it with a sense of melancholy, and Landon had half an urge to give the man a pep talk. Instead, he remained silent. It was like one of those moments in a Shakespearean tragedy where the central figure took the stage for a few moments of introspection. Who was Landon to interfere?

"Julia always struggled with depression. We had different ideas about how to raise Jake. When you come home at the end of a long and stressful day, you're supposed to feel a sense of relaxation. But I always felt like I was stepping into a war zone, full of innuendos and subtle jabs and this undercurrent that I wasn't being the kind of father I needed to be."

"So you spent more time at the office?"

"Yeah. At work, I was like this demigod. There was always plenty of excitement and danger. Recently, Erica infused a new sense of life and enthusiasm into what I did. I never thought I would be *that* guy, the one who lives a double life. And I know Erica never wanted to be *that* woman."

Elias watched his son complete a pass and shouted some encouragement to him. Jake jogged back to the huddle with a little more confidence, his head high. But the kid's footwork was still a mess, and Landon felt a pang of guilt for abandoning Jake over the summer.

Elias leaned back so his elbows were resting on the row of bleachers behind him. But then Jake overthrew a receiver and Elias leaned forward again. "What's he doing wrong?" he asked.

Landon gave a charitable analysis of Jake's footwork and decision making. He ended with a breakdown of the psychological factors. "It's mostly a matter of confidence. Jake sees the right throw, but he doesn't trust his instincts. He hesitates, and that gives defenders a chance to break on the ball. He needs to be making throws the second the receiver cuts."

Elias nodded his head and there was a long silence before he spoke again. "If we lose this case, could you spend a little time with Jake? The kid needs a steady male influence in his life. I've talked it over with Julia, and we'd want you to be his godfather or something along those lines. He could spend as much time with you as you'd be willing to give him."

The request caught Landon off guard, but he realized that this had been the whole point of their field trip. Elias King had allowed himself to think the unthinkable. What if they lost? Elias and Julia had talked. Elias was like a man with a terminal disease putting his affairs in order.

"Sure," Landon said. "It would be an honor."

Elias reached over and patted Landon on the knee. It was an awkward moment; Elias wasn't great at showing his emotions.

"Thanks," he said.

///

On the way home, Billy drove and Elias rode shotgun, with Landon and Jake in the backseat. Jake was down in the mouth, describing his performance as "pretty lousy."

"You can't let one day get you down," Landon said. "I remember some days when I threw three or four interceptions just trying to put the ball into places it didn't belong. It's better to just throw the ball away than to try and make something out of nothing."

"You talking about those days you got paid to throw those interceptions or the days you did it for free?" Billy called out from the front seat. He glanced in the mirror, a smirk on his face.

"Nobody's talking to you," Landon said. But he noticed that Jake had managed a small grin, his first one since getting in the car.

"You know what a center is?" Landon asked Jake.

"No, sir."

"A three-hundred-pound quarterback without any brains."

Jake smiled broadly. But the kid didn't dare laugh out loud. Nobody but Landon could take shots at Billy Thurston and get away with it.

68

LANDON GOT HIS OWN PEP TALK on Monday morning, the first day of the Elias King trial.

He had been awake half the night thinking about it, lying on his back, eyes wide open, worrying about a hundred tasks he hadn't had the chance to complete. For the most part, he believed in his client's innocence, though it felt strange starting a murder trial without knowing for sure what had really happened. In his law school dreams, he had seen himself defending innocent criminal defendants, Perry Mason style, the guardian of justice. Unfortunately, nothing in the real world was so black-and-white. And nothing in law school had prepared him for this.

The alarm went off at five, but the only person it woke up was Kerri. Landon was already at the kitchen table, poring over some notes. Kerri gave him a kiss, said, "Good morning," and fixed him a cup of coffee and two pieces of toast. They sat at the breakfast table and spoke softly, trying not to disturb Billy, who was sleeping on the couch, rustling around as they talked. Eventually he threw off the covers, went to the bathroom, fixed a large bowl of cereal, and joined them.

"You ready?" he asked Landon.

"Don't have any choice."

Billy snorted. "You're gonna kick butt and take names. Don't give me that poor country lawyer routine."

"I wish I had your confidence," Landon said, rubbing the back of his stiff neck. Too many hours hunched over his work.

His comment made Billy stop midbite, a highly unusual occurrence. He leaned back in the kitchen chair, which creaked in protest. "You remember that game when Dave O'Shannon got hurt?"

Landon remembered it well. It was his redshirt freshman year, and his role was to be O'Shannon's backup. It was the first time he had played when the game was on the line.

"I remember you came into that huddle with your voice all high and squeaky," Billy said, chuckling to himself. Kerri had heard the story before, but she still couldn't resist a little smirk. "You sounded like one of those Vienna choirboys. I remember looking at my buddies on the line and rolling my eyes like, 'I hope O'Shannon can walk it off.' I mean, no offense, but your legs looked like toothpicks that year."

"Yeah," Landon admitted, "I felt like my knees might buckle at any minute."

"That first series, you looked like Jake out there. Two handoffs and an incompletion. You couldn't wait to get off the field."

"It wasn't quite that bad."

"It was worse. I remember checking on O'Shannon, and he said he was out for the game. I came over, slapped you on the helmet, and told you to get your head up, the team needed you."

"I remember that," Landon said.

Kerri sat there, elbow on the table, chin in her left hand, her right around a coffee cup, taking it all in. Landon knew she loved stories like this: the good ole days, before everything went awry.

"Then at the end of the half, when we somehow managed to get into field-goal range, the coach sends in this nice little running play so that we can run down the clock and get three points before halftime." Billy looked at Kerri with wide eyes, as if he was still shocked at what happened next. "And what does my boy Landon do?"

Kerri raised her eyebrows, playing along.

"He changes the play in the huddle. Calls for a corner pattern to our best receiver. Somebody says, 'You sure?' But I nudged my buddies on the line. 'Hey, I can block for a guy like this.'"

"Yeah, and you were nowhere to be found when I went back to the sidelines," Landon said.

This brought a belly laugh from Billy. "Kerri, after he overthrew that receiver and went back to the sidelines, Coach grabbed him by the face mask and jerked his head left and right. He had a few choice words for your husband's play selection." He flipped a wrist toward Landon. "Tell your honey what you learned from that."

Landon smiled. "A lot of players jog to the sidelines after they mess up and keep their helmets on. That way the ESPN cameras won't catch the look on their face. But after that play, whenever I messed up, I always took my helmet off and carried it to the sidelines."

"Okay, so as I was saying," Billy continued, his enthusiasm for the story coming through in his tone. "We get to the fourth quarter, and we're still in the game, and Coach sends in some other cockamamy running play, and darned if your boy here didn't audible out of that one too."

"In my defense, I saw one of their cornerbacks creeping up to the line of scrimmage. I thought we could burn him with a crossing pattern."

"And that's exactly what he did," Billy said proudly. He took another bite of cereal, but he wasn't finished, so he continued with his mouth full. "He throws a perfect pass, and our guy takes it to the house and Landon comes running back to the sidelines getting congratulated by everyone except Coach. Eventually Coach comes down and stands beside him and says something under his breath like, 'You got the guts of a cat burglar, kid. But if that play hadn't worked, you'd be holding a clipboard the rest of the season.'"

"So what does Billy do?" Landon asked. He was tag-teaming the story now, his concerns about the trial far away. This was one of the great bonding moments between Landon and his center, and Landon relished the story as much as Billy.

"Billy was standing right behind us," Landon continued. "I think he heard Coach chew me out, so he steps up beside us, as if he hadn't heard a thing, and he says, 'Great play call, Reed. Coach, that reminds me of that play you called in the Tennessee game last year. Must be ole Landon here was paying attention.'"

Landon and Billy shared a laugh. "I remember Coach looked at me like, 'Oh yeah, I forgot about that. Maybe this kid's not so dumb after all.'"

Billy had finished his cereal, and he lifted the bowl to his mouth, drinking the milk. "Anyway," he said, wiping his mouth with the back of his hand, "that's the Landon that Elias King needs this week. You might have made some boneheaded mistakes your junior year with those bookies, but nobody ever doubted that you were a leader. Nobody ever questioned your confidence."

Kerri was nodding her head. "Frequently wrong, never in doubt," she said. "That's the Landon Reed I know."

Just in case that wasn't enough, Kerri orchestrated one more motivational event. Right before Landon and Billy headed off for the first day of trial, Maddie gave her dad a present. Landon opened it and stared at the maroon and gold power tie—the colors of Southeastern University.

"Have a good day in court, Daddy," Maddie said.

Landon picked her up and gave her a big hug. He was a blessed man. A few years ago he had been sitting in jail wondering if he had thrown his entire life away. And now, just a year out of law school, he was helping try one of the biggest cases the area had ever seen. It was a comeback of biblical proportions, and it reminded him that somebody greater was in charge.

"Let's pray before Billy and I take off," he said. Kerri stepped close, and Landon put his arm around her. Billy shrugged and took off his cap. Maddie squeezed her eyes shut and listened to her daddy pray.

///

The Chesapeake Municipal Complex consisted primarily of three mammoth buildings, each constructed with white stone and blue-tinted windows. The Municipal Center, which local residents sarcastically referred to as the Taj Mahal, occupied the prime real estate at the front of the complex. Behind that behemoth building was a large swath of green space that resembled a college quad. At the corners of the green space, forming an equilateral triangle with the Municipal Center, were two court buildings—one that housed the General District and Circuit Courts and the other one home to the Juvenile and Domestic Relations Court.

Landon and Billy parked in a large asphalt lot next to the J&DR Court building. Elias had followed them and found his own spot. The three men walked silently together across the parking lot and around to the front of the building, getting their first look at the media horde that had gathered on the other side of the quad in front of the circuit court building.

"Game on," Billy said.

They were all wearing Kevlar vests, and Landon was sweating like a pig. Billy was sweating too, but he looked like he was enjoying himself. He had on his new forest-green pin-striped suit, his shades covering his eyes and his Packers hat on backward. He was packing heat under the suit, and he made no effort to hide the bulge in the jacket. As they walked, he looked this way and that, surveying the crowd like a Secret Service agent.

"We need to get you an earbud tomorrow," Landon said.

"What?"

"Never mind."

They approached the gauntlet of reporters, and the questions started flying. Nobody crowded in, though, because Billy had that certain look on his face, like he might cross-body-block the first person who crossed his path.

"Will Mr. King take the stand?"

"Who killed Erica Jensen?"

"Elias, can you give us a brief statement?"

The three men ignored the questions, walked up the front steps of the courthouse, and took their places in line at the metal detector. Billy surrendered his gun to the deputies for safekeeping and stuffed his hat in a side pocket of his suit coat. The men headed upstairs and met Julia and Jake in a small conference room.

Jake looked like he was about ready to puke. "You okay?" Landon asked.

Jake nodded.

Elias reminded Jake and Julia not to show any reaction, no matter what Franklin Sherman might say. Landon noticed Julia reach out and take her husband's hand for a few seconds. Elias never changed expressions, but Landon could sense that this was the first step toward forgiveness and reconciliation.

"We ready?" Elias asked. The five of them were going to enter the courtroom together.

"I do have one small question," Landon said. He looked at Elias. "Which side of the courtroom do we sit on?"

Everybody smiled except Jake. When you're fifteen years old, there are some things that just aren't funny.

69

TAJ DEEGAN RAN AN EFFICIENT COURTROOM. The experts had predicted that jury selection would last three days. Those experts had never set foot in Deegan's courtroom.

She first ushered the lawyers into her chambers. "I'll ask a standard set of questions," she said, without sitting down. She handed both sides two full pages of questions, including ones the lawyers had submitted earlier. "When I'm done, you can approach the bench and let me know if I missed anything. But I'm the only one talking to the jury. Is that clear?"

"Yes, ma'am," Landon said. He was more than happy to let the judge do the heavy lifting.

"I'd like to reserve the right to follow up with individual jurors," Sherman said, arms crossed. He was not happy.

"We'll cross that bridge when we get to it," Deegan said. Her tone reflected a fair amount of annoyance. "But I'll be the judge of what's necessary."

Jury selection took all morning and half the afternoon, a full two days faster than the experts had forecast. Most jurors had heard about the case but promised they could still be fair and impartial. During the process, Sherman had a heavyset woman with an iPad whispering in his ear—a high-priced jury consultant, according to Elias. Elias and Landon didn't use one. Elias claimed that he had picked more juries than virtually any jury consultant in America and it was mostly guesswork anyway.

When the smoke cleared at three o'clock in the afternoon, Landon was staring at a jury composed of seven women and five men—nine whites, one Hispanic, and two African Americans. Two of the three alternates were also women.

Elias had insisted that Landon use his jury strikes on three stern-looking married women. "They'll convict me based on the affair alone," Elias had said. But that left a Baptist youth pastor and a high school principal who had a reputation for being a disciplinarian. Not exactly a defense lawyer's dream.

After swearing in the jury, Deegan read the jurors the riot act for fifteen minutes—don't talk to anybody about the case; don't form any opinions until you've heard all the evidence; don't read any media coverage or blogs about the case or watch anything on TV.

Were there any questions?

None of the jurors raised a hand.

Landon glanced around the courtroom and felt isolated. The gallery was packed. Erica Jensen's family was sitting in the front row behind Franklin Sherman. Landon had noticed that the rows on the prosecution's side of the courtroom had filled up first. Landon turned and gave a reassuring grin to Jake. The boy was too nervous to smile back.

Landon tried not to show it, but he was nervous too. His hands were leaving sweat marks on the glass top covering his wooden counsel table, and the butterflies were in full-scale revolt in his stomach. He had practiced his opening at least ten times but still wasn't satisfied with it. His remarks were counterpunches, attempts to poke holes in the prosecution's case. In his gut he knew that wouldn't be enough. He needed to somehow prove who had killed Erica Jensen. The problem was, he still didn't know the identity of the real killer.

"Does the prosecution wish to give an opening statement?" Judge Deegan asked. She looked over the top of her glasses at Franklin Sherman, who jumped to his feet.

"We do."

He walked into the well of the courtroom, a comfortable distance from the jury box, and introduced himself. He said that he represented the Commonwealth of Virginia and that it was his job to be a voice for the victim of this horrendous crime. He talked for a few minutes about Erica Jensen and the hardworking, upstanding young woman she was. "It's tragic when somebody dies," he said. "But it's especially tragic when somebody so full of potential dies so young."

To nobody's surprise, Sherman seemed supremely confident. He didn't need notes or a podium to hide behind. He had apparently memorized his entire opening statement.

He shifted into teacher mode and explained the federal insider trading case pending against Elias King. The defendant had set up offshore corporations in the Seychelles Islands, Sherman said. He had done so because you could set them up without letting the public know who the shareholders or directors or officers were. And he had used this web of anonymous corporations to set up various offshore accounts and then used those accounts to buy and sell stock.

Sherman spent a few minutes explaining the laws against insider trading—that people with inside information about a company couldn't rip off the public by buying or selling stock before that confidential information hit the market. That's why Elias King had gone to such great lengths to protect his identity. He bought options on the stocks of companies that his law firm represented. He did it when the companies were about to be sold, just before their stock price would take an enormous leap. He made hundreds of thousands of dollars.

But he didn't get away with it. An anonymous person sent the U.S. Attorney's office a package of documents that showed somebody at the Kilgore and Strobel firm was engaged in insider trading. The Feds obtained a search warrant and, through the cooperation of the managing partner at King's law firm, secretly obtained access to King's computer. They were in the process of putting together their case when King's assistant, Erica Jensen, called and asked to meet with assistant U.S. Attorney Mitchell Taylor.

"Mr. Taylor recorded that conversation," Sherman said. "When he testifies, we'll play it for you."

Landon watched as the jury took in everything Sherman was saying. As much as Landon disliked the man, he had to admit that Sherman was a master storyteller. He talked about how Erica died on the night before her appointment with the assistant U.S. Attorney. That same night, Chesapeake police received an anonymous tip about a body being dumped into the Intracoastal Waterway.

The evidence all pointed to Elias King. Strands of Erica's hair were found in the trunk of King's automobile. The car described by the caller matched King's car. King's fingerprints were on the weights found in the L.L. Bean bag. King had motive and opportunity. They had everything here except a videotaped confession.

And one more thing, Sherman said. Erica Jensen was pregnant. The baby growing inside her womb belonged to her lover—he pointed a stubby finger—"that man, Elias King."

Some people kill to keep witnesses from testifying against them, Sherman said. Others kill to avoid damage to their reputation. And still others kill because love has turned to hate, two passions that are closer together than most people think. But Elias King?

The General walked over and stood right in front of Landon's table. It was a bullying move that Elias had expected and had warned Landon about. The two of them just sat there, staring impassively at the prosecutor, refusing to take the bait.

"This man killed three birds with one stone," Sherman said, the anger boiling over, the veins in his neck pulsing. "He got rid of a witness in a case against him. He killed his ex-lover. And he made sure that his sterling reputation wouldn't be tarnished. If not for an observant motorist driving across that high-rise bridge at just the right time, he might have gotten away with it."

Sherman walked back into the well of the courtroom and surveyed the jury. It was time to wrap it up, and he appeared to be thinking about what to say next.

"It's our job to prove this case beyond a reasonable doubt. As the judge will tell you, that can be done by circumstantial evidence. We don't need eyewitnesses. We don't need a confession."

He moved a little closer to the jury box; every juror watched him. He had been talking for thirty minutes, but even to Landon the time had gone quickly.

"In fact, I once heard a prosecutor tell a story to illustrate how reasonable doubt can be proven by circumstantial evidence. He said that his son came into the house one day and had a rock stuck in his nose. The prosecutor said he asked his son how the rock got up his nose, and his son said the wind blew it up there. And I remember that prosecutor telling the jury, 'Despite the son's statement, the father had no doubt about how the rock got in his son's nose. So please, don't let the defense lawyer try to blow rocks up your nose.'"

The General turned and stared for a moment at the defense table. Once again, Elias kept his poker face. "That prosecutor was Elias King," Sherman said. "That boy was his son. And those words were his words.

"Greed caused that man to cheat his own clients through insider trading. Lust caused him to cheat on his own wife with his legal assistant. And fear caused him to kill his own lover and his own baby, the young life growing inside Erica Jensen.

"There are heinous crimes, and there are shocking crimes that make the blood run cold. But there's nothing more despicable than a man who uses his training as a prosecutor to carry out the cold-blooded, premeditated murder of a woman who was carrying his own child. There's a special place in hell for a man like that."

Landon stood to object but felt Elias's hand on his elbow. He sat back down.

"No man's above the law," Sherman said. "At the close of this case, we'll be asking you to find Elias King guilty of two counts of first-degree murder and to put him behind bars for the rest of his life."

70

BEFORE FRANKLIN SHERMAN could even take his seat, Landon was up and walking toward the jury.

"The difference between a cover-up and a setup is simple. In a cover-up, the defendant doesn't want to get caught. But in a setup, somebody wants to make sure that he is."

"Objection!" Sherman boomed. "He's arguing the case, not giving an opening statement."

Landon turned to Judge Deegan and held out his palms. "I didn't object during his opening."

"Perhaps you should have. Objection sustained."

The whole sequence threw Landon off stride. Harry had taught him to argue the case during his opening. But now, that was apparently going to be met with one objection after another.

He looked at Elias, who motioned him over to counsel table. Landon could feel his face turning red—the rookie being embarrassed right out of the gate.

"Just give the opening we planned but keep using the phrase 'The evidence will show,'" Elias whispered. "It's magic."

Landon stood up and walked back to the center of the courtroom. He took a deep breath. Good quarterbacks had short memories, shrugging off interceptions. This time he would get it right.

"The evidence will show that Mr. King was an experienced prosecutor, one of the best. And the evidence will show that there are certain things experienced prosecutors know. They know that hair testing can reveal drugs in victims for up to six months. They know that fingerprints can be lifted from objects that have been submerged in water. They know better than to dump bodies off high-rise bridges and risk being seen."

Sherman was up again. "Your Honor, may we approach?"

Judge Deegan gave him an annoyed look. "Make it quick."

The three lawyers huddled around the judge's dais, and she flipped a switch to pipe in some music so the jury couldn't hear their conversation.

"How's he going to prove this stuff if he doesn't call the defendant?" Sherman asked. "I mean, if he intends to call the defendant, I don't have any objection. But an opening statement is supposed to be a preview of the evidence. And if the defendant isn't going to take the stand, then this is hardly a preview of the evidence."

Deegan turned to Landon. "He's got a point. Is Mr. King going to take the stand?"

Elias interjected. "We haven't decided yet."

Landon wanted to give him an elbow, but it would have been too obvious. *She wasn't asking you.*

"Let's just stick to what you know the evidence is going to show," Deegan suggested. "Don't talk about anything you have to prove through Mr. King unless you know for sure he's going to take the stand."

"Thank you, Your Honor," Sherman said, loud enough for the jury to hear. He wanted to make sure they knew that the judge had sided with him.

"And keep your voice down," Deegan said.

Landon had to make some modifications on the fly, but he warmed to the task and made it through the rest of his opening with only a few objections. He concluded by reminding the jury that there were two anonymous tipsters in this case. The first sent papers about the insider trading scheme to the Feds. The second allegedly saw someone dump Erica Jensen's body off a high-rise bridge.

"Could it be that both tips came from the same person?" Landon asked. "Could it be that the person providing anonymous tips just happened to know so much because he set my client up on both matters? Think about it. How unusual is it to have not one but *two* anonymous tipsters in the same case, each one with critical information against my client?

"My client, Mr. King, was a very effective prosecutor. In that job, he made a lot of powerful enemies. He put away some angry men who have ruthless allies on the outside. Don't let them use a court of law to exact an unjust revenge."

Landon sat down, not at all pleased with his opening. There had been too many interruptions, and he hadn't handled them well. The first round, in his opinion, had gone to the prosecution.

But Elias King apparently didn't agree. He reached over and put a hand on Landon's shoulder. "Nice job," he said.

It was pushing five, and Judge Deegan decided that the prosecution should start its case the following day. When she gaveled the court closed, Landon and the King family followed Billy Thurston into the hallway and down the long escalators. They pushed their way through the reporters who were waiting outside and headed across the quad toward the parking lot on the other side of the J&DR Court building. They ignored the questions being shouted at them.

As they walked, Landon couldn't resist a quick glance over his shoulder. The General had followed behind them and was now standing on the courthouse steps answering questions from reporters. His eyes caught Landon's for just a moment, a quick look of condescension.

He smirked, or at least it looked like a smirk to Landon. And then the General went back to confidently fielding questions.

///

He hung toward the back of the crowd and watched the defense team leave the courthouse and walk across the wide-open quad toward the J&DR Court building. There was at least fifty yards of open grass between the two courthouses and a set of sidewalks laid out in a square.

During the afternoon court session, he had been checking out rooftops near the parking lot the defense team had used that morning. There was no out-of-the-way building from which he could get a clean shot. He had traced the path the defense team would take to and from court, surveying the surrounding property for a good place to hide.

He saw it as he watched the defense team walk the sidewalk next to the quad. The perfect spot.

He kept his head down, his eyes shielded by sunglasses, his ball cap riding low on his forehead. He waited until Franklin Sherman finished his press conference and the crowd started to disperse.

He walked casually across the quad, toward the back of the J&DR Court building, checked to make sure nobody was watching him, and took a quick panoramic video with his cell phone. Compared to blowing up the Cessna, this would be a piece of cake. It would take another day or two of planning, but he had a little time.

The fireworks, quite literally, would begin on Wednesday.

71

WHEN LANDON AND BILLY ARRIVED back at the office, there were five cars sitting in the parking lot. One was Parker Clausen's gray BMW. Landon didn't recognize the other four, except that the black Porsche looked vaguely familiar.

"Wait here," Billy Thurston said. He parked Landon's truck and marched inside to see what was happening.

A few minutes later, Billy reappeared and motioned for Landon to come to the front door. Landon was met there by Parker Clausen.

The three men huddled in the front portico, and Parker gave him the bad news.

The death of Brent Benedict notwithstanding, Carolyn Glaxon-Forrester was still on a rampage. She was convinced that Benedict had been squirreling money away in some offshore accounts, and she wanted her client's fair share. There had been a hearing earlier that day, attended by Parker Clausen as the firm's managing partner. Glaxon-Forrester had argued that all firm accounts should be put in a constructive trust until the judge could figure out whether Benedict had been illegally secreting money into these suspected offshore accounts.

"The court didn't grant the motion, but she did allow Glaxon-Forrester to take my deposition and yours. I tried to tell the judge that you were in the middle of a trial, but she said you could spare an hour at night."

"Are you kidding?" Landon asked. The last thing he needed—the *very* last thing—was to spend an hour being harassed by Carolyn Glaxon-Forrester. "I don't have an hour."

"I tried to tell that to the judge," Parker said. "But I think she just wanted to get Glaxon-Forrester out of her courtroom."

Landon shook his head and grunted. How did he get stuck with a managing partner who couldn't argue his way out of a wet paper bag? "Fine. Let's get it over with."

Glaxon-Forrester, along with her client and a court reporter, were already set up in the firm's main conference room. She was wearing skin-tight jeans and a body-hugging sleeveless white top. Landon threw his suit coat over a chair, rolled up his sleeves, and loosened his tie. He took a seat at the end of the long conference table and leaned forward on his elbows.

"One hour," he said. "Not a minute more."

Glaxon-Forrester sized him up over the end of her beaked nose, a contemptuous little grin on her face. She reached down and started her triathlon watch. Landon thought she did a little muscle flex just for the fun of it.

"Fair enough," she said.

Landon had never been waterboarded, but he thought it couldn't be any worse than this. Glaxon-Forrester had a list of questions that she spit out in rapid succession, each designed to make Landon look either complicit in Brent Benedict's alleged wrongdoing or, at the very least, stupid and naive.

She started off by establishing that Landon was a partner in the firm. She then asked about how firm compensation worked, and particularly about how Brent Benedict had been paid. Landon kept his answers short, his favorite consisting of three simple words: "I don't know."

"You're a partner in the firm, and yet you claim not to know that the firm paid for Brent Benedict's car, his health club memberships, golf club membership, private jet lease, health insurance, retirement plan, and life insurance premiums, all on top of his regular salary and bonuses?"

Landon's voice remained calm. "I wasn't a partner at the time. And if you know about those things, I assume they were all reported in the divorce proceedings."

"Then let's talk about some of the things that weren't reported," Glaxon-Forrester sneered. The court reporter sat next to Landon, her head swiveling from Glaxon-Forrester to Landon as she transcribed every word.

Glaxon-Forrester stood and walked the length of the table until she was standing over Landon's shoulder. She plopped some documents in front of him. Parker Clausen, who was sitting a few seats away, tried to warn Landon with his eyes.

"Do you know what these documents are?"

Landon stared at them. He thumbed through the documents carefully. He had never seen them before.

"Nope."

"You have no idea?" Glaxon-Forrester said, hovering over Landon.

"I can read what they say, but I'm assuming you could do that too. At least most of the words."

"Strike that from the record," Glaxon-Forrester said. The court reporter made a few keystrokes.

Glaxon-Forrester stayed there for a moment, arms crossed, and Landon had to crane his neck to look at her.

"Your client Elias King set up several offshore corporations in the Seychelles Islands; isn't that correct?"

"No, that's not correct. Besides, that's got nothing to do with your case."

"I'll be the judge of that," Glaxon-Forrester said. "So let's start again.

Isn't it true that the federal government is claiming Mr. King set up international business corporations in the Seychelles Islands to hide his insider trading activities?"

"That's what the federal government says. But as far as we can tell, somebody else set them up."

This brought a little smirk from Glaxon-Forrester. "As far as you can tell?"

"That's what I said."

"And that's because it's hard to tell who sets up a corporation when it's done in the Seychelles Islands; isn't that correct?"

Landon could see where this was going but was helpless to stop it. "That's correct."

"Because when you set up a Seychelles offshore company, you don't have to name the shareholders. Right?"

"That's my understanding."

"You don't have to file any public documents naming the officers or directors either, do you?"

"No."

"You can make your stock certificates—which don't even need to be filed—payable to bearer, meaning that whoever possesses them is the owner. Isn't that right?"

"I believe that's correct."

"And you can have nonresident directors?"

"Yes."

"And you don't have to file any annual returns."

"Correct."

"And lastly, there are no corporate taxes to pay in the Seychelles Islands."

"I believe that's true as long as the company is an international business company."

Glaxon-Forrester stood there for a moment enjoying her own little show. She nodded knowingly at her client, who smiled back. She asked the court reporter to mark the documents she had shown to Landon.

"You're sure you've never seen these documents before?"

"I'm sure."

Glaxon-Forrester walked to the other end of the table and took her seat. She thumbed through a pile of papers and apparently found what she was looking for. She stared at Landon for a few seconds, as if she were some kind of human lie detector who could make Landon flinch.

"Brent Benedict would have known about the allegations against Elias King for insider trading, and he would have known about these Seychelles offshore companies. Right?"

"I don't know what he knew or what he didn't know."

"But he was the managing partner of your firm, and Elias King was one of your firm's biggest clients. You don't think the managing partner would have known about the details of the insider trading indictment against Elias King?"

Landon shrugged. "Brent Benedict and I didn't talk a lot."

"Fair enough. Do you know if he ever set up any of these offshore companies himself?"

"No."

Glaxon-Forrester picked up a few of the documents, stood, and returned to Landon's end of the table.

"If you want to sit next to me, it might expedite things," he said. "I'm not contagious."

"That won't be necessary." She placed a new set of documents in front of him. These documents showed deposits and withdrawals in a number of different accounts. "Do you know whether Brent Benedict was siphoning money from the firm's operating account into an account controlled by a Seychelles offshore company?"

Landon looked through the documents, but they were Greek to him. "I have no idea."

"Doesn't that concern you—the thought that one of your former partners may have been siphoning money from the firm?"

"My concern right now is getting through this deposition so I can prepare for the second day of a murder trial."

"This account right here—" Glaxon-Forrester reached over Landon's shoulder and pointed her enameled fingernail at a document from a bank in the Cayman Islands, "has been closed out." She shuffled a few documents. "So have two or three of these other accounts. Do you know what happened to the money?"

"No."

"Did you get any of it?"

"I told you I don't know a thing about any of these accounts."

"That's funny. Your partner, Parker Clausen, said the same thing."

Glaxon-Forrester had the court reporter mark these new exhibits and then returned to her seat. She appeared to be deep in thought. Then her eyes lit up. "Harry McNaughten was the lead lawyer on Elias King's case, wasn't he?"

"Until somebody killed him."

"Do you suppose these offshore accounts were opened by Harry McNaughten?"

"No way. The man didn't care anything about financial matters and was basically illiterate when it came to computers."

Glaxon-Forrester smiled, and Landon realized he had been suckered. "So if Parker Clausen says they're not his accounts, and you're pretty sure they're not Harry McNaughten's accounts, yet it appears that some firm money was transferred into these accounts, what partner would that leave?"

Landon frowned. "I don't know anything about these accounts."

"That's your story and you're sticking to it," Glaxon-Forrester said sarcastically. "But I think you've already answered the question."

72

ON THE SECOND DAY OF THE TRIAL, Kerri woke up at four so she could be at the television station for the early morning newscast. She had taken Monday off to watch Landon's opening statement and in the last few weeks had pretty much exhausted the good graces of her bosses at WTRT. If she wanted to see the closing arguments on Thursday or Friday, she would have to show up on days like today.

Landon was already at the kitchen table, paper scattered everywhere, his hair sticking up in a dozen different directions.

"How long have you been up?" she asked.

"Not long." He didn't look up from what he was writing. She gave him a kiss on the top of his head.

"You want another cup of coffee?"

"Already had two."

When he was like this, it was best to leave him alone. She took Simba out to do his business and got ready for work. She left Landon at the kitchen table, pushing away the dog, who was determined to play tug-of-war. She could tell that her husband was getting frustrated with the case, but she knew there was little she could do to help.

Kerri hadn't gotten good vibes from the jury on day one, but there was still a long way to go. Landon was a good lawyer—he just didn't have much to work with. Some people were saying that a rookie like Landon had no business trying this case, but Kerri knew better. Landon was bright, articulate, and a fierce competitor. Elias King was lucky to have him.

The morning news focused on some national stories and, of course, the opening day of the King murder trial. It always felt surreal for Kerri to be reading copy about her husband's case, but she tried to keep it dispassionate and professional, as if the story dealt with a total stranger. She often received compliments from her colleagues about the way she handled things. Several people had told her how amazed they were at her objectivity.

Because their station had been stuck in third place in the local ratings war, the geniuses in charge had decided that the anchors should answer some live questions from callers and handle real-time text and Facebook messages during the morning newscast. It must have sounded like a brilliant idea in the boardroom.

At 6:25 Tuesday morning, a caller was patched through to Kerri, live on WTRT's morning show.

"How does it feel to have your husband defend a baby killer?" the caller asked, his voice bitter and raw.

Kerri was stunned more by the venom in his voice than the substance of the question. She sat speechless for a moment, and her coanchor, a twenty-five-year veteran of the business, bailed her out.

"Everyone's entitled to a defense under the Constitution," he said. "And the whole point of our system is that nobody is guilty until they're proven guilty beyond a reasonable doubt in a court of law. I admire Landon Reed for what he does."

The show's director had already cut off the caller, so there was no response. But Kerri's face was flushed, and she was already beating herself up. Why hadn't *she* said something? Why did her coanchor have to defend Landon while his own wife sat silently by?

The next caller asked a softball question on a well-worn political issue, and Kerri did her best to recover.

"You okay?" Kerri's coanchor asked during the next commercial break.

"Yeah, thanks. I don't know what I would have done without you."

"Haters are gonna hate," her coanchor said. He smiled, but Kerri felt sick to her stomach.

73

FRANKLIN SHERMAN'S FIRST WITNESS was Alistair Leonard, the distinguished managing partner of Elias King's former law firm. Leonard had risen to the top a few years earlier during a tumultuous time at the firm. He was a highly regarded business lawyer and a sure hand at the helm as the firm navigated through some rough waters.

He looked dignified enough on the stand. White hair, designer glasses, and a thousand-dollar suit lent gravitas to his appearance. He was rail thin, one of the top distance runners for his age in Hampton Roads. Leonard had a reputation for being precise and disciplined. Even his enemies admitted that his integrity was beyond reproach. It would be Landon's job to cross-examine the man. Elias King was saving his questioning for the one who mattered most—Detective Phillip Truman.

On direct, Leonard told the story of how assistant U.S. Attorney Mitchell Taylor had approached him about the possibility that someone at the firm was engaged in insider trading. Acting on an anonymous tip, Taylor's office had been investigating unusual stock option trades executed by offshore companies. The stock options were all for corporate clients of Kilgore and Strobel. The trades had typically taken place just a few weeks or months before a merger or acquisition that the firm was handling.

Mitchell Taylor had threatened to issue grand jury subpoenas if the firm didn't cooperate. The publicity, Leonard testified, would have been devastating to the firm. Faced with no easy options, Leonard had allowed the U.S. Attorney's office limited access to firm computers and servers, making sure he protected all client confidences in the process.

Each attorney, Leonard explained, had the option of using either a desktop or laptop computer. They were also issued iPads, which most attorneys kept with them. Elias King chose a laptop. Fortunately for the U.S. Attorney's office, he left it at the firm most nights.

To play it safe, Taylor had obtained sealed search warrants for certain information on the firm computers, including Elias King's hard drive. An independent commissioner had been appointed to review the hard drive and make sure that any attorney-client material was protected.

That process revealed that King's computer had been used to set up several offshore companies and a maze of offshore accounts. Those companies and accounts were used for the stock option trades under investigation. Sherman introduced several screenshots from the computer into evidence, as well as the Kilgore and Strobel employment manual, which reminded attorneys that all electronic devices provided by the firm remained the property of the firm.

Sherman double-checked his list of questions and smiled in a self-satisfied way. "Please answer any questions that Mr. Reed or his client, Mr. King, might ask."

Alistair Leonard took a sip of water and recrossed his legs. He was the epitome of calm.

"I'd like to ask you a few questions about the firm's security," Landon said.

"That's fine."

"When lawyers in your firm leave their offices each night, do they lock their individual office doors?"

"There's no need to. We occupy the entire nineteenth, twentieth, twenty-first, and twenty-second floors of our building. The elevators have access codes, and each floor has a sliding glass door and its own separate access code. The only people who can get into our offices at night are lawyers and staff members of the firm, and even they would have to sign in at the security desk in the lobby."

"How many lawyers are in your firm?"

"Ninety-four in our Norfolk office."

"And how many staff members?"

"Probably another ninety or so."

"What about cleaning crews?"

"What about them?"

"Do you have a cleaning crew, and do they have access to the office after hours?"

"Yes. But if you're asking about access to Mr. King's computer, you should know that much of the work done setting up the offshore corporations was done during working hours."

"Landon." It was a loud whisper coming from Elias King.

"Excuse me for a moment," Landon said.

He huddled with Elias. "Anything he knows about what's on the computers is hearsay," Elias whispered. "He didn't search the hard drive himself—he heard about it from someone else."

Landon stood and took a few steps toward the witness. "How do you know that—the fact that much of the work setting up the accounts was done during working hours?"

"That's what the FBI discovered when they downloaded the information from your client's hard drive."

Landon turned to Judge Deegan. "I ask that the answer be struck as hearsay."

Sherman stood but evidently thought better of it. The jury had already heard the answer—that was apparently good enough for him.

"Sustained," Deegan said.

"During working hours, if Mr. King wasn't in his office, two hundred or so folks would have access to his computer; isn't that right?"

"Yes. But there were never any reports of somebody sitting at Mr. King's desk typing on his computer."

"It's a laptop. Someone could have taken it out of his office and into one of your file rooms or someplace else in the firm and typed on it there. Isn't that true?"

"If we're going to play the could-have game, I suppose you're right."

"Let me change gears for a moment and ask you a few questions about Erica Jensen. When did she join the firm?"

"About two and a half years ago," Leonard said. It seemed to Landon that the witness was a little less at ease with this line of questioning; perhaps he had not practiced it with Sherman.

"Did she have prior experience as a legal assistant?"

"No. But she had a college degree, and, if I remember correctly, she had been in the military. She also had some glowing recommendations."

"How did she end up working with Elias King?"

"I think she requested the opportunity to work in our criminal-defense section."

"And your criminal-defense section was headed up by Elias King; is that correct?"

"Yes."

"Did you ever see Elias King and Erica Jensen argue with each other or have any cross words?"

"No. Never."

"In fact, did you ever see Elias King yell at any staff members or snap at anybody at the firm?"

"No."

"Before any of this happened, would you have said that Elias King was a model partner?"

"Yes. Before he had an affair with one of the firm's legal assistants and murdered her, he did just fine as a lawyer."

Out of his peripheral vision, Landon saw Elias lean forward, rising slightly from his seat. "Landon," he whispered. But Landon turned and motioned for his client to sit down. Landon might be a first-year lawyer, but he couldn't let Elias dictate every move in the trial. If Landon was going to represent the man, Elias would have to trust him.

Elias hesitated for a moment and sat back down.

"In your line of work, you don't do many jury trials, do you, Mr. Leonard?"

"I don't see how that's relevant."

Landon moved closer to the witness. "Since that didn't actually answer my question, let me try to be more precise. How many jury trials have you conducted in your illustrious career?"

Leonard's face dropped into a scowl. He didn't like being shown up by a first-year lawyer. "None," he said. "I'm a business lawyer."

"Then let me ask you to remember way back when you went to law school and took trial practice class. Do you recall your professor telling you that the ultimate question of fact—the issue of whether my client is innocent or guilty—is typically one for the jury to decide based on all the evidence?"

This brought Sherman to his feet. "Objection! He's badgering the witness."

"Sustained," Judge Deegan said. But then she leaned toward the witness and took off her glasses. "Please avoid passing judgment on the defendant, Mr. Leonard. I think Mr. Reed is making a valid point."

Alistair Leonard simply nodded. He turned back to Landon but seemed to shrink a little, as if some of the air had gone out of his inflated chest.

"Let's try again," Landon suggested. "What kind of lawyer was Elias King before the *alleged* insider trading and the tragic death of Erica Jensen?"

Leonard hesitated for a moment and spoke softly. "A good lawyer."

"Did he appear strapped for money?"

"I don't get into the personal affairs of my partners."

"Did he drive a lot of fancy cars and live in a big mansion?"

"Depends on what you mean by a big mansion and fancy cars."

"Okay," Landon sighed, "we can do this the easy way or the hard way. If you'd like, I can list your cars and describe your house and then we can compare. On the other hand, you could just answer the question as to whether Mr. King lived an ostentatious lifestyle."

Leonard glanced in the direction of Sherman, but apparently the General had decided not to draw any more attention to the testimony. "I'd say that your client is a man of relatively simple taste," Leonard conceded.

"Thank you very much," Landon said.

As he returned to his seat, Elias King leaned over and whispered, "Great job."

74

ALISTAIR LEONARD MAY HAVE STARTED things off a little rocky for
Franklin Sherman, but as the day wore on, the pieces of the prosecution's puzzle started falling into place. A computer technician testified
about the information found on Elias King's hard drive. Elias's computer, the tech said, had been used to set up several offshore companies
and accounts, and just as Alistair Leonard had said, much of the work
had been done during office hours. A financial expert tied those companies to stock trades that occurred just before news of mergers or acquisitions went public. A lab tech testified that the only fingerprints on Elias
King's computer belonged to King. And the coroner testified to the
cause of Erica Jensen's death—asphyxiation. She had been drugged with
GHB, and then the life had been choked out of her. Several hours later,
her body had been dumped into the Intracoastal Waterway.

By the time Assistant U.S. Attorney Mitchell Taylor took the stand
late Tuesday afternoon, it had already been a good day for the prosecution.

Mitchell answered the General's questions with short, clipped sentences. He was big on "yes, sirs" and "no, sirs." He recounted his investigation into the insider trading allegations, including a phone call he had received a few weeks into the investigation, while he was preparing his case for the federal grand jury.

"Did you record the call?" Sherman asked.

"Yes, sir."

"Is that legal in Virginia?"

"Yes, sir. As long as one party consents. And I was the consenting party."

"Do you record all your calls?"

"No, sir. But this one was transferred from the front desk because the caller had asked for the attorney in charge of the insider trading investigation at Kilgore and Strobel. We had kept very tight reins on the investigation, and because the caller wouldn't give her name, my instincts told me to record the call."

Landon knew the prosecution planned to bring in a voice identification expert later in the case who would testify that the voice belonged to Erica Jensen. Elias had already listened to the call several times and agreed that the voice was Erica's.

"Permission to play the call, Your Honor?" Sherman asked.

Deegan granted the request, and the jury leaned forward, knowing they would soon be hearing the voice of the victim.

"Mitchell Taylor."

"I've got some information about the insider trading case you're investigating. I'm willing to testify if you give me immunity."

"Who is this?"

"I'd rather not say over the phone."

"What type of information?"

"We need to meet in person. I'll explain everything then."

"How do I know you're legit? You need to give me something I can check out."

There was a long pause in the recording. Then Erica's voice said,

"Quarrels International Business Company. Johnson IBC. Rayfield IBC. Rajan Holding Company."

There was more silence on the line as Mitchell Taylor seemed to consider the information. Erica had just listed the names of several offshore companies that had been set up from Elias King's computer, as well as the holding company that was the majority owner in each of the others. It was information that should have been known only by Elias King, Alistair Leonard, and the FBI agents involved.

"How soon can you meet?" Mitchell asked.

"Tomorrow at 9 a.m. Show up at the short-term parking lot at the Norfolk International Airport. I'll need your cell phone number."

"That's not the way it works. I need you to come to my office at the federal building."

"Thank you for your time, Mr. Taylor."

"Wait! Are you coming tomorrow?"

"No. That's not the way it works. I'm calling the shots, not you. I have something you need."

"My cell number is 635-3197. I'll see you at the airport."

"Have a good day, Mr. Taylor."

The phone went dead and Franklin Sherman gave the jury a few moments to digest the call. He eventually turned back to Mitchell Taylor.

"Did you show up the next morning at the airport?"

"Yes."

"And did the caller ever arrive?"

"No. It was the morning after Erica Jensen's death."

"That's all the questions I have."

75

IT HAPPENED JUST AS LANDON STOOD—a Harry McNaughten flash-back.

"Remember this," Harry had said. "Unless you're watching *Perry Mason*, the purpose of cross-examination is not always to prove that the witness is lying. In fact, the best cross-examination is when you help the other side's witness tell the truth. That's when you've really done something."

Landon stood there for a fleeting moment, facing Mitchell Taylor. He had a five-page outline of questions, but he put his pad down on the counsel table and decided to go off-script.

"Who knew about this meeting between you and Erica Jensen?"

"Myself. My boss. Two of the FBI agents working the case."

"Which one of you told Mr. King about that meeting?"

"None of us."

"And you know that how?"

"We investigated it after Ms. Jensen's death."

"You did? So what did your investigation reveal about how Mr. King allegedly found out about that meeting?"

"Mr. King must have found out from Ms. Jensen. Perhaps he overheard something. Perhaps he saw something on her computer. We don't know precisely how he found out."

"You don't know *precisely*?" Landon asked, his voice rising with incredulity. "Isn't it fair to say that you have no idea how my client allegedly found out about the meeting?"

"We don't know; that's correct."

"But you know it didn't come from your office."

"Correct."

"You're sure about that?"

"C'mon," Sherman said, rising. "He's already answered that question."

"Move on," said Judge Deegan, though she looked a little amused.

"Based on your recorded phone conversation, it sounds to me like Ms. Jensen was pretty careful about whom she told. Would you agree with that?"

"She was careful when she talked to me."

"And would you agree that if Mr. King didn't know about the meeting, then stopping that meeting certainly couldn't have been his motivation for allegedly killing Erica Jensen, could it?"

"He must have found out somehow. The evidence points to him as the killer. And the timing of the meeting is too coincidental."

"Sounds like you don't believe in coincidences," Landon said.

"Most prosecutors and investigators don't."

"Then what would you call the fact that some random driver just happened to be cresting the high-rise bridge in the wee hours of the morning at the exact same time that Erica Jensen's body was being dumped into the Intracoastal Waterway?"

Mitchell hesitated and Landon did a mental fist pump. The jurors stared at the witness.

"I'd call it stupid on the part of your client," Mitchell Taylor said.

The man was smart. But he had apparently never learned that sometimes you just had to take your lumps and not dig a deeper hole.

"My point exactly," Landon said. "So I've got a follow-up question. In all your years working at the U.S. Attorney's office—the same place where my client previously worked for years as a prosecutor—have you ever heard even one person call Elias King stupid?"

Landon knew the answer even before Mitchell spoke. Elias King had lots of enemies. Drug lords. Defense lawyers. White-collar criminals. He had undoubtedly been called a lot of derogatory names. But *nobody* thought he was stupid.

Landon hoped Mitchell would try to fight him on this, too. If the witness said yes, Landon would ask for names and subpoena them as witnesses. He would quiz Mitchell about Elias King's well-documented intellect—his law school class rank, his brilliant trial briefs, his Columbo-esque way of figuring out crimes.

But none of that was necessary. "I've never heard Elias King called stupid," Mitchell admitted.

"Didn't think so," Landon said, and took his seat.

76

AS THE PARTIES LEFT CIRCUIT COURT on Tuesday afternoon, a solitary figure stood at the back corner of the J&DR building, hat low on his forehead, sunglasses covering his eyes. He watched from a distance as Franklin Sherman stopped on the steps of the circuit court building, holding forth for the media. He watched Elias King and his team brush aside the media, walk three-abreast down the sidewalk bordering the quad, and disappear around the front of the J&DR building.

They were creatures of habit—football players and a former prosecutor. People in these professions practiced the same techniques, over and over, until they perfected them. They wore the same lucky socks. They parked in the same parking lot. They took the same path to court every morning.

Habits make you predictable. Habits allow the enemy to plan.

He would have a clean shot tomorrow morning, away from the media and the other litigants crowded in front of the circuit court building. The length of the quad was about fifty yards, and the defense team would be walking down the sidewalk next to the quad by themselves, in his direct line of sight, half a football field away.

He wanted to avoid any collateral damage. He had a job to do. He would do it and be gone before anyone knew what had happened.

///

When Landon and Billy returned to the McNaughten and Clay offices, Landon's family was waiting for them. Maddie ran up to them and crashed into Landon for a hug. Simba came sliding over as well, tail wagging, panting, licking everyone in sight. *Par-tay!* In his excitement, he dribbled on the floor.

Kerri emerged from the conference room and asked how court went. After Landon gave her a quick recap of the day's events, she asked Billy if he could keep an eye on Maddie and Simba.

"There's somebody in the conference room who needs to talk with you," Kerri said to Landon.

He followed her back and was introduced to Sean Phoenix. The two men sized each other up and exchanged firm handshakes. *What is he doing here?* Landon wondered.

Kerri closed the conference-room doors and everybody had a seat. "Landon, you know that Cipher Inc. has been conducting their own investigation into the deaths of Harry, Brent, and Rachel," Kerri explained. "As part of that investigation, they also looked into Erica Jensen's death because frankly, they had some concerns about Elias King."

Landon gave Kerri the eye and was pretty sure she got his message. *Why didn't you tell me about this? We should have talked about this alone.*

"Sean called me today with some information they've uncovered," Kerri said quickly, almost apologetically. "I wanted you to know about it as soon as you got out of court."

"I asked if I could come down and explain it myself," Sean said, his gaze level, his face showing no emotion. "Very few people in our organization even know that we've been looking at this. So I didn't want to send somebody else and bring them into the loop. But also, I'm very grateful for what this firm has done for me and our company in the past. I wanted to return the favor."

Landon still suspected there was more to it than that, but he decided not to push the point. He could talk to Kerri later. They always tried to avoid airing their differences in front of people.

"We don't know for sure who killed Erica Jensen, but we have a pretty good theory," Sean said. He spoke as if the police investigation and murder trial were irrelevant—the only thing that mattered was what the great Sean Phoenix concluded.

"The police locked onto Elias King early, which caused them to have a form of tunnel vision. They didn't search for things that might implicate other suspects." He shoved a small pile of documents toward Landon. "Like, for example, a locator search on Julia King's cell phone."

Sean's gaze was steady and unnerving as he waited for Landon to react. Landon picked up the documents and casually leafed through them.

"As you may know, Verizon keeps data generated by its cell towers for up to a year," Sean continued. "By triangulating text messages and phone calls to and from a person's phone, you can roughly track their location even if they don't have a GPS device programmed in. We did that with Julia's phone."

Landon wondered how Sean had obtained this information without a subpoena, but that seemed beside the point. Apparently Cipher Inc. could get whatever it wanted.

Without time to study the documents in detail, Landon couldn't make much sense of what he was looking at. But he could see where this was headed. "She went there that night?" he guessed.

"Yes. Julia King went to Erica's apartment the night of the murder."

Landon closed his eyes and took a deep breath. Julia had lied to him and to the police. Most likely, Elias knew about her visit and lied as well.

"The police ran a locator search on Elias's phone that night, didn't they?" Landon asked, trying to remember.

"They did. If he went to Erica's apartment, he didn't take his phone." Sean glanced at Kerri. It was obvious the two of them had already reasoned through the possibilities.

"We know Julia found out about the affair on Sunday night," Sean continued. "Maybe she stewed on it for a day and on Monday night went to the apartment to confront Erica. Let's say she freaked out and dropped the GHB in Erica's drink and strangled her that night. Maybe she told her husband. He cleans up the apartment, wipes down the fingerprints, and disposes of the body. In his haste, he makes a few uncharacteristic mistakes.

"But there's another theory, one you might not like quite so well. Perhaps Julia goes there on Monday night and confronts Erica. Maybe Erica is already angry because Elias has decided not to leave Julia. Maybe Elias had originally promised Erica he was going to get a divorce but now he's backing out. So Erica tells Julia that her husband is not the man either of them thought he was. She tells Julia about the insider trading. She says she's going to the Feds. Maybe Julia runs home and confronts Elias about the insider trading allegations. You can guess the rest."

Landon nodded. Sean was right; the meeting between Julia and Erica could cut both ways. At worst, it would give the prosecution a way to plug one of the weaknesses in their case—how had Elias found out that Erica was going to the Feds?

There were still a lot of unanswered questions. The date rape drug demonstrated premeditation. Julia didn't seem capable of cold-blooded, premeditated murder. And if Elias didn't find out that Erica was going to the Feds until that night, where would he get the date rape drug so quickly? And why would Elias dump a body off the high-rise bridge?

After twenty minutes of discussion, there was only one thing that everybody agreed on. Elias and Julia King had been lying to their lawyers from day one.

"What are you going to do?" Kerri eventually asked.

Landon gathered up the documents. "Have a little talk with Elias King."

77

BILLY INSISTED ON TAGGING ALONG for security reasons, but Landon made him wait in the car. When they arrived at the King house, Julia was doing the dishes. At Landon's request, she took a break to join him and Elias in the living room.

"Where's Jake?" Landon asked.

"Upstairs in his room," Julia said tentatively. "Do we need him?" She looked from Landon to Elias. She was smart enough to know that a lawyer making house calls meant trouble.

"No, that's fine," Landon said.

When they settled in, Landon got right to the point. There was no good way to do this. "I've been doing some additional investigation in this matter," he said, watching for reactions on the faces of Julia and Elias. "I had Julia's phone triangulated for the night of Erica's death." He paused as Julia's face reddened. Elias, a seasoned pro, showed no expression. "I know you went to Erica's apartment that night."

When his accusation was met with silence, Landon had his answer. Julia looked at her husband and he answered for them both.

"Why were you checking Julia's location? That wasn't part of our defense."

"I've had a lot of investigative work done."

"Without telling me? You should have told me if you were going to do something like that."

Landon felt his blood pressure rising. He was already frustrated with Elias for lying. Now the man was trying to put Landon on the defensive? "I'm not the one who's been lying to his lawyer," Landon said, his voice sharp. His look dared Elias to take him on—Landon would walk in a heartbeat. "If you want me on this case, I'd better start finding out what happened. Why Julia went there. How long she was there. And whether Erica was still alive when Julia left."

"Of course she was still alive," Elias said.

"How do I know that? How did her body get in the trunk of *your* car?"

Elias stood, his jaw set. "This is why I didn't tell you about it before. I don't need my own lawyer jumping to conclusions. The prosecutors and media are already doing a fine job of that."

Landon held out his palms. "That's it? I ask an honest question and I get a lecture?"

"Can we just calm down?" Julia asked, looking at Elias. "Landon's entitled to an explanation. He's been with us from the beginning, and I can understand why he's upset."

Elias hesitated, torn between his pride and Julia's appeal to reason. "You're right," he said. He nodded at Landon. "I'm sorry." He sat back down.

"Julia went over there that night," Elias said, choosing his words carefully. "When she left our house, I had no idea where she was going. As I told you, she learned about me and Erica the night before, on Super Bowl Sunday, after reading a few of my text messages. We talked on Monday, argued a lot, and she drove to Erica's apartment and confronted her. When she returned, she told me what she'd done, and we got into it again. But I never went out there that night, and Julia never went back. I swear to God, we have no idea who killed Erica Jensen."

Landon looked at Julia. "Is that true?"

"Yes."

"Then why didn't you tell me about this earlier?"

Chastened by the question, Julia said nothing. Her reaction gave Landon the impression that the deception was all Elias's idea.

"This is why," Elias said, his voice softer than before. "Because nobody would believe us, not even our own lawyer."

"It's hard to believe you when you've been lying from the beginning."

For a few moments, nobody spoke. This time Julia broke the silence. "Where do we go from here?"

"I think we have to put you on the stand," Landon said. "Tell what happened that night. If we're lucky, Sherman will try to prove you're lying, thinking you're just trying to save Elias. That's when we break out the cell records."

"Sherman's not that dumb," Elias countered. His voice had a tone of resignation, as if he'd thought this scenario through already and knew the inevitable outcome. "He'll claim that Erica told Julia she was going to the Feds. That's how he'll say I found out—through Julia."

"I've thought about that," Landon said. "But it doesn't make sense. Why would Erica tell Julia about the meeting with Mitchell Taylor?"

"Julia's not taking the stand," Elias said, ignoring the question.

"I don't think you're in any position to be issuing ultimatums."

"I'm still the client, Landon. And on matters like this, the client calls the shots."

Landon tilted his head. This was unbelievable. "Why are you so unyielding about this?"

"If Julia takes the stand and we win, what do you think Sherman's going to do?"

"I don't know," Landon admitted.

"Yes, you do. We all do. He's going to turn around and indict Julia."

Landon couldn't argue with the man. Based on the evidence, he wouldn't fault Sherman for seeking such an indictment.

"I can't let that happen," Elias continued. "So she's not taking the stand."

Landon wondered what Harry would do in a situation like this. He reminded himself what Harry had said about this case many times—that they only had one client, Elias King.

"Let's cross that bridge later," Landon suggested. "We've got plenty of prosecution witnesses to focus on first."

But Elias wouldn't let it go. "I've got one other question," he said. "Who else knows about this?"

Landon swallowed hard. He hadn't anticipated this question. "Billy. Kerri. The investigator."

"Who's that?"

Harry had taught Landon a thing or two about cross-examination. You sit down and think about the questions in advance. You brainstorm how the witness might answer. You have a follow-up question for every possibility. *"It's like chess,"* Harry had said. *"You've got to think two moves ahead."*

But Landon had been too frustrated to do that. He had wanted to confront and cross-examine Elias immediately. Now Landon was the one with some explaining to do. "Sean Phoenix and some of his men are helping investigate the deaths of my partners," Landon said. At the mention of Phoenix's name, he saw Elias stiffen. "In the context of that investigation, they discovered this information."

"In the context of that investigation?" Elias shot back. "Why would they be looking at Julia's cell phone records in the context of *that* investigation?"

Even as he spoke, it dawned on him. Landon could tell by the flash in his eyes. "You think I'm somehow tied to the murder of your partners?"

Landon held up a hand to slow things down. "Not you. But maybe something about your case."

He tried to explain further, but everyone's nerves were on edge. Landon felt betrayed by a lying client. Elias didn't like his lawyer going behind his back, especially with a group like Cipher Inc. The men raised their voices, and the frustrations of the last few days came to the surface.

It ended only when Julia called them out, broke into tears, and told them she couldn't take any more of this. The men took a collective breath, and Landon quickly apologized.

"You hired me to be your lawyer," he said. "But if you want me in this case, you need to start listening to my advice. We can't win this case by just poking holes in the prosecution's testimony. The jury needs to hear from you. And the jury needs to hear from Julia."

Elias shook his head. "Maybe I'm wrong," he said. His voice, like Landon's, was now low and conciliatory. "Maybe I'm so emotionally invested in this case that I can't see what you see. But Landon, I'm the one facing jail time. And I don't want to be sitting in a cell forty years from now, having missed my son's wedding and my grandchildren's graduation and who knows what else, wondering if I should have done it my way.

"I appreciate your help. And I'm sorry that I ever dragged you into this mess. But I can't have a lawyer who's conducting investigations behind my back, one who doesn't even agree with our strategy for the case." He paused and looked at Julia for support. Finding none, he said it anyway.

"As of now, I'll be handling the rest of the case alone."

///

Landon walked down the driveway and climbed into the passenger seat of the truck.

"What happened?" Billy asked.

"I got fired."

Billy cursed—a long, creative string of words fit for the locker room. "You want me to drive this truck through his front door?"

"Sure."

Instead, Billy put it in reverse and pulled away from the curb.

On the way home, Landon vented. Admittedly, he was only a first-year lawyer, but he had never been fired before.

"What did Julia say about it?" Billy asked.

"She tried to talk him out of it."

"The man's an idiot," Billy said. Words to that same effect, though slightly more colorful, had been Billy's theme the entire ride.

"What about Jake?" Billy asked.

"That was the worst part," Landon said. "At the end of our conversation, I saw him standing in the doorway to the kitchen, listening. The kid had big tears in his eyes. When I looked at him, he just looked down and turned away."

"You think he blames it on *you?*"

"No. I just think he knows that his dad is most likely going away for a very long time."

"The man deserves it," Billy said. "What a jerk. He just fired the best lawyer money can buy."

"Maybe he deserves it, but his family doesn't." Landon said it more to the windshield than Billy. He thought about his own history—everything he had put Kerri and Maddie through. "And his family's going to suffer a lot more than he is."

78

WEDNESDAY PROMISED to be the hottest day in June with the potential for record-breaking temperatures by midafternoon. It was the type of day that made your sunglasses steam over when you walked outside. Even at seven thirty in the morning, on the short walk from his car to the office, Landon felt like he was wading through a sauna.

Landon had called Parker Clausen the night before to tell his partner that the firm had been fired by its highest-profile client. Parker took it in stride. "We already got plenty of publicity out of that one. And it looked like you guys were going down anyway."

On Wednesday, Parker arrived at the offices early, wearing his trademark jeans and T-shirt, and did his best to cheer Landon up. His theory was that Elias King had planned on firing Landon all along. "That way, he'll be able to argue ineffective assistance of counsel if he loses," Parker said. "He probably doesn't like the handwriting on the wall any more than you do."

The defense team gathered in the office at eight so they could make their way to Chesapeake Circuit Court together. Elias checked Landon's motion to withdraw and told Landon how much he appreciated what the young lawyer had done. Everybody talked in hushed tones, as if they were going to a funeral.

Before they left, there was a small rebellion when it came to wearing the Kevlar vests. It started with Billy. "I ain't wearing that thing today," he announced. "Too hot. Plus, I'm tired of wearing the same suit every day."

Kerri argued with him, but Billy had made up his mind. "Nobody's trying to kill members of the Green Bay Packers anyway," he said.

Elias decided to ditch his as well. So did Landon, but he met some fierce resistance from Kerri. She pulled him aside and prevailed on him to wear it for her and Maddie. She was going to wear hers. Even though Kerri's was specially designed for the female body and relatively thin, it still limited her wardrobe. "You think I want to wear this skirt and jacket on a day like today?"

"Then don't," Landon said. "We'll be fine. Besides, anybody who really wanted to take us out could tell we're wearing a vest and just aim for the head."

"I'd feel better if you'd wear it," Kerri said. "You can take it off in the bathroom once we get inside, just like every other day."

Landon felt like a wimp, but he put on the vest.

"Thanks," Kerri said.

"You owe me," Landon replied.

They took three vehicles to court. The King family rode together. Kerri joined Landon and Billy in the truck. And the Wolfman, as always, followed in his own vehicle, lurking far enough behind to keep an eye on everything.

They parked at the far end of the J&DR parking lot, in almost the exact same spots they had used the day before. Landon slung his suit coat over his shoulder. He was already sweating. He grabbed his briefcase and walked with the team across the parking lot toward the court complex. Billy had dressed more casually—slacks, a golf shirt, and shades. He wore his gun holster out in the open for everyone to see.

His head swiveled this way and that, like a true bodyguard, vigilant and armed for action.

On other mornings, the team had chatted about anything and everything as they made their way toward court and the waiting reporters. But today, with the specter of Landon's termination from the case looming, they were grim-faced and silent.

As always, Billy and Landon took the front of the wedge and walked side by side, with Julia and Elias right behind them. Kerri and Jake brought up the rear. The reporters saw them coming and turned their cameras in the direction of the defense team. The on-air reporters picked up their mikes and moved to the front of the media horde, prepared to shout a few questions and watch the defense team smile and say, "No comment."

Landon stared straight ahead, lost in his own thoughts. The press was in for a surprise today. Elias King would be finishing this case on his own.

///

The mastermind had set his explosives in the middle of the night. He later returned to the court complex at 4 a.m. and parked in the corner of the J&DR parking lot. He was dressed in a business suit and, except for the weird hour of his arrival, looked like a well-heeled lawyer heading to court, briefcase and all.

At this time of night, nobody else was around.

He walked casually around the J&DR building, surveyed the dark quad, and ducked behind a row of pine trees. He waited a few minutes, looking back and forth to ensure that nobody else was in sight, and then slid down the length of the building, using the pine trees as cover.

The large blue dumpster was located at the back corner of the building, next to the loading ramp, with a perfect line of sight to the quad. He slid the side door open, dropped his briefcase inside, heard a dull thud as it hit some trash, and then slipped in himself. He moved some garbage bags to form a perfect little nest and pulled the side slot nearly closed, creating just enough of a slit that he could see the entire quad. He opened his briefcase and assembled his rifle, attaching the scope, the sound suppressor, and a special plastic bag to catch the shell casings. He settled in and waited.

The heat was a problem. By the time he had been in the dumpster for four hours, it was already approaching ninety degrees. The stench of the garbage was suffocating. Sweat dripped from his face, and he wiped it away with a small towel he had brought for that purpose.

By 8:30, the quad started filling up with pedestrian traffic, lawyers hustling back and forth, defendants trying to figure out which courtroom they belonged in.

At 8:40, the mastermind got his first glimpse of the defense entourage, led by Landon Reed and his buddy, Billy Thurston. He couldn't be certain, but it looked like the only one wearing a protective vest that day was Landon. Maybe his wife was wearing one as well. But Billy Thurston clearly was not, and Elias looked too thin to be wearing his, though he had on a suit coat and it was hard to tell.

Interesting. This would require an immediate change in plans, something he hadn't anticipated. But he had been trained to deal with situations like this. And he had come too far to abort the mission now.

He knew the precise number of seconds it would take from the time the defense team first came into view until they would be in his direct line of fire fifty yards away. He had Sean Phoenix's cell number and the text message already entered in his phone. He pushed Send.

It's on, the message said.

He scrolled to the next number and put the phone on a ledge where he could easily reach it. He picked up the rifle and tried sighting in his first target. He cursed, unable to get a clean line on either Landon Reed or Elias King. First the kid, then Kerri Reed—both walking behind the others—blocked his line of fire.

"Come on, come on," he whispered.

There. It was just the right angle. Kerri and the kid out of the way.

Nobody crossing from the other direction. The media still twenty yards ahead of the defense team, preparing to ask their questions. He had two clear shots. It would all happen in rapid sequence now. His hand was steady, the crosshairs centered on Landon. He remained calm and relied on his training.

He squeezed the trigger.

79

FOR LANDON, it felt like a blindside hit from an SEC linebacker. He grunted as the force of the blow knocked him to the ground. Behind him, he heard Elias yell and saw him crumple. Billy twisted and lunged toward Kerri, tackling her into the grass, where he blanketed her body with his.

There was a loud explosion in a trash can a few feet away, followed by screams coming from every direction as tear gas filled the air. Bullets sprayed behind them, and Landon curled into a ball, covering his head with his arms.

Gunshots seemed to be coming from the other side of the circuit court building, and the press, like dominoes, had all hit the ground. The smoke stung Landon's eyes, and he could barely breathe. At the first break in the shots, Landon did a quick survey of his group. Elias was hit; the others seemed okay.

"Let's go!" Landon yelled, pointing to a small brick building away from the sound of gunfire. They had to find cover before the bullets started flying again. "Keep your heads down!"

Billy pulled Kerri up and then helped Landon pick up Elias. "It's my leg," Elias said.

Billy bent over and slung Elias over his shoulder. The whole group scrambled toward the building Landon had pointed out. Billy limped badly and fell behind.

"You okay?" Landon yelled.

The big man grimaced. "Twisted my knee."

Others were sprinting for cover in all directions as the Chesapeake police poured out of municipal buildings, guns drawn, shouting orders.

The defense team reached the front of the small brick building and sat down. There were uniformed police officers everywhere now. Chaos still reigned in the quad with people running this way and that, but the popping of the sniper's rifle had quieted.

Amazingly, as Landon looked around, he didn't see any bodies lying lifeless on the ground.

///

After firing the first two shots, the mastermind had sent a second text message. This one triggered a series of explosive devices. Tear gas erupted from the trash can several feet in front of Landon Reed and Billy Thurston. Other explosive devices were rigged to sound like gunfire coming from the far side of the circuit court building. Then he picked up the rifle and fired a few more stray shots into the turf behind the defense team.

The quad became a tear gas–filled madhouse in a matter of seconds. People scrambled for cover, confused by the explosions and the sound of gunfire. While the cops took over and focused on the opposite side of the circuit court building, the mastermind calmly disassembled his rifle and folded it into his briefcase. He opened the sliding door on the back side of the blue dumpster—the side away from the quad, the side sheltered by a concrete wall and the back of the J&DR building. He climbed out and quickly walked away, resisting the urge to break into a jog as he approached the parking lot.

As he walked, he sent his second text message to Sean Phoenix. Just before he climbed into his car, the mastermind surveyed the parking lot to make sure nobody was staring at him. Then he verified that the message had gone through.

It had. The mastermind believed in brevity, so the entire message was just six words.

Mission status—targets hit but survived.

80

IT TOOK LANDON A FEW SECONDS to calm down, but he had always been able to keep his head when everyone else was losing theirs. His ears were still ringing from the sound of the gunshots and explosions, and his eyes were watering. But with the police pouring into the municipal quad, he seriously doubted if the shooter was still around.

"How bad are you hit?" he asked Elias.

"Just a flesh wound," Elias said. He tried to force a smile, but it turned into a grimace.

Billy already had Elias's pant leg rolled up so he could examine the bullet wound in his calf. "I need your shirt," he said to Jake. "So we can put pressure on this thing and stop the bleeding."

"I'll meet you at the hospital," Landon said to Elias. He grabbed Kerri's hand. "Come on."

Keeping their heads low, they zigzagged toward the circuit court building, running past the point where they had been when the shooting started. Landon grabbed his briefcase and suit coat, which were lying right where he had dropped them. The police were clearing the quad, barking orders to everyone, but there was enough chaos for Landon and Kerri to weave their way to the circuit court building.

The place was already on lockdown, but the deputies recognized Landon. "I've got to get to Judge Deegan's chambers," Landon said breathlessly.

"Nobody comes in or leaves."

"Look—somebody shot me and my client, and Judge Deegan needs to know the details." Landon pointed to the deputy's radio. "Give her deputy a call. Tell her I'm trying to get through."

"You don't look like you got shot."

Landon turned and showed the man the back of his shirt and the bulletproof vest.

"Okay," the deputy said. He turned to Kerri. "You'll have to stay here." He told a second deputy to take Landon up the escalators to courtroom three.

"I'm going to the day care to pick up Maddie," Kerri called out as Landon was being led away.

"Good idea," Landon called back. "Make sure Billy goes with you."

Five minutes later, Landon was sitting in Judge Deegan's chambers along with Franklin Sherman while two deputies guarded the doors. Landon had his suit coat off but was still perspiring like crazy, big moons of sweat forming under his armpits.

He wiped his brow with his shirtsleeve. At this point, etiquette was the least of his worries.

"What happened out there?" Deegan asked.

"Somebody tried to kill Elias and me," Landon said. The judge's eyes widened, and Landon rapped on his Kevlar vest. "This thing works. As for my client, he's got a leg wound, but I think he'll be okay."

"Thank God," Deegan said.

Franklin Sherman said he'd been on the phone with the police officer in charge. "Elias King was hit in the leg," he confirmed. "There are a few other injuries from people scrambling to safety, but the cops have now secured the scene. So far there are no fatalities, and we don't have anybody in custody."

Judge Deegan let out a big sigh, relief showing on her round face. "It could have been a lot worse," she offered.

She stood and stared out the window overlooking the quad. From his vantage point, Landon could see the far corner of the quad next to the Municipal Center. There were police officers everywhere, and they weren't allowing anyone to move.

Judge Deegan turned back to the lawyers. "Obviously, we'll have to declare a mistrial. I think most of the jurors are already in the jury room. The others won't even be able to get through the lockdown."

"I understand," Sherman said.

But Landon had other ideas. He was feeling heroic, having just survived a sniper's attempt to take him out. And though he hadn't yet figured out who wanted him and Elias King dead or how that might play into his defense, there was no doubt somebody had just thrown a couple of wild cards into the deck. For the sake of his client, who hadn't yet officially fired him, Landon needed to keep their options open.

"I disagree," he said.

Deegan tilted her head back, regarding Landon with curiosity. "Pray tell," she said.

"I think we first need to find out whether there are enough jurors and alternates inside the building and whether my client can attend court this week. And if so, we can't let an attempted assassination of the defendant and his attorney extinguish his right to a fair trial.

"Somebody is deathly afraid of what my client is going to say if he takes the stand or what we might prove as part of our case. Judge, I know in your days as a prosecutor, you must have had witnesses threatened and even received death threats yourself. In fact, I know you personally survived that courtroom shooting in the case with that Muslim imam—"

"Kevlar vests are a wonderful invention," Deegan inserted.

"But I'll bet you never let those kinds of threats derail the trials. Why let the justice system be held hostage by a killer? I say we find out whether we have twelve jurors in the courthouse. If we do, let's sequester them overnight and make a decision on whether to proceed once we see how seriously my client is injured."

"Interesting thoughts," Deegan said. She sat back down. "Mr. Sherman?"

"Well, let me begin by saying that I'm grateful Mr. Reed is still here with us." He looked at Landon, who nodded his appreciation. "But let's give the police time to catch whoever did this. Mr. Reed is right; somebody apparently wants him and his client dead. When we find out who that is, I think we'll know a lot more about the truth of this case. But these jurors are bound to find out that somebody tried to kill the defendant and his lawyer. Do you really think we'll get a fair trial under those circumstances?"

What he really meant, Landon knew, was that he didn't want to try a case against someone the jury might consider a hero. Few things can raise a person's stock as quickly as getting shot.

Deegan turned from Franklin Sherman to Landon, and he took it as his cue to fire a shot of his own.

"Judge, let's take a step back and look at the big picture. We've got a case where my client is being accused of killing a potential witness in a federal investigation before that witness could meet with an assistant U.S. Attorney. My client's defense is that he was set up as part of some greater conspiracy. Then, in the middle of our trial, somebody tries to silence me and my client before we can prove our case. Moreover, whoever is behind this apparently sets off a bunch of tear gas canisters to create maximum chaos. In other words, they're doing everything possible to stop this trial. Why give in to that? Why not finish this case and show them that justice can't be held hostage?"

"Judge, that's ridiculous—" Sherman began.

But Deegan cut him off. "Mr. Sherman, I've spent almost my entire career on your side of the courtroom. I know what it means to be threatened and to have my witnesses threatened. And as Mr. Reed pointed out, I know what it feels like to be shot. I can guarantee you one thing. If somebody fired at a prosecution witness while I was prosecuting the case, I would have insisted that the case go forward. I would have argued that we can't let hired hit men intimidate the courts. Now, how is this different just because the shoe's on the other foot?"

Sherman started to answer, but the judge cut him off again. "That's a rhetorical question, Mr. Sherman."

He scowled but knew not to push it.

"And it's also my ruling," Deegan continued. "I'm going to instruct the deputies to bring the jury into the courtroom, and we'll see if we have enough of them to proceed. If we do, we'll sequester the ones who are here, dismiss the others, and reconvene tomorrow at 9 a.m. Mr. Reed, I'll give you the option at that time of whether or not to proceed, based on the health of your client. Any questions?"

"No, ma'am," Landon said.

Sherman frowned and shook his head. "I think it's a mistake," he muttered under his breath.

Judge Deegan stared him down for a moment but chose not to respond. Tempers were already on edge. They were in unprecedented waters.

"That's all, gentlemen," she said.

81

BEFORE HE COULD LEAVE the courthouse, Landon had to spend an hour answering questions from Chesapeake detectives. Just when he thought he had described what had happened for the last time, Detective Freeman from the Virginia Beach Police Department showed up. She made him walk through it again, step by step, as she made notes in her little black book.

"Look, my client's at Chesapeake General," Landon said, his frustration rising. "I'd like to get over there and see him. We've got a lot to talk about."

Detective Freeman scanned the faces of her counterparts from Chesapeake. "If you gentlemen are done, I can go to the hospital with Mr. Reed and complete my questioning there."

Kerri and Maddie were already at the hospital when Landon arrived. Kerri was a little sore, something to be expected after being tackled by a three-hundred-pound NFL lineman, but she was otherwise unhurt.

The Wolfman had come and gone. According to what he told Kerri, he had checked the rooftops once the bullets started flying and then had run to the parking lot on the other side of the circuit court building looking for the shooter. He had no leads but was closely monitoring the police investigation.

Julia and Jake were also at the hospital. Elias had been moved from the OR to recovery, and the police were in place to provide 24-7 protection.

"How is he?" Landon asked.

"He just got out of surgery," Kerri said. "The bullet entered the back of the calf and fractured the fibula. He's got a lot of swelling and bleeding, but it missed his major veins and arteries."

"Where's Billy?"

"He's having an MRI. He twisted his knee and we're praying it's nothing serious."

///

Elias King came through the surgery well and was grateful for Landon's quick thinking in front of Judge Deegan. "If I can't get a not-guilty verdict after getting shot in the middle of the case, there's no hope," Elias said, his mind still foggy from the anesthesia.

"Let's see how you're feeling tomorrow morning," Landon suggested.

Elias pointed a finger in Landon's direction. His tongue was thick, his smile lopsided. "You're rehired."

The worst news of the day came from Billy Thurston's MRI. He had partially torn his ACL and might require surgery followed by up to six months of rehab. The decision of whether to undergo surgery that would make him miss the season would, of course, be made in conjunction with the Green Bay team physician, but the doctors at Chesapeake General weren't optimistic. The big man had successfully protected the wife of his college quarterback, but the 2013 season may have just gone down the drain.

82

BY THE TIME LANDON got back to the office, Parker Clausen had heard all about the shootings. "I tried to call your cell but you weren't answering."

"Sorry," Landon said. "I've been a little busy."

They were standing in the front lobby of the downstairs office, leaning on the counter surrounding the work space where Janaya used to sit. Landon still had on his dress pants, though he had a small hole in the left knee, and his white shirt had a bullet hole in the back. It had already been one of the longest days he had ever experienced, and it was only two in the afternoon.

"Turn around and let me see the back of your shirt," Parker said.

Landon did, showing off the bullet hole. He had been careful at the hospital not to let Maddie see it.

"That could make Harry's Hall of Fame shelf," Parker said. "Where's the vest?"

"The police kept it. Ballistics tests."

"Oh. Sure."

Parker took a drink of his Coke and shook his head. "I'll be honest with you. When Harry first brought you to this firm, I thought he'd lost his mind. But you ended up being one of our best hires. Heck, you almost inspire me, and that's darn near impossible."

"I don't feel so inspirational," Landon said.

Parker ignored the comment and turned serious, the edges of his mouth twisting down in concern. "I'll tell you what, Landon. You've got to get out of this case, or you're going to get yourself killed." He took another swig of soda and hitched up his jeans. "We've already lost three lawyers over the King case. Let's not make it four."

Landon still wasn't sure that the other killings were related to Elias's case. But one thing he did know—whoever was trying to kill the firm lawyers had already concluded that Landon knew too much. Backing out of Elias's case now wouldn't change that.

"Seems to me that these shootings prove Elias is innocent. Our firm ought to stick with him now more than ever."

Parker finished his Coke and threw the empty at the trash can. It bounced off the edge, and he cursed. "That's why you're a better man than me," he said, leaning over and throwing his can away. "You've already done more than other lawyers would have, with the possible exception of Harry. I'm just saying you should leave good enough alone now."

"I can't do that," Landon said.

"Why not?"

Landon couldn't give the man an answer, but that didn't change the truth. He was going to see this one through. It was in his nature. He wouldn't be able to live with himself if he didn't.

Plus, what choice did he really have? Whoever wanted him dead wasn't going to leave him alone just because he pulled out of the case. The only way to get out of danger now was to help the police figure out who was trying to kill him.

/ / /

Landon spent the entire afternoon in the office with Detective Freeman, reviewing the last few weeks of Harry McNaughten's life. With the attempted murders of Landon and Elias, Detective Freeman was rethinking the entire case.

As she explained to Landon, she had previously been focused on the firm's connections with Cipher Inc. Harry had represented Cipher's top operative in the Al-Latif assassination. Brent Benedict had represented both Sean Phoenix and Cipher in numerous appeals. Plus, Benedict was a former SEAL, the type of person Sean Phoenix occasionally hired for some under-the-table work.

"I thought those offshore bank accounts set up by Benedict were for laundering payments from Cipher," Freeman explained. "And I thought somebody—one of Cipher's many enemies—was out to knock off all of Cipher's lawyers who knew about a certain project. What that project was, I didn't have the foggiest idea."

But now, Freeman admitted, her theory no longer held water. Neither Landon nor Elias worked for Cipher. On the contrary, Elias had been a sworn enemy of Sean Phoenix and Cipher. Freeman now believed that the deaths of Harry McNaughten, Brent Benedict, and Rachel Strach were all somehow tied to the King case. Harry must have figured out something he wasn't supposed to know and passed it along to Brent Benedict. Maybe to Elias as well.

Her buggy eyes zeroed in on Landon. "And somebody out there thinks you know this information too. Are you sure there's nothing you're keeping from me?"

The question frustrated Landon. She had already asked it about three times. "Why would I withhold information that would help you find the person who shot me?"

"So that's a no? You're not holding anything back?"

He blew out a breath and gave her a look, though he knew it

wouldn't make any difference. Freeman didn't care whether people liked her or not. "Yes, that's a no."

They spent a few hours trying to re-create every minute of Harry's life during his final two weeks. His time sheets were a big help, and Freeman zeroed in on two entries Harry had made a week before he died, both indicating phone calls to the secretary of Judge Zimmerman, the judge implicated in the insider trading case whose records Harry had unsuccessfully tried to subpoena. One entry read: *T/c with Zimmerman's secretary requesting a return call.* The second entry, two days later, read: *Follow-up t/c with Judge Zimmerman's secretary.*

Why was Harry calling Judge Zimmerman's secretary?

Landon read through Judge Zimmerman's subfile again, this time more carefully than before. On Zimmerman's résumé, Harry had highlighted the judge's service as senior staff counsel at the State Department. Harry had also made a few notes in the margin with the name and phone number of the judge's secretary as well as the month and year she had started working for Zimmerman. Landon couldn't figure out the significance of the data, but Harry apparently figured it was worth noting.

Harry had done a similar thing in Big John McBride's subfile, noting the starting date for McBride's legal assistant. It was within a few weeks of Zimmerman's assistant. That coincidence was significant enough for Harry to make note of it, but Landon couldn't understand why. It sure would have been nice to know what Harry was thinking.

Then a thought struck Landon. It was something he had considered before, but it now seemed more significant. "Do you know what's missing from the Elias King file?" he asked Detective Freeman.

"Yeah, a reason for somebody to kill Harry."

"That too," Landon said. "But the first thing Harry always did was to write out his closing argument. He thought that helped him focus on what he needed to prove, to separate the critical from the trivial. I thought he was working on one for the King case before he died."

Freeman thought about this for a moment and made a note in her little book. "So you think somebody took it?"

"I don't know. Maybe he threw it out. Maybe that wasn't what he was doing—I just saw him writing some notes on a legal pad. When I originally took the case over, I looked for it but never found it. If I had, it might have saved us all a lot of grief."

///

The pieces didn't fall into place until nearly eleven that night. By then, Landon had gone home and scattered the King file across the kitchen table. When it hit, the revelation was so sudden he let out a soft "Whoa," even though nobody else was there to hear.

In a flash, it all made sense. The similar starting dates for Zimmerman's secretary and McBride's legal assistant. The reason Harry had been calling the judge's secretary. The offshore accounts in the Seychelles islands.

He checked the file to make sure he remembered correctly. Erica Jensen had started at Kilgore and Strobel just six months before Zimmerman's secretary. For the first time it dawned on him why Erica Jensen, pregnant with her first child, would have called the assistant U.S. Attorney and requested a meeting. To Landon, the answer was now obvious. Why hadn't he thought about this before?

Erica Jensen wasn't going to the assistant U.S. Attorney to implicate Elias; she was planning to *exonerate* him. At first, she may have helped set him up—making the deposits into the offshore accounts and maybe even the anonymous phone call that initially got the Feds involved. But somehow, Elias had won her over. Her feelings for him were real. And when she found out that she was pregnant with his child, she had done some serious soul-searching.

Landon was suddenly energized. Billy Thurston was lying on the couch, the television on, his leg propped up. The pain pills and muscle relaxers were helping him sleep, and he was snoring like a train. Earlier, Kerri had crawled into bed with Maddie to calm her daughter's fears and then had promptly fallen asleep herself.

Landon stood, feeling like a man who had just been rescued from a mine shaft, basking in the sunlight for the first time in days. He made two cups of coffee, one for him and one for Kerri. He went back to Maddie's room and gently placed his hand on Kerri's shoulder, shaking her a little. She woke with a start and sat straight up.

"It's okay," Landon said. "It's just me."

She stared at him as if he were crazy, her eyes wide open. It took a few seconds for reality to sink in and for Kerri to relax a little.

"We need to talk," Landon said. "And I need to see the video from that first interview you did with Sean Phoenix."

"What are you talking about?" Kerri asked, rubbing her eyes.

"I'll explain everything. There's a cup of coffee waiting for you in the kitchen."

83

ON THURSDAY MORNING, security was tight at the Chesapeake Municipal Complex, a classic case of locking the barn door after the horse got out. The place was literally crawling with police and bomb-sniffing dogs. Security checks at the courthouses came as close to strip searches as the law would allow. There were no exceptions. Even lawyers who had been practicing in that court their entire professional lives had to endure pat-downs and open their briefcases so the deputies could riffle through their stuff.

The media presence had quadrupled. Nothing like a good old-fashioned shoot-out to get the American public interested.

Though it hadn't been easy, Landon had talked Billy Thurston into staying home with Maddie. He had shown enough heroism for one trial. His leg was in a plastic cast and needed to be elevated.

"I know you hate to miss the action," Landon had said. "But I'll give you a blow-by-blow tonight. Besides, there's nothing more important than knowing that Maddie's safe."

Taking Billy's place was Parker Clausen. He had trimmed his beard and put on an expensive black suit that he had apparently not worn since gaining his last ten or fifteen pounds. It made Landon hot just watching the big guy sweat as they stood in line outside the metal detector waiting to get into the courthouse.

Elias met them in courtroom three. His leg was heavily bandaged and in a cast. He sat at counsel table with it stretched straight in front of him, sticking out from under the table. *That should strike a nice sympathetic chord with the jury,* Landon thought. Elias was still on a few painkillers but said it didn't affect his thinking. To Landon, he seemed a little more mellow than usual.

Court began with a thirty-minute argument about whether the trial should go forward.

"What are we going to tell them about the shooting?" Sherman asked. "They'll certainly notice Mr. King's leg. And with all the commotion that occurred yesterday, most of them already know."

When Landon stood to offer his counterargument, he said he had a novel idea. "What if we just tell them the truth? I know that thought would never occur to Mr. Sherman, but how could it hurt? We don't know who shot my client and me. We just tell the jury the truth about what happened and instruct them that it shouldn't affect their deliberations either way."

"You really are a rookie," Sherman scoffed. "'Okay, folks, somebody tried to kill the defendant, but just ignore that.' That's really fair."

"Enough," Deegan snapped. "We don't need the attorneys acting like children." She glared for a moment at Sherman, and Landon felt vindicated. "Now sit down, Mr. Sherman."

Deegan ruled that the case would go forward. The jurors remaining on the panel had been in the jury room during the shootings, away from all sources of outside news or influence. They were already several days into the trial, and she was determined not to let whoever had carried out the shooting disrupt the administration of justice. "The less said, the better. I'm going to tell them that Mr. King was injured in an incident at the courthouse yesterday but that his injury and the underlying incident have absolutely nothing to do with this trial." Without waiting for a response from the lawyers, she turned to her deputy.

"Bailiff, bring in the jury."

///

As expected, Sherman's next witness was Phillip Truman, the lead investigator on the case. The man looked nothing like the hard-nosed detectives that populated all the TV crime shows. He had a more studious look, like a college professor. There was something about his bald pate, his pudgy nose, and his soft brown eyes that made you believe he was a man without guile, somebody who couldn't tell even a white lie without blushing. He wore khaki slacks, a blue blazer, and a dress shirt without a tie.

His demeanor had been perfected through years of testifying. He spoke in soft but confident tones, never giving Sherman more than the question demanded. Landon could tell the jury felt comfortable with the man, like he was their favorite high school teacher helping them make sense of the scientific evidence.

Landon could have scripted Truman's testimony himself. The detective first talked about his role in the investigation and his experience running hundreds of others like it. He gave a short lecture on DNA evidence and then introduced the DNA test, which showed that the prosecution was 99.99 percent sure that the strand of hair in the trunk of the defendant's car belonged to Erica Jensen. In fact, according to Truman, the odds of that DNA belonging to anyone besides Erica Jensen were less than one in ten billion. The jury seemed duly impressed. A few members nodded.

Sherman introduced as evidence a download from Elias King's cell phone showing text messages to and from Erica Jensen's phone in the weeks prior to her death, some suggesting places they could meet and be alone. All of the texts were informal and casual, demonstrating the intimate relationship between them. One of the texts from Elias thanked Erica for "last night."

There were phone calls as well. Lots of them. Even some from the night of the murder.

Shifting gears, the General asked Truman about the fingerprints found on the weights in the L.L. Bean bag. Yes, one of the prints belonged to Elias King. And to Landon's surprise, they had matched the other print as well.

"Whom did that one belong to?" Sherman asked.

"Jacob King, the son of the defendant. We were able to pick up his fingerprints on some items found in the trash."

"How did you know they were Jacob's fingerprints?"

"We only found two sets of prints on the items we tested in the trash—soda cans, a couple of old pens that were apparently no longer working, and junk mail. Because only the defendant and his son were living there at the time, and because we already had the defendant's prints, we assumed this other set belonged to Jacob. But just to make sure, we dusted the armrest of the seat where he sat Monday in this courtroom, a public place, and matched the prints."

Next to Landon, Elias grunted his disapproval. If he had been prosecuting this case, his chest would have been puffed out with pride at such a clever trick, just like the General's was now. But when you were on the defense side of the equation, it seemed a little sleazy.

"Did you ask the defendant whether he was missing two thirty-five-pound weights from his weight set?"

"Yes."

"What did he say?"

"He said they weren't missing any weights."

"Did you ask the defendant's son, Jacob King, whether they were missing any weights?"

"Yes."

"What did he say?"

"He didn't respond immediately. But when he did, he also told me they weren't missing any weights."

"Did you have a chance to check out the weights yourself?"

"Yes."

"Did they have any thirty-five-pound weights in the set you saw?"

"No. They seemed to be missing those."

This was going to be Elias's witness to cross-examine, and Landon wondered why he didn't object. Even a first-year lawyer like Landon knew that the questions called for conjecture. But Elias seemed content to stick to the game plan he and Landon had crafted the prior night. They needed to get Truman off the stand as quickly as possible.

The General changed the subject again, this time to the hair-testing evidence. According to the witness, Erica had a compound known as gamma-hydroxybutyric acid in her blood at the time of her death. "That's a date rape drug," Truman testified. "It metabolizes so quickly that you usually don't find it in the blood or urine even a few hours after its injection, but it can remain in the hair for up to six months."

Lastly, Sherman asked Truman about the autopsy. He introduced the report itself as an exhibit and had the witness read the part about Erica being pregnant.

"Were you able to determine who the father was?" Sherman asked. He tried to sound curious, but everybody in the courtroom already knew the answer.

"The defendant was the father."

"And how were you able to determine that?"

"Through the same DNA testing we discussed earlier."

"Thank you, Detective Truman. That's all I have."

It was nearly eleven o'clock, and Judge Deegan suggested that they take a brief recess before starting the cross-examination. Landon was all for it.

Yes, he was interested in what was happening inside the courtroom. But he was far more concerned about events transpiring outside. If everything was going according to plan, Sean Phoenix should be arriving in the lobby of Chesapeake Circuit Court at that very moment.

84

AT AROUND MIDNIGHT the night before, after talking with Landon, Kerri had sent a text message to Sean Phoenix. She had followed up with a phone call first thing Thursday morning. She was shaken up about the shootings, she had said. But she thought she knew who was behind them. They couldn't talk over the phone, but she had to meet with Sean right away. She needed his help.

He wanted to meet that afternoon in D.C., but Kerri was insistent. Was there any way he could come to Chesapeake that morning? She promised it would be worth his time. The guy who had tried to kill Landon had it in for Sean as well. Somehow, he knew that Kerri was now working with Sean.

"Who is it?" Sean had asked.

"I can't say over the phone. We need to meet. If you can't make it, I can just give this information to the police."

"Give it to Antonov. He can pass it to me on a secure line."

"Sean, I'm not talking to anybody else about this but you. I'm not sure who else we can trust—not even Antonov."

"You're being paranoid, Kerri. The Wolfman's been with me for years."

"Then where was he yesterday? Why didn't he stop the shooting or at least catch the sniper?"

There had been a sigh of resignation on the other end of the line. "Hang on a second," Sean said.

When he came back on the line, he was all business. "I can be there by eleven," he said.

"Great. Meet me in the lobby of the circuit court building."

"Why there?"

"Security," Kerri had said. "This place is crawling with cops."

///

As Landon watched Detective Truman climb back onto the witness stand, he knew that the reporters who had packed the courtroom were in for a big disappointment. It was nearly eleven o'clock, and the defense team needed Truman off the stand as quickly as possible. The highly anticipated showdown between Elias King and Truman would fizzle out in just a few short minutes.

Deegan called the court to order, and Elias asked for permission to examine the witness from his chair.

"Of course," Deegan said.

"Did you ever locate the witness who called in the report about somebody dumping a body off the high-rise bridge?"

"No."

"How about that anonymous witness who called the Feds and got the insider trading investigation started?"

"That wasn't my case. But to my knowledge, that person is still anonymous."

"Did you ever find any evidence that I had obtained access to the drug found in Erica Jensen's system?"

"No."

"Where would a person get a drug like that, anyway?"

"Objection!" Sherman called out. "Calls for speculation."

"Sustained."

Elias shrugged and moved on. Landon couldn't tell if his indifferent demeanor was the result of the painkillers or if he was just posturing for the jury.

"Do you have any direct evidence that I knew about that meeting between Erica Jensen and Mitchell Taylor ahead of time?"

"What do you mean by 'direct evidence'?"

"You know, a text message, a phone call, an e-mail, a notation some-place in my computer?"

"No, nothing like that."

"Did you find any of my fingerprints or DNA evidence in Erica's apartment?"

"No, the apartment had been wiped down."

"As I understand it, all of the offshore companies mentioned earlier in this trial could have been set up by somebody else using my computer; isn't that right?"

"The companies can all be set up online. So conceivably—yes."

"And during your investigation, you found that lots of folks at my law firm had access to my computer—true?"

"Federal agents took the lead in that part of the investigation. But that's my understanding."

Landon was struck by how straightforward Truman's answers were. He didn't try to fudge or counterpunch or dodge the questions. His demeanor was so calm and relaxed that even though the questions were damaging the prosecution's case, you would hardly know it. He gave the impression that this was just par for the course, that there would always be a few holes in the prosecution's evidence but it wasn't anything to be concerned about.

"As a detective, you've probably investigated what—hundreds of murders?"

"I don't keep a running count. But it would be in the hundreds, yes."

"So you know that fingerprints can be recovered from items even after they have been submerged in water; isn't that correct?"

"Yes, that's something I am aware of."

"And that this drug in Ms. Jensen's system—gamma-hydroxybutyric acid—stays in the hair for up to six months?"

"I'm not an expert on hair testing. But I do know that drugs generally show up in hair for a period of months."

"Wouldn't you expect a prosecutor who had tried hundreds of cases to know these same things?"

As expected, this brought the General out of his seat. "Objection. Calls for speculation."

"Sustained."

Elias King didn't argue the point. The jury had heard the question; that was enough.

"Well, let me ask my next question a little differently so that I don't propel Mr. Sherman from his seat again," Elias said.

The General stood again, arms outstretched. "Judge . . ."

"Mr. King, please leave Mr. Sherman out of this. Just ask your questions."

"Yes, Your Honor."

Elias waited for Sherman to sit down. He checked his notes. He leaned over and whispered to Landon.

"I want to give the jury a few seconds to get refocused," he whispered. "Anything I need to hit that I haven't already covered?"

Landon shook his head.

Elias turned back to the witness. "As an experienced investigator, didn't it bother you that a suspect like me, a former federal prosecutor with more than a passing knowledge of how criminals get caught, would choose to dump a body off a high-rise bridge on a relatively busy highway? Wouldn't you think that even a dumb criminal would know enough to take the body someplace private, like the Dismal Swamp wilderness, and bury it there?"

"He's testifying," Sherman said. "And I object."

Judge Deegan didn't look happy. "We talked about this," she reminded Elias. "And you're pushing it."

"Sorry, Your Honor."

"Objection sustained."

"Thank you, Detective Truman," Elias said. "That's all the questions I have for now."

85

KERRI STOOD BY THE ESCALATOR in the main lobby of the Chesapeake
Circuit Court building, eyeing the doors. The Wolfman was lurking
somewhere outside, and everyone else on the defense team was in courtroom number three. Kerri felt her heart pounding in her throat. She
considered the evidence one more time, turning it over piece by piece.
She prayed that her husband was right.

Sean Phoenix arrived alone a few minutes after eleven. He nodded
at Kerri from the other side of the metal detector. She smiled, and he
stepped in line behind a half-dozen people.

When he reached the front of the line, he pulled out his cell phone
and put it in a plastic dish. Kerri knew that wouldn't fly. The deputies
had their rules, and they made no exceptions, especially on a day like
today. Only lawyers could have cell phones in the courthouse. It didn't
matter if you were the president of the United States. Without a law
license, you had to leave your cell phone behind.

Kerri watched Phoenix argue with them for a few seconds and frown.
She knew they were telling him they could give him a plastic number

and keep his cell phone in a small locker, or he could take it back to his car. Kerri knew he wasn't about to hand that phone over to the deputies.

Sean looked at Kerri, held out his palms, and motioned with his head for her to meet him outside. She started walking toward the metal detector.

Just as she was approaching, a deputy handed Sean a document. He eyed it contemptuously. "What's this?" he asked, his voice acerbic.

"A subpoena," the deputy said. "Courtroom three. ASAP."

Sean looked at the document. "For what?"

"Your testimony," the deputy said. A few other deputies had gathered around, one of them standing behind him.

"Do you know anything about this?" Sean asked Kerri, who was standing a few feet away.

"I know what it is," she said. "My husband had it issued."

He gave her a look that sent a shiver down her spine. She had seen the kind of power this man possessed, his penchant for revenge. She knew that his agents were everywhere.

"You didn't give me any choice," she said.

Nobody moved for a moment as Kerri and Sean stared at each other. After a few beats, the chief deputy spoke. "We need you upstairs right away."

Sean didn't take his eyes off Kerri. "You always have a choice," he said.

A deputy gave Sean a red plastic piece the size of a quarter with the number 52 printed on it in white. "When you're done, just return this to us, and you'll get your phone back."

Kerri watched as Sean passed through the metal detectors and endured a pat-down. Two deputies escorted him to the escalators. She felt her knees go weak as she watched him ride to the top.

///

When the commonwealth rested its case, Landon stood and announced that his first witness would be Sean Phoenix. Sherman immediately objected. Phoenix had not been on the defense witness list submitted ten days before trial. Landon told Judge Deegan that new evidence had emerged since then that made Phoenix a critical witness.

As he stood next to his counsel table and presented his argument, Landon stole sideways glances at his client, who in turn checked the back door of the courtroom. When Elias nodded, Landon turned and saw Phoenix entering, one deputy on each side. They followed him down to the front, where he took a seat next to Parker Clausen—the same seat where Kerri had been earlier that morning.

"Judge, this is just a desperate publicity stunt by the defense," Sherman argued. "I ought to at least be allowed to interview this witness before he takes the stand."

Landon started to respond, but Deegan raised a hand. She didn't like it when lawyers aired out their differences in front of the jury. "We're going to dismiss the jury," she said. "And then I'll meet with counsel in my chambers."

She glanced over her reading glasses at Sean Phoenix. "Mr. Phoenix, I don't want you to leave the courtroom."

///

Kerri had followed Sean and the deputies at a distance on their way to courtroom three. When she arrived, people were streaming out for a short recess. One of them was Parker Clausen.

"What's going on?" she asked.

He nodded toward a spot a little way down the hall. The two of them huddled there. She had never seen Parker so wild-eyed.

"Landon asked me to take you home to the condo," he said in hushed tones. "He doesn't think it's safe for you to stick around here. Right now, he and the others are meeting in Judge Deegan's chambers, arguing about whether Sean Phoenix will be allowed to testify."

"Why wouldn't he be?" Kerri asked. She had never considered that possibility.

"Apparently he wasn't on Landon's witness list."

"Why should that matter?"

Parker took a quick look up and down the hall. Jake King passed by on his way to the restroom. He nodded at Kerri.

"Look, I don't know how it's all going to come out," Parker said. "But Landon says that one of Phoenix's guys has been following you around and is probably in front of the courthouse as we speak. I know a back way out of here. Landon wants you home with Maddie."

"I'm staying here with Landon," Kerri said.

Parker's face turned dour. He lowered his voice and inched closer. "Landon didn't want me to tell you this, but he just got a note from one of the deputies. Everything's all right, but somebody tried to break into the condo. Billy Thurston shot the guy, but Maddie's pretty traumatized. There's a squad car waiting at the back door."

Kerri's hands started trembling. She followed Parker as they raced down the hall.

86

BILLY THURSTON WAS NO LONGER at the condo. Bum knee or not, he had decided he wasn't going to miss the fireworks. Earlier that morning, Landon and Kerri had explained the new plan. Billy's role was to take care of Maddie. But after Landon and Kerri left, Billy called one of the high school linemen he had been working out with whose father was a Norfolk police officer. The man was off duty and said he'd be glad to help.

A half hour later, Billy dropped Maddie off at the officer's house along with a full page of instructions on how to take care of her. Among other things, she wasn't allowed to leave the house for even one minute. Billy promised he'd be back as soon as court let out for the day.

Billy took advantage of his crutches to park in a handicapped spot right next to the J&DR building. He hobbled over to the other side of the building and found an inconspicuous spot on the ground between a few pine trees where he could watch people come and go on the quad. He called the Norfolk police officer every thirty minutes.

He knew Kerri would be mad at him if she found out that he left

Maddie with some strangers. But his gut told him he might be needed at the courthouse. Landon could still be in danger, and Billy wasn't going to leave his buddy on his own.

At a few minutes after eleven, Billy saw Sean Phoenix show up and enter the circuit court building. He decided to give it a few minutes before heading over to the courthouse. That way, by the time he slipped into the back of courtroom three, Phoenix would already be on the stand testifying. Billy couldn't wait to see the look on the man's face.

///

When Landon returned from Judge Deegan's chambers with permission to call Sean Phoenix as his next witness, he quickly surveyed the courtroom. People were shuffling back to their seats, but he didn't see Kerri. Parker Clausen hadn't returned either.

The bailiff announced that court would resume in two minutes. Elias hobbled back to the counsel table. Landon took his seat and shuffled some papers, mindful of the fact that Sean Phoenix was sitting right behind him.

"I need a word with you, Counselor," Sean said, leaning forward. Landon scooted his chair back so that he was just a few inches from Sean Phoenix on the other side of the bar of court.

"You don't want to put me on the stand," Phoenix said, his voice a low growl.

Landon twisted in his chair to meet Sean Phoenix's stare. The man's blue eyes were cold, as if he could kill without emotion. "You're wrong," Landon said. "I do."

"Every man has his price," Phoenix said. "Parker Clausen, for example. You think he got to be a bestselling author because he's a good writer?"

Landon didn't respond. Was Parker one of them?

"Big John McBride wanted to get rich. Kerri wanted the big story. You—you're motivated by family."

Landon turned fully toward Sean and gave him a hard stare. "What are you saying?"

"All rise," the bailiff called out. People stood as Judge Deegan took her place on the bench. Landon's mind was racing with what Sean Phoenix had just said: *"You're motivated by family."*

"Be seated," Deegan said. "Bring in the jury."

As the jury shuffled in, Sean Phoenix leaned forward again and spoke in a whisper. "We've got Kerri," Phoenix said. "Don't make me give the order to hurt her."

The words chilled Landon as he quickly turned and surveyed the courtroom. Kerri was still gone. So was Parker. Landon wanted to tell the deputies and put out an all-points bulletin. But how far had Sean's men taken her? Once Landon said something to the deputies, there would be no turning back.

"The defense may call his first witness," Judge Deegan said.

Landon stood. "May I have a second, Judge?" he asked. The hair was standing up on the back of his neck. He had to fight back the panic and the bile in his throat. What if it was already too late? Why should he trust anything Sean Phoenix said?

"For what purpose?" Judge Deegan asked.

Landon held up a hand. "Just for one second, Your Honor. A short conference."

"Make it quick."

Landon turned and leaned over the railing, his mouth next to Sean Phoenix's ear. "So help me God, if your men touch my wife, every one of you will spend the rest of your life in prison."

"I've got people in this courtroom," Phoenix whispered back. His voice was calm and steady, authoritative. Was it a bluff? "Put me on the stand, and it will be the worst day of her life. Let me walk out of here, and I'll return her unharmed as soon as I leave American airspace."

"Why would I trust you?"

"Because one of us has to trust the other. And because you know I don't want to hurt her."

"Counsel, let's proceed," Judge Deegan said.

Landon turned and faced the judge, his head spinning. He needed a few minutes to figure things out. This was like the two-minute drill. He had to slow down the clock.

"Counsel?" Judge Deegan's voice had an edge to it.

"The defense calls Julia King," Landon said.

"What?" Elias asked, his voice loud enough to be heard by most everyone in the courtroom.

"Ms. King, please come forward and raise your right hand," Judge Deegan said.

Julia rose with a dazed look and walked into the well of the courtroom. Phoenix also stood and asked the court if he could be excused.

"Not yet," Landon said. "We intend to call him as our next witness."

JAKE KING DIDN'T UNDERSTAND everything that was going on, but he had managed to put the big pieces together. He loved football, but deep down, he knew he really wasn't very good at it. Until he had met Landon Reed—actually, until this case—he hadn't known what he really wanted to do with his life. But sitting through this trial and watching Landon and his dad tag-team the prosecution had opened his eyes.

He had always done well in school. And he could be a leader when he wanted to. He could totally see himself doing what Landon was doing now.

Sometime during the second day of trial, Jake King had decided he wanted to be a trial lawyer.

He had been trying to follow all the ins and outs of why Landon asked certain questions on cross-examination and why the prosecutor might call this witness or that witness. He had listened carefully and had over-heard enough that morning to know that the defense team was trying to get Mr. Phoenix on the stand. From what Jake had heard, he was pretty sure Landon was going to try and lay the blame for Erica Jensen's murder at the feet of Mr. Phoenix. For Jake, it was like living in a movie.

So when Mr. Phoenix came into the courtroom and sat down in the front row next to Mr. Clausen, Jake had been on high alert. The two men whispered back and forth. Jake, sitting on Mr. Clausen's other side, had leaned a little to his left and was able to pick up bits and pieces. When he saw Mr. Clausen leave the courtroom, Jake had waited a few beats and then followed.

He had seen Mr. Clausen talking to Mrs. Reed in the hallway, an intense conversation, with both of them leaning toward each other, troubled looks on their faces. He pretended to head toward the bathroom. But something told him things weren't right. It was what Landon called his "quarterback instinct." Landon was always telling Jake that he thought too much on the football field and sometimes just needed to trust his gut. He also told Jake that he was too cautious, that sometimes you just had to improvise and go for broke.

Jake had set his jaw and circled back around, just in time to see Mrs. Reed and Mr. Clausen heading down the escalator. He had hustled over to the glass railing at the top of the escalator and watched Mr. Clausen and Mrs. Reed get off at the bottom. He glanced back at the courtroom doors—they didn't need him in there—and took off down the escalator as fast as he could run.

By the time he hit the ground floor, Mr. Clausen and Mrs. Reed were nowhere in sight. Jake went to the security checkpoint, turned in his plastic marker, picked up his cell phone, and hurried out the door. He checked this way and that, frantically looking for Mrs. Reed. In the hallway upstairs, he had heard Mr. Clausen say something about Landon wanting Mrs. Reed to go home to be with Maddie. But Jake had been sitting next to Mr. Clausen all morning and had never heard Landon say anything like that.

Looking across the quad, Jake saw Billy Thurston coming toward the circuit court building on his crutches. Billy would know what to do! Maybe Jake was just making a big deal about nothing.

He started to jog toward Billy but first took one last glance around. That's when he spotted them, in the opposite direction from Billy, walking side by side. They ducked down a path through a small section of woods that led to a massive parking lot behind the Chesapeake Community Center. They were over a hundred yards away.

Jake sprinted toward Billy. Breathless, he gave Billy a quick rundown of what he had seen and heard.

"You know how to drive?" Billy asked urgently.

"Sure."

"I parked Landon's truck in the handicapped spot on the other side of that building." Billy pointed to the J&DR courthouse. He gave Jake the keys. "Here. Get Landon's truck and bring it around to this street." Billy pointed to the street behind the court building about fifteen yards away. "I'll meet you there, and we'll head over to the other parking lot."

Jake ripped off his suit coat and sprinted as fast as his legs would carry him toward Landon's truck. The more he ran, the more he convinced himself that Kerri Reed was in real danger. He found the truck right where Billy had said it would be. He wheeled out of the parking lot and drove to the street where he was supposed to pick up Billy.

Billy already had his plastic brace off and was holding it in his right hand. He threw it into the bed of the truck.

"It takes me forever to get in and out of that cab with this knee," Billy said. "I'm going to hop in the back. You drive. Head to that parking lot over there and drive around until you find them. Park right behind 'em. And don't move until I tell you to."

"Yes, sir."

Billy lowered the tailgate, sat on it, and scooted up into the bed of the truck. "Okay . . . let's go," he said.

88

NOW THAT LANDON had Julia on the stand, he wasn't really sure what to ask her. He hadn't even dared tell Elias about Phoenix's whispered threats. What if Elias said something to the police?

For his part, Elias didn't want Julia on the stand at all. "Trust me," Landon had whispered. "I just need to stall for a few minutes."

Landon started with a few background questions, but after a while he could tell that everybody in the courtroom was getting restless. He was standing facing the witness while keeping one eye on the back door. He kept hoping Kerri would walk through the door at any minute so he could end this charade and call Sean Phoenix to the stand. He also kept glancing at his phone. He had sent Kerri a text after Phoenix threatened him, while Julia was being sworn in—**Where are u?**—but hadn't received a reply.

Sean Phoenix was still sitting right behind counsel table, focused on Landon like a laser trying to bore holes into Landon's psyche. For the moment, Landon ignored him.

"Directing your attention to the night before Erica Jensen's death, Super Bowl Sunday, did you and your husband have an argument?"

"Don't go there," he heard Elias whisper. But it was too late.

Julia looked at Landon with wide eyes. She knew about the plan to get Sean Phoenix on the stand, but she obviously had no clue what Landon was trying to do right now. *It's okay,* he wanted to tell her. *I'm not sure either.*

She glanced at Elias, and Landon could sense that there were twenty-six years of marriage wrapped up in the look, a lifetime of being there for each other, of taking care of somebody even when you've seen them at their worst. Elias must have nodded or given her some sign of affirmation. When she turned back to Landon, she seemed to relax, a woman resigned to telling the truth.

"Yes."

"What was the argument about?"

"It was the night I found out about his affair with Erica Jensen."

The answer set off a stirring in the courtroom as the spectators anticipated what was coming next.

"How did you find out?"

"Through some text messages on his phone. When I confronted him, he admitted it."

At counsel table, Elias stared at his hands. Pain and regret were written on every wrinkle on his face.

"What did you do when you found out?"

"I screamed at him. I cried. I cursed the day I married him."

"What did he do?"

Julia hesitated, looking at her guilt-stricken husband. "He apologized and said he was going to break it off with Erica. He said he never meant to hurt me."

"Did you ever confront Erica Jensen about this?"

For a split second, the room was stilled. Julia swallowed, kept her head high, and looked straight at Landon. "Yes, the next night. I left the house and drove to Erica's apartment."

There was a murmur in the audience, and Deegan banged her gavel. "Let's have it quiet," she said.

"So that would be Monday night, the night of Erica's death?"

"Yes."

"Did you go alone?"

"Yes."

"To your knowledge, did your husband know you were going?"

"No."

"Did you talk to Erica Jensen that night?"

"Yes. I told her to stay away from my husband. I told her that I hadn't worked through twenty-six years of marriage to lose him now. I told her she needed to find another job at another firm and never go near Elias again."

Landon took another glance at the back door. Still nothing. Out of his peripheral vision, he noticed that Sean Phoenix seemed to relax just a little. Maybe he assumed that Landon had found a new scapegoat in Julia and just wanted Sean to watch so he would release Kerri unharmed.

"Did you threaten her?" Landon asked.

"She apologized. She said it just happened. She said she never meant to break up our family."

"But did you threaten her?"

"I never had to. She said that she and Elias were through."

"Did you harm Erica in any way?"

"Absolutely not."

"Was there any physical confrontation between the two of you?"

"No."

"Did you slip her any drugs?"

"Of course not."

"What time did you leave Erica Jensen's apartment?"

"I don't really remember. Probably sometime around 9 p.m."

"Was she alive?"

"Yes, Mr. Reed. She was very much alive."

JAKE DROVE UP AND DOWN the rows of the parking lot behind the community center, frantically searching for Mr. Clausen's BMW. He spotted it near the far corner of the lot just as Clausen was starting to back out.

"There it is," he said out his window. Billy Thurston was still in the bed of the truck but had scooted up to the front corner on the driver's side.

"And there's a man in the backseat," Jake added.

He sped down the row toward the BMW. Billy was looking through the back window of the cab.

"Ram it!" Billy said.

"What?"

"Ram it!"

Jake braced for impact and nailed the back corner of the BMW with the front of Landon's truck, pinning the car between the truck and a minivan parked next to the BMW. Only then did he see that Kerri was in the front seat, a gag in her mouth, her hands behind her back.

He held on to both sides of the steering wheel and froze, staring straight ahead. His arms and legs were trembling, and he thought he might throw up. He glanced to his right and saw the muscular guy they called the Wolfman jump out of the backseat of the BMW, gun in hand, while Mr. Clausen climbed slowly out the front. From his peripheral vision, through the cab's rear window, Jake could see Billy lying down in the back of the truck, wedged up against the passenger side rail. He had his gun out and his index finger against his lips.

The Wolfman came over to the truck and flung open the passenger door. He cursed Jake, and Jake was certain the man was going to jump into the cab and snap his neck like a twig. He wanted to run, but his legs wouldn't cooperate.

"Don't move!" Billy barked out the order from the bed of the truck. The Wolfman and Jake looked at the same time. Billy's gun was pointed at the Wolfman's head from about two feet away. "Drop it *now*—because I'd love to blow your brains out."

Without looking at Billy, the Wolfman dropped his gun.

"Now, kick it away."

The Wolfman did as instructed.

"Hands on top of your head," Billy demanded.

Again, the Wolfman complied—slowly, as if looking for an opening.

"Get over here, Clausen!" Billy yelled, swinging the gun toward Parker Clausen. With his hands up, Mr. Clausen walked slowly down the side of the vehicle. Kerri was struggling to get the passenger door open.

"Go get Kerri out," Billy told Jake. "And dial 911."

Jake jumped out of the truck at the same time that Billy, keeping his gun trained on the Wolfman, straddled the back rail and then hopped down from the truck bed. He landed awkwardly, the bad knee buckling a little, and the Wolfman took advantage.

He whirled with some kind of judo kick, and the gun went flying out of Billy's hand. A second kick landed a heel to the side of Billy's face, connecting with bone, the sound of celery snapping. Billy collapsed to the ground.

Jake was dialing 911 on the opposite side of the truck bed when Billy went down. He panicked and jumped back in the cab. At the same time, Kerri had managed to wriggle free enough to place her forehead on the car horn, which blared across the parking lot. Mr. Clausen climbed back in the front seat to push her away.

But the noise, just for a moment, distracted the Wolfman, who was bending over to pick up Billy's gun. Instinctively, Jake threw the truck in reverse and jammed on the gas. The open passenger door nailed the Wolfman, knocking him to the ground within arm's reach of Billy, who scrambled on top of him.

At close quarters, even somebody as strong as the Wolfman was no match for an angry three-hundred-pound NFL lineman. Billy had been at the bottom of more than a few football piles. He wrenched his gun from the Wolfman's hand and pistol-whipped him. As the Wolfman tried to squirm free, Jake jumped out of the cab, beating Clausen to the Wolfman's gun, which the Wolfman had kicked away earlier at Billy's command. Jake pointed it at Clausen, his hands shaking, and Clausen backed slowly away.

On the ground, Billy now had the Wolfman pinned on his stomach with one arm wrenched behind him. The barrel of Billy's gun was planted against the base of the Wolfman's skull. Blood dripped from Billy's mouth onto the back of the Wolfman's neck.

Squad cars were coming toward the scene. There were some frightened bystanders hiding behind cars halfway across the parking lot.

"Go ahead and try something," Billy said to the Wolfman. "Because I'd love to pull the trigger before the cops get here. Even if you don't, the odds are fifty-fifty that I'll shoot."

///

Sherman wasted no time attacking Julia King. He gave her a fake smile, circling like a shark with blood in the water.

"Good morning, Ms. King."

"Good morning."

"When you got home from confronting Erica, did you tell your husband where you had been?"

Julia balked at the question and looked like a deer caught in a trap. *Tell the truth,* Landon urged silently, nodding his head.

"I did."

Sherman did a double take. "You did?"

Julia looked at Elias apologetically, and Elias nodded his encouragement. For the first time, Landon thought that their marriage might still have a chance.

"Yes."

Sherman had an incredulous look on his face, a dramatic show for the jury. "Did you mention any of this when you were interviewed by the police?"

"No. I did not."

"Do you understand that it's a crime to impede an investigation like that?"

Elias nudged Landon, but he was already on his feet. "Objection!"

"Sustained."

"But you did lie to the police; isn't that right?"

Elias squirmed in his seat, and Landon hoped the jury wasn't watching his client. Julia was keeping her cool much better.

"Yes, sir. I did."

The General strutted a few steps and lowered his voice, creating a little more drama. "Isn't it true that when you confronted Erica Jensen she told you that it was over between her and your husband?"

"I think I said that already."

"Of course you did. But isn't it also true that she told you the reason her relationship with your husband would be ending was that she would be going to the prosecutors the next day?"

"No. That's not true at all."

Sherman ignored the answer. "You went home and told Elias about Erica's scheduled meeting; isn't that right?"

"No, because I didn't know about it myself."

The General scoffed, another little display for the jury. "And you expect the jury to believe you on that point even though you lied to investigators about whether you met with Erica at all?"

"I'm telling the truth," Julia said. But there was no fight in her voice.

"And for that we have your word; is that right?"

"Yes, sir. You have my word."

"That's all I have for this witness." The General sat down, a little straighter in his seat, and glanced over at the jury with a smug look of satisfaction.

90

"CALL YOUR NEXT WITNESS," Judge Deegan said.

Landon felt a tap on his shoulder. It was Detective Freeman, standing right in front of Sean Phoenix. She whispered in Landon's ear. "We've got Kerri. She's going to be fine."

He felt the emotions explode inside him—gratefulness, relief, a renewed determination to exact justice. But he didn't let it register in his expression. There was still plenty of work to be done.

"One second, Judge," Landon said. Then to Freeman, "You're sure?"

She nodded and handed him a piece of paper.

Landon turned back to the court and stood to his full height. "The defense calls Sean Phoenix."

Phoenix rose slowly, gathered himself, and stopped next to Landon on his way to being sworn in. "You and Kerri are both going to regret this," he hissed.

"I think she's going to rather enjoy it," Landon said, motioning over his shoulder.

Even Sean Phoenix, the world's master at keeping his composure, could not prevent a flicker of surprise from crossing his face when he saw Kerri leaning against the back wall of the courtroom, arms crossed. She raised her index finger in a subtle wave, which Phoenix did not acknowledge. He walked to the well of the courtroom and took the oath.

Landon didn't need notes for this one. He spent ten minutes going over Phoenix's background—his role as CEO of Cipher Inc., his former work with the CIA, his background in espionage and counterintelligence.

"When you worked for the CIA, did there come a time when your identity was compromised and you were held prisoner in Syria?"

"Yes. That's well documented."

"Prior to that capture and interrogation, were you intimate with a Syrian woman named Fatinah Najar who worked as an undercover CIA operative in Syria?"

Landon could see the storm on Phoenix's face, the flash in his eyes as he shot Kerri a look, but he didn't bite on the question. "I don't know what you're talking about."

"Isn't it true that Fatinah Najar was arrested along with you, placed in a cell next to yours, and tortured by Syrian officials?"

Franklin Sherman pushed back his chair, a noisy display, and stood. "Am I in the wrong trial?" he asked. "What does this have to do with the murder of Erica Jensen?"

Landon turned to the judge. "If the court will bear with me a few minutes, it will be quite obvious."

"Let's link it up quickly," Deegan ruled.

Landon turned back to the witness. "The CIA negotiated your release but did nothing to protect your lover, Fatinah Najar; isn't that correct?"

Phoenix snorted. "You've been spending too much time on the Internet reading gossip sites. No, that's not true."

"Okay. Let's talk about a few things we can agree on. Isn't it true that Cipher Inc. has been sued more than a dozen times?"

"Yes. All of them without merit."

"But you settled a couple of those cases; isn't that right?"

"When lawyers like you sue us, even if the case has no merit, it's sometimes cheaper to settle than it is to pay legal fees to defend."

"And you detest those types of lawsuits; isn't that right?"

Landon hoped that Phoenix would try to deny it. He had the tape from Kerri's first interview ready to roll.

"Lawsuits are the American way."

Phoenix was smart. It wasn't a firm denial, but it wasn't an admission either. "In addition to these civil suits, you and Cipher Inc. have also been prosecuted criminally; isn't that true?"

"Your client tried to prosecute us for the alleged killing of a dictator in Sudan, a man who slaughtered thousands of innocent women and children. We were found not guilty."

"John McBride, a plaintiff's lawyer from Texas who's under investigation for insider trading, sued you twice, didn't he?"

Sean Phoenix hesitated, and Landon went to his counsel table. Elias handed him the suit papers.

"Yes," Phoenix said.

"And you settled both cases, correct?"

"As I said, it was cheaper than going to trial."

"Have you ever heard of a federal judge named Rodney Zimmerman?"

Phoenix pondered it for a moment. "That name does not ring a bell."

"Let me see if I can refresh your memory. Judge Zimmerman served as one of the top lawyers at the CIA when the director made the call to disavow Fatinah Najar—your lover—a woman who was ultimately tortured and killed by her Syrian captors. Does that help place the name?"

"Actually, Counsel, it does not."

"Did you know that Judge Zimmerman is also under investigation for insider trading because he allegedly received funds from an account allegedly set up by John McBride?"

"That's a lot of 'allegedlies,' Counselor. Regardless, it's all news to me."

Sherman stood for a second time. "You've given him a lot of rope, Judge, and I still don't see how this connects."

Instead of arguing the objection, Landon just fired his next question. "Are you telling us that it's just coincidental, Mr. Phoenix, that all three men recently indicted for insider trading—Judge Zimmerman, John McBride, and Elias King—just happened to be enemies of you and your company?"

"Judge," Sherman pleaded, "this is just rank speculation."

Judge Deegan leaned forward. "Objection overruled," she said. "I'd be interested in Mr. Phoenix's answer."

"Neither I nor my company have anything to do with the charges against these men."

"Did you know, Mr. Phoenix, that new legal assistants for all three of these men started work within six months of each other?"

"Why would I know that?"

"Because Cipher Inc. placed them there. Because they were all operatives of Cipher Inc., including Erica Jensen. Isn't that right?"

"You really ought to join your partner in writing legal thrillers, Counselor, because you've got quite the imagination."

"Speaking of my partner—isn't it true that Parker Clausen also works for you?"

Phoenix raised his eyebrows. "I don't know where you're getting this stuff."

"Do you deny it?"

"Yes, of course."

"Erica Jensen was one of your operatives; isn't that true?"

Sean Phoenix crossed his legs and relaxed a little. They were falling into a rhythm. "No. It's another lie."

"But she fell in love with Elias King, became pregnant, and decided to go to the authorities and tell them the truth—that Cipher Inc. was paying her to frame Elias King for insider trading. When you found out, you had her killed. Isn't that what happened?"

Franklin Sherman stood. He sighed dramatically and held out his arms. "I know he's new at this, Judge, but that's not even a question. It's a speech."

"I've heard better questions," Judge Deegan agreed. "But I'll allow the witness to answer."

Sean Phoenix stared at Landon for a moment before answering. The look promised revenge, the same kind of revenge he had exacted on everyone else who had crossed him. "That's a lie," he said calmly. "A dangerous lie."

"Why is it dangerous?" Landon asked.

"Because it could mislead the jury into thinking that your client is not a cold-blooded murderer," Sean Phoenix said.

But both men knew what he really meant.

"You value loyalty in your company, don't you?"

"Of course. Every company does."

"And when a Cipher Inc. operative goes to the Feds and offers to testify against the company, it can cause all kinds of problems, can't it?"

Landon watched closely as Sean Phoenix calculated his answer. If he denied it, Landon would ask detailed questions about the murder trial for the killing of Ahmed Al-Latif, a trial that resulted from a Cipher operative turning against the company. But if Phoenix admitted it, he would be playing into Landon's theory of the case.

Phoenix shrugged, though his eyes fired darts at Landon. "If you say so, Counselor."

91

IN THE MIDDLE OF HIS EXAMINATION, Landon experienced a brief pang of fear. This was the CEO of one of the most powerful organizations in the world. This man had orchestrated the deaths of three lawyers at Landon's firm already. Who was Landon to think he could escape Sean Phoenix's wrath?

But then he thought about Harry. He remembered his mentor's relentless tenacity. *"There are times,"* Harry had told him, *"when you are the only person standing between your client and a lifetime of incarceration. Sometimes, in your client's defense, you may have to implicate some pretty powerful people. Never back down. And remember, if you're going to shoot the king, you'd better kill the king."*

Sean Phoenix was already wounded. It was time to move in for the kill.

"Harry McNaughten figured this out, didn't he?" Landon asked.

"I don't know if Harry McNaughten had the same kind of fertile imagination as you or not."

"He told his partners about it, and Parker Clausen called you."

Phoenix smirked. "Is that a question?"

"Yes."

"Then I deny it."

"Do you also deny giving an order to have Harry McNaughten and Brent Benedict and Rachel Strach killed?"

Sean Phoenix had heard enough. He clenched his jaw and turned to the judge. "Is this the way our justice system works?" he asked. "I have to sit here and allow this man—" he motioned derisively toward Landon— "a man who has never raised a hand in the defense of our country, a man who has served years in prison because he sold out his teammates in a football game—I have to allow *him* to make these kinds of wild accusations against *me*?"

"This is precisely how our system works," Judge Deegan said coldly. "And I'd suggest you learn to respect it."

Sean Phoenix took a sip of water and turned back to Landon. He waited for a moment and then spoke in a calm voice, barely audible. "What was the question?"

"Whether you ordered the deaths of Harry McNaughten, Brent Benedict, and Rachel Strach."

"No. Of course not. Next question."

Landon took a deep breath and walked back to his counsel table. He picked up the piece of paper that Freeman had handed him just before Phoenix took the stand.

"What about my death and my client's? Did you order those?"

Landon might as well have detonated five pounds of TNT in the courtroom. Murmurs rose from the spectators. Sherman leaped to his feet, shouting an objection, demanding a mistrial. Deegan banged her gavel.

"Approach the bench!" she demanded.

Landon and Sherman hustled forward, and Deegan began talking before Elias King could even make it to the front. She made little effort to keep her voice low enough so the jury wouldn't hear. "I thought I told you that was off-limits," she said, scolding Landon. "There was to be no mention of the attempt on your client's life."

Landon wondered if the judge would throw him in jail without even giving him a chance to explain. "We have evidence," he said quickly. "Cell phone records. I'm about to reveal them. And it fits our theory of the case."

Sherman was beside himself, pulsing with angry energy. He looked like he wanted to strike Landon. "I've never seen anything this under-handed," he sputtered. "Talk about disrespecting the court."

"I didn't mean any disrespect," Landon interjected.

"I move for a mistrial, and I move that the defendant be retained in custody without bond pending a new trial," Sherman said.

"I'm inclined to grant the mistrial," Deegan said, shaking her head. "Even after all the work to keep these jurors in place." She eyeballed Landon. "You really haven't given me any choice."

By now, Elias had shuffled to the bench on his crutches, but even he could think of nothing to say in Landon's defense.

"Judge, I can understand why the court's upset, and I apologize. But if you would give me four questions—just four—I'll show you how this all ties in. And if I don't link it up in four questions, you can grant the mistrial and I won't even object."

"But I might," Elias added.

"Four more questions?" Sherman asked derisively. "Four more of these 'When did you stop beating your wife?' questions without any evidence to back them up?"

Deegan thought it over for a second, her rage subsiding a little. "Four questions, Counsel. And they'd better be good."

Landon took his time getting back to his counsel table, formulating the precise wording for the questions.

"I hope you know what you're doing," Elias said under his breath.

Landon waited until everyone was in place, then walked to the well of the courtroom. He waited a few beats. The eyes of the jurors and the entire gallery were glued to him. Sherman was leaning forward, ready to object. The witness was staring him down. And Elias King, a man with way more jury experience than Landon, had his freedom hanging in the balance.

This was, Landon thought, the reason he had sacrificed everything to become a lawyer.

"Do you own a cell phone?"

"Of course."

"Did you leave your cell phone with the deputies at the metal detector when you came upstairs pursuant to our subpoena to testify?"

Phoenix blinked. He knew, even before Landon asked the next question, where this was headed. His arrogant defiance turned to a flicker of panic. "Yes."

"Did you know that Detective Freeman, from the Virginia Beach Police Department, had obtained a warrant to search your phone?" He pointed at Freeman. "That's her, right there."

"Of course I didn't know that."

And here it was, Landon thought. Question number four.

"Would you care to explain why you received a text message seconds after the shootings right outside this courthouse yesterday with the words *Mission status—targets hit but survived*?"

The question itself generated another stir that spread like a shock wave through the courtroom. In law school, Landon had been taught that there were some questions so damaging it didn't matter how the witness answered. And he knew, beyond any doubt, that he had just asked one of them.

///

Sean Phoenix took another sip of water.

He almost smiled as he considered the unbelievable irony of it all. Fifteen years ago, he had given up on the rule of law. Those in power had let him down and caused the death of his lover. Sean had become a renegade, a vigilante. He had been on a personal mission to avenge Fatinah's death and punish those who had been complicit in it. Along the way, he had added to his list of enemies. Men like Elias King and John McBride. Greedy and selfish men who had tormented his company in order to advance their careers.

Sean had done plenty of secret things for the good of his country and to enact vengeance on those who had crossed him. Now he was being framed for things he hadn't done. The shootings of Landon and Elias King. The deaths of Brent Benedict and Rachel Strach. Yes, Sean had framed Elias King, John McBride, and Judge Zimmerman. And yes, he had reluctantly ordered the deaths of Erica Jensen and Harry McNaughten. But someone with even less respect for the rule of law than he had was framing the great Sean Phoenix for crimes he hadn't committed.

Sean studied Landon for a moment. Did this kid really have it in him? Had Sean Phoenix been duped by an ex-jock? And what was Kerri's role? Had this all just been an elaborate setup from day one?

These were questions he couldn't answer—at least not right now. So, with Landon's devastating question hanging in the air like a guillotine, Sean Phoenix sought shelter in the only place left, a place which suddenly had far greater allure for him than it ever had before.

The U.S. Constitution. The bastion for those who believed in the rule of law.

"I refuse to answer that question," he said. "I'm availing myself of my rights under the Fifth Amendment to the U.S. Constitution."

92

ONE DAY LATER

BILLY THURSTON WAS NOT AN IDEAL PATIENT. After twenty-four hours in Sentara Norfolk's trauma center, he wanted to go home, but the doctors insisted on keeping him another day for observation. The nurses got a kick out of the guy, and he signed more than a few autographs for their kids.

The Wolfman had shattered Billy's cheekbone and broken his nose, but none of this stopped his jaw from working, and Billy was not a fan of hospital food. So on Friday, Landon grilled steaks and Kerri fixed mashed potatoes, and the former quarterback and his former center closed the door to the hospital room and had a feast.

In the last twenty-four hours, the two men had witnessed the breathtaking collapse of Cipher Inc. amid one startling revelation after another. Based on Sean Phoenix's testimony in court and the contents of his cell phone, the Feds had obtained a warrant to search the entire company's headquarters. FBI agents descended in droves, and law-enforcement sources were beginning to leak some of the incriminating information they had found. One agent let Landon know that they had found the original photos of him and Rachel. Landon assumed Phoenix had sent them anonymously to pressure Kerri into taking that job in D.C. and to pull Landon away from the firm.

"It happened just like I laid it out in court," Landon said to Billy between bites. "Cipher Inc. placed their moles at McBride's firm and Elias King's firm and in Judge Zimmerman's office. All three Cipher agents had access to their bosses' computers. They framed them for insider trading. But Erica Jensen got emotionally attached to Elias. When she found out she was pregnant, she decided to go to the Feds and tell the truth about Cipher's attempts to frame Elias. She was hoping to cut a deal and avoid jail time. She couldn't live with herself if Elias went to jail on these trumped-up charges."

"Ouch," Billy said. "I've gotta chew on the other side. That dude can kick."

"You wouldn't believe all the stuff Sean Phoenix did," Landon continued, ignoring Billy's comment. "He had an enemies list that started with the men who killed his lover fifteen years ago. Once you make that list, you're toast."

"You should have brought some A.1.," Billy said. "That way I wouldn't have to chew—it could just slide down."

"The best chefs don't want you smothering their steaks in A.1.," Landon said.

"Who said anything about the best chefs?" Billy asked. He took another bite. "Looks like you made the enemies list."

"Yeah. Ironically, I hadn't even figured out what was going on when they took their shot at me the other day. Harry, on the other hand, figured it out early in the case and went to Parker Clausen. Of course, Parker went straight to Sean Phoenix, who in turn had somebody take care of Harry. Then somehow Brent or Rachel must have figured it out too. So they were the next to go."

"I guess God decided it wasn't your time yet," Billy said.

"I guess so," Landon replied. He tried to act nonchalant, but his heart leaped to hear Billy say something about God. Until coming face-to-face with his own mortality the day before, the big man had been pretty resistant to spiritual things.

"They going to fry him?" Billy asked.

The man had a way of cutting to the chase. Virginia still had the death penalty, and they weren't afraid to use it.

"Probably," Landon said. "He's undoubtedly got a dozen different crimes that would qualify."

The two men ate for a while in silence. Billy had the TV on ESPN's *SportsCenter* even though the news channels were providing hourly updates about Cipher Inc. Billy polished off the last of his steak, chased it down with an energy drink, and wiped his mouth.

"I'm sorry about your knee," Landon said. "It doesn't seem right that you fly down here to take care of an old teammate and this happens."

Billy gave Landon a lopsided smile, the left side of his face turning up. "Poetic justice," he said. "We both know I deserved it."

93

AT TIMES IT FELT LIKE A DISNEY MOVIE. At others it felt like a Greek tragedy.

Tonight was Disney. There was magic in the air. It was the kind of night Rachel Strach had imagined four months ago when Brent parachuted out of his plane over the Chesapeake Bay. He had squirreled away enough money in offshore accounts that he and Rachel could enjoy the finer things in life. The tricky part had been creating fake passports. But when you have the money, you can pay for the best experts.

For Rachel, the whole thing still seemed surreal. Her head hadn't stopped spinning since Brent first talked to her about who had killed Harry McNaughten.

When Harry died and Detective Freeman started snooping around, Brent had been the first one in Harry's office. He had found Harry's

414

handwritten closing statement and had been amazed at how Harry had connected the dots implicating Sean Phoenix and Cipher Inc.

The one piece Harry hadn't figured out was the role of Parker Clausen. But some of Harry's notes reflected his phone call with Parker the night before the scheduled partner meeting. Harry had shared with Parker his concerns about Cipher Inc. and his plans to have the firm withdraw from representing them. That night, Harry was killed.

Brent had confirmed his suspicions about Parker's involvement by leaving the handwritten closing argument in plain sight on Harry's desk. The next morning, he noticed Parker go upstairs for a few minutes. Later that day, when Brent went into Harry's office, the papers were gone. Parker never said the first word about it.

If there was any doubt left, it disappeared when Parker argued vehemently to keep the Elias King file. If he was working for Sean Phoenix, it all made sense. Control the defense. Don't let King get new lawyers who might figure it out. Parker could always make sure that Landon didn't start connecting the dots the way Harry had done. Keep your friends close and your enemies closer.

After that firm meeting, Brent had brought Rachel into his confidence, and she had done some research on Parker's book sales. He had been a midlist author with mixed reviews until about a year before Harry's death. Then somebody—Parker claimed it was his publisher—began sinking a lot of money into advertising and book placement. Sales began to skyrocket. Reviews did not.

When Brent first suggested his plan, Rachel thought he was crazy. But he convinced her that Cipher had tentacles everywhere and that Glaxon-Forrester would never leave them alone. Why not kill two birds with one stone? Fake their deaths and live happily ever after in a tropical paradise.

Rachel was a sucker for romance and adventure. And Brent was a former SEAL.

They used a little sleight of hand when boarding the plane at the Allegheny airport. Rachel arrived in a limo as Brent was completing the preflight. The stairs to the jet were on the opposite side of the plane from the small brick terminal. She boarded as Rachel Strach—short skirt, tight sweater, something memorable in case anybody was watching. A few minutes later, she walked down the steps dressed in the black uniform of a chauffeur, silly hat and all.

A half hour later, Brent took off alone. She and Brent had prerecorded some conversations that he played during the flight so ground control could hear the voice of Rachel Strach. He bailed over the Chesapeake Bay, right after confirming his final approach, just before the explosion. A former buddy from his SEAL team triggered the fireworks from a boat and plucked Brent out of the water.

They had already started their new life in Rio de Janeiro when an unexpected twist occurred—something that even the warped mind of Parker Clausen, in his most convoluted novel, would never have dreamed up. Elias King rehired the firm. Rachel and Brent knew Parker would be ecstatic. He could now ensure that Cipher was never implicated. But they worried for Landon's safety. What if he figured out Sean Phoenix's involvement in Erica Jensen's death or the insider trading scheme, like Harry had done? Somebody, sometime, had to stop Cipher and Sean Phoenix.

She still couldn't believe they had pulled it off. Outsmarted Sean Phoenix. Beat him at his own game.

Live by subterfuge; die by subterfuge.

Rachel had wanted to act as soon as Landon was rehired by Elias King, but Brent said he needed time to put the plan together. They had argued about it, the first real source of conflict between them. But Brent was stubborn, and they waited until the trial started.

The plan was for Brent to shoot both Landon and Elias square in the middle of their Kevlar vests and frame Sean Phoenix in the process. The day of the shootings, Rachel threw up three times, sitting by the television in Rio de Janeiro, waiting for news of the events. When Brent called, he said the plan had worked to perfection except for one minor detail. Elias hadn't been wearing a vest. Brent said he felt bad about it, but he figured Elias would rather deal with a bad leg than a death sentence.

"Why couldn't you just miss?" Rachel had asked.

"How realistic is that? A sniper hired by Sean Phoenix misses entirely?"

They were both proud of Landon for the way he had quickly figured out the clues they had planted implicating Phoenix. They had been prepared to provide a few anonymous tips to help him, but it hadn't been necessary. The text message Brent sent to Sean Phoenix's phone was the clincher. Phoenix would be found guilty of conspiracy to commit murder. He deserved that and more. He had conspired to commit other murders, even if not this particular one. And there was no telling how many charges he would ultimately be facing by the time the Feds concluded their investigation of his company.

When Brent returned from that second trip, the romance was back. Rachel had always been intrigued by his special-ops background, a secret he had shared with her early in their relationship. She loved the way he never bragged about it to others. But it made her feel secure. Protected.

Still, at a time when they should have been enjoying a storybook ending, Rachel sometimes felt more than a twinge of unrest. Her mind frequently drifted to Landon, and she had to remind herself that the one thing you want is not always the one thing you can have.

There was a difference, she knew, between loyalty and love. A lasting relationship required both. She had seen it with Landon and Kerri. The way Kerri stayed loyal when Landon was in prison. The way he had returned the favor once he got out.

Now it was her turn. And the man sitting in front of her certainly deserved her loyalty. Did she love him? On some nights.

And this was one of them.

They were sitting at a quaint outdoor cafe on opposite sides of a round iron table, enjoying some of Brazil's finest wine. They had watched the sun set after a leisurely dinner. She loved the way he looked at her in the candlelight, the way his eyes conveyed his every emotion. She felt warm and loved and wanted.

Perhaps someday they would return to the States. If it didn't work between them, Brent had promised her they could both start over— brand-new identities, a whole new life. But that was plan B. Right now, she was determined to make plan A work.

"Now that Parker's out of commission, maybe *we* should write a book," Brent suggested. He was leaning back in his chair, legs crossed in front of him. He took a sip of wine. "*The Avengers.*"

"Already taken," Rachel said. "What about *Lawyers of the Caribbean?*" She smiled at the thought of Jack Sparrow and the characters played by Keira Knightley and Orlando Bloom. The romance seemed to work out okay for them.

"Not bad," Brent conceded. Another sip of wine.

He put his glass down and sat up straighter. "I've got it!" He tilted his head back and put on a stage voice. The man was proud of this one. "*Dead Lawyers Tell No Tales.*" He let the words roll off his tongue and picked up his glass for a toast.

Rachel smirked and extended her own glass, toasting his brilliance and their future together.

Forever.

She hoped.

"*Dead Lawyers Tell No Tales,*" she repeated. She took a drink and put down her glass. "Or do they?" she asked.

EPILOGUE

LANDON REED AND SEAN PHOENIX had been changed forever in prison. For Billy Thurston, it took a hospital.

Kerri left a Bible with him and was smart enough to mark it and highlight it. John 15:13—"Greater love has no one than this, that he lay down his life for his friends."

"That's what you did for Landon," she said. "And that's what Christ did for you."

It confirmed what Billy had always suspected. Even Landon's own wife didn't know. She thought Billy was a hero. Nothing could be further from the truth.

He couldn't get his mind off that SEC Championship Game—the fourth quarter, the game-winning drive. He had blocked the linebacker instead of taking out the nose tackle. Landon had been blindsided and fumbled. Game over.

But by the time the syndicate tried to pay him for it—seventy-five thousand, just as they had agreed—the guilt had taken over, and he had refused their "blood money." It was the same syndicate that had convinced Landon to shave a few points in two regular-season games earlier that year. Landon had refused to cooperate in the championship. That's when the syndicate had approached Billy instead.

Somehow, Landon had learned that Billy was bought off, but Landon never said a word. He could have earned a reduced sentence by turning Billy in. Or Landon could have at least erased all doubts as to whether *he* had thrown the championship game. Instead, he confessed to his own crimes and kept his mouth shut about Billy's. The men from the gambling syndicate only pleaded guilty to bribing Landon for the regular-season games. Billy carried on with his life.

"Greater love has no one than this, that he lay down his life for his friends."

When Billy finally took time to read the Bible, nobody had to explain to him what grace meant. He had seen it with his own eyes.

On the day of his discharge, he told Landon about his hospital conversion. Right there in the bed. Reading Scripture on his own. He explained how Landon's self-sacrificial actions had played a big role in it.

Tears formed in Landon's eyes. Billy had to blink back his own. "I've called a press conference for later today," Billy said. "I'm going to make things right."

Two hours later, standing on crutches in front of the hospital, Billy told the reporters everything. He promised to perform a thousand hours of community service in the next year alone. He would donate every dime of his annual salary to charitable organizations.

"I will spend the rest of my life trying to prove that I can be a trustworthy teammate," he said. "I apologize to every one of my teammates at Southeastern, as well as my coaches and fans. I hope you can find it in your hearts to forgive me."

He looked to his left, where Landon was standing. "And I apologize to this guy, who took a lot of heat because of me."

///

Landon had never been more proud of his teammate, and that was say-ing a lot. For a split second he caught Billy's eye, the unspoken commu-nication between two men who had been in the trenches together. *I've got your back.*

When Billy finished speaking, the reporters started firing questions. Landon held up a palm.

"Mr. Thurston won't be taking any questions," Landon said. "He looks forward to starting the healing process for his injuries and the healing process with his former teammates and the fans he let down. Right now, we'd appreciate it if you would just respect his privacy."

With that, Billy Thurston hobbled away from the mikes, and Landon fell in step beside him. The reporters parted as the two men made their way through.

Walking across the parking lot, Landon could feel the cameras rolling behind them. Billy was keeping his head high, his eyes focused on the sky in front of him. He had a long road ahead, one that Landon knew too well. But he had taken the first critical step toward redemption—an admission of wrongdoing, a promise to make things right.

Landon had warned Billy about the consequences of the press confer-ence. Legally, Billy was in the clear. Georgia had a two-year statute of limitations for nonviolent felonies, and Billy could no longer face prose-cution. But as a practical matter, this day would follow Billy the rest of his life. There would be no running from what he had done.

"You sure I can't talk you out of this?" Landon had asked. As a lawyer, he felt an obligation to protect his client. As a believer, he was secretly hoping that Billy would go through with it. There was no real freedom in living a lie.

The big man did not disappoint.

"You survived it," Billy said. "Besides, as a friend of mine once said, 'There are some things in life more important than football.'"

Coming Next Easter from Randy Singer

There have been two great trials in the history of the world. One has been studied, dissected, and analyzed for two thousand years. The second—until now—has been a great mystery.

Relive them both from the front row of history, as movements rise and fall, villains triumph, and good men struggle. The verdicts define us still.

Turn the page for an exciting preview from

THE ADVOCATE

TYNDALE
FICTION

www.tyndalefiction.com

I STOOD BEHIND Pilate at the trial of Christus, whispering advice into the prefect's ear. The man in the judgment seat was no legal scholar. Instead, it fell to me, Theophilus, Pilate's favorite *assessore*, to provide counsel on the intricacies of Roman law.

"Send him to Herod."

An hour later he was back.

"Release Barabbas instead."

At the insistence of Pilate's wife, I tried everything. But when Pilate washed his hands of the matter, I followed the would-be Messiah to Calvaria, the place of the skull, the hillside where criminals were executed.

The sight of a good man being crucified did not fade away easily. It would haunt me for years, even after I returned to Rome. *I should have done more.*

Thirty years later, as an advocate in Caesar's court, I would get my chance. . . .

///

His name was Paul of Tarsus, and I had been chosen to represent him. I had been here before, in the great marble hall, but there had never been so much at stake.

And the judge was a madman.

Nero had become emperor at seventeen. He had poisoned his brother, ordered the murder of his mother, kicked his pregnant wife to death, and married his male slave. He loved to toy with advocates. He made one beg on his hands and knees. Another time, he decreed that the man return to Nero's court the following day, properly dressed, and sent a courier that evening with a woman's gown. A third, who had the temerity to question Nero's judgment, was sentenced to death along with the prisoner. In a court-ordered suicide, he was made to drink poison the next day. Caesar smiled wickedly as the man writhed on the marble floor, gasping for his last breath.

The emperor gulped a mouthful of wine. "Next case!" he called out.

The apostle Paul and I had agreed on one thing. There would be no begging today. We would make our case and concede nothing. I was an older man now. And Rome was a mere shadow of the empire I had once admired. Thirty years earlier, I had watched another man stand up to the haughtiness of a Roman judge and the fury of a bloodthirsty mob. He was unbowed, unshaken. Today, that would be me.

I had studied this emperor, and I knew his weaknesses. The man loved drama. Almost as much as he loved being the center of attention.

Well, then, he should love this.

The idea came thirty years ago as well, at the foot of the cross, during the crucifixion of the man they called Christus. I was speaking to a woman who had been caught in adultery and saved from stoning by the Rabbi's clever defense.

"He wrote in the dirt," she said, tears streaking down her face.

"Wrote what?"

"Names."

We were both staring at the Jewish Messiah, hanging there, blood oozing from his wrists and feet, a crown of thorns creating rivulets of crimson that colored his beard and dripped from his chin.

"What do you mean, names?"

She turned, her dark eyes boring into me. "The names of the leaders who were accusing me," she answered. "And the women they had slept with."

The audacity of it made me catch my breath. I was an advocate. And as I had observed this man in front of Pilate—the give and take, the silent confidence, the questions he posed—I sensed that I might be watching the greatest advocate of them all.

"He said, 'Let him who is without sin cast the first stone,'" the woman continued. She spoke the words into space, staring again at the man on the cross, as if carried back to that time. "And then they dropped their stones and left."

And so I began my defense of Paul of Tarsus, thirty years later, in dramatic fashion as well.

The crowd formed a crushing ring on the outskirts of the marble judgment hall. I was told they had started lining up at midnight. They seemed to pulse in as the charges were read, the men in the second and third rows standing on their toes to get a better view as I rose to address the emperor.

I stood there for a moment, shoulders straight, head high, looking the man in the eye.

"Well?" he said.

I bent down . . . slowly, theatrically. I knelt there on one knee and took a last glance at Nero before I wrote the first name. I used the black ink—ground charcoal mixed with gum arabic—a nice contrast against the white stone. The crowd surged in a little, and a murmur started to spread. Nero leaned forward in his seat.

The first name created a buzz of excitement, a shot of adrenaline that coursed through the crowd on this hot, steamy day.

The second would start a riot.

ACKNOWLEDGMENTS

As you can probably tell from reading this book, I love football and even played a little "back in the day." I was an average (and that may be generous) quarterback but smart enough to figure out the number one rule: you are only as good as your offensive line. There is also a corollary to that rule: thank them every chance you get.

The same applies to writing. Which is why I never pass up an acknowledgments page.

I'll start with Lee Hough, my good friend and great agent, who provided invaluable insight at the concept stage. Thanks also to Mary Hartman, who performed her usual stellar work reviewing the first draft. Jeremy Taylor, Stephanie Broene, Cheryl Kerwin, and the excellent team at Tyndale House took it from there, bringing the story to life and devising ways to let you know about it.

Karen Watson, associate publisher at Tyndale, not only helped edit the book but literally resurrected it from the dead. I will never forget the long phone conference when I had given up on the book and suggested that we proceed on to the next project, something I had never done before. Like a good coach, Karen wouldn't take "quit" for an answer. She helped me work through the challenges and reworked Tyndale's schedule for release. Now that's somebody who's got your blind side.

In addition, this book would have never been possible without the forbearance and support of my church, my law firm, and my family. A special thanks to those closest to me for putting up with the idiosyncratic lifestyle of a man with so many fictional characters dancing around in his head.

Now allow me to take off my helmet and put on my lawyer's hat for a few disclaimers. There *is* a Character and Fitness Committee in Virginia and a Board of Bar Examiners. Both groups are composed of dedicated and superb lawyers who bear no resemblance to the ethically challenged Harry McNaughten of this book. For that matter, none of my fictional lawyers are patterned after real-life colleagues, though it might make the practice of law a little more entertaining if they were.

There is one character, however, *inspired* by a real-life client. That client showed me how much someone can truly change while incarcerated and how hard it can be to rebuild a life. But he also demonstrated that, by God's grace, it can be done. He became the inspiration for my protagonist, Landon Reed, and for that I am deeply in his debt.

Therefore, if anyone is in Christ, he is a new creation;
the old has gone, the new has come!
2 CORINTHIANS 5:17 (NIV)

ABOUT THE AUTHOR

RANDY SINGER is a critically acclaimed, award-winning author and veteran trial attorney. He has penned more than ten legal thrillers and was recently a finalist with John Grisham and Michael Connelly for the inaugural Harper Lee Prize for Legal Fiction sponsored by the University of Alabama School of Law and the *ABA Journal*. Randy runs his own law practice and has been named to *Virginia Business* magazine's select list of "Legal Elite" litigation attorneys. In addition to his law practice and writing, Randy serves as teaching pastor for Trinity Church in Virginia Beach, Virginia. He calls it his "Jekyll and Hyde thing"—part lawyer, part pastor. He also teaches classes in advocacy and civil litigation at Regent University School of Law and, through his church, is involved with ministry opportunities in India. He and his wife, Rhonda, live in Virginia Beach. They have two grown children. Visit his website at www.randysinger.net.

Keep in touch with author

RANDY SINGER

at **RANDYSINGER.NET**

→ Sign up for Randy's newsletter

→ Download discussion guides

→ Read first chapters

→ Have Randy speak to your book group

→ Discover his latest releases

→ Connect with Randy on Goodreads